13 Doors

Sometimes death goes wrong

G. J. Phelps

The Book Guild Ltd

First published in Great Britain in 2023 by
The Book Guild Ltd
Unit E2 Airfield Business Park,
Harrison Road, Market Harborough,
Leicestershire. LE16 7UL
Tel: 0116 2792299
www.bookguild.co.uk
Email: info@bookguild.co.uk
Twitter: @bookguild

This novel's story and characters are fictitious. While various real individuals
are mentioned, the characters involved are wholly imaginary and bear no
resemblance to anyone living or dead.

Typeset in 11pt Minion Pro

Printed and bound in Great Britain by 4edge Limited

ISBN 978 1915603 944

British Library Cataloguing in Publication Data.
A catalogue record for this book is available from the British Library.

For Jane, Abbie and Leo.

Contents

ONE

Bedtime Story

The scariest ghost story I ever heard – the one that frightened me the most – was also the first ghost story I was ever told.

I'm not talking about playground rubbish about broken-down cars or murdered teens, you understand. I'm not talking about the creepy house on the corner. I mean the first time anyone sat me down, looked me straight in the eye and told me what had really happened to them, personally.

What made this story so scary? It was who told it to me – my mom and dad.

My name is Joe Baxter, and as a news journalist, most people would expect me to have quite a thick skin. Which is probably true. If I do, it's been hardened over the years, because as a kid I was soft. A real wuss. But it was as a kid that I heard the ghost story that made me see the world differently.

I guess I only got what I deserved.

You see, I come from a long line of men who cry at the drop of a hat – at sentimental films, TV talent shows, retirement speeches.

Having lived with this affliction for longer than me, Dad helped me cope with it.

'It's a sign of balance, not imbalance,' he once told me, sagely.

Every now and then, being able to genuinely 'turn on the waterworks' could also be quite useful. Coupled with a vivid imagination, it was a formidable talent for a kid. Or a curse.

Which brings me to the bedtime story that changed my life.

I was around nine or ten years old. We were living in an old house in Birmingham. My parents had broken the bank to buy it as a fixer-upper and spent twenty years turning it into a family home, window by window, carpet by carpet, room by room.

Thinking back, it was a pretty impressive place, which had evidently once been quite grand, but it was not in the least bit creepy.

On the night in question, as I said goodnight, Mom and Dad were half watching a film on TV – it was Sherlock Holmes or something like that – which stamped a final image on my young mind as I climbed the stairs.

Something else, however, occupied my thoughts. School. I can't remember exactly what it was, but there was something the next day that I wanted to avoid: a test, handing in homework, a teacher I hated, a bully.

So, as I lay in bed, I hatched a plan. I would fake a bad dream. In an hour or so, I would appear at the living room door in sweat-soaked pyjamas and floods of tears. Cue parental sympathy. Tomorrow: no school, telly, and chicken soup.

For the next hour, my devious little brain lay in the dark constructing a nightmare. A theme was required; I struck upon old London Town, Holmes and Watson, Jack the Ripper, cobbled streets cloaked in fog.

Next, a ghost was needed. All small children believe in ghosts, in the same way they believe in aliens and spontaneous human combustion. They are happy to entertain the supernatural, safe in the knowledge that when push comes to shove their parents will always assure them that 'there's no such thing'.

Parents provide a protective bubble, by telling kids what to believe in and what not to believe in: ghosts aren't real but the Easter Bunny is; letters to Santa work, Ouija boards don't.

So, to work. Time to turn on the waterworks. I selected my spectre; a ghoul in a hat would climb our stairs to stand at the foot of my bed.

My imagination sparked. Eyes closed, my breathing slowed. The room fell away. My mind leapt. The apparition stepped from idea to form, from thought to flesh. Emotion began to swell. As I opened my eyes my chest juddered with the first sob. Tears came. And, for a moment I could see him, my own ghostly idea made real, silhouetted at the end of the bed, clutching an old hat, crying right back at me.

A child's imagination is a powerful thing, and soon I was a sobbing mess. Job done.

Peeling back the bedclothes I set off in the dark, creeping down the stairs – ready to open my performance with the immortal line: 'I've had a bad dream!'

I reached the foot of the staircase and stood quietly sobbing, illuminated by the light from under the living room door. Inside, the TV burbled.

An idea struck me.

What if I was still half dreaming, convinced that this nightmare was real? That would really get them. Day off school guaranteed.

So it was that, moments later, I pushed open the living room door, my face wet with fright and wailed, 'I've seen a ghost!'

That's where the trouble started.

Mom, bless her, was across the room, kneeling in her nightie, her arms around me, kissing my tears as I stood sobbing in the doorway.

Dad was sitting, fully dressed, in his armchair. I never saw him undressed, not even with his shirt off. He looked startled.

'What's up, son? What's all this?'

'There was a ghost – a ghost!' I wailed.

'You've just had a bad dream,' Mom said, pushing my hair from my eyes. 'It's gone now, it's alright.'

'No, I saw it upstairs. Looking at me.'

Mom smiled sympathetically.

'Sweetheart, it was a dream, all gone now, all gone.'

'He was wearing a hat!' I launched another volley of sobs.

'It's OK, come on, stop crying, sweetheart.'

'Come on, son,' Dad urged softly, 'you know what to do – bite down on it, deep breaths.'

Bite down on it. This was Dad's coping mechanism, shared with me so many times.

I clenched my jaw, inhaled a shuddering chest full of air and swallowed.

Mom's hands went to my shoulders. 'That's better. Listen to Dad, just breathe. It was just a dream, wasn't it?'

But Dad was quiet.

I saw him over Mom's shoulder – distant, intense.

I persevered. The tears flowed again.

'Upstairs in my room… a man, a man!' I sniffed.

'Dreams seem so real sometimes, sweetheart.'

'Jean.'

My dad, his voice flat.

'Calm down and we'll get you back to bed,' she said.

'Jeanette.'

We both looked at Dad. He never called Mom Jeanette. He gave her a pained smile, lowered his glasses, and fixed his gaze on me.

'Did you really see something, son?'

'Yes, yes I did…'

'I mean did you *really* see something, son?' He sat forward.

'Yes. I did,' I sniffed, wiping my eyes.

Now Mom was looking at the floor.

'What did you see?'

'A man in a hat. He came up the stairs.'

Dad looked at Mom, a cold exchange of glances.

His gaze returned to me.

'You know we'll always believe you. We don't lie in this house.'

'I'm not lying.'

Dad knitted his fingers, deep in thought. Suddenly the room was very quiet.

'Sit down, son.'

'Bob...'

'Jean, I think we should tell him, he should know.'

'Tell me what?' I said. I felt the hairs on my neck lift.

'Bob, I don't think we...'

'He's seen something. We should tell him.'

Another exchange of glances.

'Sit down, son,' Dad said. 'Wipe your face. Let me talk to you.'

I sat on the sofa, next to Mom, my hands in hers. Dad stood up and turned the TV sound down, then put his hands in his pockets, looking at his socks.

We both waited for him to speak. The clock ticked.

'I don't know what you saw, but I do believe you,' he said, finally. 'We always try to be honest in this family; you know that we never lie to each other.'

I nodded. Honesty was Dad's big thing.

'I would never lie to you,' he went on, 'because my father lied to me every day – about drink, about the horses, about everything – and I always knew when he was doing it. I hated it.'

I nodded. This was a familiar Dad speech. He looked at me, earnestly.

'That's why I think you're old enough for grown-up things.'

'What sort of things?'

'Me and your mom saw something once.'

I felt her hands gently stroke mine.

'What did you see?' Fear crept into my voice.

He sat down. I suddenly felt hot. 'It wasn't here, it wasn't in this house,' he insisted.

'Where was it?'

The clock ticked. Dad chewed his lip as he chose his words.

'I think it's important that you know there are some things in life that probably can't ever be explained. Things that we don't understand. People don't talk about it because it's... well, we don't talk about it. Because. But if you have really seen something tonight, then I want you to know that we saw something once too. This does happen, that's all. It's very unusual, but it does happen.'

The realisation of what he was saying hit me. Push had come to shove. This was not how it was meant to work.

'What did you see?'

Mom spoke up gently.

'It was a long time ago, in the first house we lived in,' she said.

Dad nodded.

'We had just got married; we were very young. Mom was pregnant with you. It was all we could get,' he said.

'It was just two rooms up, two rooms down. One of the old Birmingham slums. Very old, very dirty. It still had an outside toilet in the back yard. But your mom made it as nice as she could.'

She wrinkled her nose. 'It was very old, Joe. I remember it had a big metal cross on the front of the house, like a big pin holding the walls together. Inside there was no wallpaper on the walls and everything was rotten. There were no carpets at all, just floorboards. Dad was working all hours, he'd just started on the presses, so I was in this house on my own all day, every day. Well, me and the dog.'

'You had a dog?'

'Yes, we did. His name was Butch. Butch was nice.'

Dad crossed his feet.

'The house wasn't nice, though, son.'

'What was wrong with it?'

He shook his head.

'Hard to describe. It felt odd from the moment we moved in. You never felt... welcome. It was like you were waiting for something to happen.'

'After a week I told Dad that I didn't like it,' Mom said. 'When I was alone, it was like I was being watched.'

I looked around the living room, lit by the gas fire and TV.

'We just thought it was because of the room upstairs,' Dad said.

'What was upstairs?'

He took a deep breath. His eyes locked on me.

'Did you *really* see something tonight, son?'

'Yes, I did. I did.'

He sighed. Mom shook her head. He crossed his arms.

'You understand this wasn't here? It was a different house?'

'Yes.'

'You kids don't appreciate what a nice house, what a good house this is. If you could see where I grew up...'

'I did see something,' I said, weakly.

The clock ticked.

Mom looked again at Dad, then sat away from me.

'This house is completely different. This is our home. It's a good place,' he said.

'I know. What was upstairs?'

He sighed. The silent TV flickered in his glasses.

'There were just two bedrooms upstairs, that's all. The one at the front, which we used, and the back bedroom.'

Mom's hand went to her mouth. He ignored her.

'That was not a good room, and we never went in there.'

'Why?' The living room was suddenly still, the only sound the gentle hiss of the fire.

'I'm telling you this because I want you to feel safe here. This is a very different house.'

I looked at them both, wide-eyed in my pyjamas, and repeated, 'What was upstairs?'

More glances. Mom's hand gave a tiny wave of surrender. It returned to her mouth.

'The person who had lived there before us – an old man – had died in the back bedroom.'

'He died? How did he die?' I felt my heart start to pound.

Dad's brow knotted and he shook his head. 'Old age... illness... loneliness... neglect.'

'What was the room like?'

'It was awful,' whispered Mom.

'We only went in once or twice. All of his stuff was still in there. The bed, his clothes. A pile of walking sticks, pills. Old army stuff. There was a chair with a big black stain on it. It was stale and smelled and... just not a good room.'

'Is that where you saw something?'

'We agreed to lock it and never go in there,' Mom said. 'We thought that was why the house had an atmosphere, because that room was always there... upstairs, behind a locked door.'

Tick. Tick. Tick.

'So, what did you see?'

Dad wrung his hands.

'One night – the last night we stayed there – I came home very late from work. I remember it was in the winter, and it was really foggy when I drove home – but the moon was bright too, so everything outside was white. The minute I walked in I knew something was wrong. There was this sound, like a humming or a whistling noise that you could barely hear but it was there, in the air. It seemed to be everywhere. It was in the walls – you could feel it. Like a pulse. Like a charge. As soon as I was through the door, Mom came straight up to me, and I could see from her face that something was wrong. She said it had been like that for the whole day and that the dog had been going crazy.'

Mom's hand moved to her brow.

'And it was freezing, really cold. We ate and then tried to

watch the telly, but we couldn't get warm, even in front of the fireplace. So, we decided to go to bed.'

I felt Mom shift uneasily.

'What happened?'

'We went to bed,' he said, 'and I turned the light off but the noise – this humming – was still there. Then Butch, who was on the end of the bed, suddenly flew off it. He ran into the corner and started to whimper and whine, so we both sat up and then suddenly the noise started to get louder – clearer – like it wasn't a whistle anymore and you could hear it more clearly, you could hear it properly – it was muttering, like a voice grumbling.'

Mom shuddered.

'Then our bed – which was a big brass thing – started to shake, to shake from side to side… slowly at first then harder and harder and then, from the wall, there was a crack or a bang – bang! – like electricity. This was the wall next to us – the wall that joined to the other bedroom. The locked bedroom.'

His index finger twirled back and forth in the air.

'Then this… shape… appeared on the wall, or through it.' He looked at Mom. 'A shape. It was like a figure of eight – like two loops joined together – and it was blue and flickering like a flame, but it was bright, and it was throbbing with the sound, with this muttering, muttering voice.'

'What was it?'

He shook his head. 'We just sat staring at it… and then it started to float across the room towards the bed, which was really shaking now, and the sound was getting louder and louder. There was this big old wooden wardrobe at the end of the bed and this thing floated across and just hung there on the wardrobe door, right in front of us, over us. Like it was looking at us.'

'Were you scared?'

'Very,' I heard Mom whisper under her breath.

'We pulled the blankets up and held onto each other,' Dad said.

'What did you do?'

'We prayed,' said Mom firmly, taking my hand again and squeezing it.

Dad shrugged. 'It's all we could think of. We said the Lord's Prayer out loud, together, on this shaking bed, holding hands. In fact, we shouted it out, the noise was so loud.'

The clock ticked.

'It went away,' Mom said, looking at Dad. 'It just stopped. The shape just faded, like you were turning down a light. The bed stopped shaking and the room went quiet. Totally quiet.'

'What happened then?' I said.

'We left. Straight away,' Dad said. 'We got dressed, got the dog, got in the car and went to your nan's house. Your mom never went back. Never. I went the next day to get some of our things but that was it. For years afterwards, I actually avoided that street, but it's all been knocked down now.'

We sat in silence.

'What was it?' I said. 'Was it the old man?'

'I think it probably was,' Dad said wearily. 'We saw it. It happened. But I've never seen anything else, and never anything in this house. Ever.'

I thought for a second.

'What happened to the dog?'

Dad stood up and turned the TV off. 'I think it's time for bed.'

That's how I was told the scariest ghost story I ever heard, and the start of a life-long fascination. It was the moment my protective bubble burst.

I slept in my parents' bed that night. And the next. I didn't sleep properly for a week or two. Oh, and I didn't go to school the next day.

TWO

The Long Wait

The First Vigil

The knee-high wooden gate squeaked as I pushed it open, white flakes of paint peeling away into the salty evening air. The walled yard in front of the cottage – not much bigger than a dining table – was piled high with the flotsam and jetsam of Cornish life: old deckchairs, windbreaks, nests of tangled rope and old boots long abandoned to the coastal elements.

The yard next door, and all the others in the narrow, cobbled street, was dressed with nautical bric-a-brac and flowerpots. Clearly, this was the only house not being rented to tourists. Not quite 'the edge of the world' that Gus had predicted when I had showed him my train ticket.

Summer, though, was over. The September sky was grey.

The weather-worn front door clung to the tiny building like moss on a stone. Two faded words – 'Saw Porth' – were painted on the stone lintel. I took out my notebook and scribbled it down. Old habits die hard.

Time to open a new chapter. When you are a young reporter, if you're lucky, someone will teach you how to knock on a front door. The knock-knock itself, of course, is irrelevant. Most people have doorbells. Young reporters are taught the art of the introduction, of gaining trust, reading a face, being prepared. It's a pantomime refined over generations of tense doorstep encounters, and not for the faint-hearted.

Most of all, seasoned journalists pale at the memory of their first 'death knock', a rites-of-passage visit to a bereaved family hit by tragedy, requiring tact, empathy and serious balls. The empathy I could do, the rest took training.

Now, with my career about to kick the bucket, I found myself on the doorstep once more. Back to square one. This time, though, I was expected. Or so I thought.

There was no bell, so I knocked. Nothing. I knocked again. Nothing. Leaning across an old deckchair, I peered through the window. Somewhere, a light was on. I rapped on the glass and then again on the door. Nothing.

Not an auspicious start, I thought. I took out my phone, searched recent calls, found a Cornish number and dialled. As the handset reached my ear, an old-fashioned telephone bell rattled beyond the door. I let it ring five or six times, then hung up.

I inspected the screen, considering another try.

'Missed call' blinked at me. Just a few seconds before. The number was familiar – but not Cornish. I looked with hope to the single upstairs window, then flicked to voicemail. No messages.

OK, call them back, I thought. But the number was gone, vanished into the digital ether. 'This is what happens when you try to use a mobile phone on the edge of the world,' I muttered.

With a sigh, I reached for the neatly typed letter that was folded inside my jacket. Like I said, I was trained.

I was about to slip the letter under the door when it suddenly shunted inwards with a scrape of wood on stone that echoed down the street. A small, white-haired lady, squinting through thick glasses and her mouth hanging limp, peered down at me.

'Mrs Angwin?' I stood up, brushing the sandy dirt from my suit trousers and tucking the letter back into my jacket pocket. 'Mrs Angwin, my name is Joe Baxter – I spoke to your daughter on the phone…'

She tightened her squint and raised her chin, inspecting me carefully.

'Mrs Angwin? Is Emblyn in? My name's Joe – Joe Baxter.'

She looked me up and down. Not a word. Then, with a well-practised kick, she forced the door wide open and shuffled inside, leaving me in the open doorway. Those years of training were being put to the test.

I followed. The door opened onto a dull little living room. An unlit coal grate squatted coldly in front of the threadbare sofa and chairs. In the corner an old TV, unused for years, groaned under a stack of curled-up magazines. A little lamp glowed. The smell of waxed wood mixed with mild disinfectant.

At the back, the day's last light lit a tiny kitchen through narrow windows.

Mrs Angwin was sitting down. She ushered me in, limply rolling both wrists at the sofa opposite. I turned to close the open door, but she dismissed it with a feeble wave.

I left it open and sat, sinking deep into the old upholstery, my hands rising on my knees. Mrs Angwin studied me, slack-jawed.

'Mrs Angwin, thank you for seeing me. Is…'

She raised a bony finger, and shook her head slowly from side to side, side to side, side to side. Her eyes slid to a clock above the fire. 'Not yet,' she seemed to say.

We sat. Her face, sand-blasted by seaside life, was deeply lined and drained of colour, her wispy hair almost translucent. Behind her cloudy spectacles wet, distant pupils observed me as if from a different room.

'Sorry! Sorry! Mr Baxter, is it?' A large, middle-aged woman bundled through the front door, her head wrapped in a scarf and her arms weighed down with shopping bags.

'Yes, you must be Emblyn?' I stood, offering a hand.

'Yes, that's right, yes,' she said, barging past me into the kitchen. 'Sorry I wasn't here. Mam, I've got your things, everything but the Guinness.'

She began emptying the bags onto the kitchen table as her mother sat expressionless, her eyes still set on me.

'I tell you what,' she went on, 'it's a miracle I've never run a tourist over. I know St Ives wasn't built for cars but it's like they leave their brains at home when they come down here.'

'It is a bit confusing,' I said. 'Glad I came by train.'

Emblyn Angwin marched past me, removing her scarf to reveal fine blonde hair and a clear family resemblance. She shut the old door with a shove and turned with a toothy smile.

'Well, don't you look smart!' she said. 'Don't get many in suits round here. Weddings and funerals!'

I blushed.

'Well, sit! Sit, Joe Baxter! Let's talk!' She marshalled me expertly back to my dent in the sofa and then sat, with a thump, next to me. Her mother's squint moved between us.

'Did you call me just now? I had a missed call.'

'Not me, love, no signal here at all. You alright, Mam?' she said, her head nodding with every syllable. 'Deaf as a post, she is. Doesn't speak much either these days. Two strokes, they reckon, in quick succession, all in one night. She's still in there, though, still my mam.'

She sat forward, reaching for her mother's knee. 'You're still going strong, aren't you, Mam!'

The wet eyes flickered. A roll of the wrists.

'That's right, who needs ears, eh? Shall we have a cup of tea, and talk about you-know-what?'

*

14

While her mother wasn't much of a talker, Emblyn Angwin certainly was. After she talked me into a cup of tea, she talked me into a seafood stew and a glass of wine.

Afterwards, the three of us sat around the wooden dining table in the little kitchen. The sun had set as we ate, painting the room red as my host talked jovially about everything apart from the reason for my visit: the cost of cockles, the difference between homeless people and tramps, why the Stranglers were better after Hugh Cornwell left.

Finally, as she was clearing away the plates, she fixed me with a serious glance and switched on the light. She took her seat as the bare bulb cast deep shadows beneath our faces.

'Why are you doing this?' she said, her wine glass paused.

'I don't know really. It's been a fascination since I was a boy. An obsession, really. But this is the first time I've done this – actually gone somewhere to do it, I mean.'

She considered her next words. Her mother stared into space.

'It's your funeral, I s'pose,' she shrugged, finally.

'Can you tell me more about it?'

'What do you know?'

'Only what I read in the *Cornishman*.'

She snorted. 'Well, that wasn't entirely accurate.'

'They exaggerated?'

'No, they downplayed it. The reporter looked embarrassed when I told her. She thought I was a loon. Nobody believes us, you know. Which is why nobody will believe you.'

'So, what did you tell her?'

Emblyn took a sip of wine and studied me for a moment.

'And that's what you do, is it? Reporting?'

'It is, yes, but probably not for long.'

She raised an eyebrow.

'It's a disrupted industry,' I said. 'I've been disrupted.'

'Shame.'

15

Outside, a sea breeze brushed leaves against the dark window. It was starting to rain.

Under her breath, the old lady began to make a noise, a soft 'humph... humph... humph... humph'. I watched as the loose skin of her throat moved up and down, then blushed to find Emblyn studying my surprised face.

She smiled. 'I think she's humming to herself, bless her. She does it all the time. I reckon she can't hear what we can hear, on the outside. It's probably a lovely tune inside her head.'

I drank a little more wine and took out my notepad.

'Do you want to tell me about it, then?'

'Well, Mr Baxter, that depends on if you're going to be embarrassed too,' she said. 'It's pretty hard to believe.'

'Why don't we find out. Tell me about what you saw.'

'You won't *see* anything here. But you will hear it. If you listen.'

'It's not a visible thing?'

Mrs Angwin hummed her tune. Humph, humph, humph.

'The house talks to you,' her daughter said. 'That's the only way I can put it.'

'And you've heard it yourself?'

'Yes, but only a few times. But Mam used to say she heard it all the time, almost every night. Said it was worse when the weather was bad. I thought she was barmy; told her she was going senile. Fact is, I only heard it after she went deaf, if you can believe that.'

'What happened?'

'The night she had her stroke – I mean strokes – I was over in Mousehole, visiting friends. I came back the next day and found her on the bathroom floor. Been there hours, bless her.'

Mrs Angwin's wet eyes slid to mine. Humph, humph, humph.

'Anyway, when she was in hospital, in Truro, I came back here to get her some things to keep her comfy. And that's the first time I heard it.'

'What did you hear?'

She tapped the side of her wine glass.

'I tell you what, I'm not going to tell you what I heard. You're going to stay here tonight – that's the idea, isn't it? I don't want to put ideas in your head. If you hear it, you'll know for yourself.'

I put my pad away. 'Fair enough. The report in the paper said something about a window.'

'That's right. Upstairs in the back room. Lovely sea view. That's where I heard it and that's the room that Mam used to talk about.'

'And it's a bedroom?'

'It was Mam's. It's your bedroom tonight.'

Outside, the rain came.

*

The window was unremarkable. The view wasn't. The land fell away behind the house, revealing a handful of moonlit, stepped rooftops that led down to a small cove, which was being lashed by the worsening downpour.

Beyond, a great swell of black sea rose and fell, the surface puckered by rods of rain. The thin glass of the old window rattled in its soft wooden frame as the wind noisily pushed and pulled against it, testing the latch.

I wasn't sure what to do. I had excused myself quite early – just as the clock over the fire had struck eleven – and Emblyn had led me up the narrow staircase, her sense of the dramatic clearly piqued.

Arriving at the room she said, 'Here we are then,' and invited me, mischievously, to enter first. The white panelled door was small, like everything in the house. It gently tapped inside its frame, animated by draughts that were stealing their way in as the storm grew outside.

The room was cold. Emblyn lit some kindling in the lop-sided little fireplace, which lazily flared to produce a block of yellow warmth in the chimney breast. It coloured the white walls of the cell-like room. She picked up the pillow from the bed and plumped it.

17

'Right then,' she said, 'Mam's in the room opposite – you won't get a peep out of her – and I'll be downstairs.' The window rattled. 'Going to be a noisy one, I think!'

Then she turned and left me, shutting the door behind her.

Three hours later, I stood in the dark, watching the sea and waiting for something to happen. The fire had died down, reduced to a glow that occasionally broke the silence with a delicate crack.

I had changed into jogging bottoms and T-shirt, placing my notepad and phone on the bare floor.

What was I doing here? I was in a stranger's spare bedroom, miles from home, listening – that's what I was doing. I smiled to myself. I clearly hadn't thought this through. I wasn't even sure I could stay awake all night.

I sat on the end of the bed, framed in moonlight, the sea and sky wrestling in front of me. Tin-tack waves of droplets swept across the windowpane, reverberating through the silence of the room.

An hour passed, two, three. I had slid back along the bed, sitting against the headboard to watch the storm pass. In the dark, the silence of the room pressed dully against my ears, weighing on my eyelids, pushing my shoulders. The fire was almost dead; red ridges clung on in the blackness, like the leaves of a burnt book. Outside, the storm was moving away. It had been a big one. The rain faintly tapped the glass. Beneath, the sea roiled into bigger and bigger swells.

The moon, gliding behind dark clouds, cast flickers of blue onto the crests of the waves and whipped ribbons of light across the walls of the room, across my face. I felt myself nodding.

Sinking.

Falling.

Suddenly, the moon broke through, unfurling a luminous furrow across the waves that seemed to reach out from the horizon. It bathed the room in light. The window glowed, a block of white. I forced my eyes open, dry and blinking, as the shaft of light clung to the rising water.

That's when I felt it. Something deep and heavy fell across the room.

From the pit of my stomach, from my toes, from my fingertips, from my teeth, from my throat, from my… from my… *heart*, I felt a fathomless sorrow swell, soaking me in sadness, in regret, in loneliness.

In its shadow came an immense, deep silence – a deadening hole that muffled everything, hushing the rain and the wind, smothering the waves and leaving only my thoughts audible.

I looked around the soundless room, as if in a dream – at the dying fire, the raindrops on the glass, all submerged in absolute silence.

Nothing.

From the void came a tiny whisper – female, young, desolate.

'*Ty a fyll dhymm.*'

I felt my heart sink, my stomach turn. My shoulders sagged. Such sadness. Such sadness. Salt welled in my eyes.

Did I really hear that?

The voice came again, from the window, a dry, hoarse whisper. A girl.

'*My a'th kar.*' I felt my heart jump.

I groped around for my notepad and sat up.

'Hello?' My mouth was dry.

'*Ty a fyll dhymm.*' This time she was louder, more desperate. I scribbled on the page, more alien words below 'Saw Porth'. Outside, the dark sea rolled and banked angrily, the moon skipping quickly across the waves as the wind rose.

'Hello… can you hear me?' I whispered. Nothing.

Suddenly, the old glass in the window shook violently, rattling through the room and shattering the silence.

'*Ple'th esos ta! Prag nag esos omma!*' the voice wailed.

With a crash, the window flew open, sending a bitter wind whistling around the room, a hissing swirl of salt and grit and foam. I leapt across the room and onto the window shelf, the rain lashing against my face, and forced it shut. I hammered the wooden latch down with the side of my fist.

Silence again. The sea rose under the moon.

'*My a'th kar,*' came a cold whisper in my ear.

Terror jolted down my spine. I had to get out. As I turned to the door, a blast of cold air rushed down the chimney, and the square hearth of the ancient, lopsided fireplace seemed to glow blue in the moonlight.

'*Ty a fyll dhymm!*' she screamed.

I bolted through the door, then bent double at the top of the stairs, my hands on my knees, as my heart raced in the dark. The door tapped gently in its frame behind me.

Breathe. Breathe. Slowly, the fear subsided.

Rubbing my face, I stood and opened my eyes. A flash of terror.

Two beady eyes watched me.

Old Mrs Angwin stood outside her room, shrouded in the dark.

'She misses him,' she croaked.

As I opened the door at the bottom of the stairs, the warmth from the living room fire welcomed me. Emblyn was sitting on the sofa in the firelight, a glass of wine in her hand, her face grave. She gave me a pitying look.

'Just be thankful you don't speak Cornish,' she said.

THREE

The Rules

Gus Harper squeezed his rotund frame behind the desk and lowered himself into his chair with an involuntary groan.

I eagerly offered him my notebook. He waved it away, then bent down to remove his shoes, sliding his feet into a pair of well-worn slippers. This was Gus's morning ritual, a sign that he was ready to start the day's work.

His face reappeared from beneath the desk to find my notebook still waggling in front of his eyes.

'Really, can't this wait until I've at least had one cup of tea? I'm too old to put up with this juvenile nonsense at this time in the morning.'

'Gus, I'm forty-two and it's nearly 10am. You're an hour late.'

He looked around the deserted newsroom of the *Midland Echo*.

'Well, what are they going to do, sack me?' he said, scratching his beard.

Gus Harper was a long-in-the-tooth hack who had gone to seed but rather enjoyed the process – what is known in the trade as a 'Cardigan Sub'. Once, these beasts prowled every newspaper office, instantly recognisable by their comfy knitwear and disdainful countenance.

As experienced sub-editors – responsible for editing reporters' copy – they were the quality control behind the news. As industry grandees, their main role seemed to be to complain about how things used to be better. At their best, they were inspirational. At their worst, they could be poison.

Gus was both my chief tormentor and my mentor in chief. He was the man who taught me how to knock on a door.

He snatched the notepad from me and immediately dropped it onto his desk.

'You look terrible,' he said, 'even worse than usual.'

'Well, I've had an eventful weekend, haven't I?'

He took off his glasses and began to polish them with the tip of his tie.

'Joe, when are you going to grow out of all this crap? Pretty soon you'll be old enough to vote, drink, drive and you'll probably start getting interested in girls too.'

'Again, I'm forty-two. I think I'm onto something here, Gus, really I do.'

He put his glasses back on with a withering look.

'This isn't news, Joe, you know that. It's bunkum. It just doesn't stand up and frankly, publishing any of it would make any newspaper look ridiculous – unless the whole thing was written tongue-in-cheek, and what's the point in that? It's embarrassing.'

'I told you on the phone what happened. It actually happened.'

'You drank some wine. Some daft old girl told you scary stories. You tried to stay up all night – in a bloody storm too. Then, not surprisingly, you thought you heard something.'

'I did hear something. And it scared the living daylights out of me.'

'Joe, what have I taught you? You know the rules. How are you going to stand it up? Where's your evidence? Remember, your

22

credibility – and the credibility of the paper – depends on the credibility of the stories. So, where's the credibility? Think about what you're asking the reader to believe. This isn't journalism, is it?'

'I'm not thinking about news, I'm thinking about a book.'

'A book, he says! A pop-up one, or one of those ones you colour in?'

'Again, I'm forty-two. And no, a real book. Seat-of-the-pants stuff, reportage. Supernatural claims under proper journalistic scrutiny.'

Gus thought for a second.

'And which one are you, Velma or Daphne?'

Two mugs of steaming tea appeared on the desk between us. Helena Hart, the newsroom's youngest reporter, looked dejectedly down at us, her short brown bob silhouetted against the strip lighting.

'Brown and nasty for you, four sugars for you,' she said.

'Helena sweetheart, what are you doing here?' asked Gus, kindly.

'I work here,' she said, returning to her desk, 'and don't call me sweetheart.'

'But, sweetheart, they told us we didn't have to come in today,' he went on.

Helena shot me an irritated glance. Her thin young face was pale and tired.

'Then what are you doing here, Gus?' she said, tapping on her keyboard.

'Force of habit. Muscle memory. Autopilot. Nothing better to do,' he replied, sipping his tea and winking at me. 'Anyway, after *sixty years*, I'll be the one to decide if I'm finished.'

'You haven't done sixty years,' I scoffed.

'Fucking well feels like it,' he smiled.

Helena stopped typing. 'I know I'm new to all this, but I'm pretty sure he'll decide if you're finished – and I suspect he already has.'

She nodded across the newsroom to the open door of the editor. The light was on.

'Is the prick in?' Gus said, standing.

'Yes. He was on time. He does that.'

'Right!' Gus squeezed from behind his desk and set off across the room, weaving between the empty desks, his slippers gently flapping against his heels.

'What are you going to say?' I shouted.

'I haven't a clue, but it's going to be fun.'

As he reached the door, the dishevelled figure of Seth Nash sidled out. He gave Gus a guilty look and then headed towards us.

Gus marched into the editor's office, boomed 'Good morning!' and angrily shut the door behind him.

Nash sat on the edge of Helena's desk, ran his fingers through his long greasy hair and took out a battered packet of cigarettes.

'Well, that's that,' he said, inspecting the contents.

'What's what?' I said. 'I thought I was in first. That's what was agreed.'

'You are in first. I'm not in the pool anymore. My name's off the list.'

Helena and I exchanged glances.

'Why?' she demanded.

He smiled, stood up and slipped a bent cigarette into his mouth.

'What can I say? I'm going up in the world. Promoted to digital content editor.'

'Hang on – he can't promote someone during a redundancy consultation,' she said.

Nash shrugged. 'He didn't. It was agreed last week – we just finalised it. Things are going online first now, folks, so he knows he needs my kind of content. It gets the clicks. They can use it to fill the paper after it's been on the website.'

My tea suddenly needed more sugar. 'Sounds like a quality read,' I said.

Nash rattled a box of matches. 'Got to shake things up, mate. Got to go viral. No one wants community news anymore. No one cares. Anyway… I'm safe. Best of luck. I'm working from home. You should too.'

We watched him as he scurried out of the office, lighting his smoke as he reached the door.

'Fucking ambulance chaser,' I muttered, as Helena returned to her typing.

I watched her index fingers pecking at the keys, then said, 'You know he's right.'

'About what?'

'Working from home. You needn't have come in today. I've been through this whole thing before – twice. The consultation takes four weeks at least, but they've already said the office is closing. That decision has been made. So, even if we keep our jobs we'll be working from home from now on.'

'We're not keeping our jobs,' she said, eyes fixed to her screen, 'apart from Nash.'

'The consultation hasn't even started.' I looked at my watch. 'In fact, it starts in about ten minutes, with me. There's a lot of talking to be done yet.'

She rested her hands on the desk.

'I'm still at college, technically on probation and – frankly – inexperienced. You're, like, in your sixties or something, you're paid more than they can afford these days and actually too good for what they need.'

'I'm in my forties.'

She corrected me. 'You're forty-two.'

'So, why are you here?'

'For all the high-brow debates, obviously.'

'Ah, the magic of the newsroom,' I said and sipped the sweet tea.

Helena smiled then, for a moment, seemed to drift off, her eyes floating across the empty desks and boxes, listening to the silence.

Raised voices. The editor's door swung open, and Gus stalked out, his face red.

He loped back to his desk and sat with a broad grin. We both looked at him.

His eyes flicked between us.

'Is he trying to groom you? I did warn you about him, didn't I?' he said.

'How did it go in the office?' I refused to rise to his bait. Helena refused to sink to his level.

'Well, I feel a lot better, that's for sure. Where's that toerag Nash?'

'He's gone home. But he says he's safe. He's been promoted to digital content,' she said.

'That ambulance chaser? That just about sums this place up. What a fucking joke.'

Helena tutted. 'So much swearing in here.'

'The magic of the newsroom,' I said. 'How's the course going? Will you get to finish it?'

She nodded. 'Yes, I think so. We're just covering data journalism, and about how you can apply it to investigative stuff.' She looked at Gus. 'Computers. I'm talking about computers.'

He shrugged. 'There's nothing new about data journalism, it's just in my day you did the legwork yourself, we didn't leave it to R2-bloody-D2. All we needed was a phonebook, the *Encyclopaedia Britannica* and half-decent shorthand. Speaking of which…'

He picked up my notebook. 'Now that I'm in a better mood, you can tell me about your magnum opus.'

I rolled forward on my chair.

'Well, it's very simple, really. I'm just going to find places that are supposed to be – you know – haunted, stay there overnight and then write about each one.'

'How many of these are you planning to do?'

'Well, I thought that thirteen seemed like a suitably creepy number. I reckon I could have them done by Christmas.'

He nodded. 'And what about if – sorry, *when* – nothing happens?'

'Then I'll write about that, about the experience, about the people.'

'They'll be a bunch of nutters,' Helena said.

'You might be right, but that'll be half the fun,' I said. 'That's what I like about this job. Which is why I'm going to find them through newspapers, through the people I know at other newsrooms. I sent off a load of emails this morning. I'm looking for stories where someone has had the balls to call up a reporter and say, "There's this really weird thing happening, that I can't explain." I'm not interested in castles or tourist stuff. I want to apply proper journalistic rigour to it and see what happens. Cornwall was eye-opening.'

'What happened in Cornwall?' Helena asked.

'Don't encourage him,' said Gus, leafing through my notebook. 'He's always been crazy about this stuff. Anything even vaguely unusual and he turns into Fox Mulder.'

'Who's Fox Mulder?' she said.

He held up the pad. 'I mean, what's that supposed to mean?'

I shrugged. 'It's Cornish, I think. That's what I heard. I just scribbled down what it sounded like.'

'How much wine did you have?' he said, throwing it back to me.

'Come on, Gus, you know every newsroom has a tale like this. I've already got my next one lined up, in Nottingham. A mate on the *Post* told me about it. You must have seen some weird things over the years.'

He shook his head. 'Nothing surprises me, Joe, nothing.'

'What is the weirdest thing you've had?' asked Helena.

Gus sensed the spotlight fall on him. He thought for a moment, stroking his beard.

'OK – two things, actually. The first was this woman – a young mum – who came in one day with a toddler, asking if she could look through our archives. Years and years ago, this was. She said that every time she drove down a certain road with the kid, and went past a certain point, the kid said, "I died here, Mummy." She wanted to look in the archive to see if there had been an accident there.'

'And had there?' Helena asked.

Gus nodded, smiling. 'There had, yes, about ten years before – although it was a bad one, and lots of people knew about it so…'

'And what was the other one?' He had my interest.

'Ah well, this is a mystery that even freaked out the police – but I reckon I solved it. This was a long, long time ago, back in the days of hot metal and paste-up men. Not long after I came out of the press room to be a reporter.'

'Why have I never heard this story?'

'You never asked. There used to be this thing called the police voice bank – have you heard of that?'

'Like an answer phone for the police?'

'Sort of. Back when there used to be policemen in police stations overnight, and newspapers had early shifts for reporters, the voice bank was a message service that you could dial up and it would tell you what had happened overnight.'

'A recorded message? Like on a tape?' Helena smiled.

'Yep. So, every night, throughout the night, as crimes happened the police press office would update the voice bank – usually burglaries, road accidents, punch-ups outside pubs at the weekend. They used it to appeal for witnesses, give updates on running stories; it was great actually – very useful.'

'Before my time,' I said.

'Anyway, the desk sergeants were very careful about what they put on it, as they knew it would go straight into morning editions. But there was this one morning where they had left a message which was pretty weird. They took it down pretty quickly afterwards too.'

He leant back with a satisfied smile, knowing he'd hooked us.

'Well, go on then!' Helena laughed.

Gus grinned. 'So, this happened in the winter, in the run-up to Christmas and it was snowing. Lots.' He turned to Helena. 'It used to do that.'

'Get on with it,' I said.

'Yes, so… it had been snowing all night, a real white-out blizzard. It was really thick when I got into the newsroom. I was on earlies, so it was my job to ring the voice bank at about 5am.'

He looked at us both, hanging on his every word.

'Joe, you know Witton cemetery, right?'

'Yes, the big one near the motorway?'

'That's it, that's the one.' His eyes flicked to Helena. 'Biggest cemetery in the city, huge old Victorian place with six-foot walls all the way round. Thousands and thousands of graves, all crumbling away. It's surrounded by roads and housing now.'

'So, what happened?' she said, reluctantly taking the bait.

'The message was an appeal for witnesses,' Gus went on. 'Apparently, a workman – like a plumber or an electrician – had been driving home in his van very late, through this thick snowstorm. It was the early hours of the morning and the roads were quiet, no other vehicles at all. Then he reached Witton. As he was going past the old cemetery, he was struggling to see what was ahead because of the blizzard. Then suddenly – WHAM! – he smashed into someone standing in the middle of the road – and he went right through him. He skidded to a halt and jumped out, expecting to find someone lying dead in the street. But there was nobody there.'

Helena and I exchanged glances.

Gus went on: 'So, this fella panics. He looks at the front of his van and there's a bloody great dent in the front where he's hit this man, but no blood, no footsteps and all the time the snow's still coming down thick and fast. He starts to look around the roads nearby because he's worried that the bloke's limped off and is lying somewhere, dying in the snow. Here's the best bit: he went into

29

the cemetery too, through the old iron gates, and stands there in the blizzard calling out – which must have freaked him out even more. Nothing. So, he ran to a phone box and called the police.'

'And what did the voice bank say?' I asked.

'Well, they had to take it seriously, didn't they? There was a dent in the vehicle, so he must have hit someone, but no one had turned up in hospital and they'd searched the area and the cemetery for hours. Nothing. The driver was proper shaken up, and adamant that he'd run someone over. It was apparently him who suggested he might have hit a ghost. The police aren't going to say that, so they tried to make light of it. The message said they were looking for the press's help with solving a "spooky mystery" near the cemetery and appealed for witnesses to come forward. But after an hour the message was erased, probably because it sounded so ridiculous – but the chap was adamant it had happened. It was wiped before anyone else got in that morning, so I was the only one to hear it. It's the only time I know of where the police have put out an official appeal after a ghost sighting.'

Helena sat back in her chair. 'Did the paper run the story?'

He chuckled. 'God no... it was too ridiculous, just not the sort of thing the *Echo* wrote about. These days we'd be all over it online, I suppose. Brilliant click bait. But no – not then, not in print. But it was a real mystery, and people talked about it that Christmas quite a bit...'

He raised a finger. 'And I solved it.'

'What do you think happened?' I asked.

He paused for effect, savouring his moment.

'Some silly fucker built a snowman in the road,' he said, dismissively.

We both groaned.

Across the room, the office door closed with a click. The editor was pulling on his suit jacket and looking at me with a forced smile.

'Joe, we'll be ready for you in five minutes in the boardroom,' he said, and slipped through the double doors to the stairs.

'I wish someone would run him over,' said Gus.

I gathered up my things. Helena wished me 'good luck' as I headed for the stairs.

Outside the boardroom, the company's founding family stared down at me from dusty portraits. The awards cabinet that had reflected the paper's fortunes over the years stood half empty, boxes on the floor filled with pitted silver cups and slabs of Perspex. Only photographs remained behind the glass, group shots of shaggy-haired reporters and Brylcreemed printers in horn-rimmed spectacles. My eyes fell on their usual mark: a black and white image of young men in overalls, raising glasses of beer in front of a gleaming new press. At the front, my dad was caught, mid-laugh. At his shoulder, a shiny-faced Gus whispered in his ear.

'Hard to believe it's all over,' said Gus quietly from behind me. He had followed me up the stairs.

'It's been coming for a long time,' I said, 'but it's only over for me and you. It will carry on, just not like this.'

Gus picked up a silver cup and ran his finger across the engraved front.

'It doesn't have to be over for you, Joe, they'll keep you if you want to carry on.'

'I don't think so, not this time. I don't fancy the new era. Working from home, trawling social media for leads. That's what news is these days, I get it. Nash might want to do it, but it's not for me.' I looked at the boardroom door. 'I think it's time to duck out, gracefully.'

Gus put the cup back in the cabinet and inspected the photograph.

'If you're sure that's what you want. Your dad would have hated all this, but he would have loved you being a reporter. You know he wanted to do it, but never got the chance.'

'I know.'

He put a hand on my shoulder. 'You're so much like him, you know that, don't you? The thing is, Joe, after what happened to him, I need to know you're OK. That you're happy with this, that you're dealing with it.'

I felt emotion begin to swell, just as the boardroom door opened. The editor's eyes met Gus's. He nodded gently and retreated inside. At the back of the room, a fierce-looking woman from Human Resources sat, pen poised in her hand.

I cleared my head.

'Gus, it's fine. I'm OK.'

'Good, good,' he said, straightening my tie. 'Now get in there and give him hell!'

FOUR

The Lock-In

The Second Vigil

The ancient arched entry to the Old Tunns sulked inside the glazed porch, like a museum exhibit trapped behind glass. I peered inside. The building was dark, the glass reflecting my silhouette on the pavement as the last shoppers of the day passed behind me.

Over one of the windows a banner flapped in the breeze, proclaiming in an unsuitable font: 'Under renovation – opening soon'. The distant buzz of an electric drill drifted from a propped-open window on the top floor of the thin three-storey building.

I pressed my face to the glass, eyes shielded by cupped hands, just as a tall figure sauntered out of the darkness towards me, a phone pressed to his ear. He unlocked the door without giving me a second glance, then turned away as I stepped in behind him, my overnight bag on my shoulder.

'Hi,' he said loudly.

'Hi, I'm Joe Baxter,' I said to his back.

He spun around and looked at me in faux surprise. 'Hi, this is Jordan Newbould from the New Old Tunns in Nottingham,' he continued into the phone, 'I need to speak to Maxim, please. About a delivery date for tiles. Bathroom. The Old Tunns. The New Old Tunns. They should have been here this morning.' He rolled his eyes at me and turned away to continue his conversation.

I was standing in a short tunnel. It cut straight through the old building before opening up into a broad cobbled courtyard, stacked with wooden picnic tables to the rear. Red metal trap doors stood open at the far end, thirsty for the next delivery of beer. Above, the hive-like frame of a glazed roof was taking shape over the yard. On either side of the tunnel empty doorframes gaped awkwardly, their doors confiscated. Power leads crept like vines across the cobbled floor to disappear into the two bars that flanked it. I dropped my bag on the floor.

Jordan Newbould paced around, speaking into his phone in an abstract tone while inspecting his latest project. He was tall and thin – like every twenty-something of his generation seemed to be – with a tower of blond hair extending from shaved temples to provide unnecessary extra altitude. Below a carefully shaped beard his lean body seemed to swing, pendulum-like, wrapped in T-shirt, tight blazer and skinny jeans. Marching about the historic coaching tunnel, he looked as ill-placed as his intentions for one of Nottingham's oldest buildings.

He finished his call and swivelled in his Converse trainers to face me full on.

'Joe? Jordan.' He offered a limp handshake that briefly clutched the end of my fingers, then extended a long arm across my shoulders to lead me into one of the bars.

'I'm not really a newspaper person,' he said sympathetically, 'but I'd really like to explore the story of the Tunns and how it is evolving.'

This didn't look much like evolution to me. The room, which had obviously once been a cosy saloon, was being stripped back to the brickwork. One wall of panelled joinery was half gone, the nicotine-stained woodwork prised away to lie in piles of plaster-caked, splintered timber. Paintings and pictures leant in stacks in the corner, facing the wall like out-of-favour children.

'I think I know what you're hoping for,' he went on, 'so I've lined up some people who you can talk to, who will help you get what you need. Beginning with... Darren.'

We arrived at an alcove where a large, red-haired man was kneeling to strip panelling. He stood and removed his glove to offer a calloused hand and an uneasy smile.

'Darren. Joe,' said Jordan Newbould. His phone rang. 'Maxim!' He was gone.

'I have no idea what's going on,' I said to Darren.

'He wanted me to tell about the things moving,' he said, sheepishly.

We sat on barstools, our elbows finding room among broken tiles and screwdrivers.

'I wasn't expecting to talk to anyone,' I said. 'I only really arranged to stay overnight – so I'm grateful for your time. You're obviously busy.'

He shrugged. 'That's alright. I don't know what to say really. I feel stupid even talking about it.'

'So, what's moved? Jordan hasn't really explained anything.'

Darren smiled and shook his head. 'Yep, sounds about right.' He pointed along the bar. 'You see that yellow crowbar?'

'Yes.'

'Well, that moved.'

'It moved.'

'Yes.'

'Did you see it move?'

'Nope, but it moved alright.'

'But you didn't see it?'

'Nope.'

'Then how do you know it moved?'

Darren gestured to the piles of splintered wood and rubbed his short-cropped hair self-consciously.

'Well, because I was using it over there. And then I put it on the floor. And then I looked back at the wall. And then I reached for it and it was up on the bar, right where it is now. Like, in the space of two seconds.'

'Just like that?'

'Just like that.' He smiled again. 'Look, that's just the tip of the iceberg. I'm the foreman, and I lost two staff this week because of this. They just got up and walked out because their stuff kept moving. And they did see it.'

Instinctively, I took out my notepad. 'Can I speak to them?'

'Maybe.' He looked at the pen hovering above the page. 'Two Polish lads, so I'd have to find them. But it's been going on for a few days, well, since we started.'

'And what did they see?'

'Well... Antoni said his hammer slid across the floor, right in front of him. Aleks said his van keys flew across the room.'

'And you believed them?'

'They're professional lads, good workers – and they needed the money. You don't come all the way from Poland to walk off a good site like this over nothing. And there was no persuading them to stay, that's for sure. And then my crowbar went walkies.'

I looked around the stripped room.

'Can I ask you a question? Is this allowed? I mean, this is obviously a historic building.'

'It's all been signed off and approved,' Darren said. 'It's a listed building but all these fittings – the panelling, the doors, the décor – it's all just post-war reproduction of what was here originally, so it can come out, as long as the fabric of the building is respected. That's why all the new structural stuff, like the porchway and the roof, is just glazing. It can just be unscrewed and removed in the future... and the Old Tunns is back to how she was.'

Jordan reappeared, his index finger scrolling across his phone as he approached.

'All good?' he smiled, inviting me from my stool. We were off again.

'Thank you,' I said to Darren, as Jordan steered me back across the tunnel into the other bar. A woman and a man, both middle-aged, waited grim-faced at a table. Sharing the guilty demeanour of co-conspirators sitting outside a headmaster's office, they both had a half-drunk pint of beer in front of them. They also seemed to be wearing matching grey cardigans.

'This is Margaret, our shift manager,' Jordan said, ushering her to her feet. Margaret obediently offered a firm, cold handshake and sat back down without a word. '… And this is Malcolm. Malcolm used to work here too, but now he's one of our most loyal regulars – and something of a history buff.'

Malcolm glared at me. 'Evening,' he said, throwing a contemptuous glance at Jordan, whose phone began to chirp again.

He looked at the name on the screen. 'Sorry… got to get this.' He flicked long fingers at his two captives. 'These guys will tell you all about it, ask them anything. Maxim!' And again, Jordan Newbould was gone.

'I'm Joe, by the way,' I said, sitting down as Jordan disappeared back into the tunnel.

'And you're from the *Post*, are you?' asked Margaret. She had the steely eyes and thin lips of a pub landlady used to cutting drunks down to size. Her mousy long hair was tied into a ponytail.

'Actually, I'm from the *Midlands Echo* – but I'm not here for the paper really, I'm working on a book.'

They both let out a little groan.

Malcolm spoke up: 'We were hoping you'd write a story about what's happening here, the bloody mess they're making of this place.'

'You're not happy with the changes, then?'

'No one is,' Margaret said, 'and it's all happening so quickly. Two weeks ago, I was the landlady here, now I'm a bloody shift manager and the builders are pulling my pub apart.'

'They're ripping the soul out of the place,' Malcolm interjected. 'This is a historic building not a bloody greenhouse.'

I took out my pad. 'I'm researching a book about paranormal stuff, but I can have a word with a friend on the *Post* if you like. I'm sure he'd talk to you about your concerns.'

'I can't say anything anyway,' said Margaret, 'not if I want to keep my job.'

'I bloody can,' said Malcolm.

'Well, I'll get your details before I go tomorrow and see what I can do,' I said, waving the pad. Malcolm stuck out his bottom lip, gave a begrudging nod of his head and reached for his beer.

'So, you're staying here tonight? The rooms upstairs aren't ready yet,' Margaret said, crossing her arms.

'Well, Jordan has said I can stay but I'm not sure where. I was hoping you could tell me where the best place is to – you know – see something.'

They looked at each other. A little smile passed between them.

'Let me tell you a little bit about the history of this place,' Malcolm said, sitting forward to carefully place his glass on a beermat. Margaret looked at her nails. She had heard this before.

'The Old Tunns is the fourth oldest pub in Nottingham – after Ye Olde Trip to Jerusalem, Ye Olde Salutation and the Bell Inn – and in its day was a very important coaching stop on the Great North Road. The coaches would come through that archway to be stabled at the back – where they are now building that bloody great sunroof – and the passengers would stay in rooms upstairs. This bar, the lounge, was for travellers and the other one, the saloon, was for the locals.'

'It's an amazing building,' I said.

'Was,' Margaret muttered.

'She's seen everything, the Tunns has, and survived it all – Hitler's bombs, plagues, recessions. It's a bloody disgrace what's happening now, it's upset everyone,' Malcolm added, sitting back to inspect his pint.

'Tell me about the things moving,' I said, 'the haunting. Is it part of the pub's history?'

'Well, he's clearly upset too,' Margaret said, 'and not for the first time.'

'Who's he?'

She looked up from her nails. 'The drummer boy.'

'The drummer boy?'

Margaret's eyes prompted Malcolm to continue, then returned to her nails. He sat forward. His pint found its beermat again.

'This is the story,' he said, clearly warming to the task. 'This was a coaching inn during the English Civil War, and Nottingham was where King Charles I set up base – at the castle – after the war started. So, this was a Royalist town and all the pubs and inns were used as digs, and for recruiting, by his soldiers. You know, Cavaliers and what not. But the Roundheads – Oliver Cromwell and the Parliamentarians – were making constant attempts to take the city and force old Charlie Boy out into the countryside. Nottingham was right at the centre of the war. Anyway, the story goes that the Old Tunns was being used by a small group of Royalist troops, with the Cavaliers and officers staying upstairs and the foot soldiers down here and in the stables. Perfect place for them, strategically, as it's on one of the main routes in and out of Nottingham, and there's lots of ale and food to eat. Happy days. They made themselves at home.'

He cast a glance at Margaret. 'Suddenly, they hear word that there's a massive column of Roundheads marching up the road from Newark, with the intention of stopping right here, at the Tunns. So, the Royalists drink all the beer, grab all the food, gather up all their things and get the hell out – they scarper into the centre of Nottingham where the rest of the King's army is. Safety in numbers, you see.'

Margaret picked up her glass. 'Problem is, they didn't all leave,' she said, taking a sip.

'Am I telling this or what?' snapped Malcolm.

She rolled her eyes and replaced the glass. 'Get on with it, then,' she said to her nails.

Malcolm sat forward again. 'Problem is, they didn't all leave.

'In their haste they left behind a young drummer boy, all done up in blue velvet and white ribbons, who had drunk a bit too much beer and was asleep in the stables. When the Roundheads got here, after marching for hours and hours, they found the beer barrels were all dry and the pantry was empty and they weren't best pleased. And then this poor young boy comes wandering out of the stable block dressed up like Little Lord Fauntleroy, nursing a sore head.'

'What happened to him?'

Malcolm grimaced. 'They beat him to a pulp,' he said, 'used him for target practice, did all manner of unspeakable things to him, and then tossed him into the cellar and locked it. Then they smashed the place up and set off down the road for the next inn, looking for beer and food.'

'And the boy?'

'Nobody knew he was down there, poor little sod. I think he probably tried to escape by crawling along the old drains, trying to get to the next cellar along the road – the road is riddled with them. But he wouldn't have been able to get through, they're too narrow. Most likely he starved to death. They found his body months later, in the cellar, when the Royalists took the area back.'

'And he's the one that moves things?'

'That's what they say,' said Malcolm, sitting back, his job done. 'He usually plays little tricks, nothing spiteful.'

Margaret spoke quietly. 'I think… he doesn't like change. He's been here a very long time, and he doesn't like people messing with his home. This trouble that's going on with the workmen – well, that's happened before. When I first started, back in the 1980s, that's when the toilets were upgraded and he did exactly the same then, moving tools and throwing things. But this is on a different scale. He's not very happy at all.'

'Has anyone ever seen him?' I asked.

'I've seen him,' she said.

'She's seen him,' Malcolm confirmed.

'Where was this?' I placed my phone on the table. 'Sorry, do you mind if I record this – my shorthand's not what it was.'

Margaret shrugged. 'It was upstairs, years ago. About ten years ago, I should think.'

'In one of the bedrooms?'

'Until very recently it was a flat – my flat – that I got as landlady.'

Malcolm nodded. 'The Tunns stopped being a hotel after World War I, and became just a pub. But now it's going to have rooms to rent upstairs again.'

'I see. So, tell me what you saw.'

Margaret took the last swig of her pint and looked at the ceiling. Malcolm sat back. It was his turn to listen.

'Well, we had closed and cleaned up after a lock-in with some of the regulars, so it was very late. I'd gone to bed. I was pretty boozed up, if I'm honest. You don't really drink when you're behind the bar, so you make up for it quick-sharp after the doors have closed. Anyway... I was asleep and then I woke up – because I had this feeling that someone else was in the room. You know that feeling you get when you sense someone is standing behind you? Like that.'

Margaret pulled her cardigan tight around her.

'It was totally dark and I couldn't see a thing, so I sat up in bed and said, "Hello?" Nothing. Nothing at all. When you live over a pub sometimes you worry that you've left a door open or a window – or one of the punters has got locked in when you've closed up. So, I called out "hello" again. Nothing. But I still had this feeling that there was someone in there. In the dark.'

Malcolm raised his eyebrows. We were clearly coming to the good bit.

'I stared into the dark at the end of the bed. Just stared and stared. And slowly my eyes started to adjust to the darkness so I could see little outlines of things, like the window frame and the door. And in the corner, I notice this cross shape – like a little "X" shape – hovering in the dark. *That's odd*, I thought, so I stared at it harder, for ages. And as my eyes adjusted the X got bigger and whiter and wider and I started to make out shoulders above it in the dark too.'

She looked at Malcolm. 'I wasn't frightened at all, though, it wasn't threatening in any way.'

She put her glass down with an awkward smile. 'I must have stared at that corner for an hour. And as my eyes got used to the dark he just emerged, outwards from this little "X" shape. He was just standing there, this little boy. The "X" was the straps across his chest – you know, straps like would hold a drum or something. By the end I could even see the shine on his velvet jacket.'

'Did he say anything?' I asked.

'I don't think he even knew I was there,' she said. 'His eyes were just looking around the room, like it was the first time he'd seen it, like he was surprised to be there. He was smiling.'

'He's supposed to be quite playful,' Malcolm said.

'And then he just sort of stepped back into the darkness, and he was gone,' she added. 'I got up and had a cup of tea, and then went back to bed and slept like a baby. Never saw him again.'

They both sat looking at me, their arms crossed in their matching cardigans.

'That's quite a story,' I said, reaching to touch 'stop' on the phone's recorder app. 'So, do you think upstairs is the best place for me to stay tonight, or in here? I'm a bit concerned about all these tools and power lines lying about.'

Malcolm chuckled. 'Oh, you won't be sleeping up here. You won't find him up here.'

He jabbed a finger playfully towards the ground. 'He's down there.'

*

There's a theory that Americans wrongly think the British like their beer warm because inn keepers here kept their barrels at 'room temperature' – when the room in question was actually the pub's cellar. The cellar of the Old Tunns was anything but warm.

Malcolm led me, followed by Jordan and Margaret, through an old wooden door that lay beyond public view and so had survived the aesthetic cull. In the dimness behind the bar, the door appeared a dull red colour, but decades of bashing by beer crates had left the paint pock-marked with craters, revealing older coats in ridges of green, white and blue like multi-coloured rings in a tree trunk.

At the bottom of rickety stairs, the maze-like cellar was cold and damp but well-lit, with dusty strip lights strung across an impossibly low whitewashed ceiling. A smell of earth and beer cloyed the air, which hummed gently with the noise of pressured pipes and electric circuit boards. If the Old Tunns had been a ship, I was standing in the engine room. It felt alive, almost alert.

We stood just inside the cramped doorway, next to a threadbare settee and a battered desk, an old radio sat forlornly in its centre.

Directly ahead of us, in a dank corner, stood the remains of a long-abandoned kitchenette, with a filthy sink and rusting metal hob. On the floor, an ancient iron grate jutted upwards.

Jordan, who was trying his best not to touch anything, took charge. 'This was Malcolm's lair, when he was the pub's...' He searched for the word.

'Pop man,' Malcolm said.

'Pop man! Love that!' Jordan exclaimed. 'Malcolm, would you give Joe a quick tour? Show him what he can't touch, health and safety and all that? You'll be alone all night, Joe, but the first shift starts upstairs at 5am on the electrics. Lots to do!'

He placed a hand on Malcolm's shoulder. 'Sorry to be cheeky, but a couple of barrels have just been delivered at the back – I don't suppose you'd mind rolling them down the runners for me?'

Malcolm gave him an incredulous look, prompting Margaret into action.

'I'll help with that,' she said, 'I still work here after all.'

An oblivious Jordan was already disappearing up the stairs, pausing only at the top to wish me 'good luck'.

The cramped cellar was a labyrinth of walkways and shelving which seemed to cover the entire footprint of the pub. I placed my bag on the desk before Malcolm and Margaret led me along one of the side walls, which changed from white-painted brick after a few yards to reveal rough-hewn sandstone that was wet to the touch.

Malcolm slapped it. 'The whole of Nottingham is built on a bloody great slab of this stuff, so all of the old pubs have cellars that are carved out of the stone. Keeps everything nice and cold.'

Along the floor steel kegs of beer were lined up, plumbed into the arteries of the building, while crates of bottles rose in stacks everywhere. Wires and piping snaked along the walls, rising to disappear through holes in the ceiling to the bars above.

Halfway along the wall, a bricked-up arched doorway appeared. Malcolm pointed to another one directly opposite on the far side of the cellar. 'They were all linked up at some point in the past,' he said. 'All the cellars along the road.'

In the centre of the room an old, domed boiler sat blackly next to a mass of modern electrical equipment, which hummed and blinked over piles of dusty boxes, broken chairs and solidified sacks of cement.

We reached the far end of the cellar, turning the corner to find two squat tunnels cut into the stone. Narrow rails ran up the centre of each one. Malcolm clicked on a light, which flickered to reveal a small room at the end of the tunnels. Two kegs of beer stood on a wooden platform. Beyond, a ramp led up to the red trap doors in the yard above, now closed.

'Give us a moment, Joe,' Margaret said, and they scurried up the nearest tunnel. I watched as they expertly upended the barrels and eased them off the platform onto the metal rails. Then they each rolled a barrel along the two tunnels, the sound of the steel kegs whirling around the sandstone with a grinding metallic echo.

'Just leave them on the rails for now,' Margaret said as she stepped out of the tunnel. 'I don't know why he ordered them anyway, we don't reopen for a fortnight.'

'Probably got them cheap,' said Malcolm, dusting his hands.

They led me back to our starting point along the other side wall, stepping over boxes and crates and past the other bricked-up doorway. I noticed that, above eye level, a single brick was missing, revealing the quiet blackness of another space beyond. Along the way, Malcolm dutifully pointed out fuse boxes and trip hazards. We emerged near the defunct kitchenette, opposite the stairs.

He pointed to the rusting metal grate on the floor. Beneath it was a coffin-like stone-cut gutter which disappeared under the floor in the direction of the wall.

'Mind out for that,' he said. 'That's one of the original drains. You don't want to trip over that in the dark.'

*

This time, I had come better prepared. After making sure that I had everything I needed, Malcolm and Margaret looked down from the top of the stairs like nervous parents and asked, 'Lights on or off?'

I clicked on my heavy LED torch and said, 'Off.'

'Rather you than me,' muttered Malcolm, flicking the switch and shutting the heavy door behind them.

I popped the top of the torch open and stood it up on the desk. It cast a warm yellow circle of light around the immediate area, illuminating the settee and radio and almost reaching the old sink.

The contents of my bag were already spread out across the desk: spare batteries, my phone, a woolly hat and gloves, a notepad, a sleeping bag, a flask of tea, water, chocolate and sandwiches. I plugged my phone charger into the ancient power outlet used by the old radio. Next to it lay a clear plastic bag containing sticks of chalk and the shiny metal playing pieces from a game of Monopoly: a little dog, a racing car, a top hat, a boot, a boat, an iron.

The sleeping bag was quickly unzipped and unfurled across the settee and hot, sweet tea poured into the cap of the flask. Then I spread out the Monopoly pieces on the desk and carefully drew around each one with the chalk.

'Your move,' I said under my breath.

Then I sat down on the settee, wrapped the sleeping bag across my legs, picked up my tea and turned off the torch.

The cellar was immediately swallowed by darkness but then, almost as quickly, the room reappeared – developing like a photograph, dimly lit by dozens of different lights blinking on the machinery that ticked over as the Old Tunns slept above. The phosphorescent light show was backed by the quiet buzzing, chirping, humming and whirring of technology. The dark cellar had an eco-system of its own, a sandstone cavern on stand-by mode yet still strangely awake. As the little green, yellow and red lights took turns to throw shadows across the walls, it looked a little like a fun fair. Or a playground.

My sandwiches didn't last long. Afterwards, I set out on a slow and careful expedition to explore the nooks and crannies of the cellar, taking the torch with me but not switching it on; I wanted my eyes to get used to the dim glow given off by the equipment. I stepped carefully over the grate of the old drain, then moved along the wall, inspecting the second bricked-up doorway and staring up into the blackness beyond the little missing-brick cavity. When I turned the corner I felt the first chill of fright at the site of the two loading tunnels, the pregnant silver barrels still sitting toad-like on their rails. The half-light of the equipment only reached midway down the tunnels, glistening dully on the red sandstone walls, giving them a wet, flesh-like sheen. I peered down them. Pitch black. I would not be venturing into the tunnels, I decided.

By the time I returned to the settee my eyes had fully adjusted to the dimness. One by one, I inspected my Monopoly piece control experiment. None of them had moved during my little safari.

So, I sat back down, pulled on the woolly hat and gloves and wrapped the sleeping bag back across my knees. My ears were filled with the background thrum of the cellar now; I was confident of staying awake all night. Sleep, however, had other ideas.

The dream I fell into was aural and smothering. A heaving tide of bleeping gadgets, distant, flapping banners and buzzing drills washed around my head, a whirlpool of drifting noises into which I sank. From the depths, voices bubbled up: Jordan exclaimed, 'Pop man!'; Malcolm muttered; my smiling editor beckoned me into the boardroom, down the rickety stairs, into the sandstone tunnels, into the dark. Then suddenly another voice – no, a new presence – began to float up, an unknown, a stranger, lifeless and limp, rising from the sediment up and up and up; it dragged my consciousness in its wake, clinging to its long, buckled shoes, chasing behind in a rising panic that pushed past the interloper to burst through and scream in my own voice. Someone else is here. Someone else is here!

I sat up with a violent jolt, my elbow jarring the desk, shunting the Monopoly pieces from their chalk pools. I forced my eyes wide and glared into the dimness, breathing heavily. My heart was pounding. Margaret's voice came to me, certain and stern: 'Someone else was in the room.' Electricity charged the cellar's thick air.

I was no longer alone. I knew it.

My eyes landed on the scattered Monopoly experiment.

Get yourself together.

Pulling off the gloves, I began to quickly place each piece back in its chalk circle, willing my eyes to focus on the trinkets, but they refused, jumping to scan the room as I moved each one – first the little silver dog, then the racing car, the top hat, the boot, the boat. I reached across the desk for the last piece – the iron – when a tiny scraping sound drifted up, breaking the spell. I looked down. My eyes widened as the little dog slowly slid back out of its circle, pushed by an invisible force.

I was on my feet.

'Hello?' The little dog fell over.

Sshhft. Somewhere in the labyrinth of boxes, chair legs and crates, something moved – a shuffle above the background hum.

'Hello?'

Ssshhhft. Another shuffle, longer, bigger, in a different place. I swallowed hard and pulled off my hat, suddenly hot. I grabbed up the torch but resisted the urge to flick it on.

Get it together!

Edging forward, the old sink and hob loomed out of the dark. Finding the far wall, I began to pick my way along it, stepping over boxes and sacks with the unused torch clutched to my chest.

'Hello?' I called again. 'Hello?'

Another shuffle, followed by a dull metallic 'clang' near the boiler. I peered at the black, domed shape. For just a moment the silhouette seemed to bulge, as if something moved behind it. A shoulder?

Ssshhhft.

I took two more steps along the wall, my free hand feeling the cold sandstone until it touched the dry surface of the bricked-up doorway.

I froze.

Near my ear – from the wall – came the distinct sound of footsteps. The hole. The hole in the brickwork. Footsteps from the cellar next door?

The rectangular hole was a foot above eye level. A deep, velvet blackness pressed against the other side of it, like water at the bottom of a well. I dragged an old, broad paint tin and stood on it, teetering for a second as my eyes came level with the gap. Then I took a deep breath, placed the torch into it and flicked it on.

It was not another cellar. Six feet ahead of my strained eyes was another hand-cut sandstone wall. It blushed a skin-like red in the torchlight, garish, wet and glistening. Putrid air escaped from the cavity. It was silent in there; hollow, encased. I realised I was still holding my breath. Carefully, I moved the flashlight left, right and back to the centre within the little hole. The sandstone wall extended as far as the beam would reach.

A sob.

A soft, pitiful sob.

My body tensed, my feet pushing down on the paint tin. Had I heard that?

Again. A soft, gentle sob drifted up from the foot of the red wall. I exhaled; my heart raced. I *had* heard that.

Carefully, I began to tilt the back of the torch up, the beam descending slowly over the red stone in front of me, my eyes following it down, down, down. I lifted onto the tips of my toes as the light sank below floor level, the red wall shimmering deeper and deeper. My brow pressed to the brickwork, I peered down my nose, straining to see the bottom of the pit as the light slid down, down, down.

I gasped. There. A head. Shoulders. Real.

His face was against the wall. I blinked, blinked again, my hot breath against the brickwork. He was there, below me. Long, curly yellow hair shone matted and wet in the torch light. His shoulders, hunched and tightly strapped in yellowed leather, shuddered gently up and down as he sobbed quietly to himself, trapped, alone. It was a pathetic, intimate sight.

Emotion filled my chest. Not now, not now. Bite down on it.

I teetered on the paint tin, the beam swinging away and then back to him as I wet my dry lips.

'H-h-hello?' I whispered through the hole.

Slowly, as if awakened from sleep, the quivering blond head began to turn. Little lips pouted beneath a mop of damp hair as the figure shuffled around, to face away from the wall, chest-deep in a pool of shadow. Then, from the bottom of the pit, he lifted his gaze to look directly at me with black, empty eye sockets. The little boy smiled. Playtime.

The paint tin gave way. I tumbled back into the cellar with a crash, as the torch slipped from my grasp and fell through the hole, clattering into the darkness beyond. I lay, breathing heavily in a pile of old cardboard boxes, staring at the ceiling as my eyes fought to refocus in the dim light.

With a sharp screech, a harsh, grinding metallic sound suddenly roared through the cellar, rolling around the walls, overpowering the ticks and whirrs of the room, filling my ears. I knew immediately what it was. One of the barrels was on the move.

I clambered to my feet and started to pick my way back to the wall, consciously avoiding the bricked-up doorway, as the sound of metal on metal vibrated through the dark room, grinding the air. It stopped, dead, as I turned the corner to the loading tunnels. One of the barrels was gone.

I stood at the empty rails, staring into the darkness of the tunnel, as the metallic echoes faded and the cellar fell silent.

'Hello?' I said into the void. My voice bounced back at me. 'I'm sorry if I scared you. My name is Joe.'

A sob. A giggle. Slowly, the barrel began to roll out of the darkness towards me, propelled invisibly, its steel rim shining as it moved, filling the room with sound again. It halted, halfway along the rails, like an unsure dog offered food.

'My name is Joe...' I repeated, speaking to the barrel. '... I wanted to say hello...'

With a jerk the steel keg trundled back into the darkness, disappearing to the far end of the tunnel. I heard it rock against the wooden platform at the rear. A shuffle in the dark.

I edged towards the loading ramp's light switch, my hand hovering over it.

'Are you still there?' I called.

Another shuffle. I hit the switch.

The strip light beyond clicked and flickered, the two tunnels blinking like eyes and I saw the boy's hunched little silhouette caught in a yellow flash but, just as the lights caught, they died, instantly, with a paper-bag 'pop', followed by every piece of equipment in the cellar – the pumps, the electrics, the meters, the little lights – going out behind me, one by one, like a city at night.

For the first time that evening, I found myself in absolute darkness, absolute silence, absolute stillness.

A rush of air from the tunnel. A giggle. I felt the boy push past me in the dark, brushing against my side, my hip, to then run on across the inky black room, his heels clicking tap, tap, tap against the floor in little strides as though the cellar was empty, as though it was yet to be filled with centuries of junk, stacked with crates, plumbed with pipes, strung with lights. I wanted to run with him.

I followed him, feeling my way along the other wall, past the first bricked-up doorway, towards the settee and desk. As I reached the bottom of the stairs, the sound of his footsteps halted, abruptly. Across the cellar, a block of dim blue-white light rose from the old drain, projecting the grid of the iron grate onto the low ceiling, and throwing dark shapes onto the walls. The long shadow of an outstretched hand reached towards me across the desktop.

My flask stood in its centre, one of my gloves carefully placed on its top to offer a friendly wave. In front of it, the Monopoly pieces lined up like little soldiers.

As the light from the drain flickered and died, the faintest giggle rose from its rusting grate.

*

Nothing else happened that night, and I didn't stay in the cellar any longer. It wasn't fear that forced me upstairs, but rather a sense that I was now intruding, that playtime was over – and a feeling that I had been sent a message which I was yet to decipher.

When Darren unlocked the Old Tunns at 5am, I was waiting on the other side of the new glass door, my bag on my shoulder. I sheepishly greeted him, avoided his questions, and set off in search of an early train.

FIVE

Sleeping with the Dead

Remember me.

Remember me.

Remember me.

Remember me. Remember me.

Remember me. *Remember me.* Remember me. Remember me.

Remember me.

As always, the pleas of the dead fell on him like a cold shower: at first solitary, lonely voices calling in the dark, then a clamour of confused and tired cries – male, female, young, old, some muffled by soft, damp shrouds, others thinned by wooden lids or echoing inside cavernous stone voids.

Remember me. *Remember me.* Remember me.

He did what he always did. He couldn't remember why he did it. His huge frame rolled over in the bed, his pyjamas pulled taut across his bulbous stomach as he curled into a ball. Then, as they did every night – every time the calls of the dead fell – his thick fingers slipped into his mouth, his tongue pressing hard against their gnawed nails, as if he could gag the voices filling his head.

Remember me. Remember me.

Then, as always, their faces surfaced from the gloom: pale waxen masks, eyes closed, lips sealed thin and tight.

He shut his eyes as his fingers, wet and sticky, slipped from his lips, sliding down his thick beard, combing through the matted hair, pulling on knots.

Remember me. Remember me.

He tried to resist. He couldn't. His legs swung from the bed onto the soft floor. Now his fingers were moving up the side of his head, through the thick mop of hair, squeezing it tight, pulling at the roots, his teeth clenched. He opened his eyes.

In the dark, the faces of the dead, hundreds of faces, stared down blankly from the walls.

Remember me, they said.

Slowly, his hands moved down to hover in front of his face. Ready.

Remember me.

He stood and moved to the table.

'I will,' he said. 'I will.'

SIX

The Good Doctor

It was the day after my thirteenth birthday and New Street Station was the usual maul of rushing businessmen, overladen shoppers and confused out-of-towners. I held my breath against the diesel fumes as Mom tugged me in zigzags through legs and bags, across the platform and up the steps.

Out in the city centre, the pavements moved with a steady stream of heavy-coated people, endless processions that changed course to flow around a barking newspaper vendor, stare impassively at a busker or avoid the gaze of a street preacher.

The gruff rattle of idling double-decker buses filled the air. Wrapped in my duffle coat, Mom pulled me on.

The offices of Dr Sabapathy were above a women's clothes boutique not far from the station, announced discreetly by a stained brass plaque at the foot of narrow stairs. At the top waited a vinegar-faced receptionist whose bored disposition never changed when she greeted Mom, but usually cracked into an insincere smile when she spotted me peering over the counter.

Each week, after sitting in silence in the small waiting area, the starched grey suit of Dr Sabapathy would appear at the office door, and he would usher us in with a broad smile. His warm brown hand would slip onto my shoulder and direct me to the leather seat in the corner, where I would stare absently at certificates and bound volumes, my legs swinging gently as their voices blended across the room.

This had become a ritual in the months since Dad's death, something which I knew was necessary, yet didn't really understand.

Today, though, the routine changed. This time, the warm hand directed me to the sofas in front of the big desk, while Mom slipped quietly into the leather chair.

'Today, Joe, I want to talk to you,' he said in a soft Indian lilt.

My eyes darted nervously to Mom, who cast an encouraging look in my direction. I suddenly felt scared, and tears welled in my eyes.

'What do you want to talk to me about?'

'Oh, I just want to know how you are, how you are feeling these days,' he smiled.

I looked to Mom. 'I don't want to. I don't know what to say. I'm alright!'

'Joe, Dr Sabapathy just wants to talk to you – that's all, you haven't done anything wrong. It's OK.'

There was a soft tap on the door. The receptionist held it open to reveal Gus, lean and clean-shaven.

'Sorry I'm late,' he said, bounding in to shake hands with Dr Sabapathy and nodding towards Mom.

He sat next to me on the sofa. The unmistakable odour of the press hall clung to him. He smelled like my dad.

'We had to pull an overnighter,' he said to Mom. 'Breakdown on one of the towers.'

He turned to me. 'Came straight here, sorry if I stink.'

'That's alright,' I giggled.

'What's up, Doc?'

'Well, I was saying to Joe that I want to talk to him about how he's getting on, how he's feeling.'

Gus elbowed me gently. 'What do you say, Joe? It's good to talk, you know.'

'I don't know what to say.'

'Just be honest, darling,' Mom said.

'OK,' I agreed, sheepishly.

'That's the spirit,' Gus winked.

Dr Sabapathy crossed his legs and opened a notepad on his lap.

'Do you have lots of friends, Joe?'

'I think so, yes.'

'Your mother tells me you have a special friend – a pretend friend?'

'Er no, I'm not a little kid, you know,' I objected. 'I don't pretend anymore.'

'Of course, I mean a friend in your imagination.'

'No, I don't.'

Gus leant against me. 'Mom says you talk to yourself, is that it?'

'I do sometimes... but everyone does that, don't they?'

'Yes, mate, we all do that,' Gus agreed.

Mom spoke up. 'You get angry, though, Joe, when you're talking to yourself sometimes.'

'Do you feel angry when you talk to yourself?' Dr Sabapathy asked.

I fell silent, conscious of their eyes on me.

I screwed my face up. 'I get angry if we disagree.'

Sabapathy tilted his head. 'If you disagree with whom?'

'With Wilko.'

Mom leant forward. 'Who's Wilko, Joe – someone at school?'

'No, he's my friend. He talks to me.'

I felt Gus's arm slip around me on the back of the sofa. 'When does he talk to you?' he asked.

'All the time.'

I sensed them exchanging glances.

Dr Sabapathy rested his hands on his pad. 'Joe, can you see Wilko?'

'No.'

Mom chipped in, 'So he's pretend?'

'*No*,' I protested. 'He's real.'

Gus shifted to lock his eyes on me. I could tell he was genuinely interested. 'And he's not in your imagination?'

'No. He's real.'

'How do you know he's real if you can't see him, mate?'

I thought about this. It was a good question. 'Because I know when I'm imagining something – like a game, because I think it up. Like pretending. Wilko's just there.'

'Where?' asked Dr Sabapathy.

'He sounds like he's behind my shoulder most of the time.'

Gus stroked his chin. 'How do you know he's called Wilko, Joe?'

'Because that's what he says. Wilko.'

The doctor wrote something down, thought for a second, then asked, 'What else does he tell you?'

I shrugged. 'What he thinks, what he thinks about people. Sometimes he tells me what to do, and that's when we disagree.'

'Do you like talking to him?' Gus asked.

'I don't know. He makes me feel tired sometimes. I get tired.'

'Is he talking to you now?' the doctor asked.

'No, he's quiet today. He hasn't said anything.'

Sabapathy sat back and gave me a reassuring smile. 'OK, Joe, that's fine – thank you. Gus, why don't you take Joe down to the sweet shop, while I have a word with Mum?'

As Gus led me down the stairs, the receptionist closed the door with a leathery smile. Behind her, I saw Mom stand to talk to Sabapathy. The colour had drained from her face.

★

The concrete steps leading up to my flat smelled, as usual, of urine. As we passed the loading bay of the shop below, Gus paused for breath, leaning back against the wall with the cumbersome monitor screen resting across his belly.

'Why couldn't they have let you have one of the laptops?' he said.

I shifted the desktop computer and keyboard awkwardly in my arms.

'Because the poor sods who'll be working from home will need the laptops, when they're filing stories from their kitchen tables. All this stuff is obsolete now, that's why they're letting me have one.'

'I thought you had a bloody laptop. I've seen it.'

'I do, I do but it's ancient. Anyway, I need something to write the book on, with a proper screen.'

'Oh well... that's different... I wouldn't want to stand in the way of literature! Come on,' he said, heaving himself up and heading for the last flight of steps.

At the door to my flat I set the equipment down on the floor and Gus watched as I searched for my key, his red face resting on the top of the screen.

'Gus, put it down, I'll carry it from here.'

'No, no, I'll bring it in, that's OK,' he said.

I found the key and slipped it into the door. 'No, mate, really, I'd rather you didn't come in. It's a mess.'

He gave me an incredulous look. 'Don't be ridiculous, Joe, it can't be that bad. I've got it, just open the door.'

'No, really, Gus, I'd rather you didn't – maybe next time.'

'Why, what's it like in there? Are you hoarding cats? Shitting in bags?'

I pulled the key back out. 'No, it's just... maybe next time, OK?'

59

He eyed me with suspicion, then placed the monitor on the floor.

'Alright… but it hasn't escaped my attention that no one has been in there apart from you in a very long time. Just looking out for you, kid, just looking out for you…'

He headed back to the steps. 'And don't forget, we've got to empty our desks before the office shuts.'

The key went back in the door.

My flat wasn't a mess. There were no stacks of newspapers reaching to the ceiling, no piles of out-of-date food or tied-up bags of rubbish. Quite the opposite.

As I stood in the tiny hallway, the computer equipment at my feet, I got the same feeling I had every time I walked through the door: an emptiness that matched the cold, sterile rooms.

Still here. Sparse furniture, unused plates and cutlery, bare walls and a bed that was too big.

How many years had I lived here, with my life on pause? How can you plant yourself somewhere for so long, but not put down roots? As a kid I'd spent my days trying to get outside, but I'd somehow ended up living here, without a garden to even look out on, just an expanse of concrete and passing cars.

I was resigned to losing my job, but the thought of spending my days here filled me with dread. It felt more like a mausoleum than a bachelor pad.

Got to plan ahead. Plan to get out. Get outside.

In the quiet living room, my old laptop screen glowed. I checked the email, and my heart sank.

Two replies from old colleagues, but not what I needed. One, from an old friend now working for an agency in Africa, another who was a big noise on the nationals. Suffice to say messages from high-flyers, while well-meaning, did little to raise my spirits.

But then another pinged into the inbox, from a friendly face up north.

The subject: Fancy a night at the pictures?

SEVEN

Mr Saturday Night

The Third Vigil

It looked like a mouth. A cavernous, gaping mouth with row upon row of teeth poking out of red-carpeted gums. As I sat on the dark stage of the old Regal cinema, my sleeping bag wrapped loosely around me, hundreds of stained seats stared blankly back.

I had stopped checking the time, but it must have been around 2am and the auditorium was cold and silent. I swallowed a yawn. A week had passed since my visit to the Old Tunns and I hadn't been sleeping well. Every time my eyes closed, I struggled to square my experiences with years of scepticism drilled into me by Gus and half a dozen gruff chief reporters. I hadn't spoken to anyone about it, partly due to the office closure, but mainly because I knew how unhinged I would sound. After all, I had spent my teenage years having my sanity probed and my honesty gently questioned. I had no appetite to reopen that can of worms.

In fact, other than talking to an old colleague now working on the *Middlesbrough Gazette*, I hadn't spoken to anyone about anything.

A long coach journey had carried me to the North East and a sprawling suburb called Brambles Farm – which was considerably less picturesque than its name suggested.

Just a few hours before, I had looked down on the estate from the roof of the Regal, which rose above the houses like a medieval keep. I pulled my suit jacket tight to keep out the cold.

'You're not going to believe what he said to me – my own solicitor!' shouted my host, Jaz Singh, as he braced his legs against the wind.

He put one hand to his powder-blue turban and shook his head. We were either side of a man-sized hole.

'He told me, "Don't be surprised if he sues you!" Sues me!' he laughed, his beard lifting in the breeze.

'So, this trespasser, who is trying to break into *my* premises, falls through *my* roof and then he can take me to court for health and safety? So, I tell him that I think we've got a pretty good defence – that you shouldn't go walking about on the roof of a building that's been derelict for fifty years – and he asks me if we have got any warning signs up here!'

He gestured to a big – and clearly new – sign which screamed 'UNSAFE ROOF' in large red lettering. 'We bloody well have now!'

I peered into the hole, and the void below. 'What happened to him?'

'He broke both his legs and a couple of ribs, but he could have broken his neck! His camera equipment wasn't quite so lucky,' he added. 'Totally smashed in the fall.'

'Camera equipment – he wasn't a burglar?'

'No, no, he was – what do you call it – an "urban explorer". He sneaks into places like this to take photos and then sticks them up online. Abandoned spaces. Apparently, it's a thing. He should have just asked, I wouldn't have minded at all – it might have helped us with the fundraising.'

He looked at his watch. 'Let's go back in,' he said. 'It's getting dark.'

As I followed Jaz back across to the ladder, Middlesbrough's skyline jutted into pink and grey streaked clouds around us. Ahead, the angular silhouette of the Transporter Bridge rose above the rooftops. The lights of the chemical works at Redcar blinked in the distance.

We clambered down the rusted ladder to the fire escape, and then slipped back into the building, emerging into the musty, red-carpeted upstairs foyer. The ornate ceiling sagged above our heads like a pregnant belly, its mouldings stretched and cracking. Open blisters of paint, popped like over-ripe spores, peeled away from the wall either side of a filthy blue door set back into the wall.

Jaz pushed it open, releasing a putrid waft of damp air. 'In case nature calls!' he smiled.

It swung shut with a soft *swish-thud*. I checked the stained brass sign above the doorway: 'Gents'.

I won't be using that, I thought.

In the middle of the back wall stood tall dark double doors. The silver-edged rays of a rising sun spread from their centre with elegant art deco symmetry – old Hollywood chic now deeply pitted with black, powdery mould.

'They open onto the Upper Circle,' he said. 'I don't recommend you go through there. I wouldn't.'

Hastily, he led me down the sweeping marble staircase to the main lobby, where an ankle-deep carpet of litter and leaves covered the chess board floor. Only the glass-fronted box office remained amid the debris, waiting like a confessional, my overnight bag sitting on its counter. I ran my finger around the little circular hole cut into the glass, through which generations had bought soft-blotted tickets to escape their lives, whispering wish-fulfilment as if to an oracle – weekend sweethearts, matinee housewives, Saturday morning schoolboys with pockets full of sweets.

'They probably used to have problems with burglars once but there hasn't been anything worth stealing in here for decades,' Jaz went on. 'When we took over the place the only thing left worth anything was the equipment in the old projector room, vintage stuff, but we sold all of that to pay for repairs to the fabric of the building. Everything else worth anything was gone. It's sad really. Over the years the place has been stripped of all the things that made it special, all the trimmings, all the glamour. Perhaps people took mementos of what it used to be like. These days, if someone gets in, it's just curious kids who want to mooch about, or the occasional rough sleeper trying to get out of the wind.'

'And the plan is to restore the building?'

'That's the idea,' he said, holding open another art deco door, which led into the main auditorium. I slung the bag over my shoulder and followed him in.

It was enormous. The long, stepped central aisle split the dark halfmoon room, descending through hundreds of mouldering yellow seats, up-ended and brocaded, hunched in tight rows like military gravestones. The side walls towered into the gloom above, draped with red curtains which sagged and twisted with age. At its centre, the remains of the Regal's silver screen hung in tattered ribbons behind a small stage.

'It's a listed building – very listed in fact, Grade II,' Jaz said, leading me swiftly down the aisle. 'It was a one-off design, a real palace in its time. The pictures of what it was like in its hey-day are amazing.'

As we descended through the silent rows, I looked at the expanse of ceiling above; its ornate patterns were interrupted by the black hulk of the overhanging balcony, from which hundreds more seats stared down out of the darkness.

'I had no idea it would be so big,' I said as we reached the centre. 'Do you own it?'

'Yes, my family bought it a few years ago.' He climbed onto the stage and surveyed the room. He was clearly nervous.

'Why?'

'What?'

'Why did you buy it?'

'Oh... well, it's important to the local community, and this is our community.'

He said it like he had answered the question a million times.

'My father opened our first shop here in the 1970s, when the estate was really something, really alive. We started out with the little unit at the end of the shopping parade next door, and people really took to us. Of course, there was a bit of bother every now and then – this was the 1970s, after all – but we made a real effort to be a part of the community. And all the time, at the end of the parade, was this old cinema – just rotting away. It had been shut for years even then, but customers always talked about it when they came in to buy a paper or some cigarettes. Over the years, my dad got sort of attached to it, I suppose.'

He kicked some leaves from the stage, his hands on his hips. 'The estate isn't what it was, but people still look out for each other. Most of the shops here closed down, so we bought all the units, one by one, to try to stop them falling into the state that this place is in.

'In the end, the only thing left to buy was the Regal, and my dad just stood up in a local council meeting one evening and announced he was going to buy it, to say "thank you" to Middlesbrough. To protect it and try to give something back, you know, to the community.'

He rubbed his neck. 'To be honest with you, I wish we had never got involved now. We're in the middle of setting up a trust to get it restored, so we can hand it over to volunteers. Not to be a cinema, to be a community hub, or an arts centre. That's the idea anyway.'

'That won't be cheap.'

'No, it won't be cheap – but we're taking it one step at a time. The first thing is to get a grant to secure it and keep the weather out.'

He pointed to the hole, high above. 'It doesn't help when social media explorers fall through your roof.'

I put my bag on the stage. Jaz looked at his watch again.

'Look,' he said abruptly, 'don't take this the wrong way, but I want to get out of here. Quickly.'

He smiled awkwardly. 'You're welcome to stay – just don't go into any rooms that are taped off for safety. But I'm not staying here much longer, not once it's gone dark. So… do you want me to tell you about the Upper Circle?'

I took out my phone and hit record. 'Go for it.'

'Right.' He rubbed his hands together. 'So, there have always been stories about this place being… you know… haunted. The Upper Circle in particular – the balcony. But we never paid them any attention, we're businesspeople, sensible people. But then last month, after the incident with the trespasser, well – let's just say I'm a believer.'

I looked up at the balcony. 'Tell me what happened.'

'OK,' he said with a smile. 'But quickly. Then I'm gone.' He poked both index fingers to the door.

'I understand. Tell me what happened.'

'Well, I got the call from the fire service at about ten o'clock on the night that it had happened. Someone had been walking past outside and heard the trespasser screaming, so they dialled 999. They sent an ambulance, police, and the fire brigade came out as well, because the building's derelict – and they had my number as owner. I drove down straight away. When I got here the police and ambulance people were up there with this bloke – on the balcony, that's where he landed. He was in a right mess. He fell right across the seats and was screaming the place down till they gave him some serious pain relief. It was horrible, to be frank, so I left them to it and came back downstairs. I waited while they

66

got him out into the ambulance, which took a very long time. Eventually, they all went.'

Another glance at his wrist. He steeled himself.

'So, I'm getting ready to go too – it was about 1am by then – but when I went to lock up, I found that the fire service had smashed open the main entrance to get in. The lock was wrecked. I had to call up someone to come and replace it, and board up a hole they had smashed in the door too, to make the building secure. I rang the 24-hour locksmith we usually use, and he said he'd be about an hour. I came and sat on the edge of the stage and waited for him.'

'Right here? Why on the stage?'

'This is the only place with a working power socket. I had to charge my phone.' He glanced for a fleeting moment at the balcony. 'That's when I saw him.'

'Who did you see?'

Jaz puffed out his cheeks.

'A man, sitting in the Upper Circle.' His eyes stayed fixed on mine. 'On the right of the centre, eighth row back, in the seat right next to the middle aisle.'

'A man?' I looked up to pick out the seat. Jaz didn't.

'Yes, a tall man, sitting upright. Bolt upright.'

'What did he look like?'

'It was very dark, so I couldn't see his face, but I could tell that he was wearing a suit; a shirt and tie too. He had short hair – smart. He looked smart. And he was just... sitting there. Straight as a board.'

Jaz swallowed and stroked his beard nervously.

'Part of me wanted to believe it was one of the emergency people still here, maybe a policeman, a scene-of-crime officer – but in the back of my mind I knew. I knew. Since we bought this place we've spoken to lots of people, old people, who used to work here. Every one of them told us about the Upper Circle. I just froze. I must have sat and stared at him for twenty minutes. The more I looked, the more I saw. I could see his tie, the shape of his hair. At first, I actually thought he was looking right back at me, but then I realised he wasn't – he was looking at the screen. Like he was watching a film.'

'And you're sure he wasn't someone who had come in from the cold?'

'Oh yes, oh yes.'

'Why?'

'I called out to him. I shouted at him. "What are you doing here? This is private property!" – that sort of thing. But he didn't react at all – I mean, at all. Nothing. Like he didn't hear me, he just carried on looking down, past me. Then he suddenly stands up, in one movement, straight up, and I can see that he's tall and thin, thin like a stick.'

'He stood up?'

'Yes, he stood up and then he turned and stepped out into the aisle up there, and started to very slowly climb the stairs towards the double doors – the doors upstairs that I showed you. I was absolutely terrified. Never been so scared in my life. I didn't know what to do.'

'What did you do?'

'Like I said, I just froze with fear. I didn't want to go out into the lobby, and I didn't want to stay put here but I couldn't take my eyes off him. Then, when he got halfway up the steps he just vanished, disappeared, gone – which really freaked me out, I'm getting goose pimples just thinking about it – and suddenly this voice shouted "Hello!" from the lobby and I jumped out of my skin. I screamed out loud.'

'It shouted at you?'

Jaz shook his head and exhaled.

'It was the locksmith. That was it for me, I told him what to do and was gone.' He jumped down from the stage. 'And I'm gone again now.'

Jaz pretty much bolted from the auditorium. Reliving the experience had clearly made him even more nervous.

So, I had set myself up on the stage, plugging in my phone, and eating my sandwiches as the room got progressively gloomier. Then I spread the contents of my bag out on the stage, including a replacement torch and my latest toy: a little video camera with a 'night vision' function.

After fiddling about with it for a while, I settled down to wait to see if the Regal would provide any entertainment for the night.

*

Auditoriums are designed to both muffle and carry sound, to direct it in waves across the heads of the audience while blocking out noises from outside. Sitting perfectly still and alone in such a huge, dark space is an unsettling experience. True silence – the absence of any sound at all – starts to take form after a while, and your ears fill with a soft, acoustic hiss that's moulded to the shape of the walls, the furniture, the ceiling, clinging to the inside of the space like plaque. The tiny ticks and clicks that are inevitable in such a big building, as drapes shift or hinges settle in natural air currents, are amplified and echo across the air. You can almost feel the soundwaves wash over you at the slightest noise.

My eyes, however, were only really interested in one thing. They waltzed lazily around the room over and over again, but always darted back to that seat in the Upper Circle, each time finding it empty and then slowly moving away.

This dance went on, first as minutes ticked by, then hours. Every now and then I would focus intently on the empty chair, trying to will a change in circumstances. Nothing.

Then, deep into the small hours, I felt a temperature change in the room; a chill rippled across the air towards me, like mist over water.

I pulled the sleeping bag tighter around me. Had I fallen asleep?

Instinctively, my dry eyes rose to the Upper Circle, to the chair. Empty.

It was suddenly freezing cold. I stared at the seat. Still nothing. My shoulders rose as a shiver shuddered through me.

Then, in the corner of my eye, I caught something at the very back of the balcony – in its dead centre – in the dark block of the rear wall. A tiny, rectangular block of light appeared, like a fluttering, flickering brick of soft luminescent blue-white. I squinted at it and, as I did, my eyes picked out another smaller square light, just a little to its right. Flickering.

The projector room.

My eyes darted back to the seat.

He was there.

I sat up. Awake. Alert.

Illuminated from behind by the flickering light, I could see his narrow, tailored shoulders, the outline of his slicked hair, the white edge of his shirt collar. He sat silently with his hands on his knees, bolt upright, a solid presence, just as Jaz had described.

My hand fumbled for the video camera. I turned it on, flicking it onto night vision, then pressed the viewfinder to my eye. With shaking hands, I turned the lens to the balcony and quickly scanned the rows to find the seat. It was empty.

I pulled the camera away and looked up, my eyes widening. There he was. I tried the viewfinder again – nothing.

The camera couldn't see him. I could – and in more and more detail now: the subtle dip in his hair where it was expertly parted, the dull shine from the points of his lapels, the neat tie knot below his obscured face.

Was I dreaming? Instinctively, I rubbed my eyes and looked again.

Now the seated figure seemed to be moving, just very slightly, his left shoulder dropping here, twisting there, his head tilting with gentle beats to the side, the flickering light rolling across his combed hair. He was talking to someone unseen. Whispering in the darkness.

I suddenly felt his eyes on me. I was looking at him. Was he looking at me? His head turned to the seat next to him and nodded gently, whispering, whispering.

I swallowed.

I called out. 'Hello?'

No reaction.

Louder: 'Hello, can you hear me?'

Slowly, the silhouetted head rotated, turning to face me. Not the screen. To face me. Now a hand was lifting from his knee, rising into the dark void of his face, as if to press a finger to his lips. The figure leant forward. A soft sound drifted down from the balcony.

'Shhhhh.'

I dropped the video camera.

Get a hold of yourself, Joe. This is happening. You've got to go up there. Go up and check it's not a prank, it's not Jaz trying to make headlines. Credibility!

I eased myself down off the stage, grabbed the torch and began to climb up the central aisle towards the door, all the time keeping an eye on the shadowy figure above, whose gaze stayed fixed on the screen.

Out in the lobby, I turned on the torch and made my way past the box office to the foot of the marble staircase. Slowly, but with my heart beating fast, I began to climb towards the foyer and the doors to the Upper Circle.

The torch threw a deep shadow off the low, sagging ceiling of the foyer, light catching on the cracked cornicing and illuminating the fungus-like blisters on the painted walls.

I edged towards the double doors. This was it. I knew the seated figure had been just a few rows inside the doorway, maybe six steps down the aisle on the left. I had to look. I had to.

I put the torch down on the floor, and placed both my hands on the double doors, ready to open them wide with one push.

Through the crack between the doors, I could see the flickering light from the projector room. I've got to look. I held my breath, gritted my teeth and shoved both doors open wide.

Nothing. Upturned chairs.

The Upper Circle was deserted, the all-important seat empty. I exhaled, peering down at the stage below.

Swish-thud.

A noise from behind me. The smell of putrid, wet air wafted past me.

Slowly, I turned, letting one of the double doors go. The blue door to the toilet. The torch flickered at my feet.

He emerged from the doorway.

He walked across the room in front of me as if in slow motion, like a marionette worked by invisible strings – tall, upright and proud. A broad smile spread across his face.

But he was dead, long dead.

His skin was thin, blue-green and broken, sinews showing through his collapsed throat, his black teeth shining dully through almost transparent cheeks.

His clothes – the expensive suit, the crisp shirt, the smart tie, his black shoes – were decayed too, broken down by the same entropy that gripped the Regal itself, filthy and tainted, the fine cloth disintegrating, the stitching undone, the leather dried and warped. The remains of a flower poked brittle and withered from his buttonhole. These were the clothes he was buried in, his pride and joy. His Saturday night best.

Only his hair was immaculate: jet black, slicked with Brylcreem, expertly parted and combed tightly across his rotting scalp.

He took four silent steps, still smiling as he moved across the foyer then stopped and gave a little nod, as if greeting someone.

He turned on his heels to face me, and gently presented his right elbow. A person unseen slipped her arm into his. He nodded graciously to her. Slowly, he began to walk. Towards the doors. Towards the Upper Circle. Towards me. Escorting his companion back to their seats, he proudly promenaded her across the crumbling room.

As his face fell into focus, I felt a visceral revulsion rise in me – the long, straight nose below his arched eyebrows, his taut nostrils, the hollow cheeks pulled back into paper-like folds by his blackened grin.

I pressed my back against the open door, trying to make space, trying to get out of the way, trying not to look, hoping not to be seen as he stepped closer, and I held my breath and turned my head away, pressing my cheek hard against the door.

He stretched out a cadaverous hand, the skin hanging limp on his fingers, and gently pushed open the other door, turning on his hip to squeeze by me, his invisible companion in tow, his face just inches from mine. As he passed, still smiling broadly, the sickly-sweet air of decay brushed my senses. Repulsion leapt inside me, damming my throat, thickening my tongue, pulling back my ears.

For a fleeting moment, his eyes met mine.

They seemed to recognise me, to welcome me; they gleamed, full of joy, full of life. They seemed to say: 'Isn't this wonderful?'

He swept past. The doors swung shut. I fell back into the foyer, exhaling. The flickering stopped. The show was over.

I ran down the stairs, heading for the main doors.

*

I asked Jaz to mail my things back to me the next day, offering to pay him for the inconvenience. I had taken a taxi straight to the coach station and caught the first one south. On the back of the seat in front of me, a little TV screen was showing a movie. I didn't watch it.

EIGHT

The Bad Patient

A week after turning fifteen, I was slouched in my regular spot in Dr Sabapathy's office. My duffle coat had given way to a denim jacket stitched with embroidered patches, tribal totems to heavy metal bands. My sensible school shoes had been replaced by trainers. Gus sat in the corner, now my weekly chaperone.

'How have you been this week?'

I chewed my lip, petulantly. 'Same as every other week, really.'

'And how have you been getting on with your mother?'

'Fine.'

'And school?'

I looked at Gus. 'School is school,' I said.

There was a silence as Sabapathy consulted his notes.

'Your mom tells me you have been suspended from school. From Monday. How do you feel about that?'

'It was an overreaction. I didn't do anything. We were just messing around, that's all.'

'The letter I have here says that one of your friends got quite upset.'

'I can't really help that; it wasn't something that I did. I told the headmaster that.'

'It says here that you and four others tried to hold some sort of séance in one of the common rooms and lots of people were very upset about it.'

'We were just messing about.'

Gus spoke up: 'Lots of kids do this sort of thing... it's just natural inquisitiveness.'

Sabapathy raised a calming hand. 'Of course, I'm just interested in what Joe finds interesting about it all.'

'It was just something to do. Spur of the moment.'

'Your mom tells me you made a Ouija board and took it into school. Did you think it would impress your friends?'

'No!' I scoffed. 'It was a joke, we were messing about.'

He eyed the patches on my jacket.

'Do you find yourself attracted to the darker side of culture – music, art, films?'

'What do you mean?'

'I want to know what kind of young man you're becoming.'

'It's just music,' I said dismissively.

He shifted on his seat. 'Tell me about how a séance works, Joe. Is it like in the films – do you call out? What's the phrase... is there anybody there?'

'I just find it interesting, that's all.'

'And do you try to contact anyone in particular?'

'Like who?'

'I don't know... a rock star, famous people?'

I smirked. 'We were just messing about.'

'And why did the other boy get upset?'

'I think he got frightened.'

'Do you get frightened?'

'Not really, no. I think I've been frightened enough.'

He made notes.

'We spoke, a long time ago, about how you felt you were very

75

sensitive – like your father was. Do you remember that? Do you think that you've lost some of that sensitivity?'

'No, I don't. I'm just not frightened of things like the others are.'

'And why do you think that is?'

'I don't know.'

He made more notes.

'Do you still feel sad about your father?'

'Of course I do. All the time.'

'And do you talk to your mom about that?'

'No. I don't want to upset her. She's got enough to deal with.'

'You obviously weren't thinking about her when you got suspended from school,' Gus interjected.

I ignored him.

Sabapathy tapped his pad with his pen.

'You know, this is where you can speak about it, here in this room. That's why we do this. Do you talk to anyone else?'

I looked out the window behind him, at the dirty windows of the tall buildings opposite, stacked high with colourful boxes which coloured the glass red, green, blue.

'There is someone who talks to me. But I try not to listen.'

I felt Sabapathy and Gus exchange looks.

'Tell me…' the doctor asked, 'do you recall the first time you heard Wilko?'

My eyes, fixed on the windows, slipped out of focus. My mind looked back.

Sabapathy persevered, gently: 'When was the first time you heard him, Joe?'

His voice was distant. The windows across the street glinted and fell away.

'Joe?' Gus said softly.

I blinked and studied the coloured glass. The shapes. The faces.

'Joe?'

Gus was leaning down over me, his cleanshaven young face close to mine. He followed my gaze to the stained-glass windows.

'Joe, are you feeling better?' he said, holding out a warm hand. 'Do you want to come back in now?'

I nodded. I felt uncomfortable in the suit. The new shoes were too tight.

'I'll come and sit with you,' he said.

I took his hand and he led me through the oak doorways, then down the aisle of the church, towards Mom, towards the priest, towards the coffin.

She smiled softly, wiped a tear from my cheek, then patted the pew next to her, as Gus sat down.

I took my seat and the priest began to speak, but I couldn't hear him. I couldn't hear him.

I felt the room shift.

The gravelly voice came from somewhere behind me.

*

From across the boardroom table, I sat watching Helena stare into space as the union rep prepared his slides on a laptop. Worry was etched on her young face as she vacantly turned a pen over in her fingers.

Gus sat down with a thump next to me and followed my gaze to her.

'Poor thing,' he said quietly, 'she seems to always be away with the fairies these days.'

'She's got a lot on her mind. She told me this was her dream job. It's over before it's started.'

The union rep was fiddling with an overhead projector now.

'She'll be alright,' Gus replied. 'She's got talent. And she doesn't take any shit from anyone.'

The pen continued to turn as Helena stared into the distance.

'She's a lot like I was at her age,' I said. 'I don't know anything about her, really, but I suspect she's had quite a hard time. She presents this tough image, but she's just a kid really.'

'Well, you've done a good job of taking her under your wing. I have noticed.'

'Just passing on what you taught me.'

For a second, he eyed me with what looked suspiciously like pride. Then he clicked his fingers.

'That reminds me...' He delved into his suit pocket. 'I found this.'

A faded laminated card was slapped on the table.

'Where did you find that?'

'At the bottom of my drawer – it was your desk for a while, wasn't it?'

I picked it up and rubbed the greasy, brittle plastic with my thumb. 'Yes, years ago. Amazing. I'd totally forgotten about it. This is where "The Rules" started.'

The Rules were something of an unwritten, ever-expanding constitution; pearls of wisdom from Gus that he usually prefixed with a wagged finger and an earnest 'first rule of journalism...' They teetered between advice that was genuinely helpful in the day-to-day job to dodgy dictums that simply stopped you doing things that annoyed him.

So, they covered everything from 'exclamation marks are for fiction' to 'Never stir tea with a spoon you just made coffee with'.

On my first week, he gave me the card, featuring Kipling's words:

'*I keep six honest serving-men*
They taught me all I knew;
Their names are What and Why and When
And How and Where and Who.'

'Ask those and keep asking them,' he had said, 'and you won't go far wrong – but ask one more. Ask them how it made them feel. It's got to be about people, not facts. People are the story. That's your intro.'

The projector blinked into life, throwing a live table of online stories onto the wall, the entries jostling up and down as their audience figures danced. The rep tutted and stroked his chin.

'It seems so long ago now,' I said. 'It all feels a bit of a waste.'

'What do you mean?'

'Well, what have I achieved here, really? Maybe I should have moved on years ago.'

'Rubbish. Think about all those stories, all those people. What do you want, a medal?'

I slid the card across to Helena, her hand pinning it to the table as she looked up, dazed.

'What's this?'

'Call it an heirloom,' Gus smiled.

'It's gross,' she said.

At the top of the chart, Nash's name blinked next to the top five stories of the day.

'I notice he's not in here,' Gus said. 'He's managed to save his hide.'

'Well, he's top of the pops, isn't he? Gets the clicks.'

The table disappeared, to be replaced by the rep's first slide. He clapped his hands in triumph.

Gus sat back. 'Clicks. If that's the future we're better off out of it. First rule of journalism: it's not a competition.'

NINE

The Competition

The Fourth Vigil

Mulvaney Tower looked lonely. The high-rise block sulked in the middle of a huge building site, orbited by the rubble of three others that had been demolished in recent weeks. Most of the windows of its twenty storeys were smashed and dark, their rain-soaked curtains curling outwards to stick to the grey concrete.

I made my way to the main entrance, my bag slung over my shoulder, past sleeping mechanical diggers corralled behind chain-link fences, their hydraulic limbs dipped, cabins empty. Their keepers had clocked off after a dusty day's work dismantling 60s Grimsby, their hard hats and gloves left pressed against cabin windows among cigarette packets and red-top newspapers. It felt like they were watching me.

Inside the doorway, my host for the night stood under a dim yellow ceiling light, which illuminated his bright red hair with a pinkish halo. He extended a tattooed hand, tipped with black-painted fingernails.

Mo Spooner was an ageing Goth, whose long leather overcoat, tight black jeans and high-laced boots sat uneasily with his sunny disposition. His most prominent feature – a large, rounded chin – supported a crooked, nicotine-stained smile below pinched lived-in eyes.

'Joe, great to meet you, thanks for coming,' he said in a nasal voice, shaking my hand vigorously.

'Not at all, thanks for inviting me,' I replied, swinging my bag from one shoulder to the other.

'I'll take you straight up,' he carried on, leading me towards a lift door which was propped open with a fire extinguisher. We stepped in and he pulled the red cannister inside, allowing the doors to slide shut.

'Don't worry, we won't get in trouble for that,' he said, thumbing the button for the fourteenth floor. 'It's our personal elevator now, we're the only ones left in the building.'

The lift was small, its inner walls lined with a tinny metallic finish that was studded with shallow dimples. As it lurched upwards, a knee-high compartment at the base of the back wall swung gently open, its door tapping against my heels.

'I'll get that,' Mo said, quickly kicking it shut again. He offered me another broad smile and jabbed an enthusiastic finger at the compartment. 'Know what that's for?'

I shook my head.

'Coffins!' he said crossing his arms sagely. 'Makes the lift floor big enough for a coffin. Well, you can't stand 'em up, can you?'

'Well, I never knew that,' I offered. 'Have you lived here a long time?'

'We've been here… fifteen years. I'm sixty-two, you know, the missus is younger, she's fifty-five. No… fifty-six. Met her when I was in a band. She was my groupie!'

'And you're the only ones left in the whole block?'

'That's right, we're holding out for a better offer. Most of the flats were council-owned, so they got evicted, but we own ours –

it was me mam's, she was here for twenty years before us. So, we're playing hardball.'

'How's that going?'

'Well, we're still here. We're big believers in fate, Joe, the universe will sort us out. Here we are!'

The doors slid open, and we headed down a dingy narrow corridor, our footsteps echoing as we passed flats sealed up with steel sheeting.

A purple painted door waited at the end of the passageway, a shiny number 21 stuck on in gothic lettering.

'Home sweet home,' he said, producing a key. 'Now, you wait out here for a minute, Joe, and I'll get Ellie – she can explain it all a lot better than me.'

He disappeared inside. I stood, my bag between my feet, listening to voices from beyond the door. Male. Female. Another male? It went quiet.

Across the corridor, on the facing wall, a square hatch with a white-painted handle rattled on its hinges. I stepped over and pulled it; it opened from the top, swinging downwards to reveal a drop that disappeared into the floors below. An old rubbish chute? A draught of cold air rose, and I closed it, leaning back on the wall. Still no sign of Mo.

Absent-mindedly, I took out my phone and tapped in my passcode. Missed call. I rolled my eyes. A missed call, just a few seconds ago. I flicked onto the call register. The number at the top was unfamiliar. 02135… It blinked, then disappeared. Bad reception? I clicked the phone off and then on again. The number was gone. Was that the same number I missed in Cornwall?

For the second time that night, I had the feeling I was being watched.

The purple door opened suddenly, and I slipped the phone into my suit jacket as a glamorously plump woman in a long black lace dress squeezed by me.

'Joe, I'm Ellie,' she said. 'Or Elvira if you like.'

She offered an aristocratically curled hand. I wasn't sure whether to shake it or kiss it. I shook it.

Ellie's long, raven hair framed a marble-white face and a vivid pout of shiny red lipstick. She fixed me with a sultry smile.

The door swung open again and Mo emerged, dragging a large duffle bag which he lifted over mine with some difficulty, easing his way past us both.

'Excuse me, babe, don't mind me!'

'Are you going somewhere?' I asked.

'We're staying down the road tonight with friends, gonna leave you lot to it.'

'You lot?' I was confused.

'You're the last one to arrive,' Ellie said. 'After the story went in the *Telegraph*, quite a few people got in touch. So, we thought we'd kill a few birds with one stone and see what you all come up with.'

I looked at the door. 'So, I won't be alone tonight?'

Mo chuckled. 'It's like Ghostbusters in there, mate! Look upon them as the competition.'

Ellie raised her hands theatrically. 'We want to see if you all reach the same conclusion as me.'

'And what is that?'

'There is a presence in there, I know there is.'

'My mam always said it was haunted,' Mo interjected.

'Yes, but... *I* have a sense for these things, and I have felt it myself and seen it manifest,' she continued, undaunted.

I took out my phone and hit record.

'And what did you see?'

She looked at the phone and spoke directly into it. 'You'll see it yourself, it's on the kitchen wall.'

'Bloody great stain,' Mo said.

'It might be a stain, it might be something else, a shadow, a shade, a revenant... but that's where it manifests, that's where I sense it most strongly, right there by the table. Above the fridge.'

'It appeared a few weeks ago, when they started to dismantle the flats upstairs,' Mo added, heaving the bag onto his back, 'but there's always been a funny feeling about the place.'

'I think it's reaching out,' Ellie said, 'across the astral plains, through the fabric of the universe.'

'And above the fridge,' Mo said. 'Babe, we gotta go, they ordered the curry twenty minutes ago, it'll be waiting for us.'

This broke Ellie's mystic reverie and they rushed off, Mo throwing a 'see you tomorrow' over the duffle bag and Ellie offering a little wave.

I looked at the door. It was plain, cheap and flimsy, probably an original from when the block was built in the 1960s. The thin purple paint was crudely applied, with broad, visible brush strokes that ran over the edge of the door handle and wooden frame.

I picked up my bag, grasped the handle and gently pushed the door open to step into a dimly lit but surprisingly large hallway.

I wasn't alone. A tall man stood in the centre of the room, his legs spread far apart, his back to me. His head seemed to be bowed; I could see the end of a stubby blond ponytail riding on the back collar of his black blazer.

'Hi,' I said, dropping my bag again.

At first, he didn't react, but then turned dramatically to look at me with piercing blue eyes. His arms were projected downwards, his fingertips touching to form an upside-down pyramid across his jeans.

'I'm getting an old-fashioned name,' he said, 'a man's name... Harry or Henry or Harold or Albert or Arnold or Arthur or...'

'It's Joe,' I said.

'Is it? Is it? Is it Joe?'

'No, I mean I'm Joe.' I offered him my hand.

'Oh, I see.' He grasped it and placed his other hand on top. 'Adam Zacharanda – you must be the journalist.'

'Writer – and you're a medium?'

'I prefer clairvoyant – less baggage,' he smiled.

I looked around the square hallway. Three closed doors were decorated with gothically psychedelic posters. Another was open, revealing a small bathroom.

'So, what are your first impressions? Anything going on here?'

'Oh yes, yes. No doubt. A number of spirits, all different, in here and in the kitchen. Lots of energy.'

'And you're getting a name? They're speaking to you?'

He looked around the room. 'They were, yes. Listen… what do you think about working together on this? I've spoken to the others and they're up for it.'

He gestured towards one of the doors.

'I tell you what,' I said, 'I'll have a word with them and get back to you on that.'

Adam Zacharanda nodded earnestly, turned, and bowed his head.

The living room was unoccupied, but I barely noticed, distracted by the view which reached out to the Humber estuary as the lights came on across Grimsby below. My eye was drawn to the horizon, where the grey sky and calm sea blurred into one through layered bands of cloud and wave, broken only by the vague outlines of distant ships.

The TV was switched on in the corner, the neon blues and reds of a Saturday night quiz show reflecting garishly back in the large windows at the end of the room, giving Grimsby's skyline beyond a Vegas-like aura. The room's décor was Lord of the Rings meets Gypsy Rose Lee, all dream catchers, Afghan rugs and incense burners.

Another purple door lurked in the corner, its clumsy paint job creeping over a porcelain sign, decorated with dancing fairies and a couplet in romantic script: '*No matter where I serve my guests, it seems they like my kitchen best*'.

I put my bag down and noticed three others – large khaki camera bags, bulging with pockets and compartments – lined up in front of the TV screen. Whoever 'the others' were, they were packing some serious kit.

The purple door swung open, and a balding, thick-set man in his fifties stepped silently out, holding a silver stick-like device at arm's length, which he was studying with slack-jawed concentration. He took two more steps, as if following the device's lead, before noticing me out of the corner of his eye and quickly waving it at me, as if to check I was real. Satisfied, he slipped it into one of the numerous pockets on his khaki flak jacket and pointed a friendly finger at me.

'The man from the fourth estate!'

'I beg your pardon?'

'You know, stop the press, hold the front page. Are you the reporter?'

'Yes, that's right – well, I'm a writer. Used to be a reporter, now I'm a writer.'

He looked crestfallen. 'Oh, I thought this was for the paper...'

'Sorry, no.' I changed the subject and pointed to the silver handle protruding from his vest. 'That looks like an interesting bit of kit.'

He took it out. 'This? Yes, great bit of tech. It's a... it's a... thingy. EMF Meter, Electromagnetic Field Radiation Detector. Only got it yesterday but seems to be doing something. I'm Brian, by the way, Brian Wiley. Cleethorpes Paranormal Society. CPS.'

'Nice to meet you. And you tried it in the kitchen?'

He glanced back at the door. 'Yes, yes – same result there, it went a bit crazy actually for a second.'

'Near this famous stain?'

'That's right, the stain – have you seen it? My assistant is collecting a sample right now.'

He turned to the kitchen again. 'Cameron! Cameron, did you get the sample? I want to try it in the...' He gestured to the kit bags on the floor. 'In the thingy.'

The purple kitchen door swung open again and a callow-looking youth held up a little transparent plastic tub. 'Got it, Mr Wiley,' he squeaked.

Cameron had long brown hair, parted like curtains across his oily brow, and he was also wearing a flak jacket – the apparent uniform of the CPS. Behind him in the cramped kitchen I could see a large West Indian woman sitting at a table, watching him with some amusement. Her eyes met mine through the doorway – her brows flicking upwards with a friendly 'hello'.

Brian waved Cameron through the door. 'Yes, yes, good, bring it in then, lad, bring it in then.' His gangly young sidekick strode through, handing over the tub and letting the door shut behind him.

The tub was held up to the light and they both stared intently at it for a few seconds, not quite sure what they were looking at.

Brian broke the silence. 'Is there actually anything in it?'

'Yes, Mr Wiley.'

'Well, there's not a lot of it, is there, lad?'

'I didn't know how much to take.'

'Well, enough to test would have been a good idea,' Brian said, looking at me in bemusement.

'I didn't want to hurt it,' Cameron responded.

'Hurt it? It's a stain.'

'Is it though?' the young man said. 'Is it though?'

Brian thought about responding, then thought better of it. They returned to staring in silence at the tub.

I said, 'I think I'll take a look at the kitchen, then.'

'Of course, of course.' Brian stepped aside. 'By the way, did you meet Adam? He's of a mind that we should work together, compare notes – get our stories straight as it were – what do you think?'

'Let me have a look at the famous stain first,' I said, heading for the purple door. 'I'll get back to you on that.'

The kitchen was cramped but warm, with a small window that cast pink light across the worn white cupboard doors and dishes piled in the sink. The West Indian lady was sitting at the small table, a thick, apple-green coat buttoned up to her chin. A shopping bag sat at her feet. Playing cards were set out in a game of Solitaire in front of her, with half a deck clutched in her soft-looking hands. She smiled as I entered but carried on with her game, placing cards and turning them with a soft *flick-flick-flick*.

I inspected the V-shaped stain that climbed the wall opposite her. It was, indeed, above the fridge and had a cloud-like appearance with blooms of rusty red and dirty grey wheeling into small clusters from the bottom. It was about five feet tall.

'What do you make of that then?' I asked.

'It's a stain, darlin', she responded, without breaking concentration.

'You don't think it's anything else?'

The cards paused as she turned her deep brown eyes on me. 'I think it's what you get when you take out a kitchen in the flat upstairs and don't need to do it properly.'

I laughed. She went back to her game, gently shaking her head. I watched as her hands moved, the cards flicking quickly into their lines. It didn't seem like any game of Solitaire I'd ever seen. It was dizzying.

'What are you playing?'

'The rules are different where I come from.'

'And where's that?'

'St Lucia, darlin'.'

'It looks confusing.'

'It's frustrating, that's what it is.' She sighed, scooped all the cards up and stacked them neatly into a pile to one side. 'I never seem to finish,' she smiled, inviting me to sit down.

I pulled up an empty chair. 'I'm Joe, what's your name?'

'Nice to meet you, Joe, my name is Patience. Patience Dubois.' She cocked her head towards me. 'And that's my *real* name. Adam Zacharanda!' She rolled her eyes.

'So, what's your job in tonight's activities, are you a medium too?'

She scoffed, 'No, darlin', I'm not a medium. I don't believe in mediums, no such thing.'

As if on cue, the door opened. Cameron gave me a sheepish look as he propped it open with a ceramic Buddha. Zacharanda poked his head around the open door, briefly inspected the stain and then strode back out into the middle of the living room to adopt his wide-legged, head-down stance. Brian circled him studiously, waving his silver wand. Patience and I exchanged glances.

'So, he can't talk to the dead?' I said, unable to avert my eyes from the spectacle.

'No, he can't speak to the dead,' she said, carefully putting her playing cards back into their box. 'No one can speak to the dead, because they're dead.'

I drummed my fingers on the table. 'You know, I've had a few experiences over the last few weeks that might make you change your view.'

'Is that so? You're the writer, right? I would have expected you to be a little more analytical.'

'I believe what I can see, and the things I've seen lately have left me questioning pretty much everything, including my sanity.'

Patience tutted. 'Don't worry about questioning things or questioning yourself. Not everything has to make sense. Leave that to science, it'll catch up eventually, it always does.'

'What do you mean?'

'What I mean is life isn't perfect, and people shouldn't expect it to be. Don't get me started on science!'

'Go on, explain.'

She shrugged. 'Well, isn't that what science teaches us? Isn't that how we went from crawling on our bellies to walking up tall; a billion, billion, billion lucky mistakes that selected the survivors? The problem is that science tells us that life is all about imperfections, but science can never see its own imperfections. Scientists tell us what is real and what's not these days, but they only see what they can measure. They can never admit that they've got a lot of measuring left to do, measuring the things that fall outside their reach. Darlin', it's not so long ago that they were feeling the bumps on your head to tell you what kind of person you are.'

In the living room, Adam Zacharanda's face was now gently vibrating as Brian and Cameron recorded him with video cameras.

'So, they're wasting their time?' I asked.

'Well,' Patience said, 'the dead *can* speak to you – if they want to. I know that for a fact. From experience. But no amount of mumbo-jumbo can persuade them to speak if they don't want to.'

'So, if you're not a medium, what are you?'

'Where I come from, people used to say that some folks are between two places. That's me.'

I looked around the kitchen. It was nearly dark now, and the window no longer illuminated the room; the single light bulb in the centre of the ceiling bravely cast a yellow glow that seemed to make it warmer, cosier. Outside, matt grey clouds muffled the stars, but Grimsby twinkled below as the brake lights of cars swarmed like fireflies up orange-lit streets.

'And what about this place?' I asked.

'Oh, this place is in two places, that's for sure,' Patience said. 'But it's nothing to do with that.' She nodded at the stain. 'It's in here, and out in the corridor too. Believe me, I know it.'

I rubbed my face, suddenly very tired. 'I believe you. The last few weekends I've been doing this, going to places like this and... I never expected it to be like this. I thought it would be little bumps in the night, maybe funny noises, creepy feelings... but I've *seen* things. Seen them. I think I'm losing my mind.'

Her eyes wrinkled with sympathy. 'Oh, Joe, Joe, you're a sensitive soul, I can tell. You're an open door, darlin'. If you have seen things, it's because they wanted you to see them. They chose you; they don't choose many. What you have to understand is that when you see them, you see them with your feelings as much as your eyes. That's because feelings are stubborn, they last forever, they stick around places... like that stupid stain. You can't see the past, but you can feel it. You must be an emotional man.'

'You don't know the half of it,' I said, with a weary smile.

Patience crossed her arms and observed Adam Zacharanda, who was now sitting on the sofa, his head thrown back, eyes shut tight.

'I feel sorry for him,' she said, 'he's got the wrong end of the stick. He's spent his whole life thinking he's got some kind of ability, that he's connected in some way, that he's special, when really he was probably just a lightning rod for a brief moment. Someone must have reached out to him once, spoke to him, touched him – and he assumed it was all about him. It rarely is.' She looked me up and down and smiled. I blushed.

'I need a drink of water,' I said. 'Want one?'

'No thank you, darlin'.'

I found a glass in a cupboard and filled it from the tap, then leant against the worktop and drank it down in one.

'You look like you need to sleep,' she said, inspecting the box of playing cards as it rotated in her hands.

'I can't sleep. Nobody knows what I've seen – I haven't told anyone. I'm a rational person, but every time I close my eyes, I see them or hear them again.'

'That's got to be natural. It's a shock to the system, it'll pass. Anyway, sleep's overrated.'

I sat back down. I felt comfortable with this woman. 'So, what are they then, Patience? The things I've seen. They're all so different. Explain to me.'

She looked confused. 'What do you mean "what are they"?'

'I mean why are they like that? What are they?'

'They're people, Joe. They're still people.'

People are the story, I thought.

'But… how?'

She exhaled deeply, then took the cards out of the packet.

'Listen,' she said, 'it's actually very simple.'

She began to place the cards down again, building rows, turning them over, *flick, flick, flick*.

'Think about what we know for sure, what the scientists tell us. Life isn't perfect, in fact life is all about the imperfections. That's the game of life. That's evolution.'

The cards seemed to blur as her hands moved back and forth.

'Just as we learn from our mistakes in life, life learns from its mistakes to repair itself, to grow and to change.' *Flick, flick, flick.* 'The only thing certain in life is change, that things *will* change, and we happily accept that, most of the time. But the biggest change we go through is at the end of life, and we struggle to accept that.'

The cards stopped. She tutted and scooped them back up ready to start again. Patience looked at me, the deck poised. 'The thing is, Joe, life goes wrong all the time – and sometimes death goes wrong too.'

Flick, flick, flick.

'Death goes wrong?'

'Everything natural goes wrong, all the time, and death is the most natural thing in the world. So sometimes, it goes wrong.'

'How does it go wrong?'

'Well, lots of ways. People get left behind; people get frightened. Some don't realise they're dead. Some get confused, some refuse to change, they want to carry on as they were. Some are searching for something or bound to a place by ties they can't break. Some get stuck in a loop. Some stick around to warn other folk. Some are just so comfortable they just can't summon up the energy to move – like a cat lying in a sunbeam.'

Her hands moved quicker and quicker, the cards landing at a bewildering speed.

Flick, flick, flick, flick, flick.

'Some of them – just a few – refuse to go because they are wicked, they are bad, and they are frightened of being judged, because they know what they'll face. But only they can choose to move on. You can't make them go, at least nobody from this side can – all that "walk towards the light" nonsense. Mediums. Exorcists. Charlatans. You see, they're in the wrong place, they can't do anything. But if you meet them, Joe, remember… they are all people. Dead people – but people.'

She paused and looked at the cards, before resuming her game. *Flick, flick, flick.*

'What I've seen so far,' I said, tapping the table, 'there doesn't seem to be any rules, they're all different.'

'As different as the leaves on the trees, darlin', as different as snowflakes. Some stay the same, some change with time. Some are like smoke and some look so real you can't tell if they're alive or dead. Some can see you, some can't. Some have been around so long there's barely anything left of them; they mix with the air, like noises or perfumes. They are all different, just like everything in nature is different.'

'So, are they tied to a place?'

'Yes, or maybe an object. Usually near where they passed on.'

'I'm trying to find places to visit – for my book – so any suggestions would be good.'

Flick, flick, flick.

'Sounds like you are doing pretty good on your own.'

'But I don't know where to look, really. I want to avoid the obvious things. You know, castles, graveyards.'

'You'd be wasting your time in a graveyard. I mean, whoever died in a graveyard? Besides, the dead need the living. Stay away from graveyards. Where I come from, they say the only thing that haunts graveyards is death. Or elementals.'

'What's an elemental?'

Flick, flick, flick.

'Never seen one. Never want to. The things *you* have seen,

93

they need to be around life, around the living. That's why you see them. There's no life in a graveyard. The things that you'll find in a graveyard need the dead.'

She stopped and looked at the window. 'When I was a girl – a long time ago – we all used to play in the graveyard near our home. That was the way it was then. It was a happy little place, on the hillside outside our village. It was always in the sun. It was beautiful, bright... I remember some of the tombs were like little houses, with picket fences. We loved it. Then one day, even though the sun was shining there, it just suddenly turned cold, grey – we all felt it. When we went back the next day, an elder from the village was waiting at the gates. She stopped us going in. She told us not to go there no more, because there was an elemental in there, among the graves, inside the tombs. I asked her how did she know – and she said someone had seen it and that it was a soucouyant, an elemental that had never been alive, which slept with the dead. I asked her what did it look like. She wouldn't say, but said it had no interest in us, only the dead, as long as we stayed away. I never went back there.'

'I've never heard of an elemental.'

Patience resumed her game.

'Sure, you have. There's just lots of names for them, depending on where you're from. Juju, soucouyant, chondo, demon. Stay away from graveyards, that's all. What you're looking for is drawn to the living. Whoever died in a graveyard?'

'You make it sound so simple.'

'It is. It's natural. It's science, really, when you think about it.'

'I think the scientific community might disagree.'

She stopped and scooped up the cards again.

'*Scientific community.*' Patience practically spat the words out. 'Until World War I the "*scientific community*" thought there were giant canals on Mars, dug by Martians. They thought man would never fly. They've still got no idea how your brain works. They only accept what they can measure. Some things can't be measured because they exist in two places.'

94

She wagged the deck at me.

'If you were to listen to science and only science, they would have you believe that *you* – whether you call it your mind, your personality, your consciousness, your essence, your life force, or your *soul* – is just biology, nothing more than neurons bouncing backwards and forwards. How can that be? It's obviously too simple an explanation, but it's the only one they can give, because it's all they can explain.'

Flick, flick, flick. The cards started again.

'Talk to other scientists and they'll tell you everything is made of stardust, and that you, me, these cards – everything – is just one big soup of molecules bumping into each other, and that it's only our perception that separates me from… this table, or you from that chair. Science wants to deal in the definite, but it leaves as many questions as any religion or belief system.'

I rested my chin in my hand, and smiled at Patience, lost for words. She laughed and put away her cards again.

'Anyway, Joe darlin', try not to think too much about the things you have seen. You should feel privileged. Now, listen to me: nothing is going to happen now tonight. I know it. Trust me. Go and get some sleep in one of the bedrooms. I'm not going anywhere.'

*

I slept like a rock. I found a single bed, covered in soft toys in a room that seemed to double as a home studio. I climbed into my sleeping bag among the velour dragons and fluffy black cats and fell into a deep slumber for the first time in weeks.

I only awoke when I felt someone sit on the end of the bed.

'Joe?' It was Patience's voice.

I lifted my head groggily from the pillow, my body trussed up tight in the sleeping bag. 'What time is it? What's going on?'

The sun was about to come up, and the room was caught

in that dreamlike moment between night and day, where the darkness seems to shine like water under moonlight. I could see the unmistakable silhouette of Patience sitting at my feet, her coat still buttoned up, her face turned to the door.

I undid the sleeping bag a little and lifted myself onto an elbow. 'Patience... what's up? Did something happen? What did I miss?'

She spoke softly, without turning. 'It's alright, darlin', you didn't miss anything, nothing happened, nothing at all. Everyone's asleep. I just... need to tell you something.'

Intrigued, I hauled myself up further, rubbing my eyes. 'What do you need to tell me?'

'Something you ought to know,' the silhouetted figure said. 'Something you need to know.'

'What's that then?'

'Someone is trying to reach you.'

'You mean...'

'From the other place.'

'Who?'

'Don't know.'

'What makes you say that? How do you know someone's trying to reach me?'

'It's just there. All around you. I think that's why they all notice you. It's all over you. Someone wants you. Someone is looking for you.'

'Someone wants me? What for?'

The silhouette suddenly turned, to look me straight in the eye.

'I don't know, Joe, but I don't think it's good. I think you need to be careful, you're too open.'

'What do you mean it's not good?'

She shook her head. 'Just... not good. Not happy. Not friendly. Bad. Guilty.' She paused to think and looked at her hands. The box of playing cards rotated slowly in the dim light. 'Do you know who it might be? Can you think of anyone?'

I paused momentarily, withholding my answer.

'Joe?' she persisted. 'Have you got anyone in the other place?'

'My dad,' I whispered.

'Your dad passed on?'

'He killed himself.'

She seemed to slump a little, nodding her head gently. 'Bless you, Joe, bless you. Just be careful.'

'Is it him?'

'I don't know,' she said, standing up. 'I don't know. Go back to sleep, darlin'.'

When I awoke early the next morning, I was alone. As I shut the purple front door behind me, the old rubbish chute rattled, sending a metallic echo down the corridor, up the elevator shafts, through the deserted floors of Mulvaney Tower. As I pressed the button for the ground floor, I knew I needed advice.

TEN

Family Patterns

Whenever I visit Mom's house I'm taken back to my childhood. It's as if a knot, pulled tight at my core by adult life, loosens as soon as I step over the threshold; when I hear the doorbell echo off the hall's high ceiling, smell the wood polish or fit my hand instinctively round the contours of the worn doorknob.

As I took off my shoes, I watched Mom shuffle busily into the kitchen to lift the whistling kettle. I remembered when the big old house – it seemed even bigger then – was a never-ending project; rooms closed off while money was squirrelled away in jam jars for wiring, for windows, for plasterwork, all to restore them to their original splendour. The hallway had been one of the first rooms to emerge from a chrysalis of dust sheets, newspaper and masking tape to a chorus of 'oohs' and 'ahs' from visiting relatives.

Even the feel of the old hallway carpet underfoot grounded me. I knew every twist and turn of its elaborate pattern, after kneeling so many times to command toy soldiers on missions through its maze of swirls and squares. Once, as a boy, I visited the identical house across the road, hunting for a missing cat. Their hallway glowed amber with parquet flooring – it turned out that Dad had decided to carpet over it at our house, as bare wooden floors reminded him of his poor upbringing.

So, this grand old house stood as a testament to his determination to better the family, and my mom's determination to carry on after he was gone. Change may indeed be a constant in life, but for me that house seemed to stay resolute and certain – an anchor that I could cling to whenever the tide pulled me harder than usual.

There was an edge, however, the bright memories of my early life soiled by a sense of shame, the result of my behaviour as a teenager.

Mom reappeared, a stacked tray clutched tight under her chin, and drew me into the lounge with a smile. She wanted to talk.

She put down the tray and stood to inspect me in the way mothers do, gently brushing fluff from my suit lapels.

'Very smart – have you been to work today?'

'No, I haven't actually. I just put this on through force of habit, I think.'

'I like you in a suit,' she said, pulling out a chair, 'you look like your dad in a suit.'

Over the years, our chats had evolved into a chess-like game. We sat at the oak dining table in the big bay window, the light picking out scratches in the deep brown wood; just like us, it bore the wounds of family life.

Mom's kind blue eyes, framed by long grey hair, watched me as she poured the tea, the milk, then passed me a cup. A dramatic frown followed as I added four spoons of sugar.

'Really, Joe, it's a wonder you have any teeth left in your head.'

'I need the energy, Mom, got lots to do, lots to think about.'

'You've been doing that since you were a teenager, and you certainly didn't need the energy then.'

I stirred the tea and smiled. 'Well, let's just say I needed it as a mood enhancer.'

We sat in comfortable silence for a moment, watching a family of magpies skip on the lawn.

'You look tired, Joe,' she finally said. 'What's happening with your job?'

'We're coming to the end of the consultation – it's all over really.'

'That's sad. Gus called me yesterday, he said the building was nearly empty.'

'Yes, it's all being stripped out. It is sad, but there's no point fighting it. I'm getting quite a decent pay-off, Gus too.'

The magpies hopped as we fell silent. It was evident that we both had something to ask, something to say.

Mom made the first move, pushing a plate of biscuits towards me. 'He also said he was worried about you. Said he hasn't heard from you in a few days.'

I took a biscuit and bit into it. 'I've got a new project, been working on that. I was planning on seeing Gus next week actually – we've all got to go in to get our stuff from our desks, but I thought I'd ask him his opinion on it.'

'He told me what you were up to. Sounds… interesting.'

I looked at her, sensing in her voice the protective edge I had relied on so many times during my childhood. The steel behind her blue eyes was glinting.

'It is. It's going very well, fascinating in fact – I think it will make a book.'

'A book. That would be good.' She gazed into her teacup. 'It sounds like you're revisiting some… old interests. That's what Gus was worried about.' Her eyes rose to mine. 'He said you might be getting into it over your head. Getting… carried away.'

The suggestion needled an irritation I hadn't felt for years. I swallowed it with a mouthful of tea.

'That's a fair concern. It's something I've always been interested in – you know that – and I'm different now. All grown up.'

'All grown up and still having four sugars in your tea,' she said, pulling the biscuits back.

'I knew you'd be concerned, Mom, don't be. I know what I'm doing with this.'

'You look so tired though, Joe.'

'Well, it does involve late nights, put it that way. But I'm used to that from working on rotas all these years. I'm going to do some more; I've got a trip to London lined up in a couple of days. I've only been able to do it on weekends so far, but that won't be a problem from now on. I'm a free man.'

She nodded and we both looked out of the window.

My move.

'It has given me a lot of time to think, though,' I said.

'Oh yes? What about?'

'Lots of things really. I've been thinking about Dad a lot.' I glanced at his armchair, next to the fire. The room had been rearranged many times over the years, but the chair always remained in place.

Mom shifted uneasily. It was her turn to feel needled. She sipped her tea.

'I think about him every day. All the time,' she said. 'Everything about this house reminds me of him. It's good to think about him.'

'Do you feel like he's still here sometimes?'

The steel glinted again.

'You know, Joe, I hope I'm not part of your little project. I'm not sure it's something I approve of.'

'What do you mean?'

'I feel like you're interviewing me.'

'God no! Sorry, that's not what I meant. I just… I don't know. Do you ever feel like he's close by or…'

Mom sat up straight.

'Joe, I'm beginning to see why Gus said he was worried. You're acting like you did… when you were younger.' She raised a palm towards me. 'I want to know that you're not slipping back

101

to where you were, because if you are we can sort that out, we can get help – we've done it before.'

'Mom, I'm fine,' I snapped. 'I know how to deal with this stuff, I've spent all my adult life dealing with it. I'm *OK*. I've just got a lot going on.'

A withering look. I had overstepped the mark. She sighed.

'Every few years, Joe, you need to talk about your dad. I understand that. But it doesn't change anything. Your dad was unwell, or he became unwell. It's something that had probably simmered in him since his childhood – but you are not him, Joe. There's so much of you that you get from your dad, you know that... your sensitivity, your stubbornness. But what he did – what happened to him – had nothing to do with you.'

She reached across the table and grasped my hand.

'It's very hard to explain... for you to understand... what a difficult childhood your father had. He grew up after the war, when a lot of men came back different, which led to a lot of broken families. He survived it. I think he wanted to make sure that the cycle was broken, that the pattern changed... that you would have a proper chance, a nice home, an education... and lots of love. In the end, I think it still took its toll, it caught up with him. But he'd be so proud to see the man you have become, and how you've overcome your own problems.'

Our eyes met properly for the first time that day.

'I have struggled a little lately,' I admitted.

'I know. Are you sure this project of yours is a good idea? You should be careful you don't reopen old wounds.'

'I don't think I can stop now,' I said. 'I'm hooked. But I know what I'm doing. Don't worry.'

'And do I need to worry about your home life? How's that flat of yours?'

She had changed the subject. The game was over. A respectable draw.

'What do you mean?' I said, munching another biscuit.

'I can't remember the last time you let me inside – you're like a hermit. It's no wonder no woman is interested in you.'

I rolled my eyes. 'Don't start. I'm a busy man.'

'Well, I'm not getting any younger. I want to see you settled down.'

Mom seemed to consider something, then produced car keys from her pocket.

She gently placed them in front of me.

'These might help with your travels. They're spare ones for the car. I hardly use it now, I don't need it really. So, if you need to borrow it, just take it. Your dad would have loved you working on the paper. I think he would have loved the idea of you writing a book, too.'

The magpies skipped.

ELEVEN

A Night's Watch

The Fifth Vigil

Back when I was in primary school, we had an 'ant farm' in our classroom. Just dirt sandwiched between two sheets of glass, it was populated by a colony of ants, who had carved an intricate labyrinth of tunnels into the earth: an insect city in cross-section. I loved watching them swarm up and down the long diagonal climbs to the surface, to collect the titbits we dropped in for them. Whenever I visit London, I'm reminded of that ant farm.

As I emerged from the Underground station at Canary Wharf, everyone else was heading in the other direction, into the subterranean network below the capital – eyes cast down, bags held tight, collars turned up. October had arrived, bringing the first chill of winter.

At the top of the steps, I moved to one side, letting the river of people flow past. Above, the lights went out in office blocks, as their occupants drained into the tunnels below.

To an out-of-towner, London seems to be populated in shifts, the tube, taxis, trains and buses ferrying the daytime masses home at closing time to suburbs on the outskirts, or farther afield into Buckinghamshire, Essex, Kent. They leave behind nightshift Londoners, the people who work through the dark hours, walk its neon-lit streets, or sleep in its urban heart.

As office hours end, you can sometimes see them observing the exodus, leaning on walls and standing in alleyways, waiting to reclaim their city once the herds have cleared. With my bag between my feet, for a few moments I joined them: an old man clutching a newspaper, a sleepy-looking woman in a headscarf, a gang of six black lads sitting on railings, their hooded heads bobbing in animated conversation, shoulders bumping and elbows nudging. Within an hour or two, the city would be theirs for the night.

My destination was a new dockside building, whose five-storey glazed frontage squatted beneath the forest of skyscrapers like unassuming foliage. On the neat concourse outside loomed an eight-foot-tall fibreglass Viking wielding a ridiculously oversized axe, his comic book features airbrushed in bright colours. Behind the glass, a neon logo shone out, its curling, conjoined letters reflecting across the water – a single word that automatically shaped in my mouth: 'Phatt'.

The tall glass door was locked, but inside I could see a security guard behind a reception desk, laughing with a long-haired kid in shorts and T-shirt who was leaning lazily against his counter. I pressed the intercom and he buzzed me straight in; their laughter was still ringing around the foyer's marble walls as I stepped inside.

'Hi, I'm here to see the CEO,' I said, my shoes squeaking as I approached the desk. He and the kid exchanged mischievous looks.

'The CEO or the COO?' the guard asked. 'Chief Executive Officer or Chief Operating Officer?' The kid stifled a giggle and then crossed his arms to study my response.

'Er… CEO I think… Charlie Blake?' Another exchange of glances.

'Well, that makes it easier because Mr Blake is the CEO and the COO,' he said. 'And you said you were here to see him?'

'Yes, that's right.'

A broad grin spread across his face. 'Well, you've seen him. Anything else I can help you with?'

The kid laughed and offered me a hand. 'Hi, I'm Charlie. You'll have to forgive Otis, he gets bored easily. Joe, isn't it?'

'I'm so sorry,' I said, 'I didn't recognise you.'

'Good!' he said, leading me across the foyer and throwing a friendly nod back to the desk, adding, 'Otis, we're taking over your lair!'

Charlie Blake was in his mid-twenties, not much more than five feet tall and had the build of a sixteen-year-old boy. Standing next to him in my shapeless suit, I suddenly felt old. He was also one of the most successful video game developers in the world, the founder of Phatt, and someone who kept a famously low profile. In recent weeks, though, that had proven more difficult than usual.

'Your email was incredibly well timed,' he said. 'I have something which I think you may find interesting.'

He led me through a heavy door, flicking on the light to reveal a small security office. A desk and two chairs sat in front of a large screen surrounded by smaller CCTV monitors, all of which buzzed with the crystal-clear colour interiors of offices, kitchens and corridors.

We sat, and he logged onto the system. 'Your email really grabbed me,' he said as he tapped the keyboard. 'I don't usually speak to the press – and that's not a habit I intend to break – but after the events of the last two weeks your book idea intrigued me.'

A podium appeared on the main screen, the Phatt logo behind it. Carefully turning a broad dial, Charlie began to whizz through the footage, with figures blurring in and out of shot, setting up microphones and checking lighting.

He spoke as he worked, his eyes never leaving the screen.

'It struck me that you could provide me with a more... measured... way of responding to recent accusations. Unfounded accusations. Ah, here we go!'

The footage froze as the Hollywood smile of actor Ethan Butler appeared behind the podium, his symmetrical features suspended between immaculately parted hair and a tailored black shirt.

Charlie turned to me. 'You'd think I'd be sick of the sight of this by now, but I can't stop watching it, so you're going to have to bear with me. You've seen it, I take it?'

'Yes, a couple of times – but not on a screen like this.'

He smiled. 'It's a bit better than watching it on your phone, that's for sure.' He hit play and turned up the volume.

A trumpet fanfare blared over polite applause and Butler waved as camera flashbulbs lit up his face. 'This is downstairs, right below us,' Charlie said, transfixed as the actor settled his audience down.

He spoke in a warm Texan drawl: 'Ladies and gentlemen, ladies and gentlemen, thank you so much for coming along at this ungodly hour to help us launch the next chapter in the *Runes of Eternity* franchise...' he reached below the podium to produce a sword, which he held aloft '... the *Ghosts of Valhalla*!'

Another fanfare. Flashbulbs fired. The audience clapped.

Butler lay the sword across the podium and leant forward to speak into the microphone, clearly reading from an autocue.

'Since Chapter One launched three years ago, *Runes of Eternity* has broken all records for a role-playing game, making the leap to the silver screen twelve months ago in the first of a movie trilogy featuring the quests of Harald Arne. *Ghosts of Valhalla* will give fans, followers and fellow travellers a chance to once more visit Lundenwic and play their own part in this timeless saga.'

He looked straight into the camera.

'Wait for it...' Charlie said, his hand hovering over the dial, 'wait for it...'

Butler flashed his teeth. 'And as a life-long gamer myself, I can't wait to find out what happens, before shooting starts on the next movie!'

'There!' Charlie slapped the dial. The picture froze. Next to Butler's grinning face, just above his right shoulder, a small, golden orb-like light hung in the air.

Charlie turned to me. 'That's the first one, right there. I've been over this footage so many times, I know it almost frame by frame. There's at least six on it, and at one point five in one frame.'

'And did you notice them at the time? During the launch?'

'God no!' Charlie said, running his hands through his long hair and pulling his feet up onto the seat. 'No one did, or at least if they did they just assumed it was a trick of the light, lens flare or something like that. I didn't have a clue until it went viral.'

'And that's when the accusations started...'

'Got them all here,' he said, his fingers working quickly on the keyboard. A slide show of web pages began to flick across the screen, each with screen grabs of Ethan Butler and his orb. 'We held the launch at 2am partly to give it a bit of mystery, but also so we could live stream it in other markets around the globe, and as far as we can see the first person to spot the lights – the orbs – was a gamer in Montreal who started talking about it on social media while the show was still going on. It just took off from there.'

Charlie flicked back to the frozen footage of Butler and began to wind it forward, silently, in double speed. The camera angle broadened as the actor made his way down steps to meet costumed characters. Freeze frame. Two more orbs hung between the people on the screen.

He shook his head. 'First thing I heard about it all was in the morning. It started off with people sharing this idea that, because of the ruins downstairs, because of the bones, there was a real supernatural apparition at the launch of *Ghosts of Valhalla*. It spread like wildfire. Which, I suppose, was fun. Great publicity. But then, pretty soon, it turned a bit nastier.'

He rolled the footage forward again. Butler moved in double time across the screen, talking to the moving camera before arriving at a waist-high glass wall with an open door in it. Freeze. Two more orbs, behind the glass.

Charlie sighed. 'So, then people start saying, "Hang on, Phatt make movies now, they do CGI, this is their thing – it's a fake. Charlie Blake's faked it to get publicity. Blake the fake." Then the legacy media – the papers, the TV, the old farts who like nothing better than to have a pop at the gaming world – they get involved. It was crazy.' He pointed to the screen. 'This is the money shot, by the way, coming up.'

The footage rolled again. Butler spoke to the camera, then turned to the glass door, stepped through it and began to descend steps out of view. The screen cut to an overhead shot. Butler was climbing down a ladder into the red dirt of an archaeological site dug into the floor, where a camera man awaited. An elderly gent, smartly dressed in a three-piece suit, offered the actor a hand at the foot of the steps, his neat grey moustache twitching. Freeze.

'The ruins,' I said.

'Yes, and look...' Charlie leant forward and tapped the frozen image. 'One, two, three, four, five. Five orbs in one shot.' He sat back. 'It's probably fair to say that we *could* have faked it, but to be honest I'm not that clever. And my marketing monkeys would *never* have thought of something as off-the-wall as this.'

'So, can I see the dig? Is that where I'm spending the night?'

'I'm not sure just yet,' he said, tapping at the keyboard again. 'I'll take you down in a moment and explain when we get down there. It's complicated, but I'll try to sort it out for you. That's actually not what I wanted to show you. This is.'

He hit return and a large, dimly lit room appeared on the

screen. In the centre, the low glass wall surrounding the dig glinted.

'So, after all this fuss died down, I wanted to get to the bottom of it. We analysed the footage forensically but that was no use, didn't explain the orbs at all. So, then I thought I'd try to get more footage.' He nodded at the screen. 'I've had cameras set up down there all week, 24/7.'

'And?'

He rubbed his childlike hands together with glee and hit play. We watched as looped footage, clipped together from numerous angles, captured pinpricks of light gently floating through the air, some glowing like candles, others blinking and arcing in and out of the gloom.

Charlie pulled his knees up and wrapped his arms around his legs. 'They never last long and they always appear in the middle of the night.'

'Are you going to release the footage? Clear your name?'

He shook his head. 'They'd just say we'd faked this too. Anyway, I did it for my own curiosity, not to prove anything. But then your email arrived, and I thought… maybe this could be a better way to share this, through your book.'

'Well,' I said, sitting forward, 'just to give you some background, I've been doing a few of these overnight vigils, at places I've sourced through my contacts at local newspapers. This is the first time I've approached a place after I saw it in a paper myself.'

'And these other places… anything like this at all?'

I looked again at the looped footage. 'No, not at all. This is very different.'

He stood up. 'Let me show you the ruins.'

*

Leaving my bag with Otis, we made our way down a broad staircase off the foyer and emerged through double doors into the building's large, brightly lit basement, which was furnished with soft seating, vending machines and a pool table. Vintage video games lined the white walls, punctuated by framed posters advertising Phatt's greatest hits. A large black granite bar, its shelves fully stocked with booze, filled the far corner. In the centre of the room, the glass wall surrounded the site of the dig. I followed Charlie across the polished concrete floor.

'It's a really big space, so I thought it would be a perfect break-out area,' he said. 'We call it the "rumpus room" – that's a Simpsons thing. Although, to be honest, the team aren't quite as keen to come down here alone anymore.'

We reached the glass and looked down into the rectangular dig site. I felt myself rock back on my heels, surprised by the dizzying drop. It was a huge void, sunk into the floor, its sides contained by walls of interlocked steel piles. About the size of a tennis court, the dig descended at least thirty feet through different levels – carefully cut platforms whose sides exposed layers of stone and brick, all illuminated by discreetly placed lights. Sets of simple wooden steps linked each level. At its deepest point, I could just see a metal sheet lying in the black dirt.

'That's amazing,' I said. 'You'd never think something like this would be here.'

'It's quite the conversation starter,' chuckled Charlie, 'but it can be a bit of a headache. Any buildings put up in London, particularly in an area like this, require an archaeological survey before any construction begins, and they started finding stuff almost straight away. There wasn't anything hugely important, so they said we could bury it again and start building. Then I thought, let's keep it – make it a feature and build around it. We could have our own slice of Old London Town in the building, something to show the Yanks when they come over.'

He pointed to the deepest part of the dig. 'Problem is it hadn't given up all its secrets. We were halfway through putting the building up around it when there was a sudden collapse at the bottom, which must have been caused by all the heavy machinery. All of a sudden, we had a site of major historical importance in the middle of our new HQ.'

'And that's when they found the bones?'

'The bones, yes, but it was the age of the new levels that made it so important.' He leant against the glass wall. 'So, what we have here, in the centre of our rumpus room, is an officially scheduled ancient monument. I own it, but I have to be very careful about what happens to it, because it's of proper significance in historical terms. It's still being studied now.'

'What are they still studying?'

'Specifically, the bones. They sorted through all the pottery and other stuff quite quickly, but there were so many bone fragments, and they were in such a state, that they've been working through them for months. Other than the fact they are human, I haven't been told a great deal.'

He gave me a conspiratorial glance. 'That's another reason why your email was well timed. I was told by the powers-that-be that preliminary results were due yesterday, and I was hoping to be able to tell you about them tonight. Might add a little background to your writing.'

'Can we go down?' I asked.

'Yes, we can have a look around it, but I don't think you can spend the night down there. I was hoping you would be allowed to. I put in a request for advice from Professor Holliday – he's the one overseeing the research – but he's not got back to me. He's a decent chap, but quite erratic – works all hours. So, you may have to make do with a bird's eye view from up here.'

I looked around the rumpus room. 'Trust me, I've stayed in worse places,' I said.

The little glass door swung open, and we descended the first set of steps to a flat platform next to exposed, brownish brickwork.

Charlie touched it gently. 'Obviously, this is the more recent stuff – early Victorian dockside buildings probably.'

As we dropped another level, the air began to dampen. An exposed cross-section of earth revealed a dull rainbow of layered colours.

Charlie resisted the temptation to touch. 'So, we've gone down another hundred years or so, and this is apparently evidence that at that time this was underwater, or part of an earlier manmade dock, because these are layers of silt. It starts to get a bit more interesting from here downwards.'

Another set of steps took us down to a thin ledge next to a broader area where the outline of a building could be made out in the dark soil. 'That's properly old,' Charlie said. 'Medieval – and evidence that people were living here before the area became a dock.'

He pointed to the top of the final set of steps, which disappeared into a much darker, deeper space. 'That's the level that was exposed by the collapse, that caused all the trouble.'

'Where the bones were found?'

'Yes, the bones and the really old stuff – the stuff that suddenly made the British Museum sit up and take notice.'

'Can we take a look?'

He grinned. 'I don't see why not. But be careful – there aren't any of these little lights down there and stay off the metal sheeting. And if Professor Holliday shows up, don't tell him you've been down there!'

Again, Charlie led the way. These steps were practically vertical, and we descended backwards, climbing down them like a ladder. The walls were different too – no steel piles, just black, inky earth rippled with chalky loam, newly exposed after centuries of darkness. A peaty fug of decay hung in the air. The ant farm forced its way into my thoughts again. This was no longer a dig. It was a pit.

We reached the bottom. The close, steep walls seemed to press inwards, their dark soil absorbing the light from above. Large, yellow chiselled stones lay in a pile against one of the sides, an ancient wall which had evidently collapsed. The steel sheet on the floor glistened in the gloom, straining to reflect the lights of the rumpus room high above.

Charlie put his hands on his hips. 'This is old. Very old. Not quite Roman, which is what they first thought, but not long after they left. This is London in the Dark Ages, well over 1,000 years ago.'

He tapped one of the stones with his toe. 'The academics got very excited when they began to look at these. This is some serious masonry, and it continues into the side for a few feet too. Back then, we only really built things out of wood. Professor Holliday said it was so substantial that it could only be for defensive use, military even. He thinks this was part of the defences of an Anglo-Saxon settlement that was here, on the outskirts of London.'

'And this is where the bones were?'

Charlie nodded towards the steel sheet. 'Under there. We can have a look, if you help me lift it – but be careful.'

The square sheet was heavy and had sunk into the dead soil at the bottom of the pit. Our fingers dug into the earth and we heaved it up on one side. As we did, a natural seal broke, and the hole below exhaled. It was a well.

'Mind your footing,' Charlie said, struggling to get a grip on the sheet. 'We're not sure how safe it is. It's another ten feet deep, but there isn't any water in it anymore. The bones were found at the bottom, hundreds of fragments.'

'A plague pit?'

'No, far too early for that. The professor said there's evidence that bodies were sometimes placed in water as part of pagan rituals, but not smashed up like these were.'

'And how many bodies were there?'

'That's one of the things they're trying to work out. Let's put it down, it's too heavy.'

We eased the sheet back into place and stood rubbing our hands. Charlie wagged a finger at me. 'Like I said, you never came down here.'

'Of course, I understand.'

'I'd never hear the end of it if the professor found out.' He looked up the ladder. 'Speaking of which, I think I'll give him a call, see if there's any news. Let's go back up top and have a drink.'

*

Otis dropped my bag on the sofa next to me and gave me a thumbs-up before heading towards the double doors. I was just unzipping it when Charlie appeared with two bottles of beer grasped in one hand and his phone pressed to his ear with the other.

He handed me a beer as he finished his call.

'OK, Professor, hope to see you in the morning, thanks.' He sat down and took a swig. 'Well, he sounds excited. He said he'd be over at about nine o'clock to tell us about the bones, if you think you'll still be here.'

'I don't see why not.' I raised my bottle to him. 'This will be the most comfortable vigil I've done yet.'

Charlie chuckled and took another swig. 'Make yourself at home,' he said.

I looked at a bank of 80s video games which were quietly buzzing and beeping on the wall next to us.

'Would it be possible to get some stuff turned off before I start? I need everything to be quiet – and dark too.'

'No problem. If you don't mind, we'll leave the cameras running, though – then we can take a look together in the morning. They have a night vision function which is pretty good. I'll be in early, I tend to start at seven.'

'You won't be joining me tonight, then?'

'No. I'm intrigued by all this but not enough to forgo my bed!'

'Fair enough,' I said, slightly relieved.

'Otis will be upstairs all night, though, of course, if you need anything. Would you like me to ask him to pop down and check on you at any point?'

'Actually, no. I'd rather stick to how I've been doing things up to this point. My experience shows that if there's more than one person then, frankly, nothing happens.'

'OK, I'll tell him. Look, I asked the professor about you going into the ruins and he said you shouldn't. To be honest, from a health and safety point of view it's a no-no too, especially if you've got the lights turned off. So, you'll have to make do with the view from the top.'

I sat back and took another swig of beer. 'I think I can manage that.'

*

So far, all my overnight stays had been a waiting game, but this was the first time it felt like I was waiting to catch a flight. The low lights, soft seating and concrete floor combined with the hum of the bar's refrigerator to make the rumpus room feel like a departure lounge at Heathrow.

The contents of my bag were laid out on the sofa next to me, the rolled-up sleeping bag rendered redundant by the room's warm temperature and soft cushions. My sandwiches had been relegated down the menu too, the contents of the vending machine by the door proving more enticing. Only my flask of super-sweet tea retained full privileges, providing a familiar injection of energy as the small hours arrived.

Charlie had left me at around 7pm, and I had wandered around the large room aimlessly for a while before pulling a sofa up to the glass wall overlooking the dig. Then I had spent twenty minutes locating his CCTV cameras – I found six in all, dotted around the room to provide maximum coverage.

Then I made myself comfortable on the sofa, stoically resisting Charlie's parting offer to help myself to more beers. I was becoming more practised at my sleepovers; they were now called vigils. I needed to be alone, I had to try to stay awake, it had to be quiet, dark. I regretted the three large glasses of Merlot I had sunk in St Ives before settling down to watch and wait for the first time. Call it a schoolboy error, or Dutch courage. From now on, only polite libation would be allowed. Sweet tea would be my fuel.

One thing I was getting good at was sitting still. When you're trying to listen out for the subtlest sounds your ears tune themselves to a room's silence, eventually pushing aside ambient noises, like air conditioning, to focus on the space between, like finding the empty frequencies on a radio dial. There's a zen-like nature to it. Even a small movement can release a rustle or a click that echoes into the empty void, sending out waves that scramble all your hard work doing nothing. So, you sit still. Really still. And listen.

This time, my big city location provided a challenge. Despite being below ground, the noises of urban life began to dig their way through: a police siren, raised voices in the street, wolf whistles – even the rattle of the passing tube somewhere beneath, even deeper than the pit.

But I concentrated. Tune them out, tune them out. Listen. Listen.

I don't know whether it was the sweet tea or the more comfortable surroundings, but my energy levels stayed high as the night lengthened, my eyes open, my ears alert. As 2am approached even the noises from above seemed to fade.

I stood and stretched, then leant over the glass to peer into the dig site, testing how far I could see into the dimness. Each of the higher levels was just visible, the cut soil looking like patches of dark brown leather or velvety cloth in the half light. All was quiet.

However, while you can tune out noises, I was learning that light cannot be ignored. As your eyes adjust to a room, the smallest light source only gets brighter.

Darker. I needed it darker. A soft glow rose from behind the bar, the fridge glinting through the shelves of glasses and bottles above. I made my way over and, finding the switch next to the power socket, flicked it off. Half the room was swallowed into a deeper blackness, the other half dully lit by the glass-fronted vending machine by the door. In for a penny, in for a pound.

I edged into the light, skirting around the pool table, and making a mental note of its position. I took one last look at the rows of chocolates and snacks in the machine then bent down and switched it off at the wall. Blackness enveloped me. The room felt much bigger.

Now I needed to return to the sofa, to my vantage point above the pit. I shut my eyes tight and counted to ten, then opened them wide in the hope that they would adjust to the darkness. No good. Still pitch black. The night had suddenly got more interesting. I pointed my body in the rough direction of the pool table and began to edge slowly forward in the blackness, my hands grasping gently at the air in front of me.

A step, another step, another, another.

I stopped and felt around me. I should have reached the pool table by now. My heart jumped a little. I had missed. I was adrift in the dark. I wet my lips and pressed on slowly, slowly, slowly, stepping forward with my best foot, my right shoulder slightly forward, my hands sculling warily around me.

A step, another step, another, another.

I stopped and closed my eyes tight again, then opened them wide, blindly scanning the void. Darker. It seemed to be getting darker. How could that be? My heart began to race. Planting my feet firmly, I tried stretching an arm out to my left, then to my right, then forward. Nothing. I was lost. I felt myself squat slightly. I suddenly felt exposed, vulnerable.

Get yourself together. Where next? Carry on straight ahead or turn? Where was the pit? I decided to carry on. I took another step.

Hhhhhhhhhh.

I froze. Somewhere in the dark, behind me, a long, dry breath had been exhaled. My head turned to stare pointlessly in the direction of the sound. I blinked.

'Otis, if that's you it's not fucking funny,' I whispered.

Hhhhhhhhhhh.

Another dry, desiccated breath – long, thin, like a collapsed lung releasing papery air.

I started to edge into the blackness again, away from the sound, a feeling of panic beginning to drown me as I grabbed at the darkness.

Hhhhhhh. To my right. Shit, to my right, to my right!

Hhhhhhhhhh. Behind me. My entire body tensed. Press on, move. Move!

A step, another step, another, another into the dark, moving the black around me, my arms swimming in ink, my eyes blinking furiously, my lips dry. I juddered as my hands finally hit a wall, feeling the cold surface, pressing against it. I put my back to it and looked back into the void. I realised I was panting loudly, and clasped my hand over my mouth, holding my breath to listen. Listen. Listen. Silence.

Now I needed light. I needed to get to the sofa, to get my torch, my phone, anything! I tried to find my bearings in the dark – where was the pool table? Where was the bar? I turned forty-five degrees on the spot to my left, aiming into the darkness. I stepped away from the wall.

A step. A step. A smell. Peat. Soil. Damp. Old. Black.

Was I near the pit? Another step into the dark. I felt my weight sink a little. What? I rocked on my feet, testing the surface of the floor. A lick of noise. Wet? Slowly, I crouched down, my fingers lowering to touch the floor. Thick, oily dirt bloomed around their tips, under my nails. I knew that smell. The bottom of the pit.

Hhhhhhhhhh.

I stood up, shoulders tight, eyes wide, heart racing, mouth frozen open. How could I be in the pit? I needed light, I needed to see, I needed to get out. I shut my eyes tight, pressing my palms into their sockets, drawing the darkness into my head, balancing it, absorbing it, hoping to reopen them and see anything. Anything. I peeled them open.

Deep in the dark, a pinprick of light meandered briefly through the void, glaring gold and white, rolling slightly as it faded. I swallowed.

Silence.

Silence.

Hhhhhhhh. Right in front of me.

I staggered backwards. Another orb, bigger – closer – loomed out of the black, past my shoulder. My back crashed against the wall. Real wall, hard. Not the pit.

My palms pressed against the surface and I stood breathing heavily into the smothering darkness.

Slowly, an orb emerged to my left, at shoulder height, as if stepping from behind a curtain. I stared at it as it curled and rolled, glinting, almost metallic. It lingered, as if observing me.

Another appeared, to its right, a little higher, moving slowly left and right, a fiery bronze droplet that seemed to slip back and forth along an unseen groove.

Another. Three now, lined up, moving in the air, watching me, trapped like a specimen. Another, another. Five orbs, in a line, shifting in the blackness, wavering, as if on unsteady feet. A crack of static. Behind them, across the room, a vertical beam of blue-white light cut through the darkness from the base of the pit.

'Hello?' I stammered.

In unison, they exhaled a long, melancholy breath – *Hhhhhhhhhh* – and as they did, I felt an ancient fatigue drift over me, embracing me, ageless exhaustion clinging to me, burying me like black soil, tendering my tense muscles, slowing my heart, withering my will, ageing my eyes, my teeth, my bones. So tired. So tired. Nothing left.

I slowly blinked and looked upon them.

In the gloom the orbs gently moved and rolled, slipped and slid, golden and bronze, emerging, forming, arcing around shoulders and chests, metallic and solid, gleaming on forearms and legs, shining on swords and shields, rippling across armour, illuminating the sunken cheeks of warriors, faded, bound together, eternally walking together, lost in the dark.

For just a second their eyes saw me properly, their dirty faces marvelling at the man pressed against the wall.

'Are you alright?' The room glared white. Otis was at the door, his hand on the light switch. 'I've been watching you on the screen – are you alright?'

*

Charlie shook his head in wonder as he rolled the footage back again.

'I can't see them,' he said. 'You definitely saw orbs?'

'I saw a lot more than orbs,' I said, wearily rubbing my eyes. 'You wouldn't believe me if I told you.'

We watched as I edged across the screen, glowing green under the night vision cameras, my arms waving frantically, my eyeballs white with fear.

Otis was by the door of the security office, his coat pulled on, ready to head home. 'That's what he was doing for ages,' he said. 'I was worried he was going to fall down into the archaeological site in the dark, so in the end I went down.'

Charlie spun on the chair to face me. 'OK, tell me what you saw.'

'I saw orbs, but I saw people too and they saw me – I'm sure of that.' I stifled a yawn. 'I have genuinely never felt more tired than I do now. Nothing like that has happened before.'

Charlie held his hands up. 'I tell you what, Joe, save it for the book.' He turned to Otis. 'This is just between us three, right?'

'Yes, boss,' Otis said. 'See you this evening.'

As he stepped through the heavy door an elderly gent appeared, a thick folder of documents clutched beneath his twitching moustache.

'Professor!' Charlie stood up. 'I wondered if we would see you today.'

'Yes, Mr Blake, I'm sorry. Late night. Lots to report, a real breakthrough.' The old academic eyed me with suspicion.

'It's OK, Professor, this is Joe – the writer who spent the night in the rumpus room last night.'

'Oh!' the old man said, peering at me over his spectacles. 'How did it go?'

'Illuminating,' I said.

'Not my field, dear boy!' he said with a wry smile, opening the folder on the desk in front of Charlie. He tapped a photograph of hundreds of pieces of bone, spread out on a table. 'We have news on your fragments.'

'Go on.'

'Well, as we thought, they are human, and they are Anglo-Saxon, which fits with the masonry and time frame. Dated to around 840–860AD – well over 1,000 years old. The fragments of pelvic bone found suggest there are only men present in the pit. But here's the really unusual part: there are no skulls, no fragments of skull, no heads at all.'

Charlie and I exchanged glances.

'Why would that be?' I asked.

'Good question. My guess would be that they were defending the wall when it was overrun, probably by Norsemen. The Vikings sacked this part of the city lots of times.'

'Vikings,' Charlie said. 'That's amazing. Vikings!' He looked at the photograph, at the mass of white, chalky fragments. 'How many men were buried down there?'

'Five,' I said. 'There were five of them.'

The professor looked at me. 'How did you know that?'

TWELVE

Archive Material

Newspaper reception offices used to be bustling places. All local life was there: reporters interviewing with notepad on knee, readers trawling archived issues, reps selling space, advertisers writing cheques to fill it, newly-weds presenting pictures, parents revealing babies, the bereaved announcing deaths.

My heart sank as I entered the *Echo*. The reception had been emptied, the counter torn out, the clocks taken down, even the carpet ripped up.

In the corner, on two dusty office chairs, an elderly couple sat holding hands. Their eyes fell hopefully on me as I headed for the newsroom. Gus emerged, wearing a blue hooded top and carrying his belongings in a box. His slippers peeped over the edge.

He stopped by the couple and said, 'Sorry, someone will be down to see you in a moment. Thanks for your patience.'

'That's alright, we'll wait,' the old lady replied softly.

Gus looked me up and down. 'Jesus Christ, I know I always say this but this time I mean it – you look *terrible*. Where have you been?'

'London,' I said. 'Just got back. I'm exhausted. Long day. Long night.'

'Job interview?'

'No.'

'Then why are you wearing a suit?'

I looked at my clothes, then at Gus's. It occurred to me that it was the first time I'd seen him without a shirt and tie in decades.

'Er, it was for the book. I always wear a suit when I'm working. You taught me that. It's in The Rules.'

He shook his head. 'I'm not sure I had your current mode of employment in mind. We've been waiting for you for ages – they are literally locking up in twenty minutes.'

I smiled at the elderly couple. 'Who are they waiting for?'

'They came in to see a reporter – I told Nash to deal with them, but I can see that's not happened yet.'

'Where is he, then?'

'Up there, with Helena.' He looked around the room. 'It's all over here, Joe, finished. Time to try a different outfit on. I've emptied your cupboards for you, it's all in a box on your desk. I'll wait for you and Helena in the car park. I'll give you both a lift home.'

Through the doors I found Nash sitting with his feet up. Behind him, Helena was standing next to a large cardboard box staring vacantly around the room, thinking about her future, listening to the silence.

'Have they gone yet?' Nash asked.

'Who?'

'The people in reception. The old ones.'

'No, they're waiting to see a reporter. Didn't Gus tell you to do it?'

He stifled a sneer. 'He didn't *tell* me to do it. I'm on digital now, he's not my boss anymore. He's not anyone's boss. He's done.'

'Do you know what they want?'

'No.'

'Well, it could be a story, couldn't it, Nash?'

'Since when did a decent story just walk in off the street? Besides, I could spend an hour talking to them or I could get a dozen stories from social media in the same amount of time.'

'But what if they need help? Or advice?'

Nash stood and lifted a box from the floor. 'What do I look like, the Citizens Advice Bureau? You talk to them if you want, I'm going out the back. I work from home now anyway.'

I wandered over to Helena as Nash scurried towards the rear car park.

'Hello, stranger,' she said, snapping out of her reverie and motioning towards another, smaller box. 'That one's yours. I think we got everything.'

I peered inside at the sad collection of dog-eared notepads and dried-up pens.

'You hardly had anything,' she added. 'You know, I think you can tell a lot about a person from the number of books they have.'

I picked out a notepad. 'I just need this. I won't be too long – then I'll carry your box out for you. Gus will wait. One last story!'

I disappeared into reception, the old man rising to his feet and extending a nervous hand to me.

Twenty minutes later, Gus was waiting with boot open as I struggled across the car park, weighed down by Helena's personal library.

'I thought you Millennials were supposed to be digital natives,' I said, levering the box into the back of the car using my knee.

She daintily placed my box next to it. 'How is it that I've only been with the paper five minutes, and I've got more to show for it than you?'

I placed my hand on my heart. 'My legacy is in the archive.'

Gus opened the door. 'Then your legacy is currently shrink-wrapped in the back of a van on the way to Watford. Shall we go?'

We drove in silence before Gus asked, 'Did Nash see those people?'

'No, I did. Nice couple, called the Bentleys. Sad story. They've got a disabled grown-up son, and he's lost his funding for day care. Apparently, he's no longer disabled enough to qualify. They can't manage.'

'Oh… one of those stories,' he replied. 'Did you tell them you were leaving?'

'No, no… I'll do the story. People ought to know, and it won't take long. I might get a councillor involved or the local MP. See if we can sort it out.'

Helena piped up from the back seat, 'Nash wasn't interested.'

Gus cast a glance into the mirror. 'Not enough clicks, sweetheart.'

She thought for second. 'I'll help you with the story, Joe, if you like. With the Bentleys.'

Gus looked impressed. 'Any chance you could help me… and tell me where I'm going?'

She sat forward and thumped his shoulder. 'Yes… and don't call me sweetheart.'

Helena directed us to the upmarket suburb where she lived, in a small, cosy-looking house at the end of a paved driveway.

Gus popped the boot open. 'Would you mind doing the honours, Joe?'

As I followed Helena up the driveway the front door opened and a slim, attractive woman stood in the doorway, gently rubbing lotion into her hands. She was wearing light blue medical scrubs.

'Evening, Mother dearest,' Helena said, sliding past her. 'This is Joe.'

'Hi,' I said, putting the box down, 'nice to meet you.'

Helena's mom stared back at me, her smile sliding sideways, her eyebrows arched. Then she crossed her arms and leant casually against the doorframe.

'Joe Baxter, you don't remember me, do you?'

Her head tilted as a bemused expression spread across my face. I was on the spot. Her voice was instantly familiar, her intelligent blue eyes, her warm smile.

126

'Kate? Kate... Bailey?'

'Kate Hart now.'

Helena reappeared, hanging her coat up inside the door. She sensed the awkward silence. 'What's going on?' she said, suspiciously.

Kate and I exchanged conspiratorial smiles. She turned to her daughter. 'Well, it turns out that Joe and I knew each other in school.'

'What?' Helena looked mortified.

I nodded in confirmation, unable to hide my glee at her embarrassment. 'It's true. Me and Kate – I mean your mom – were friends.'

'Friends?'

Kate grinned at the floor. 'Actually, Joe, there was at least one date.'

'Was it a date? Was it? A date?'

'Oh, it was date,' she said.

The colour drained from Helena's young face.

'Joe was a bit of a bad boy,' Kate went on. 'I seem to remember him being the school rebel.'

'Is that right? I seem to remember you being a bit of a square. Goody two shoes.'

'This cannot be happening,' Helena said, disappearing into the house.

We stood for a second on the doorstep, looking at each other.

'You look great,' I said.

'Thank you. You look tired.'

'You always were observant. I can't believe you're Helena's mom. Didn't you marry...'

'Darren Hart.'

'Helena Hart, of course. How is Darren?'

'Oh, I should think he's happy enough,' she said, 'he's living in Spain with his latest bit of fluff.'

'I see.'

127

'And you?'

'Me?'

'Married, kids?'

'No, no, not me.'

A beep from the end of the drive. Gus aimed a sarcastic wave in our direction.

'I think you've got to go,' she said.

'Yes, looks like it. I'll just lift the box inside...'

'No, it's OK, I'll get that. I'm not the shrinking violet I used to be. Thanks for carrying it up.'

'No problem, my pleasure. Good to see you.'

'Good to see you too, Joe Baxter.'

I began to jog back down to the car when she called after me.

'Sorry about the "tired" comment. Just joking.'

I turned, suddenly feeling bashful. 'You're right, I'm exhausted. Been up all night.'

'Still a rebel, then.'

'Not quite – I was working.'

We lingered for just a second, like awkward teenagers, before I walked to the car and climbed in.

'Not interrupting you at all, am I?' Gus said.

'I went to school with Helena's mom,' I said, glancing back as we pulled away. She was looking at me, then pulled her eyes away shyly as the front door closed. 'First time I've seen her in years.'

*

That night I slept fitfully. I don't know if it was seeing Kate, but my dreams carried me back to my youth, to school corridors, to classrooms, to friends and foes and discos and dates. A party. A church hall dance floor. First cigarettes stung my throat again, sickly cheap booze filled up behind my eyes and clouds of aftershave stung my cheeks.

It was one of those dreams where you joyfully reinhabit your old self, slipping perfectly into the emotional skin you once wore: the excitement, the anxiety, the naivety, the wide-eyed expectation of a life ahead and the green summer brightness of friendships that shaped your character.

My senses, stretched and shredded by the experiences of the last few weeks, pulled the warm nostalgia close and tight; I fell into the memories, the faces, the places and the voices, shouting to be heard over the music, huddled in happy groups and talking at a million miles an hour. My cheeks ached with laughter.

But from behind the shifting figures, something else. My smiling cheeks fell, the shine dulled in my eyes. Cutting through the sounds, deep, gravelly and cruel, a voice I had hoped never to hear again.

It mumbled from the back of my head:

'Where have you been? Wilko?'

THIRTEEN

Remember Them

Tonight, his thick hands moved quickly, darting so quickly that the charcoal slipped in his wet fingers. They scratched and swirled as the dead looked on, staring down in rows from square upon square, their eyes shut, pale and waxen, yet still watching, seeing, pleading.

His fat fingers smudged and rubbed to shape the faces, first nose then eyes, mouth across, full lips, thin lips, smooth for children, lined for the old, faces, faces, faces. Night after night he made them. Night after night they called.

Another one finished, held up and tossed to the floor as his fist pulled at his hair in frustration, still more to do, always more to do. Honour them. Remember them.

He worked and worked, his massive body stooped over the small table, caught in a pool of lamplight, as the faces watched from the walls or lay piled next to his bedclothes, staring out, staring up, staring in with closed eyes. Always closed.

Then, with the last sheet he tried again, to capture *the* face, the face they all saw, that slumbered with them but would never let them sleep.

The slab-like cheeks and rod-straight nose, the empty eyes, open – open – but white like eggs, eyes that had never seen; the flat, chiselled chin and smooth lifeless brow beneath a hooded cowl. He stared at it from beneath the thick mop of brown, dirty hair. Nearly, but… no, no, no, not this time!

He tore the picture in two and slumped onto the table.

FOURTEEN

The Queen and the Princess

The Sixth Vigil

Her pear-drop eyes, young and ringed with smoky black make-up, tried their best to outshine the tiara that gently pinched her short-cropped hair. Although the old photograph was black and white, you could tell the bud-like lips, stark and black against the ivory skin, were painted the deepest scarlet. A long cigarette holder, poised with impossible delicacy close to her cheek, completed the look.

'Have you seen her?' I asked, testing the thick, powdery card between finger and thumb.

'I haven't, no, not personally,' he said haughtily, brushing the sleeves of his white steward's tunic. 'But I've heard her, and I believe I've smelt her too…. Chanel, I believe…' He leant forward and pecked a manicured finger at the picture. 'And very strong cigarettes.'

Jeremy Wood-Jones was tall and barrel-chested, with the kind of white hair and ruddy red complexion usually found on landed aristocrats. While he stood with a youthful confidence, the deep lines under his milky grey eyes gave away his considerable age.

I turned the picture and held it under one of the small jewel-like lamps that lit the narrow passageway. The inscription, in blue pencil, had almost entirely faded away. 'Mimi Von Busen'.

He eyed me down his substantial nose with stiff-backed detachment. I handed the photograph back and, with a curt nod, he deftly slipped it into the menu folder clutched to his side.

'*Mimms* to her friends,' he said, 'of which there were many.'

'Could you tell me more about her?'

'Of course, Mr Baxter,' he said, turning on his heels slightly. 'Shall we walk and talk?'

I slung my bag over my shoulder. The walk was brisk, shuffling along the endless red carpet past teak cabin doors edged with rose gold.

'My initial role on the *Queen Alexandria* was as a steward, then after she was decommissioned and moored here, I became a tourist guide – and Mimms' story was one of my specialities.'

'When was the boat decommissioned?'

He stopped. 'Ship, sir, or liner. The *Alexandria* is not a boat.'

'Apologies.'

'Quite alright.' We shuffled on.

Our footsteps rebounded off the walls ahead of us, drowning out the background drone that told us we were on a lower deck.

Wood-Jones spoke over his shoulder: 'The *QA* made her last Atlantic crossing in 1959, after more than thirty years of service. Even then she was quite a thing of beauty, the last of her kind, so the decision was made not to scrap or refit her for some more.... utilitarian.... purpose, but to turn her into a tourist attraction, here in Bristol.'

He stopped and spoke reverently into the air above our heads. 'There was a sense, I believe, that the golden age of transatlantic travel was coming to an end, and that preserving the *Alexandria* would provide a glimpse of a bygone era that people would pay to see.'

We shuffled on.

'And did they... pay?' I asked.

'Yes, at first, she did very well indeed. Some areas were mothballed of course, entire decks in fact, and the engines were decommissioned and sold, but the ship's best attributes – the ballroom, the restaurants, the bridge – they are just as impressive now as when she made her maiden voyage.'

'*Why... why can't I leave?*'

'Mr Baxter, are you alright?' Wood-Jones asked.

I looked up. I had stopped, my knees slightly buckled, my arm against the wall. My shirt collar felt tight against my neck. I looked over my shoulder. The voice – female, withered and frail – had gone right through me.

'Did you hear that?'

His eyebrows arched. 'Mr Baxter, I believe she likes you!'

I straightened up and dropped my bag.

Wood-Jones chuckled. 'Don't worry, I had the same reaction the first time I heard her. Gets under the skin, doesn't she? I think this is a good start! Come along, much to see!'

I gave my head a shake as he held out an arm, inviting me to take the lead. On we shuffled along the passageway.

'So... you were saying, you were a tour guide?'

'Indeed. Very happy times.'

'And now?'

'Oh, quite different now. Quite, quite different. We had something of an Indian summer after that dreadful *Titanic* film, but in the last decade or so it became clear that returns from tourism alone couldn't fund the upkeep of the *Alexandria*. So, now she is also a "conference centre" – and I once again find myself setting her tables, although this time it's not with silver service but with cheap pens and notepads. I suppose that's what happens when a tourist attraction fails to attract tourists.'

'International travel has changed a bit,' I said. 'There's not a lot of mystery left when you can get a flight to Europe for less than £50. And perhaps the *Alexandria* isn't what people expect of luxury cruise ships these days.'

He stopped abruptly and fixed me with a cool stare.

'Mr Baxter, the cruise ships of today cannot be compared to the *RMS Queen Alexandria*, or any ship of her era. Yes, today's liners are bigger, more powerful and more spacious, but what they offer in terms of scale they lack in terms of finesse. They are effectively floating tourist resorts – practically cities in some cases – while the *Alexandria* was an exquisitely appointed ocean-going luxury *hotel*. Don't misunderstand me – I am someone who spent his youth on the ocean wave, and I fully appreciate the wonderful service, and the considerable cost associated with modern cruisers. They do deliver luxury, if you pay for it. But while they may be the Ferraris and Lamborghinis of the oceans, this...' he touched the wall of the passageway tenderly '... is a Rolls Royce Silver Ghost.'

We pressed on, and he led me through a door and up a steep flight of steps, emerging into a broad, wood-panelled lobby. It was dominated by an impressive, red-carpeted staircase that swept theatrically to the upper decks, splitting in two beneath a glass-domed ceiling.

We stood for a moment, admiring the carved opulence.

'This is the grand staircase,' Wood-Jones said, 'designed to be the centre point of the *Alexandria*. All First Class passengers, on boarding, came through here on the way to their cabins, and the stairs led up to the ballroom and the main restaurant.' He looked at me apologetically. 'I'm afraid you came aboard via one of the service gangways, so you didn't get the full effect.'

I nodded. 'It's spectacular. Is this one of the places she has been seen?'

'It is…. and heard. This is also where I smelt Mimms' perfume, oh…. fifteen years ago? It was as if she was standing right next to me, and then it was gone.'

He nodded to himself, as if acknowledging the memory, then trotted up the stairs. I followed, my bag swinging on my back.

In the restaurant, Tiffany lamps bloomed like gemmed mushrooms on round tables, whose legs splayed delicately to the polished wooden floor.

He led me to a side table, draped with a white cloth, on which waited cheap teacups, sachets of sugar and instant coffee and a selection of teabags. Behind them, two modern hot water flasks backed guiltily against the wall, like gatecrashers from the twenty-first century.

'I thought this might be a more comfortable place for us to talk,' Wood-Jones said. 'These were laid on for an afternoon conference but were not required. Shall I be mother?'

'Yes… tea, please,' I said, grabbing a fistful of sugar sachets.

He selected a table next to two small windows. Outside, one of the *Alexandria*'s three huge red funnels towered into the evening sky. Wood-Jones placed the menu in front of him and opened it, revealing a small selection of photographs and ageing news clippings. He began to sort through them.

'Tell me, Mr Baxter, what is it you hope to achieve this evening?'

'Achieve? Well, I'm aiming to stay awake all night, hopefully in a place where I'm likely to experience something unusual or supernatural… but I have done a few of these vigils now, for my book, and I want to assure you that I'm applying proper journalistic scrutiny to everything. I want to write a book that people will take seriously, even if nothing happens.'

His eyebrows arched.

'The press officer seemed to think you might get us some much-needed publicity, which I understand, but I have my reservations.'

I took a sip of my tea. 'Please, go on.'

'Well… I consider myself to be a custodian of the *Alexandria*. I've been with her longer than anyone else. Except Mimms, that is.' He gazed down at the picture on the table. 'I wouldn't want you to write anything that was in any way... unfitting.'

'How do you mean, unfitting?'

He frowned, gently, and passed the photograph to me.

'The thing is, I'm not just a custodian of this ship – I also consider Mimms a friend. We're fellow travellers. I feel like I should protect her honour, or her story at least.'

Her round eyes stared up at me. I placed the picture gently down.

'Actually, I have to be honest, this is a new experience for me.'

'How so?'

'This is the first time where I have a photograph to use as reference, or where I know a name.'

He tapped the clippings. 'That's because all of this happened almost in living memory. A lot of it happened in my lifetime – in terms of the things that people have seen, or felt, or heard. Mimms has been part of my life for a long time. I want you to be fair to her.'

He looked around the room, at the walls, the ceiling, the floor, as his fingers subconsciously followed the grain of the tabletop. 'When you have spent so many years on a ship, Mr Baxter, you become attuned to her. You sense changes... and I feel a sadness creeping into the *Alexandria*, and into Mimms too. This ship was built to be filled with people. It was a happy place, which existed to see the world – not to sit idle. If you could have seen her in her heyday, out in the Atlantic under the stars, her lights catching on the waves, the music – the voices – floating out across the water! Each trip was fifteen days of utopia, a floating island of happiness. The fact is people don't come here anymore. The *QA* is, for the most part, an empty vessel – even her memories fade with each coat of new paint. It is a lonely place, and a place that is lonely.'

Wood-Jones looked at the pictures on the table and tilted his head sadly. 'May I ask, what was it you heard earlier?'

'The voice said, "Why can't I leave?"'

He gave a resigned smile and nodded. 'You may hear that Mimi Von Busen is playful, flirtatious even… but my sense is she pines for people, just as the *Alexandria* does. I'm quite sure all of this sounds perfectly mad, but I would like you to be kind to her.'

I took out my phone and notepad.

'Why don't you tell me about Mimms?'

*

Wood-Jones bent over the old gramophone, his silhouette hunched against the windows behind. He lowered the needle onto the record; it crackled like kindling before an orchestra struck up, instruments muffled and warm, drifting across the room in a stately foxtrot. A genial male voice warbled:

> *'Where is our star tonight,*
> *To light our way to love?*
> *Lost in the canopy so bright,*
> *That watches from above.'*

'Forgive me,' he said, adjusting the volume. 'I do so love to tell Mimms' story. Best to do it properly.'

He took his seat and passed over a brown-edged newspaper clipping. Mimms stared up from a grainy picture, smiling broadly, a tight-fitting hat wrapped around her head.

'Mimi Von Busen was the closest thing America had to a princess,' he said. 'She came from old blood – old by American standards anyway. The family traced their lineage back to the days when New York was called New Amsterdam, when Dutch colonists owned the farmland where much of Manhattan now stands. However, she was really seen as American royalty because of the fabulous wealth she inherited, and the company she kept.'

He passed across a photograph, sepia-tinged, showing Mimms curtseying deeply in front of a large, bearded man in morning suit and top hat. Despite his imposing figure, the crowd of onlookers behind only had eyes for the young American girl.

'I suspect I ought to know who that is,' I said.

'King George V,' he said, 'taken at Royal Ascot. It's hard to explain in today's terms just how wealthy Mimms was – today's tech billionaires are probably the best comparison.'

'Where did she get her...'

He raised a finger. 'Please, Mr Baxter, allow me to tell the story. I rarely get to these days.'

He went on, with a smile.

'Mimms' great-great-great-grandfather, a humble farmer, built a mill in New Amsterdam, which her great-great-grandfather converted to work metal. By the time her grandfather had taken over the business, it was operating steel mills in New Jersey that provided the metal for railroads, bridges, buildings. When the twentieth century arrived her father, Ernst Von Busen, was supplying steel for motorcars and household items, as well as the girders for the New York skyscrapers on what was once their farmland. The family was fabulously wealthy, rubbing shoulders with Rockefellers, Carnegies, Rothschilds.'

Another ancient photograph moved across the table: a formidable-looking woman awkwardly holding a baby.

'However, Ernst and his wife Elizabeth only had one child – Mimi – meaning for the first time there wasn't a male heir who could be readied to take over the business. Mimi was a very bright and intelligent young girl, but there was never any question of her actually running the family firm... Instead, Ernst decided that she should be married into another great family, preferably a European dynasty of some kind, who could provide a suitably business-minded husband to head the Von Busens' interests.'

A postcard of the *Alexandria*, her red funnels coloured by hand, moved between us.

'So, in 1930, at the age of twenty-two, Mimi was dispatched on the *Alexandria*, across the Atlantic for her introduction to

British high society. The voyage took two weeks and she enjoyed every second of it, finally out from under the judgemental eye of her parents. She danced, she drank, she sang, she swam every single day. However, the two months she spent in England were less successful, at least from the family's point of view.'

He tapped the picture taken at Royal Ascot on the table in front of me. 'She was mystified by the protocols and formalities of the English elite, and horrified by the priggish, old-fashioned businessmen who were wheeled out to meet her as prospective husbands. So, almost inevitably, after a month of stuffy introductions she threw her itinerary out of the window and headed for the West End of London in the hope of finding some fun. She found some like minds.'

Another picture slid across the table. Mimms and another woman held champagne flutes aloft between two tall, dapper-looking men in dinner jackets, their hair slicked above sardonic smiles. Wood-Jones leant across and placed a digit on the photo.

'You may recognise Noël Coward, who apparently was the first to call her "Mimms".… and this is Sir Robert Peel and his wife Beatrice Lillie, who was a Canadian-born film star. Sir Robert was the great grandson of the famous Prime Minister, but he had chosen a quite different profession – he was a big band leader, and something of a playboy. I've often thought that his decision to choose his own way in life must have made quite an impression on young Mimms. They all got on like a house on fire, and for the final weeks of her time here they were rarely apart – and rarely out of the gossip columns.'

Next, a newspaper clipping was placed down solemnly – the headline read, 'STEEL MAGNATE DIES'.

'The news came through the day before she boarded the *Alexandria* to return. A heart attack. She was devastated. She had lost her father, was leaving behind her new-found freedom and friends and she was steaming back to an uncertain future – so on the return voyage she threw caution to the wind and drank and danced for fifteen days. Back in New York she had no interest in the steel business or finding a husband.

'Within six months, she was back on board the *Alexandria*, steaming back to England.'

*

I soon realised that for all her outward beauty, the *Queen Alexandria* had plenty to hide. Wood-Jones led me down another pristine passageway, past doors whose polished cabin numbers glistened like mirrors, but then we took a sudden turn through a service door into a dank gun metal compartment whose walls rippled with rivets. Iron ladders dropped down to the deck below. Stripped of carpet and wood, the room gently reverberated with the true sound of the steel ship: a dull interior hum that closed around you. The smell of oil hung in the air.

'Just a quick shortcut,' he said, disappearing down a ladder. I followed, and soon we were standing in another, perfectly preserved but shorter passageway.

'The Day Deck,' Wood-Jones announced.

Through double doors waited a small, intimate cocktail bar, lined with cosy booths. A handful of white-topped tables surrounded a grand piano on a corner stage.

'This was one of her favourite places,' Wood-Jones said, leaning against the counter. 'It's said that when she was onboard, she would hold court in here every evening, taking the stool at the end of the bar or singing at the piano.'

'How many times did she travel on the ship?' I asked. 'You make it sound like she lived here.'

'In a way, she did,' he said. 'After inheriting the family's steel mills, she left the business to run itself and headed back to England and her friends for six months, then returned to the States on the *Alexandria*. Over the next twenty years she criss-crossed the Atlantic, always on this ship, always staying in the same suite of cabins. Each time she had the very same valet, the very same flowers. It was a home from home. Mimms never bought a property in England either, but instead stayed at the Ritz, the Savoy or Claridge's – a constant tourist, a permanent passenger. She was even booked onto the *Alexandria* for her first voyage after the Second World War – she was a hospital ship during hostilities, and thankfully survived unscathed. Her valet was waiting for her the day she came onboard, with her cabin waiting for her, just as she liked it. The sad thing was that, as the years passed by, her friends either died or fell away, and there was very little waiting for her in England, yet still she came. It was almost as if Mimms was making trips to Europe and back simply to be onboard the *QA*, to relive that first crossing and the sense of freedom she felt. I think she felt alive when she was onboard.'

'And she never married?'

'No, she never met the right man.' He looked at his watch. 'I have two more places to show you – where she spent her days, and Mimms' cabin.'

We stepped back out into the passageway.

'Just for a while, just a little fresh air.'

Her voice came again, feeble and sad, gripping me like the tendrils of a creeping plant. I rocked on my feet, and instinctively I grabbed Wood-Jones's wrist.

He steadied me. 'You need to work on your sea legs, Mr Baxter.'

'She said she wants fresh air.'

He took my bag. 'Come along, nearly done now.'

We shuffled further along the passage, the carpet giving way to blue mosaic tiles, which sent the sound of our steps clattering into a dark, open doorway at the end. The echoes seemed to bounce around in the void. Wood-Jones pulled up and wagged a cautionary finger.

'Now do be careful in here, Mr Baxter, it is quite dark and surprisingly slippery underfoot.'

He flicked a switch. We entered. A square swimming pool, empty and cavernous, was dimly lit by lights embedded in the blue tiled walls, which reached up high above. After the tight confines of the ship's passageways, it was disorienting to stand in a space that both rose into the dark and sank deep to the bottom of the cube-shaped pool. At the far end, a short diving platform stretched out in the empty air. Sandalwood benches lined the pool side like pews. It felt cathedral-like.

Wood-Jones whispered. It seemed appropriate. 'The First Class pool. Everyone else used the pools on the upper decks, but this was reserved for the more discerning passengers. She swam here every day. We don't allow anyone to come in here anymore, because... well, frankly it's not safe. There hasn't been water in the pool for decades, and you wouldn't want to fall into it, believe me, as you'd struggle to get out. However, I am happy for you to spend some time in here tonight, if you are careful. This is one of the places where Mimms has been seen.'

My hopes of spending the night in one of the *Alexandria*'s more exclusive suites sank as Wood-Jones led me down flights of stairs, deeper and deeper into the ship. With each level, the surroundings became colder, the gold and teak finishes replaced with dull greys and metal floors, the golden wall lamps usurped by bare yellow-white bulbs behind wire cages. The atmosphere changed too, as if the decks above were pressing down on us, amplifying the background hum that hung in the recirculated air. I tried hard to memorise the route as we descended into the ship's bowels. Wood-Jones was quiet and grim-faced.

At last, we arrived at a plain, blue-grey metal door, its rounded edges sealed with a rubber trim. A wide and heavy-looking hatch was clipped shut in its centre. A small table and wooden chair stood guard outside. Wood-Jones slumped down in the seat and mopped his brow with a handkerchief.

'I'm sorry,' he said, 'I apologise. I'm getting a little old for all these stairs, and I really don't like coming down here.' He waved the hanky at the door. 'This is what is known as Mimms' cabin. I don't like the name – she wasn't the only person to use the cabin, by any stretch – but it's stuck. This isn't where she stayed on all those happy journeys across from New York, but it is where she spent her final crossing.'

He looked up at my bemused face. 'Mr Baxter, this is the ship's quarantine cabin. This is where she died.'

*

I sat on the cot-like bed, the white metal railing that ran along its edge digging into the back of my knees. The cabin was tiny, more of a metal box than a room. A square ceramic sink nestled in one corner, within arm's reach of the bed. Along with my bag, a small metal bedside table filled the remaining floorspace.

Wood-Jones's frame filled the doorway, his elbows resting against the metal edge.

'I should warn you that when the door is closed it is pitch black in here,' he said. 'There's no porthole because we're below the water line. The whole point of this cabin was to keep its occupant as far away from the rest of the passengers as possible.'

I ran my hand over the rough blanket on the bed. 'What did she die of?'

He shook his head. 'A most terrible thing, Mr Baxter – rabies. It was a return voyage. The ship's doctor was hopelessly out of his depth and didn't have a clue what it was, but it was clear that she was very, very ill – fever, confusion, all manner of horrible symptoms. So, they locked her up down here for the voyage, with only her favourite valet feeding her through the hatch in the door. She died two days before the *Alexandria* reached New York. Her body was kept in here until the ship docked. It was only days later that the cause was established – she had been to a shooting party in England the day before embarking. There was a dog, a ridiculous, angry little lapdog, which had recently returned with its owners from France. It nipped Mimms on her ankle, which everyone found hilarious. It was a death sentence.'

He stood straight, flattening his tunic with his palm. 'So, after all those happy times travelling in luxury, this is where she died. The terrible irony is that rabies isn't contagious in humans. She could have been cared for in comfort, in her own suite.'

Mimms' cabin was anything but comfortable. Two hours later, with the door shut, I was enveloped in its blackness. Wood-Jones had bid me goodnight, with a final plea to be careful when making my way around the ship – and had then pulled the door shut with an airtight squeak.

The rubber-edged door not only kept the light out, it also kept the sound in – and in the dark the little room seemed to throb gently, the trapped air and metallic hum of the ship contained and compressed. It was hot too, the air heavy with moisture. I sat on the bed, listening to my own breathing, my eyes wide open despite the blackness. I didn't know if it was the background hum or subtle air currents in the cabin, but despite the deep darkness I could still sense the walls, close to me, within touching distance. I felt a bead of perspiration run down my face.

Time to listen.

An hour passed.

Mimms' cabin hummed and hissed in the dark, but nothing happened. Just after midnight, I decided to explore. The door opened with a gentle 'woosh' and I blinked as I stepped out into the dimly lit corridor. I left it open, hoping to let in fresh air.

On the little table lay Wood-Jones's white tunic, a hand-written note tucked under the lapel. 'Put this on, it might help.'

I did as I was told, and headed for the stairwell, fastening the stiff buttons as I began climbing the metal steps.

As I moved up through the ship, passing double doors to each deck, music began to drift down. A familiar voice sang:

> *'Lit by our own private moon,*
> *As we sail off to romance*
> *Lost in the endless moving swoon,*
> *Of the ocean's timeless dance.'*

Wood-Jones had propped open the door to the unlit Day Deck with a fire bucket. I stuck my head through to peer along the corridor. Light shone from the cocktail bar, the source of the music. I didn't recall seeing a gramophone in there.

> *'Where is our star tonight,*
> *To light our way to love?*
> *Lost in the canopy so bright,*
> *That watches from above.'*

Slowly, I made my way to the double doors, tensing slightly as I passed the spot where the frail voice had gripped me earlier. I stepped inside. The music stopped.

The little cocktail bar was dark except for a spotlight that aimed a warm pool of light at the stage, illuminating the piano. My eyes searched the booths, the tables and then fell on the stool at the end of the bar. The room felt expectant, like an unseen audience was awaiting the night's main attraction.

'Well, aren't you just darling.'

I span around. Her voice. Behind me. But different: young, clipped and eloquent, full of mischief. And it was here too, present in the room, pricking my ears, not jolting my bones like earlier. A breath of rich tobacco smoke drifted across my face. I had company.

'Hello… Mimms?' I said.

A girlish giggle flitted past me on the air into the bar, weaving between the tables.

I took a step forward. The room fell quiet again, the faint buzzing of the spotlight underlining the silence.

Slowly, the stool at the end of the bar moved outwards to face me. I watched as a smooth, feminine indentation sank into the upholstery. I was being observed.

'Mimms, my name is…'

'*Now, who told you you could call me that?*' the playful voice floated out of the darkness above the seat.

'I'm sorry…'

'*I don't care.*' She cut me off.

I took another step forward. 'I can't see you.'

I waited, biting my lip.

'*I can see you. It's quite a sight.*'

I felt myself blush. 'I'd like to see you.'

Quiet again. Now I was holding my breath.

A sigh in the dark.

'*Tell me… why can't I leave?*'

'Where do you want to go?'

The light flickered. '*Up top,*' the voice whispered, '*but you can't help me, can you?*'

SLAM! The piano lid crashed shut, rattling the keys and jolting a wave of noise across the room. My heart skipped a beat. The light flicked off.

'Mimms?'

A giggle behind me, outside the door. It disappeared down the passageway, towards the pool. I followed.

After flicking on the dim lamps I carefully made my way along the side of the drained pool, sitting on one of the sandalwood benches. To my left, the white diving board reached into the black. Suspended in front of the tiled walls, it loomed like a mortuary slab. I don't know why, but I stood and returned slowly to the door and turned the lights off, then carefully edged my way back to the bench. I sat in the dark, trying to sense the cavernous room, the empty void just a step away from my feet.

'*Thank you.*'

Her voice came from the doorway. Then, across the void in

front of me, soft, bare footsteps padded over the tiles, echoing gently around the walls.

To my left: step, step, step.

She exhaled.

SPLASH! Pinpricks of moisture jumped into the air, frosting my cheeks – w*hump, whump, whump* – powerful strokes chopped and scooped, pulling through water, thundering around the tiles; kicking feet bubbled foam into the air to cascade down, fingertips flicked arced droplets behind, as the bouncing waves of her wake slapped against the pool side and rose over the tiles. Mimms reached the end of the pool and I listened as she pulled herself onto the side and stood, dripping and shivering in the dark.

Another giggle. I heard her creep out of the pool room.

Outside, a trail of perfect, wet footprints glistened on the tiles and carpet, past the cocktail bar to the stairwell door, still propped open. It was time to return to the cabin.

I found the rubber-edged door shut. I put my hand on the handle and began to turn it.

'*You can't come in.*' The voice, frail and weak once more, whispered from the other side of the metal.

I pulled the wooden chair up to the door and sat, then carefully unclipped the catch and gently lowered the hatch. A bright block of light projected across the box-like cabin. I peered in. Heat. Sweat. The stench of vomit. An angular hump rose in the rough blanket. The bed was occupied.

'Mimms?'

'*Bertrand, is that you?*' her voice was tired, fractured.

'… Yes…' I said, searching for movement in the dark. The hump shifted in the beam of light. Her neck, drawn and soaked in sweat, glistened briefly.

'*Bertrand, when can I leave?*' she whimpered. '*I don't want to stay in here anymore. I want to go above.*'

She lifted onto an elbow, the bottom of her face falling into the light. Her skin was yellow and tight.

Patience's words came back to me.

'Mimms,' I said, 'I believe you can leave now if you want to, if you really want to.'

Slowly, she sat in the bed and blinked into the light. She was a corpse. A beautiful corpse. *'Really? I can leave? It's safe?'*

'I think it's time to.'

'Will you open the door? Will you?'

'If you want me to.'

'I would, I'm ready, Bertrand, I'm ready. Will you help me?'

'I will, if I can.'

She reached out her arm into the beam of light, towards the hatch, towards me, her fingers moving painfully in the blue-white glow – then the light seemed to grip her skin, seeping into her pores, to spread over her, up her arm, glowing brighter and brighter as it reached her face, her eyes. The light pulsed bright and round as she reached for me. Then she was gone.

Instinctively, I turned. At the foot of the stairs, Mimi Von Busen stood, beautiful and youthful, her short-cropped hair pinched under that chic tiara. She smiled radiantly.

'Don't listen to him, Joe,' she said, 'don't listen to him.'

And then Mimms climbed the staircase for the last time.

FIFTEEN

In With the Out Crowd

Birmingham at the end of the 1980s was not a pretty place. It may have seen the birth of the Industrial Revolution, but it also heard its death rattle – the moment when the twentieth century first started to run out of steam. The city was littered with the decaying remnants of its Victorian heyday: derelict factories, boarded-up pubs, empty churches abandoned by congregations who had fled to the suburbs.

Like most teenagers, my waking hours were spent finding reasons to get out of the house, to get outside, away from Mom's worried glances, and I was drawn to the crumbling older parts of the city. Outwardly, I hoped this looked like a rebellious fascination with the darker side of life, like the Iron Maiden patches stitched to my denim jacket. Inwardly, I knew I was actually seeking the solitude to be found among the weeds and broken bottles.

That solitude brought blissful silence; escape from disinterested teachers parroting irrelevant facts, classmates yapping inanities and TV and radio that frothed with trivial white noise. My life was filled with voices, and I just wanted to shut them all out, so

I could think. Unfortunately, one voice was harder to shake off than the rest.

I always knew when he was about to speak. I felt a shift in gravity, a tiny, dizzying shoulder-tap of vertigo – like the fluid in my skull had swilled around my brain.

Then, his guttural, raspy voice would whisper:

'*Alone again – Johnny-no-mates? Wilko?*'

I needed to be alone, to be out. First, I explored the old canal network. The city boasted it had 'more canals than Venice' but the fetid waterways of Brum, festering in the shadows of motorway flyovers and windowless warehouses, failed to live up to Continental comparisons. I loved them.

But it was another Italian-inspired import that really gripped my imagination – and then dragged me into deep trouble.

Near the centre of the city, in the old jewellery-making quarter which made the cheap trinkets that the city exported to the empire, I came across two crumbling Victorian graveyards, sprawling on overgrown slopes next to each other. The final resting place of the city's industrial founders but long closed to new burials, they were filled with moss-covered tombs, toppled gravestones and lopsided, headless angels, their arms outstretched as if to question what had become of the once hallowed ground.

And deep in the centre of these necropolises lurked Birmingham's catacombs.

Like the canals, these were brick-built recreations of the Italian originals, engineered to create extra burial space for the great and the good as the city's population exploded. Cut into the hillside of the graveyards, they provided family vaults and public shelf space for lead-lined coffins, their arched doorways sealed for eternity with lime mortar. Engraved metal plaques and ornate stone memorials recorded the names of the occupants.

The grandest of these catacombs formed an immense horseshoe, with sealed vaults rising on two tiers, like an amphitheatre from which the wealthy deceased could overlook the common graves below. They must have been an impressive sight once, but by the time I discovered them, on a bright Sunday afternoon in May, they were crumbling at the edges and overrun with crawling nettles. They were not, however, deserted.

As I climbed the narrow, worn side steps that crept up to the top tier, the silence was broken by one of Birmingham's other exports: Black Sabbath. This was my kind of music. Voices, one high and excited the other sharp and sneering, penetrated the slow, distorted thrum of guitars. So much for solitude.

I stopped near the top and peered over. More outsiders. A tall kid – my age, maybe older – stood holding a packet of cigarettes out to a small boy with straw-blond hair, who was squeezed into a skin-tight AC/DC T-shirt. His young hand hung in space, poised to take a smoke. Beyond, I could see the leather-clad back of a long-haired girl, who was hunched cross-legged on a long tomb. Mournful guitar droned like a bell from a large cassette player beside her.

'Are you going to have one or not?' the big kid sneered, before plucking a cigarette and lighting it. He took a deep drag and nonchalantly blew out a cloud of smoke as the smaller boy looked on in awe.

I watched from my sunken vantage point. I knew this kid. He went to my school. He was a prefect, the year above. His name was ... Perch? Yes, it was him – different hair, no smart uniform, but it was him. I marvelled at the transformation.

His usually neat red hair was swept back, revealing a pale, angular face pock-marked by teenage acne. His skinny white neck disappeared into the collar of a leather biker's jacket, which jutted box-like from his silhouette. His long, thin legs were planted in heavy motorcycle boots.

Perch took another long, hard drag, his cheeks hollowing inwards, pulling the embers down the cigarette. He blew the smoke at his little disciple. 'I thought you said you smoked?'

'I-I-I do, I do,' he responded, finally snatching one from the pack. Perch smirked, his cigarette sliding to the side of his thin lips. He produced a box of matches, lit the boy's cigarette and then observed as he nervously sucked on it.

The boy removed it from his mouth, clamping his lips tightly together, then blew out a small puff of white smoke.

'He's not even taking it back!' Perch scoffed, repeating it to the disinterested girl over his shoulder. 'He didn't even take it back!'

She gave a silent shrug.

'I-I-I did, I took it back,' the boy protested.

'Yeah, but you're supposed to hold it in,' Perch sneered. 'Otherwise, it's not smoking, is it? Go on, take it back. Hold it in.'

The boy looked at the cigarette, nervously licked his lips then took a big drag, pulling the smoke into his lungs so that his chest rose. Lips pursed. Eyes bulged. He exploded into a hoarse, retching cough, dropping the cigarette in the long grass as he bent double.

Perch roared with laughter and flicked his cigarette into a nearby grave, as the girl turned her head.

'Perch, you're such a dick,' she said.

'He's alright, he's a smoker!' he grinned, his hand thumping the boy's heaving back. He picked up the cigarette and held it out. 'Go on, finish it off.'

The boy straightened up and wiped his streaming eyes, looking at the cigarette.

The girl turned again. 'Leave him alone, Perch. You don't have to smoke it, mate.'

The boy stifled another cough. 'I do smoke, though. All the time.'

'Well then, carry on... finish it off.'

The boy looked from the cigarette to the girl, who offered a subtle shake of her head, her eyes flicking to Perch.

'I said finish it,' he growled.

The boy's eyes widened in fright.

Perch jutted the cigarette at him with his pale, thin hand. 'Finish it!'

'I'll have that,' I said, stepping up from the undergrowth.

All three of them looked at me, their mouths open. I felt Perch's eyes scan me, with a flicker of recognition.

I ambled forward, took the cigarette, sucked on it and blew smoke in his face.

'Not really my brand. Bit weak.'

He curled his lip and puffed out his chest. 'Do I know you?'

'Dunno. I know you, though. You look a bit different without your prefect's badge.'

His eyes thinned. 'I recognise you. I know you. From school. You got a problem?' he loomed over me.

The girl swung her legs over the stone tomb to face us, turning off the tape deck. The graveyard fell silent.

She smiled. 'I wouldn't if I were you, Perch. That's Baxter. He's fucking mad.'

There was another flicker of recognition in his eyes.

'Baxter? Barmy Baxter? You're that kid that talks to himself, shouts in lessons. Mad Bax. What do you want?'

'I want you to leave him alone.'

I dropped the cigarette, crushing it into the grass.

'I-I-I'm alright,' the boy said. 'We're mates, isn't that right, Perch?'

'That's right, Nipper,' Perch said, his eyes still fixed on me, 'mates. Good mates.'

The girl stepped between us, the tape player swinging at her side. 'Leave it out, boys. Nobody's impressed,' she said flatly, looking at my jacket. 'Nice patches. Did your mom sew them on for you?'

She pressed 'play' and walked off as 'Iron Man' rose into the air.

'Slut. She's a slut. Wilko?'

Instinctively, my eyes flicked shut as the voice washed through me.

Perch sniggered. 'You on your own, or did you bring your invisible friend with you?'

I leant in close and whispered, 'I've dealt with bigger fish than you, Perch,' and winked at the young boy who was eyeing me up and down. A wine-coloured birthmark, partly hidden by his blond fringe, spread across his forehead above his young blue eyes. I knew him too, I was certain – I'd seen him bullied in the playground. A fellow outcast.

'You alright, mate?' I said.

'I-I-I'm OK – your jacket's ace. Do you like Iron Maiden? I've got *Maiden Japan*. It's a live album, really rare.'

'He's a waste of skin.'

'I've not got that one,' I said, 'but I've seen it at Readington's on the wall. Is it good, then?'

'What's Readington's?'

'Readington's Rare Records.'

'Oh right, yeah, it's brilliant, b-b-brilliant. You can hear the crowd and everything – I can tape it for you if you w-want. I'm Nipper – Nipper Mitchell.'

Perch shook his head. 'Iron Maiden. Def Leppard. Too soft for me. All that prancing about and hair spray. I like it heavy and dark. Like Priest. Like Sabbath.'

'Listen to him. I like this one. Like him. Meat for brains. Wilko?'

The girl was wandering along the sealed archways of the catacombs, one hand running across the rough, crumbling mortar as the cassette player swung at her side.

Perch shouted to her. 'Turn it up, Lou!'

She gave him a surly glare, twisted the volume knob then turned to inspect an iron door set in the wall between the tombs. Guitars reverberated around the crescent. She rattled the door.

'Now, that's real metal,' Perch said, lighting another cigarette. She rattled the door again.

'True,' I agreed. 'But you can't compare it to new wave stuff – it's a different generation.'

The voice rasped angrily:

'Who cares what you think?'

'Hey, look at this.' The girl switched off the music, put the cassette player down and pushed the gate. It swung inwards with a thin metallic squeal. 'It's open.'

We all peered into the black void of the catacombs. The air was damp. Six feet away, a rotting wooden door waited at the end of a short tunnel.

'Worm food. Let's go in.'

SIXTEEN

No Words

A wasted night. I'll make this one short. I don't want to give him the publicity he obviously craved. I don't have the words to explain how pissed off I am, and I wouldn't waste them on him if I did.

Part of me wants to put it all down in excruciating detail, name and shame, publish and be damned. The more sensible part of me knows that he would milk that for every bit of publicity he could get.

I should have suspected something was not right when he insisted I stay on Halloween night.

So, this is all I have to say.

I'm trying to apply proper scrutiny to all this stuff, these stories, at my own expense and in my own time, and frankly it's exhausting.

Not only that, what I've experienced so far has shredded my nerves and had me questioning my sanity for the first time since I was a teenager.

So, I don't need fucking charlatans inviting me along to

their squalid little Yorkshire B&B in the hope that they'll have something entertaining to mention on their website.

You don't have to be Hercule Poirot to spot a piece of fishing line making a picture frame move. The food was shit too.

SEVENTEEN

Just to Sleep

My head nodded with the dull, hypnotic thud of the car's wipers, as orange streetlights streaked across the wet windscreen. I vaguely remember staring, unblinking, at dark banks of trees as they swept by.

'I know you can hear me.'

Mom was sitting next to me on the back seat, tightly squeezing my hand, as the dark countryside streamed past. In the front, Gus leant over the steering wheel to wipe condensation from the inside of the glass. Outside the rain poured. I looked down at my hands. Black soil was still trapped under my fingernails.

Mom sniffed and wiped her eyes. Gus glanced in the mirror.

'It's not far now, Jeannie,' he said. 'I think it's just round the next corner.'

I stared ahead into the rain.

'Are you receiving, Wilko? I know you can hear me.'

I closed my eyes.

Mom brushed dirt from the cuffs of my denim jacket, then gently moved the hair back from my eyes.

'Joe, I need you to listen to me now, I need you to pay attention.'

I looked at her, blankly. Her face was lined with worry. I had done this. Had I done this?

She squeezed my hand. 'Dr Sabapathy will be waiting for us. He says this is the right place for you. Do you understand?'

I nodded.

The car pulled to a halt and Gus wound down the window. The rain spotted his sleeve as he reached out to press an intercom button. Illuminated in the headlights, tall gates loomed out of the darkness. A nondescript sign above offered one word: Westcroft.

I watched all this as if it were happening somewhere else, or on TV.

Pale, wet hands appeared on the gates, pulling them open and beckoning us through. Gus wound his window shut and raised a thumb as we drove past the gaunt-faced guard and up the long driveway.

Another sign – Westcroft Psychiatric Unit – stretched across the canopy covering the entrance. Through the double doors Sabapathy, his face a study in drawn sympathy, waited under yellow strip lighting. He was flanked by two male nurses.

Talking. A shower. Food. More talking. Signatures. Some pills, just to sleep. Mom held me tight then let go, her hand trailing as she released mine, being led away by Gus.

For the first time in my life, I was unable to cry.

Now I was alone, in a bed with paper-crisp sheets, in a room somewhere between hospital and hotel, the air sharp with pine disinfectant. The only sounds were the soft squeaks of nurses' shoes as they paced the scrubbed corridors beyond the locked door. The pills pulled my shoulders down and weighed on my eye lids. I waited.

'I know you can hear me.'

The choked, gravelly voice was quieter.

'Are you ignoring me? You can't ignore me. You know that by now,
Wilko?'

I shut my eyes, tipped my head back onto the pillow and swallowed. Mom's face appeared, so worried, so frightened. This had gone too far.

'Boy. Boy. You know you have to listen to me.'

I felt my jaw tighten.

I whispered, 'I'm never going to listen to you again. Ever. I'm finished. You're finished.'

The room fell quiet. The pills pulled at me again. Drowsy. Somewhere, I heard him exhale, coldly.

'Your choice. Waste of skin.'

The voice rasped bitterly.

'Just listen to me one last time, boy. Listen to me and see what you can hear. Listen. Listen. Listen...'

The word repeated again and again as the bed began to sink ... *'listen'*... clinging to me as I plunged into unconsciousness, ringing in my ears as I felt sleep rise like water around me ... *'listen'*... and as the fog of the sedatives lifted, the gravelly voice unspun ... *'listen'*... slowly clearing, crystallising with each repetition, unravelling.

I let go, adrift, as one final *'listen'* brushed my ears – a clear, clipped, malevolent whisper. It touched me to the core, in my marrow. I heard something new. Something in the voice I somehow recognised. This was a family voice. It was the voice of... my father?

'Listen.'

A long, deep creaking sound, tightly woven like a clenched fist, swung forwards and backwards in the blackness.

Eyes open. Follow. I swung my feet out of the bed. They dangled in the air above my bedroom carpet. A child's feet.

The creak came again, a bristling, coiled pendulum that swung in the dark.

I stood at the top of the stairs, listening to the TV burble from beneath the living room door below. I was home.

'Listen.'

The creak. Follow. I took the stairs slowly, one at a time, my small fingers holding on to the banister, until my toes glowed pink with the light from under the door.

The creak came again, swinging slowly closer then away around the corner, through the kitchen, the old scullery, into the dark garage with its high, wooden eves. Follow.

The soles of my bare feet peeled softly from the linoleum. I stepped down onto the concrete step. The smell of petrol and oil.

'Listen.'

The creak. Tight. Slow. Bristling. Rope gripping wood, its cords grinding into the grain. I looked up. His feet swung slowly above my head, back and forth, back and forth, back and forth. I reached up.

Flash! A crack of electricity, bright blue light washed the walls, his limp legs cast in silhouette. Behind him rose a shape, glowing like neon, scratched into the air, burnt on my retinas, fizzing, jolting, buzzing. A figure of eight.

Far off, the gravelly voice began to laugh.

'So much life… So much life.'

My eyes opened. Pine disinfectant. Paper-crisp sheets. I was alone. I cried all night.

EIGHTEEN

The Black Abbot

The Seventh Vigil

I spotted him – just a fleeting glimpse – as the bus pulled away, dragging a cloud of dust and leaves behind it down the wet village street. A thin, small figure in a flat cap shifted uneasily in the rain, lingering behind a red telephone box. Our eyes met, then he stepped back out of sight. Odd.

Massop, like many English villages, was an uncomfortable jumble of old and new, where biscuit-tin cottages and their weather-worn outbuildings jostled for space with drab 70s homes that looked like they wouldn't last another decade. Above the rooftops, the dark green hills of the Peak District watched, huddled over the small settlement like giants around a board game.

In the centre the grey tower of the abbey rose, dark against the cloudy sky.

I sucked in country air. I was still angry about my wasted night in Yorkshire. I needed Derbyshire to deliver.

I dropped my bag and looked around, just as the sound of a power drill cut through the quiet. A workman leant heavily on metal sheeting, his shoulder pushing it against the wooden window frame of a pub, before sealing it tight with another *fripp* of his drill.

I watched as he moved to another window, lifting more wet sheeting onto the ledge of the redbrick building. Window by window, he was sealing it shut. I swung my bag onto my shoulder and wandered over.

'Excuse me, mate – do you know how I can get to St Cuthbert's?'

He looked at me blankly, then pulled an ear protector away from his head. 'Sorry, what did you say?'

My eyes flicked up to the tower.

'I'm looking for St Cuthbert's, do you know where I get in?'

An involuntary scowl fell across his face. He jabbed the way with his drill.

'Gate's round the corner – you've got to ring the bell, buzzer's broken.'

I left him with a nod but could feel his eyes on my back.

'Don't overstay,' he called after me, 'shuttering it tomorrow! 7am!'

He squeezed a couple of shrill twists from his drill into the air. 'Looking forward to it,' I heard him mutter.

The wrought-iron gates were rusted, the hand-painted wooden sign faded.

'*St Cuthbert's Preparatory School – boarding and day school for boys aged 3–13 years*'.

Inside, across a cobbled courtyard, a heavy oak door squatted under a stone arch, its wood gripped by curling hinges which spread like the veins of a leaf. The silver intercom box on the gate post was taped up, but on top of it an old brass handbell glistened in the wet, its handle chained to the gate.

A soft step from behind. I turned. The little man, his old

face grim and unshaven under the peak of his cap, glared at me through bloodshot eyes over crossed arms.

'You going in there?' His voice was thin and sharp.

'I am, yes.' I held out a hand. 'Are you from the school? My name's Joe...'

'I know who you are. I hear you're looking for a story.'

'That's right, yes, for a book...'

'You won't get the story in there, at least not the real story.' His eyes slid upwards to the tower overhead. 'And it's not in any book either, never has been. Only those around here know this story. The proper story.'

Rain dripped from his cap as he studied me.

'Someone I know at the *Derby Telegraph* told me about the lights at the abbey...'

'Not in any newspapers neither.' He shook his head impatiently. 'Older than that. Old as those hills. It's not in newspapers because it doesn't want to be.'

'What doesn't want to be?'

He nodded at the tower. '*That* doesn't want to be. This place.' He slid his hands into his pockets and took a step towards me, his shoulders hunching as he leant closer. 'This is a bad place. Worse than that, those who go into this place come out bad. I hope you don't find that out yourself.'

'What do you mean they come out bad?'

'It makes them bad. *He* makes them bad. That's the story. Can't prove it, but everyone knows it. Everyone around here. So, you can't write that story, can you? Can't put that in a book. You can only pass it on. Down the years, drip, drip, drip.' He looked up at the sky. 'Like rain.'

I reached into my jacket for my notepad. 'Will you tell me the story?'

He shook his head slowly.

'I tell you what. You go in there first and hear *her* story. Nice cup of tea and a slice of cake and hear the fairy story. She likes books too. Then I'll meet you – just you – later and tell you the rest. The real story.'

'OK, great – thanks. I'm staying overnight, so… tomorrow?'

'No, tonight, it has to be tonight because I won't want to tell it tomorrow. I'll meet you at the mercy stone.'

'What's the mercy stone?'

He chuckled and turned to walk away. 'You'll see.'

'What time shall I meet you?'

'Clock in the tower rings at eleven. I'll meet you then. Name's Swift.' He nodded at the gate. 'Buzzer's broken.' He raised his collar to the rain and walked briskly away.

'Ring the bell,' I said to myself, grasping its wooden handle, feeling the weight of the brass. The metallic clang echoed around the village, bouncing off the whitewashed walls, rattling windows and rising to the hills above. The great oak door shunted open.

*

Penelope Larkin marched stiffly ahead of me into the dim lobby, the heels of her sensible shoes hammering on the tiled floor. She placed her handbag on the wooden reception counter before slipping behind it to rummage in a drawer.

The room was small, square and smelled damp. Ahead, an arched stone doorway stood between two stout-looking visitors' chairs. Whitewashed walls were decorated with wide, framed photographs: row upon row of blazer-clad boys, standing shoulder to shoulder or sitting cross-legged to squint at a distant photographer.

Set into the tiled floor was the St Cuthbert's coat of arms – four emblems on a shield: the tower, a sword, a hammer and a quill. The motto *scientiae libertas* scrolled elaborately below. I ran my toe along it.

Ms Larkin looked up as her search moved to another drawer.

'*Knowledge is freedom,*' she said in a clipped, frosty voice. 'St Cuthbert's put the physical development of the boys on a par with their academic progress. It was part of the attraction of the school that it was in the National Park, so pupils could get out into the hills, into nature. Vigorous, daily exertion – work the body as well as the brain. It wasn't quite as spartan an existence as Gordonstoun, but my father said it made men of them.'

She pulled open a third drawer, grasped a set of keys and emerged to study one of the photographs.

Penelope Larkin was unusually tall but carried it with an obstinate detachment. Despite clearly being in her sixties, she stood with a rod-straight back, as if she were balancing something on her head, with hands tucked neatly behind and feet planted firmly on the ground. Dressed in tweeds and a high-necked blouse, she had cold, hooded eyes that drooped over an upturned nose and prominent front teeth.

'There I am,' she said, tapping the glass.

I stepped to her shoulder and peered into the faces. Among the boyish frowns, a little girl stared vacantly out.

She gave me a sideways glance, a glint of pride in her eyes.

'I was the only girl to ever attend St Cuthbert's – the perks of being the headmaster's daughter and the founder's great-great-granddaughter.'

'When did the school close?'

'We had our last boarders ten years ago, and our final day students finished a year later. Very sad. A combination of softening attitudes, competition and, frankly, government interference. It's hard to explain to inspectors the character-building benefits of your pupils constructing a drystone wall.'

This was a million miles from my own school experiences. 'And the building's been closed ever since?'

She stared into the picture. 'Yes. I've tried to sell it, of course. But there are so many restrictions because of its age, and it's so remote. Now, if it were out in the countryside, like a manor house, then it could have become a hotel, but sitting in the middle of Massop as it does makes that a non-starter. And the locals have never been keen on this place, either, so any new owners would have to deal with that too. Can't get the staff, always been a huge challenge.'

She turned, picked up her handbag and slipped it over her arm.

'So, tomorrow, it's going to be closed up, along with all the other old buildings that used to be part of the estate – the stables, the pub next door. You'll be the last person to spend the night here.'

'And where will I be staying?'

Ms Larkin looked at her watch. 'That's up to you, Mr Baxter, you can have the run of the place – it's quite safe. Just avoid the tower, there are some concerns over its stability. I've made up one of the old beds in the dormitory for you, so you should be quite comfortable.'

She jingled the keys.

'Why don't I show you around, and tell you the famous story?'

*

There was no disguising the old school's previous life as an abbey. Its stone-walled corridors held up elaborate vaulted ceilings, and every doorway peaked into an arch. Steps and staircases were worn down by centuries of soft shuffling feet, while high stained-glass windows threw light that coloured walls but left corners in shadow.

Above all, I was struck by its solemn silence, which seemed to absorb the echoes of our footsteps as Ms Larkin led me along.

'First of all, I think it's important that you know that there is absolutely no evidence that any of this actually happened,' she said.

'Right, so it's like a legend.'

'I would call it a folk tale, little known beyond this part of Derbyshire,' she said, leading me into a corridor lined with portraits and plaques.

'History is my subject, Mr Baxter, and evidence is everything to the historian. It was always my intention to write a history of St Cuthbert's – and the abbey before it – but there simply isn't enough material to work with before my family came along and took over the estate. That's unusual, because this was clearly a significant ecclesiastical centre, but it was quite remote from the rest of the church. So, without evidence, we only have stories – and the Black Abbot is just a story, one which, in my opinion, overshadows much more important events and characters connected with the site.'

We stopped in front of a bronze memorial set into the wall, bearing a dozen or so names.

She clutched her handbag to her chest and offered me a raised brow. 'A case in point. These are the St Cuthbert's boys who gave their lives in the Great War – all officers, all killed leading their men.'

She walked me along a little further to a small portrait of an elderly man, a broad moustache clinging to his gaunt face.

'This is Brigadier Archibald Fawcett, another St Cuthbert's boy, who was instrumental in setting up refugee camps during the Boer War, and that…' she pointed to a black and white photograph of a young soldier in shorts and shirt sleeves, 'is Captain Martin Fleming, who attended during the 1940s, and grew up to help quell the Mau Mau uprising in Kenya. These are real characters, who were instilled with resolve and leadership here at St Cuthbert's. There are more too – scientists, politicians, doctors, industrialists. Their accomplishments are rarely talked about, while everyone fixates on something that probably never happened.'

We both stared ahead into the glassy eyes of the portrait.

After a moment, I asked, 'So, why did you agree to my request to stay?'

Ms Larkin blinked as she chose her words. She seemed irritated. 'Well, I suppose I expect you to debunk all this nonsense. My initial reaction was to tell you to clear off, if I'm honest, but when you explained your approach to your work – and in particular the way you described your last experience – I was persuaded of your objectivity.'

I shifted on my heels. I had called Ms Larkin the morning I got back from Yorkshire, and she had borne the brunt of my irritation.

She gazed into the vaulted ceiling above us. In the corner, a carved face grimaced down from the stone. 'You won't get any funny business here, I can assure you, Mr Baxter. But I also believe the only thing you'll come away with is an appreciation of what a formative place this was. It left its mark on everyone who passed through. This is a place that changes people, and my hope is that you will help change people's minds about it, especially around here.'

We walked to the end of corridor, past more paintings and photographs, to rain-flecked glass doors which led outside, where the light was already fading. She unlocked them, as I cast a final look back at the faces on the walls.

'With so many influential old boys, why didn't any of them help when the school got into trouble?'

'Oh, they never come back,' she said, opening the door, 'they never come back.'

*

The playground was desolate. A gravel-topped expanse edged with high iron railings, it felt more like a prison exercise yard than a place for children to play. Crouching gargoyles stared down from the abbey's walls, like guards on watch. In the far corner, a small, crumbling chapel nestled where the railings met.

The air was still thick with rain, so Ms Larkin led me under the cover of a narrow cloister, where we sat on a cold stone bench.

'I'll tell you the version of the story that I grew up with,' she said, fixing her eyes on the hills beyond the railings.

Penelope Larkin straightened and took a breath.

'Most folk tales are impossible to date but if there is a kernel of truth in this one, it can be pinned down to an actual period in local history. That's because it involves the Black Death – the bubonic plague – and we know that there was an outbreak in Derbyshire in 1346. At the time, Massop was a tiny place, which was dominated by the abbey. There were around 120 monks living inside here, and a few dozen families living in the village outside the walls. In the Middle Ages, you see, the poor would flock to big ecclesiastical centres like this, because the church would look after them. So, the villagers relied on the abbey for everything – water from the well, meat and eggs from livestock, vegetables from the gardens – and the abbot was happy to share his produce with the villagers.'

She gestured to the playground. 'I should explain – this was originally the churchyard, where monks were buried. The graves were moved in Victorian times to a new cemetery outside the village, which is when the old perimeter walls were pulled down and replaced by these railings. The only things left were this cloister and the original Chapel of St Cuthbert.'

The night was beginning to draw in over the hills now, bringing a chill breeze. I shifted on the stone seat. 'So, there was an outbreak of plague in Massop?'

'That's how the story goes, although there is no written record of one, unlike others in the county. According to legend, a monk returned from Leicestershire with a bundle of cloth, which he generously gave to a family in the village. But the cloth was infected. Within days the family showed symptoms of the plague and that's when the abbot decided to act.'

Suddenly, there was a loud, metallic grinding noise. A bell in the tower behind us began to chime, its dull throb rolling out into the countryside. I looked at my watch. 7pm.

171

Ms Larkin cleared her throat. 'Seven o'clock. I'm afraid the old clock is a little hit and miss these days – it strikes at seven, nine and eleven and sometimes at three. A consequence of the structural issues in the tower. I see little point in getting it fixed with the school closed.'

She stood. 'Let me show you the chapel. It's an important part of the story.'

Our feet crunched the gravel as we crossed the yard, the light rain swirling around us in the breeze. Ms Larkin continued.

'So, the abbot, being a pious man, visited the infected family and prayed with them. He told them to isolate in their cottage and promised to personally deliver food to them every day. He told the monks to remain inside the abbey, to avoid infection, saying that he would be the only one to venture out until the outbreak was over. He believed that God would protect him.'

As we approached, the Chapel of St Cuthbert seemed to sag with its immense age. Its door was unremarkable compared to the grand arches of the abbey – just a plain, wooden door of rough, planked wood, held shut with a piece of string. Its walls were a patchwork of pitted dark stones, broken by two small, glassless windows and knitted together by centuries of moss.

Ms Larkin unhooked the string and we ducked as we entered. Inside, the small room smelled of peat. Four wooden pews faced a rough-hewn stone altar. Shafts of light from the two windows mingled with a third, which cut into the room from a round hole in the wall that looked out onto the outside world. Next to it, the remains of a long-bricked-up second door scarred the wall. We sat.

'You can tell this is old... really old,' I said.

'It's by far the oldest part of the site,' she said. 'This was probably considered the holiest place here, somewhere to commune with the saint. It fell into disuse as the abbey expanded.'

Outside, the rain was falling steadily now.

'So, what happened with the abbot? The outbreak?'

'Well, the plague spread, from family to family, and the abbot still visited them every day, bringing prayer and food. The villagers would come into this chapel to worship, using the door that used to be in that wall, and he would lead them in prayer. But the outbreak kept getting worse. Every day he found families dead or dying. Eventually, he decided it was too dangerous to let them into the chapel, so he locked the door. He would say mass through the hole in the wall and bless the dying through it. That's why the villagers called it the mercy stone.'

The mercy stone. My meeting place with old man Swift.

She looked at her shoes and took a breath. 'But the abbey began to run out of food, and the remaining villagers – mainly the men – began to blame the abbot for the plague, saying he had cursed the village. They said he was spreading the Black Death by going from house to house; he was the Black Abbot, they said, the walking plague. Then, one Sunday, as he began the mass in here, the men of the village smashed down the door and carried him away. They killed him, but his body was never returned. He was never buried. Then they ran wild through the abbey, grabbing anything edible, until the monks forced them back outside. The door was sealed up not long after.'

She looked at me steadily. 'And that's the story.'

'And the ghost?'

She stood up, brushing herself down. 'Well, the boys would say that he walked the corridors of the abbey at night, whispering in their ears as they slept.'

'And has he been seen?'

'There were boys who said they saw him as they lay awake in bed, but they were just boys trying to scare each other. That's what little boys do. Believe me, I know.'

'And you've never seen him?'

She gave me a withering look and a gentle shake of the head. 'I am aware of the story that appeared in the *Telegraph* last month, about lights being seen in the building at night, but I've no doubt that was some wag in the village pulling the reporter's leg. I, of course, declined to comment.'

'One last question… who told you the story?'

Her eyes searched for an answer. 'You know, I don't remember. Seems like I've always known it.'

We walked back across the barren playground in silence. At the top of a narrow, uneven staircase, the dormitory stretched into darkness, with rows of plain metal beds pushed against the wall. One had been made up with stale-smelling sheets and blankets, ready for my night as St Cuthbert's final boarder. I dropped my bag onto it and watched as Ms Larkin disappeared down the stairs.

*

The abbey at night was a new experience, its deep walls and stone-flagged floors projecting a dense, cloak-like quiet as I sat in the dark. Hushed air seemed to seep from the building, as if pockets of silence had been trapped in its fabric by years of prayer and solitary study, only to bleed from the pores of the stone. Despite the close confines of the dormitory, I was also acutely aware of the size of the building, sensing the empty corridors, classrooms and cloisters below and the tower above. Through the windows, the black outlines of the hills skimmed the clouds.

Alone, I exhaled and felt my shoulders relaxing, and I knew why. My vigils were beginning to provide much-needed structure to an increasingly disjointed life; supplying the purpose of work – however unorthodox – and a place to think, to focus my thoughts. And while previous experiences were thickening my skin, I also had to admit that the prospect of another encounter, in fact the *expectation* that something would happen, made me feel frightened, but alive. I was choosing to do this, and I was doing it.

At 11pm the clock in the tower chimed and I looked out over the playground. Rain was still falling. A dim, yellowish light flickered from the small windows in the chapel. Time to get the other side of the story.

Down the stairs the empty corridors, bathed in moonlight through the high stained glass, seemed bigger, wider, longer. Past the dead glares of the portraits and photographs, I opened the glass doors and crunched across the gravel, conscious of the tower looming behind me, watching my progress towards the little building in the corner.

I unhooked the string and entered. An old-fashioned paraffin lamp sat in the round hole of the mercy stone, its bright little wick illuminating the whole of the chapel and filling it with oily fumes.

I stepped up and spoke into the void. 'Hello?'

'I'm here.' The old man's voice was tense. He was on the other side of the wall. I could see the top of his cap, soaked with rain, just below the hole. He was standing with his back to the building.

'You must be freezing cold,' I said. 'I can let you in the main entrance now if you like – there's no one else here.'

'Not one person from this village has set foot inside that place for more than 600 years. I won't be changing that tonight, believe you me,' he said sharply.

I took out my phone, hit record and placed it next to the lamp. 'What is it that you want to tell me, Mr Swift?'

'What we've been telling each other for generations. Do you know what mummering is, Mr Baxter?'

'Can I ask how you know my name?'

'My boy told me about you. My son, Danny. You met him earlier, shutting up the old pub. He's doing the abbey tomorrow – *she* told him your name.'

'Right. So, he works for the school?'

'No. No one round here works for that school, never have done. He's the village handy man. He can shutter it up without going in, and he'll make sure it's done properly. Permanently. Do you know what mummering is, Mr Baxter?'

'I don't, no.'

'Fine old tradition. In most villages mummering is just at Christmas. Families visit each other's homes, to sing songs and do little plays. All good fun. We do it differently here. We do it all year round – at Christmas, New Year, at funerals, wakes, weddings. You see, in Massop, mummering has another purpose – to keep the story alive. When the day is over, we pull up chairs and recite the words. I told it to my boy, him to his. When Massop children are naughty, they are told the Black Abbot will get them. It's the same in every family.'

'Ms Larkin said the story was never written down.'

I saw his head move gently from side to side.

'And who was there all those years ago to write it down? Could anyone outside these walls read or write? A bunch of illiterate peasants? The only ones capable of recording what really happened here were the black-hearted devils inside – and why would they write it down, why would they record their shame? That's why we keep it alive.'

'So, what did really happen here?'

'A crime against God, Mr Baxter, a crime against God – perpetrated by a man of the cloth.' He cleared his throat. 'You'll have been told about how *he* was pious and righteous, about how he went from home to home helping the afflicted. That story has been shaped inside the abbey over the centuries, poison he has dripped into their ears every night. All lies. The truth is still told here, every year, unchanged and out of his reach.'

'And what is the truth?'

'That he had a black heart, black as those hills. That he hated the villagers. He hated the poor, who he saw as leeches feeding on his abbey. But the monks lived like kings inside these walls, while the villagers lived in abject, filthy poverty. Did she tell you about when the graves were moved?'

'She did, in Victorian times.'

'But did she tell you about the skeletons that ended up in Cambridge?'

'No.'

Another shake of the head. 'When the graves were moved, many of the bones were sent to Cambridge University, to historians at Pembroke College. A few years ago, they were rediscovered in a cupboard, and analysed, with proper modern science. You know what they found?'

'What did they find?'

'That all the holy brothers of Massop abbey – all of them – had been fat, overfed pigs. None of the usual signs of malnutrition or illness found in medieval times, just bones and joints worn away from lugging their fat carcasses around.'

'Ms Larkin said the abbey shared its food with the villagers.'

'More lies. The villagers were made to work like dogs for scraps from the table, and even then he wanted rid of them. That's why he saw the plague as an opportunity. An opportunity to wipe out the village. The moment he heard the infection had arrived, he bolted and barricaded the great doors of the abbey. Not a soul stepped outside for six months – including him. He wanted the village to wither and die, and he left the people to rot. As for food, some monks dropped turnip peelings, eggshells and rotten scraps through this hole for a few days, but he put a stop to that. He'd rather give it to his pigs.'

The light from the lamp flickered.

The old man's voice dropped. 'This is what we know. What we remember. The words we recite. With no food, they had no strength. The Black Death came, knocking on every door, the Black Abbot at its side. With no strength, they let him in. The crops rotted in the fields. The flesh rotted on their bones.'

He took a breath, as if preparing for a new chapter. 'First, the old ones died. Then the children died. Then the women died. The good men of Massop, too weak to work the land, saw their families die around them. And all the while they could hear the monks over the wall sing, smell the bread cooking, hear the pigs being slaughtered for *his* table. There were no prayers said, no masses held for the villagers. No last rites, no Christian burial. The Black Abbot tried to send this village to hell. But he didn't reckon on the men of Massop.'

I saw him turn and look at the wall of the little chapel.

'Our mummers' plays – the stories we tell each other – say that this is where the men breached the abbey, where they finally got in. They all knew the Black Abbot would not set foot in the ancient chapel. This was older than his abbey, you see, a site of pilgrimage. He couldn't corrupt it, so he feared it. *She* no doubt told you it's always been part of the abbey, that the village grew around it. Wrong again. The men of Massop built this chapel – a Celtic shrine to the Saint – long before the monks showed up and encased it within their walls. The men knew this was their way in.

'So, every night, for months, they would take it in turns to come here in the dark and work at the lock and the hinges, weakening the door. Then, one night when they knew they could finally open it, they took up their pitchforks and axes and quietly entered. They had only one thing in mind – not bread, not meat, not beer, but to find the Black Abbot and to exact retribution. They crept across the graveyard, following the sound of laughing, of singing voices, through the abbey until they found him, seated with his bloated, cruel monks around a great feast. The story says that the room fell silent when the monks saw these skeletal, deathly men emerge from the shadows, with weapons in their hands and murder in their eyes. Terrified, the fat godless cowards fled to the hills. And they left their abbot behind.'

'And the men of the village killed him?'

'No. No, they didn't. That was their great mistake, a mistake which haunts us to this day.'

'Ms Larkin said that the villagers killed him and took his body. That no one knows where he is.'

'I know where he is. We all know where he is.'

'What do you mean?'

For the first time, Swift looked up to the hole in the mercy stone. Our eyes met.

'Death was too easy for a man who tried to murder the entire village. These men knew exactly what to do with him. The Black Abbot locked himself away behind this abbey's walls while the Black Death devoured their families. So, they dragged him, screaming, up the stairs of the tower, to where the belfry was still under construction and, brick by brick, they walled him up in it, locking him away inside his bloody beloved abbey for ever. When the monks returned, the men warned them not to look for the abbot, or they would raze the abbey to the ground and kill them all. Then they took all of the food, every last morsel, every last scrap and returned to their homes. That happened in 1346, and no villager has set foot in the abbey since.'

'And why was it a mistake? I don't understand.'

The little man fell quiet. He turned his face away. 'Because he's still here, that's why. Up there in the tower, watching over the abbey, over the village. When he went into the wall, as the men put each stone in place, he cursed them and their village. They did not realise it, but they were sealing his evil soul into the abbey. Now, he *is* the abbey. He's in the air, in the stone, in the wood, in the water. It is no longer sacred ground, it is his. Only this chapel, which once held the bones of a saint, is free of his influence. This is a soul so malevolent that he persuaded more than a hundred holy men to abandon the weak and the dying, to turn their backs on God. He sent them to hell. Now, when he can, he still feeds on the innocent, blackening their souls to sustain himself.'

'How does he still do it?'

'I told you earlier. Those who go into this place come out bad.'

'You mean the boys at the school?'

'Just like those innocent young monks he turned into godless gluttons. You'll have seen how proud she is of the way this school turned out callous, cold men?'

'She says they were leaders.'

179

I heard him exhale a cold, short laugh. 'Oh, I've read all about them. Pioneers? Captains of industry? Monsters. Monsters to a man. What did these golden boys grow up to do? Bankrupt banks? Finance war? Hang children for stealing bread? Torture Kenyans? So many cruel men. Judges, doctors, soldiers who revelled in pain. She told you about Fawcett? The Boer War? He's the pick of the bunch.'

'She said he built camps to help refugees.'

'They weren't refugees, they were starving women and children, forced out of their homes. And we call those camps something else these days too – we call them concentration camps. One of the golden boys of St Cuthbert's invented the concentration camp. Put that in a frame and hang it on the wall.'

The old man turned back to face the hills. 'And it's all because *he* was in there, whispering in their young ears every night, filling their hearts with evil. Poor little sods. I used to see them when I was a boy, you know, coming down from the hills every day, soaking wet, drained of life. They had a permanent look of fright on their faces. Then they'd go back in there – to *him*.'

'How do you know he's still in there? The school has been shut for a decade, empty.'

'We've all seen the lights, candles being carried behind the glass at night, up and down the stairs, along the cloisters. Looking for fresh souls to corrupt, looking for life to feed on. I think he knows he's on borrowed time. He's going to be sealed in again, but this time for good. It's his turn to starve.'

His hand reached up and took down the lamp, its light slipping through the hole into the night.

'That's it,' he said, bluntly. 'There's not many outside of this village been told that story, Mr Baxter. Whatever you decide to put in your book, I trust it will be the truth. And I hope when you leave here tomorrow, you'll not be affected by this place. Don't let him in.'

And then the little man was gone, trudging away into the darkness, the halo of the lamp guiding his way.

Back in the long, dark dormitory, I stood over the little bed that had been prepared for me. The old man's words returned.

'*Poison dripped into their ears every night.*'

I had to get ready. Focus. The headboard was pushed against the wall, so I stacked it up with pillows, giving me a view of the doorway and the windows. I emptied my bag onto the next bed: flask, sandwiches, chocolate, notepad. Then I sat, placed my phone next to me and looked across the rows of bare metal bedframes.

'*Whispering in their young ears every night, filling their hearts with evil.*'

Buzz. My phone shook noisily. Instinctively, my hand darted to it, and I blinked at the glowing screen. It throbbed again.

I squinted at the number, then the time. 11.35pm. Who could be calling me now? *Buzz.*

I held it to my ear. 'Hello?'

The line crackled. A sniff. A little boy. 'I'm sorry. I will do better,' he said weakly.

'Hello? Who is this? Are you OK?' I said, reaching for my pad.

'I know, yes I know,' he said. 'I will try harder, I promise. I will.' He seemed to be talking to someone else. There was fear in his voice.

'Hello, can you hear me? Did you call me?'

A crackle of static as the line fell quiet.

'Please don't say that. I'm trying my best,' he said softly. Another pause. My ears strained – was there another voice?

Suddenly, the boy cried out, his voice shrill with fright. 'No, don't do that, don't do that!' A sickening thud pulsed down the line. *Click.* It went dead. I felt my stomach turn.

'Hello? Hello?' I looked again at the number.

02135652108.

Was this the number I had missed before, the one that kept

vanishing from my phone? I scribbled it on the pad, then hit redial and pressed the phone to my ear.

My feet swung onto the floor. The line clicked.

'*This number is not recognised.*'

Dial again.

'*This number is not recognised.*'

The phone screen dimmed, as if in defeat. Check recent calls. The number was gone. Gone again! I placed the phone on the bed and inspected the pad, rubbing my eye with the heel of my palm.

02135652108.

0213. I didn't recognise the area code. At least this time I'd written the number down.

I sat back against the pillows, staring at the number. Tired. Rain gently rattled the windows. I ate a little, drank tea. Waited. Tired eyes. It was inevitable.

I slept on the old bed, the thick blanket's musty smell swaddling me in dreams of half-forgotten wet Sunday afternoons, park rain puddles and warm maternal hands drying my hair with rough rubs of a towel. But then the wet hair stung my eyes and cold rainwater rolled off my frozen shoulders, cascading from hand-built walls on a windswept hillside and there, pinned to the old stonework, gripping it tightly, was a black iron cross.

'*Brothers, boys, boys, brothers…*'

Somewhere, distant and disconnected, a high, wavering voice called – soft, elderly, searching for hidden playmates.

The pitter patter of rain drifted in, percussing gently in tiny waves on glass and wood, carrying me on the bed beneath the clouds and through the hills, past the endless walls of the abbey. Now another sound emerged from the rain, this time on stone, on oak, rippling along click-click-click-click-click, like drumming digits down the corridor walls.

'*Brothers, boys, boys, brothers, let us speak.*'

Click-click-click-click-click,   click-click-click-click-click   – fingers, yes, but brittle against the soft sound of the rain.

Now I saw the bloated hand as it slid along the wall, its dimpled blue knuckles rippling as the fingers drummed stone, click-click-click-click-click, but the sound was wrong – wooden, lifeless. The hand stopped, spiderlike, on the wall and stretched out. The fingers. The blue flesh was gone from their ends, halfway down, exposing tendril-like bones, dry and yellowed with age. Scraped away in desperation. Chewed off in despair.

I opened my eyes. I was lying on the bed, curled up on my side, half of my face pressed into a pillow. Beds stretched out to the doorway like stepping stones, their metal glinting dully in the moonlight.

My eyes focused. A shape, round and low, shifted silently between them, bending briefly to each one, inspecting, searching.

I felt the hairs on my neck stand. Broad shoulders stooped over a bed in front of me. They sagged, dejected. Silently the shape swept to the door and disappeared in the direction of the stairs. A flicker of amber light glanced across the doorway. A candle. I had to follow.

Downstairs, stripes of moonlight stretched along the corridor, falling from the windows to form pale blue pools on the sandstone floor. I paced hesitantly through them, my eyes on the tower ahead. I was entering a deeper part of the building now, one I had not been in before: a labyrinth of galleries and cloisters, lined with dusty, darkened windows behind which mothballed classrooms sat, desks empty and faded notices peeling from their walls. I was beneath the tower now. I felt my pulse quicken.

At the end of the corridor I stopped, suddenly aware that I couldn't see what was around the next turn. A shuffle, out of sight. A cold, dry sigh.

Click-click-click-click-click.

That noise. The half-skeletal hand crawled out of my dream. Then the high, faltering voice drifted around the corner.

'*Boys, brothers, where are thee? Where are thee? Will thou come out?*' The voice was sing-song soft; sickly sweet. I pressed my back

183

against the wall where the corridor turned, held my breath, and listened.

More soft shuffling noises. The dull flicker of candlelight caught in the ridges of the stone floor. I heard a door slowly opening, then closing again.

Click-click-click-click-click.

'*Brothers, oh brothers, how long has it been? Days or years, years or more?*'

Now, silence.

Carefully, I turned my chest to the wall, and moved an eye past the edge. Another corridor. Empty. No, wait! At the end, I saw a heel disappear around another turn. It was him.

I felt like I should pinch myself, slap myself, check I was awake – it was happening again. What had Patience said?

'You're an open door,' I whispered. My pulse raced. I felt alive.

Steeling myself, I stepped round the corner and listened. This corridor was windowless, darker. I could hear him somewhere, shuffling away beyond the next turn, his soft, pleading voice disappearing into the distance.

'*Will thou come out and talk, will thou listen? Boys, brothers?*'

I crept to the next turn. Out of sight, a different door opened somewhere in the dark, then slowly closed. The glow of a candle danced briefly on the wall opposite. Another door, heavier, opened.

Again, I edged my gaze around the corner. Down a short, broad passageway, an arched door into a larger room was wedged open. Candlelight flickered on metal pans hung on the far wall. The kitchen? The high, fluttering voice drifted out. He was humming to himself.

I crossed the passageway and peered around the doorframe.

The Black Abbot had his back to me. He was enormous, like a bull, the cloth of his dark cassock pulled tightly across his huge form, his head dipped and out of view. He was real, present, solid. Bare calves, braced apart to carry his weight, sunk to the floor, their blueish mottled skin visible below the rough cloth. He seemed to be inspecting a stack of empty, dusty plates piled on a table, his high, wavering hum filling the room.

His hand crawled across the top plate. Click-click-click-click-click.

A broad, round candle glowed dimly on the table, its edges set thick with pustules of wax. I gripped the doorframe.

The old wood creaked.

I froze.

The Black Abbot stopped humming.

His bald head lifted slowly, then turned to the side, listening with thick, fleshy ears. I could see bloated cheeks, a snout-like nose, fat wet lips. His eyes were pure white. Blind.

He whispered into the air, '*Boys, brothers, are you there? It is so dark. Will you come and listen, hear my sermon?*'

My heart jumped in my chest. He knew I was there; I could feel it.

He listened, waiting. A sickly smile. '*So it is…*' he sighed. I saw the bones of his flayed fingers wrap slowly around the candle and lift it, then he turned to face the door. To face me.

His features were broad and bovine, with stiff white whiskers bristling from a neck that sagged, bag-like from his chin. A large misshapen cross hung on a chain around his neck, its gold dullened by time. By dirt. By stone. By digging. A huge stomach hung over a coarse rope that stretched around the matted cassock. A dry white tongue ran around his lips, as he padded forward on fat bare feet, the candle held high.

I stepped back as he passed by me, then swallowed a gulp of air as my lungs gave out. He stopped at another arched door and ran his fingerbones across the wood. Click-click-click-click-click.

Then he gently pulled it open and paused, as if for my benefit, before squeezing through it. I heard his high, wavering hum begin again.

Again, I had to follow.

Steep steps rose in a spiral up through the floors of the tower. The sound of his humming echoed around the curved walls as the light from his candle flickered down. I began to climb.

Up, up, through the tower, past the small windows that looked out onto the playground and the village beyond.

The rain had stopped, and the clouds cleared, revealing a bright moon and a spectacular canopy of stars, massing like scattered glitter above the distant hills. Below, a few dim lights hovered in the village, framing locked porches, or picking out pathways, but the iron railings seemed to act like a barrier, separating light from dark. Despite the bright night sky, the little chapel in the corner was barely visible. Within the abbey's confines, all was black.

His hum drifted down. I pressed on, up the worn steps.

At the top, a door stood ajar. The belfry. I stepped in. It was empty, quiet. Broad openings on three sides let the starlight in and a breeze whirled gently around my feet. The moon seemed impossibly close. The black wall ahead was partly collapsed, with bricks missing next to a large copper plate which clicked and whirred quietly. The back of the clock?

There was no sign of the abbot. I looked out of the front opening, down at the expanse of the playground. As my eyes reached the little chapel, a blue-white light emerged from its two windows, drifting like fog. The hills seemed to watch.

Crack! A harsh metallic grinding filled the little room. Three o'clock. The bell rang out.

A voice whispered from behind.

'*Brother?*'

I swung around. He was there, inches from my face, smiling with his thick, fat lips. I felt my body straighten, stiffen, as if grabbed by a great hand.

'*Brother!*' he said. '*Brother! Thou hast joined with me! How good it will be to imbibe thy thoughts and share thy love of life, your very essence of being. We shall feast on ideas.*'

His white tongue licked his lips, as his blind eyes darted excitedly. I tried to move. Paralysed. The wind began to rise, swirling around our feet.

Slowly, he raised his skeletal fingers to his mouth and sucked their bony ends. *'We shall talk of what truly lies in men's hearts and the divine blessings of the Earth's bounties – and I would offer unto thee the secrets that I have divined, about the strength of a man's eternal character and the sinful weakness of mercy.'*

I felt his breath on my face. I couldn't move. I couldn't blink. His white eyes gleamed. The bell rang out again.

'But these are secrets that only we brothers should share, our own private gospel, not lessons to confuse witless sheep. All is within these walls; all is here for us.'

I couldn't look away from his white, dry eyes. He raised an arm, reaching slowly out. Wind rushed around us. I felt the bony ends of his fingers grip my shoulder. His face moved closer.

'My brother, we are the chosen few, where heaven can be here upon Earth if we choose to stay, to sustain ourselves through the secrets I have learned. A love of life itself shall be our sustenance.'

His eyes drew level with mine. *'I will share them with thee now. Come, brother, let me whisper this sermon to thee...'*

Unable to breathe. Unable to scream. Unable to move. I felt gravity pull at me, draining me, squeezing the air from me, draining the life from me as his bloated face edged forward, the great thick lips moving silently, sliding towards my ear, his cheek touching mine, his breath on my neck, the wind lifting the stench of decay around us, a cloud of dust, bitter and caustic, the dust of centuries in the dark, centuries of hunger, as he inhaled to speak...

The bell rang out.

'This one is not for you!'

Wilko's voice rasped angrily in the air.

'This one is mine!'

The abbot stepped back, his head darting blindly from side to side with confusion.

'*Who speaks to me so?*'

'*This one is not for you – you fat weak-willed fool! Back in your hole! Back in your hole!*'

Terror streaked across his face. He turned and lumbered towards the collapsed wall, crashing into it, crashing through, seeping into the stone. Gone. The wind fell.

'*This one is mine...*'

I felt my muscles loosen, my breath pour out. I lunged at the door, to the stairs, to safety. I stumbled down the steps, then bolted through the abbey until I reached the double doors to the playground. Out across the gravel I ran to the chapel, towards the blue-white light that lit up the little windows.

Inside, the light was gone. The little building was dark and peaceful. Breathing heavily, I sat on one of the ancient pews, and looked up through the mercy stone. The stars shone in the night sky above the village.

*

I stayed in the chapel for the rest of the night, grateful for the protection of its thick walls. In the morning, I let myself out of the main entrance. Across the road, Danny Swift was unloading metal sheets from the back of a van.

He saw me and nodded, before raising his drill in the air. Seven o'clock. High above, the bell in the tower remained silent.

NINETEEN

Chapter and Verse

The taxi idled on the kerbside as I rang Kate's doorbell again. I was looking at my watch when her little car bounced up the drive and she jumped out, offering me an apologetic glance as she retrieved her handbag.

The key slid into the front door, and she shook her head. 'I am so sorry, Joe – such a long day. I will be two minutes, just wait.'

Kate was wearing blue scrubs again, her hair pulled back into a ponytail. As she disappeared up the stairs, she left a fresh bloom of perfume behind. She smelled good.

'It's alright, don't rush,' I called after her. 'If you like, I can send the taxi away and we'll go on in a bit.'

I could hear her moving about upstairs, her feet running from room to room. Somewhere, water splashed briefly into a sink.

'No, no, I'm nearly done – just wait.'

An awkward wave to the taxi driver.

And then she was coming down the stairs, the scrubs replaced by a simple summer dress, a small clutch bag in her hand and a big smile across her face. 'See – two minutes!'

She paused at the hallway mirror, producing lipstick, and locking her eyes on me in the reflection. 'You always were an impatient sod, Joe Baxter.'

Then, Kate swept the band from her ponytail and turned to me as her hair fell across her shoulders. 'Shall we?'

Déjà vu washed over me. This was going to be fun.

The drive into the city was noisy and exhilarating, as the yellow lights of the expressway rippled across the cab's windows. Two days had passed since my night at St Cuthbert's, and I still felt the energy of the experience pulsing through me – fright, confusion, excitement – but also an acceptance that something was happening to me. A line had been crossed. I had talked to the abbot – or he had talked to me. And Wilko's words hung onto me, his anger, his vitriol. Connected, that's the word. I still felt connected to what had happened. I had spent the last day locked in my flat feverishly writing about the vigil, getting it onto the page, recording it, making it real, tying it down before it could fly away. I just wanted to tell someone about it, all of it.

Kate applied make-up but looked agitated as she stared into her compact.

'Tough day?' I asked.

'Sorry, yes. I'm a bit pissed off, to tell the truth. There's a new wing being built at work – which is great, big investment and all that – but it's such a hassle, the whole place is a building site. Then, to cap it all, management used our rest room to store a load of paperwork while the work is being done and some of it got lost. They had the audacity to question the nursing team about it. If you don't want confidential files to go missing, don't leave them in a big pile of boxes in a nurses' rest room!'

'I take it you shared that thought with them?'

She flipped the compact shut and slipped it into her clutch bag. 'Yes. Yes, I did,' she smiled.

'Good.'

'So, where are you taking me?' she asked, brightening. 'I hope it's going to be as awesome as our last date. I remember you made a real effort. No denim or leather jacket or anything.'

'How can I forget? I never managed to wash the sauce from the ribs out of that shirt.'

'The ribs!' she snorted, with laughter. 'I forgot about the ribs! You really were a vision in that plastic bib! Very alluring.'

'In my defence, I was only seventeen, and I really liked ribs. I mean I *really* liked ribs. And the Exchange did the best ribs anywhere. Everyone knew that. I planned that date for days, I spent a fortune – well, a fortune for a teenager.' Kate offered me a sympathetic nod. I persevered.

'I had no idea that eating ribs on a date would be anything less than attractive. I thought it would look rugged and windswept. I thought it would look cool.'

She sniggered. 'Joe, it was all over your face. Washing your fingers in that little bowl of water! Very rock 'n' roll. Very cool. Actually, I was referring to the music.'

I gritted my teeth, guiltily.

'Like I said, I was... what? Fifteen? Sixteen? I thought everyone liked what I liked.'

'What were they called? War...'

'War Pigs. Sabbath tribute act. Again, sorry. At least it was a memorable night.'

'Oh. It was memorable alright.'

'Well, we're going somewhere a little more upmarket – the Posthouse.'

'Ooh very posh. A regular haunt of yours?'

'No – hardly – but I'm told it's very good.'

'And have you been planning this for days too? It's very exciting.'

'Trust me, it's all in hand.'

The city centre was the usual hubbub of noise and movement. Music bounced off passing cars and rattling buses, as groups of people clutched each other's elbows under neon and shopfront canopies.

All, however, was not in hand.

The teenaged *maître d'* at the Posthouse looked at the night's bookings and then at me, his pencil-line moustache pinched to one side of his nose and one eyebrow arched, before informing me that there was no table in my name. I could feel Kate giggling softly behind me.

Back out on the pavement she clutched her bag behind her back and inspected her feet. 'So… where now, Romeo?'

'It's going well, isn't it?'

'Like a dream,' she smiled. 'Like dream.'

'There might be somewhere on Broad Street where we can get a table.'

Kate exhaled and looked around. 'I'm not sure I want to go anywhere posh, to be honest. I just want to be able to relax. It would be nice just to talk to someone sane…'

'Not sure I can help you with that.'

'Wait.' Kate's eyes came to rest over my shoulder. 'I think I've found the perfect place.'

She jabbed a finger. I knew before I looked.

In the distance, over low tin rooftops, a tired-looking neon sign winked. The Exchange.

Inside, we slipped into one of the painted booths, sitting either side of the chipped wooden table. We ordered two rum and cokes, and Kate expertly herded the sauces and condiments aside as the waitress delivered them, ice cubes tinkling gently against glass. Kate took a sip and then visibly sank into the bench with a happy sigh.

'This is what I need,' she said. 'I'm sorry, I couldn't face a night in a swish restaurant, I hope you don't mind.'

I looked around the dimly lit diner. A handful of people were propping up the bar, as an old juke box played unobtrusively in the corner.

'Not at all, this is much more my kind of place – style-wise, and price-wise.'

'You calling me a cheap date?'

'No, I mean I'm a cheap date... So this is a date, then?'

Kate tilted her head, considering the question. 'Not sure. Thought it would be nice to catch up, to be honest. That's why I called you. Although, for the purpose of torturing my daughter this is *definitely* a date.'

I nodded in agreement. 'Agreed. How's Helena dealing with the job situation?'

'I think it's playing on her mind. She seems to be thinking about it all the time. But she'll bounce back. She's already looking at college courses – I think she's going to do investigative journalism, digital stuff.'

'Data journalism. That's where the future is,' I said. 'She'll be great at it.'

'If you hear of anything that might be of interest, though, let us know – or if she can help you with anything.'

'That reminds me!' I said, pulling a folded printout from my pocket. Kate opened it.

The worried old faces of the Bentleys looked out from the front page of the *Echo*, their gaunt-looking son sitting between them. The headline screamed: 'ABANDONED'.

'It won't sell much, but it's important,' I said.

Kate looked at it, confused. I pointed at the by-line beneath the photograph. Her eyes lit up.

'Oh wow!'

'Helena's first front page. Quite possibly her last too, but she's done an amazing job on a tricky story. She's made of strong stuff, that daughter of yours. She's turning into a very good reporter, I know that. She was all set to do her first death knock until all this happened.'

'Death knock?'

'Really tough job – visit to a bereaved family.'

Kate screwed up her face.

'Sounds awful. She didn't mention it.'

'That doesn't surprise me. She wasn't fazed at all. But this is a really good piece of journalism. You should be proud. She's fearless.'

She folded the printout and slipped it into her bag. 'She's a nightmare, but I love her.'

I laughed. 'Her generation get a lot of stick for being snowflakes but they're much more together than I was at that age.'

'So true. Sometimes I think Helena's a lot more "together" than I am now,' Kate said. 'When I've had a tough day, she's the one who sits me down and talks to me like she's the parent. We would never have done that when we were kids, would we?'

'Definitely not. So... nursing's a tough job. I'm impressed.'

She picked up the menu. 'Psychiatric nurse. It's challenging, but you get used to it, I suppose. The secret is not to normalise the stress, but to see it for what it is, so you can carry on the next day – and to focus on the fact that you're helping people. That's why Helena's so brilliant at it. She just dusts me down. She helps me switch it off.'

'Where do you work?'

She studied me as she answered. 'Westcroft.'

I nodded.

'It's where you went for a while, isn't it? I remember.'

'It is, yes. Long time ago now. I was banged up there for six months. Expect it's changed a great deal.'

'Well, we don't... bang people up there anymore, put it that way. You wouldn't recognise the place, or the staff, from when you were there. Come to think of it, there's probably only one person who's been there that long anyway – and he's a patient. It's very modern now, friendly. I was a general nurse before this, on the wards, and Westcroft certainly doesn't even feel like a hospital. Well, it's more like a building site right now, but you know what I mean.'

'Sounds like a change for the better.'

Kate screwed up her face a little. 'Sorry, I don't know how we got on to this subject. Do you mind talking about it?'

'Erm, no, I don't think so. I haven't thought about it for years, to be honest.'

'My fault, still trying to switch off after today. It's hardly a suitable topic of conversation for a date.'

'So, it is a date, then. Excellent.'

She conceded a laugh, then looked me up and down wryly. 'You've really changed, Joe.'

'*I've* changed? *You've* changed.'

'Oh, I know I've changed but you... I almost didn't recognise you the other day.'

'What do you mean?'

'You were the bad boy, the rebel. I found you a little bit scary at school – I think everyone did. Not nasty, just... unpredictable. Is that fair?'

'Mad Bax? I think I was a walking cliché.'

'It was the 80s. Everyone was a cliché.'

'I mean it was an act – a front. You remember what happened with my dad? Well, it was a reaction to that. The rebel bit, I mean. At the time I swore blind that it wasn't affecting me, but... in the end I had to get help. That's it really.'

'From my experience,' Kate said quietly, 'when someone has a trauma like that in childhood, they often spend years telling themselves it had little impact – in fact, sometimes they feel guilty about not being upset enough – and then, when they're older, they realise that it was the single biggest event in their life. At least you faced up to it. Dealt with it then. Otherwise, it becomes baggage.'

'Well, I've plenty of that,' I said, sipping my rum and coke.

'And anyway, cut yourself some slack. You were a pretty sensitive kid; it was bound to have an effect on you. I remember when you had to read aloud in front of the class and you just started crying – not because you were frightened, but because you were moved. It was really sweet.'

My head fell into my hands. 'Oh God, I forgot about that. *I Know Why the Caged Bird Sings*. Jesus. So embarrassing.'

'You were always crying.'

'I still do, can't help it. It's genetic.'

'It's sweet.'

'I suspect it undermined my legendary tough guy image, to be honest. But what about you! You've changed so much. Don't get me wrong – you look great...'

'Thank you.'

'... but I mean you were so shy, so quiet. You were the classic wallflower.'

'You make me sound like I was a real catch.'

'Well, you know what I mean. You were so sensible and grown up.'

'All teenage girls are grown up compared to teenage boys.'

'I mean I could really talk to you. That's why I liked you. But – let's face it – you were a square. God, you were a square. Proper goody two shoes. I always thought you'd settle down, get married, have loads of kids.'

Her jaw dropped in faux offence. 'Now who's the walking cliché?'

'Yeah, but that's my point. You didn't, did you? Look at you – you're raising an amazing daughter on your own, doing a tough job and you're so confident. That's what I mean – I've calmed down, you've toughened up.'

'Yes, well, divorce will do that to you.'

We sat in comfortable silence for a moment, both suddenly aware of how quickly we had reverted to our teenage selves.

'This is going to sound corny,' I said, 'but it's nice, isn't it, when you meet someone after a long time and nothing's changed? Do you know what I mean?'

'You just said I had changed.'

'You know what I mean.'

A hint of a blush. 'Yeah, I do.'

The waitress reappeared, pen poised over paper pad, but retreated to the bar as Kate went back to scanning the menu. I sipped my drink.

'So, what happened with Darren?'

She shrugged softly. 'Not much to say. We were married. He cheated. Quite a bit, it turns out. Darren ran a travel business and was away a lot, but I wasn't aware of what he was up to when he went on one of his trips. Basically, as soon as he unpacked his suitcase, he reverted to being single. Then the last one – who's barely older than Helena – followed him home and knocked on the door. Helena answered. So, I kicked him out. He's living in Spain with her now.'

'That's shocking.'

'It was. It knocked me sideways. Really messed with my head. I was so… angry.'

'I'm not surprised.'

'But I wasn't angry at him. I think I was angry because I felt stupid, that I'd allowed it to happen by just accepting things. I realised I had just been… passive. So, I was angry at myself, not him, which I knew was ridiculous. I couldn't be angry at him because, after all, he was just a dickhead, and I'd known that all along. He was just pathetic. But I was supposed to be the sensible one and shouldn't have let him do it to me. Or to Helena.'

'That's really screwed up.'

'I know. I had a bit of a meltdown. So, I had to get help too.'

She put the menu down and wrapped both hands around her drink.

'But you know what? It made me stop being passive, made me open up a bit. And how they helped me with my mental health rekindled my passion for work – non-judgmental, just listening. It was a revelation. That's when I decided to start again. I retrained and switched to psychiatric nursing. So, in a way, it did me a favour. The marriage was a joke – we never actually listened to each other at all – and I'm much better off without him. So is Helena. And I'm not such a shrinking violet anymore. Or a goody two shoes. I don't really care anymore.'

'So, I've become more square and you've gone more rock 'n' roll.'

'Something like that,' she said, swirling the ice in her glass. 'So anyway, I got the house, he kept his sordid little love nest in Spain. He sold his business, cleared out his home office and scurried off. Haven't seen him since.'

Another silence.

'So, what's your story?' she asked softly. 'Your turn to open up.'

'What do you want to know? Ask me anything.'

'Was there ever a Mrs Baxter? Kids?'

'No, not me. A couple of partners but nothing that lasted.'

'Why?'

'Erm...'

'Come on, I've just given you chapter and verse.'

'OK. I guess, if I'm honest, I don't think I've ever committed to a relationship. Properly.'

'Why?'

'Is this how they roll at Westcroft these days?'

Kate grinned. 'Like I said, I retrained. Come on, answer the question.'

'OK, OK. I think that... I'm not equipped to deal with it. I don't want to let them down.'

'Why would you let them down?'

'I don't know... maybe it's just that I don't know how to handle things when life goes wrong. Because I'm not equipped.'

She changed tack. 'Who have you let down?'

'Oh, my mom. You know that. It seemed like the whole town knew that.'

'That was a long time ago. You were a kid.'

'Are you going to charge me for this? Dr Sabapathy used to do quite well.'

'Sabapathy? He was your psychiatrist?'

'He was, why?'

'The new wing they're building at Westcroft is going to be called the Sabapathy Wing.' She raised her glass. 'Cheers, Doc.'

I took a swig. 'It's what he would have wanted. It actually is.'

'So, you're afraid of commitment? I take it back – you really are a walking cliché.'

'No, I don't think I can be trusted with other people's emotions. That's different. I've had a lot of time to think about this, believe me. I'm OK with commitment. I was committed to my career.'

'That went well.'

'It was going well.'

'Have you got any thoughts on what you'll do next?'

'I've got a bit of breathing space, because of the redundancy payment. But I'm working on a book.'

Kate sat forward. 'Oh yes, Helena mentioned that. What's it about?'

I pursed my lips. 'I'm not sure I want to tell you.'

'Why not?'

'Partly because it's going well and I don't want to jinx it, but mainly because it will probably sound infantile. I think I've been pretty cool on this date so far, and I don't want to put on another plastic bib.'

'Intriguing,' she said, sinking back into her seat.

The waitress reappeared, her pen waving like a metronome.

Kate pushed the menu away across the table. 'There's really only one choice,' she said. 'I'll have the ribs.'

'Make that two. And two more drinks, please.'

We ate and talked and talked and ate and had a few more drinks. Over ice cream, we fell into a slightly exhausted silence.

'It's about the paranormal,' I said eventually, laying my spoon on the table.

'The book?'

'Yes.'

Her eyes thinned. 'Fiction or non-fiction?'

'Non-fiction.'

She pushed her bowl away and leant forward on the table.

'I hope you're not hanging around in graveyards again.'

'I sort of am.'

Kate exhaled slowly. 'Can I ask you a question?'

I nodded. Cautiously.

She shifted on the seat. 'The truth is, after I went through my... episode... with Darren, and certainly after I switched to mental health work, I've thought about you quite often. Thought about what you went through when we were kids.'

'Right?'

'I hope you don't mind, but... what was the name of the voice you used to speak to? Waldo?'

'Wilko.'

'Wilko... Wilko... that's right. Do you mind me...'

'Go on.'

'I'm just interested...'

'It's OK, go on.'

'OK. So, did it just stop? No more voices?'

I took a beat and thought. 'Yes, it just stopped. At Westcroft. Nothing since.'

'Liar.'

I felt my toes curl inside my shoes.

Kate smiled, her head shaking gently. 'Right. Good. Fascinating, actually – see, that's really quite unusual. From my experience.'

'Is it? It's all so long ago.'

'Liar, liar.'

'You were a proper legend at school, you know. An enigma. One day you were there, then you were gone. Everyone talked about it for months.'

'I dread to think what was being said about me.'

'There was some pretty outlandish stuff. What was his name... Perch. He was full of it.'

'Was he. About what?'

'About what you did. What he said you did. And that Goth girl.'

'It was a very long time ago, and it's all a bit sketchy to be honest,' I said.

'More lies. Liar. You know. You know. I know.'

'Of course, sorry. I'll leave it, I was just curious after all these years. I'm not judging, trust me I'm beyond that!'

'No, that's OK... what did you want to know?'

'Well... did you really do it?'

TWENTY

Alfred's Boy

The Eighth Vigil

A good reporter can tell when they are struggling to win someone's confidence. Gus called it his 'Spidey Sense', a knack for picking up subtle signals from a contact or interviewee; micro facial expressions or vocal inflections that display mistrust or unease. It's all part of the training. Douglas Fairfax wasn't sending subtle smoke signals. He may as well have used semaphore to flag his displeasure at my presence.

'I will be here at 0800 hours to let you out,' he said, jutting his chin in a military fashion.

'Would it be possible to let myself out? I tend to finish earlier than that.'

'Out of the question, I'm afraid. I'm the only key holder to the buildings and the main gate of the base. Some of the items in the collection here in the museum are of great value.'

I looked at the dust-covered objects scattered around the room: a battered ARP helmet, faded ration books and reproduction

'Keep Calm and Carry On' posters. A gas mask, its glass lenses scratched and fogged, stared back at me from the corner.

I gritted my teeth. Training. Rule One: persevere, reassure and don't give up.

'Of course, I understand, Mr Fairfax, I appreciate your time.'

'Captain Fairfax,' he corrected me, coldly. 'Retired. Would you like to leave your bag here, and I'll show you around? Briefly?'

Group Captain Douglas Fairfax (retired) was short, thin and coiled tightly, like a primed spring. Dressed in pressed black slacks and a dark blue sweater with epaulettes, he had a countenance that sat somewhere between caretaker and scout master. He walked ahead of me in sharp impatient steps, like a clockwork toy wound and released.

A flight of concrete stairs led to the top of the control tower, and a panoramic view that looked out onto the deserted airfield. I was drawn blinking to the windows.

The cluster of low buildings cowered under a huge expanse of Lincolnshire sky that was becoming streaked with grey and pink as night approached. Only two enormous hangars – one new and angular and the other old, curved and ribbed like the tail of some great hidden beast – dared to encroach above the horizon.

Fairfax was still standing at the door.

'I must admit, I don't fully grasp what it is that you hope to achieve tonight, Mr Baxter,' he said, his voice edged with irritation.

'Well, I'm writing a book on hauntings, and an old colleague at the *Grimsby Telegraph* told me about the apparition that was reported at the ceremony last week. The closing ceremony?'

'Decommissioning ceremony. For the airfield, not the museum. It's not clear what is going to happen to the museum.'

'Right. So, I contacted the trustees to ask if I could spend a night. Soak up the atmosphere.'

Fairfax slipped his hands behind his back and rocked on his heels.

'Well, I don't understand why they didn't run it past me. I'm the curator after all.'

My Spidey Sense was tingling. Persevere, reassure and don't give up.

'I'm sure it was just a breakdown in communications,' I said. 'And I only want to cast the museum in a positive light. I'm doing this properly, it's not some sensationalist tabloid book.'

Fairfax nodded dismissively.

'You know, the thing I've never understood about this sort of… thing… is how people can get so excited when there's so little to get excited about.'

'I'm sorry, what do you mean?'

'Well, RAF Binton, along with quite a few other RAF airfields, has developed this… mythology… that it is haunted, when in actual fact you could count the number of so-called witnesses on one hand. I've been here for a very long time, with the RAF and then as curator, and I've never seen anything. Anything. Come to think of it, the fuss last week was the first example in decades.'

'So, you don't think it's haunted?'

He gave me a slightly pitiful look. 'No, Mr Baxter, no. A very long time ago, after the war, there were stories about a ghost. I suppose these things have a way of becoming accepted as fact; they get included in local history guff and repeated in newspapers over and over again. But my father served here during the war, and afterwards, and he always said that it was rubbish – just people seeing something out of the corner of their eye.'

'An airman?'

'You'll find the same story repeated at bases up and down the country. It's always a young airman in World War II flight gear. Funny that. And as I said, last week's business was the first time in decades. I don't know what all the fuss is about. I genuinely can't remember the last time this came up. If he is haunting the airfield, he's hardly prolific, is he?'

'My friend told me two people saw it last week – two local councillors, in fact.'

'Apparently so. But again, they *think* they saw it. No doubt they were already aware of the stories. I know this place like the back of my hand, Mr Baxter. Nothing. I've seen nothing.'

'So, what do you think is going on?'

He squared his shoulders. 'Emotions. After the war lots of this sort of thing went on. Not surprising given what the country had been through. Last week was an emotional occasion too. We had VIPs, ex-personnel, former flight crew – who you will understand are very old. Even their children are old. There were speeches, a bugler. It was held in the old hangar too, where the Lancaster is. I think it got to people, that's all. Emotions.'

'I'm told these councillors were adamant.'

'Well, it got them in the paper, didn't it?' He looked at his watch and sniffed. 'Shall we move on?'

*

We entered the old hangar through a plain wooden door, which had clearly been replaced since the airfield's wartime heyday. Inside it was dark, but the space still betrayed its cavernous size, the air hanging damp and heavy and open. At the end, the dying day leaked in around the edges of the huge main doors, throwing highlights along the tops and sides of shapes hiding in the gloom.

And, in front of us, a huge black presence lurked unseen. Fairfax flicked on strip lights and the Lancaster Bomber blinked into reality.

Instinctively, I stepped back. Everything about it was enormous, exaggerated – and bestial. Its huge wingspan reached over our heads and away into the distance; its smooth, black fuselage stretched in front like a vast whale. The nearest engine loomed above, smooth and shark-like with puckered exhausts rippling like gills down its side, a black propeller blade jutting upwards like a fin. And multiple eyes, of bubble-blown glass, looked out from the front, the top, its back, its rear. But the insect stare was empty. The monster was dead.

Fairfax walked into the shadows beneath, glancing back to check that the bomber had made its usual impact.

'This is the *So Long Betty*,' he said, 'our star exhibit. The museum's collection was built around her. She has a direct link to RAF Binton. Lincolnshire was known as "Bomber County" during the war, with airfields up and down the coast, but this beauty made Binton special. She was the plane that completed the Miracle Mission of 1943... and she landed here. She has been here ever since – she never flew again. If you look closely, you can see the bullet holes left by two Messerschmitt fighters.'

'The Miracle Mission?'

He gestured to information boards standing in a semi-circle around the plane's wheels.

'There's plenty of detail here to fill you in. Basically, her squadron was on a bombing mission to the Ruhr Valley when she was picked off by two German fighters. They strafed the plane, killing some of the crew, and took out three of the four engines, then left her for dead as she went into a dive. But the pilot managed to pull her up – and she limped all the way home to Binton on just one engine. An incredible piece of flying by the pilot, a chap called Alfred Trowton – who's still alive and living in the village. It made national headlines, featured in newsreels, and was mentioned in Parliament.'

My eyes picked out a bullet hole on the bottom of the plane, then another, then another. It was riddled with them. 'And the pilot is still alive? He must be ancient.'

'He's in his nineties but still compos mentis. He was here last week for the ceremony, one of our guests of honour. Alfred is one of the most important figures in Binton's history – after the war he was in command of the airfield for a few years, before my father took over.'

'I'd like to meet him. He sounds fascinating.'

Rule 2: If you're still getting nowhere, find someone else.

'I'll give you his address before you go – I'm sure he'd be grateful for the company. But you should know, he's not exactly what you'd expect of an RAF man. Quite the free thinker. But then again…' he looked me up and down, 'I suspect you'll get on.'

*

In fairness, Fairfax was right. My vigil at RAF Binton failed to get off the ground.

At 2100 hours I ate my sandwiches.

At 2230 hours I tried the hangar door, only to find Fairfax had locked me in.

At 2345 hours I explored the exhibits in the dark and fell over a vintage military bicycle.

At 0200 hours the only faintly interesting thing happened: I was at the far end of the hangar when I noticed a dim blue light reflecting on the ribbed roof, from the direction of the *So Long Betty*, although when I returned to the plane, all was normal.

At around 0400 hours I fell asleep.

At 0800 hours, on the dot, I heard the jingle of Fairfax's keys.

*

The wire gate closed with a rattle behind me. There was a hint of sea spray on the November air on the lonely road outside RAF Binton. All around, endless blue rose above low-lying hills lit green and yellow by shafts of morning sunlight, which fell in columns from behind towering, billowing clouds. Bomber County.

My hand found the scrap of paper in my pocket: Alfred Trowton's address. Pulling my bag tight to my shoulder I began the short stroll down to the village.

The morning was quiet, and my mind drifted to Kate, to Gus, then the gates of Westcroft as I trudged along the grass verge. The road looped down towards the village, with a small pub marking the halfway point to the base. It was shuttered as I walked past, its pub sign swinging gently in the breeze – The Tame Otter.

Wait. Someone watching me? Across the road, a crumbling brick-built bus shelter cut a box-like silhouette against the sky. A figure in apple green sat alone. A familiar, friendly hand waved. It can't be. I crossed.

'Patience?'

'Joe, is that you?' she beamed.

'It is! Patience, what are you doing here?'

She looked sarcastically around the little shelter. 'Er... waiting for a bus! What do you think I'm doing?'

Patience moved along the little wooden bench as I sat down next to her, lifting the shopping bag at her feet, and adjusting her thick green coat.

'I mean what are you doing in Binton? It's the middle of nowhere.'

She sucked her teeth, shook her head and pointed down the road. 'We're twenty minutes from Grimsby. That way. I'm just visiting. What are you doing here?'

'Another vigil – up at the RAF base.'

'Oh, I see. And how was that?'

'Complete washout. Waste of time.'

'And how is the book going?'

'Well, I've started to actually write it now... since I last saw you, so much has happened. It has been amazing, really. How long has it been?'

She shrugged. 'I don't know, it's all a blur at my age. So, what have you seen?'

'All kinds of things. And I've talked to them too, and they have talked to me.'

Her brow knitted into a frown. 'Talked to them? And they answered?'

'Yes, I think so... yes, they did.'

Patience looked perplexed. Instinctively, her hand dipped into her pocket. The familiar pack of battered playing cards appeared. She began to turn it over and over in her hands, like a rosary, her frown fixed on the hills ahead.

'You know, I think it's a good thing you found me like this,' she said slowly. 'I told you before to be careful, but I think you're beyond that.'

'You said someone was looking for me.' I shifted to face her. 'I heard a voice say, "This one is mine".'

She glanced at me, the cards turning slightly faster, then nodded. 'Then maybe he found you.'

The cards stopped and she fixed me with her deep brown eyes. 'Things are getting serious, Joe, I can sense it. You have to know what you are doing is dangerous. If they are talking to you, then...'

'Then what?'

'They could get too close. They could get attached.'

'Attached?'

'Yes, attached to you. They can follow people, walk in your shadow, by your side. You don't want that.'

'How does that happen?'

'If they are talking to you, then they are connecting to you. You are allowing them in. Have any of them touched you?'

I felt the skeletal fingers of the abbot on my shoulder. 'Yes. At least once. Why?'

A slow shake of the head. 'That's not good. Not normal. I told you before, you are a door, Joe. An open door. You need to be careful who you let in.'

'What should I do, then? How can I tell if they are attached to me?'

'You can't, unless they want you to know. It's like I said before, they are all different, different like leaves on a tree – sometimes you might be able to spot them, but sometimes they just look completely normal. You might sense they are there, but sometimes you wouldn't notice them if they walked past you in the street.'

'And if they get attached?'

She thought for a second. 'Let me explain it to you. These are people with no life left, like a flat battery, you know? So, if they want to stick around, and not just fade away, they need to get their energy from somewhere. Most are harmless – they get it in a good way, by drawing from happy memories, or watching over people they love, or maybe from a place that's filled with people all the time, that's full of life, like a theatre.'

'Or a pub?'

'Yes, like a pub.' Her eyes darkened. 'But others, the ones that refuse to leave – well, they can drain you, feed on you. Feed on your fears, your emotions, your energy. That's how they sustain themselves. They have no life left, so they take yours. But you can't always see them, Joe. That's why you need to be careful.'

'I'd certainly notice the ones I've met,' I said. 'They would stand out quite a bit.'

'Maybe,' she said, suddenly standing up. A single-decker bus was approaching. Patience slipped the cards back into her pocket and picked up her bag. 'This is my ride. Be careful, Joe, don't leave yourself open. This isn't about buildings, houses, bricks and mortar. It's about people.'

The bus pulled up and the doors opened with a hiss. I watched as she climbed aboard and moved down the aisle to take a seat.

The tired-looking driver stared at me. 'You getting on or what?' he said.

'Sorry no, I'm walking down to the village.'

He rolled his eyes, shut the doors and pulled away.

*

Morphic Resonance & The Presence of the Past: The Memory of Nature.
ESP, Hauntings and Poltergeists: A Parapsychologist's Handbook.
Schizophrenia: Cognitive Enhancement.
Shell Shock: Trauma, Neurosis and the British Armed Forces.
The Phantom World: The History and Philosophy of Spirits, Apparitions, and c., & c.
Spiritual Nomads: Supernatural Traditions of Indigenous Peoples

My eyes widened as they swept the bookcases of Captain Alfred Trowton, which lined all four walls of his small living room. Thick dust coated the books, which jostled for shelf space with dozens of framed photographs of a happy, pretty woman; she smiled with youthful shyness in black and white, and with middle-aged contentment in rich Kodachrome colour. The frames and glass gleamed, lovingly cleaned every day.

I heard the captain softly enter and watched as he stooped, his stick-thin arms slowly and carefully depositing mugs of tea onto the low table.

'You and I appear to have shared interests,' I said.

Trowton looked up quizzically, his head shuffling gently from side to side.

'Your books. Quite the collection.'

'Oh,' he said, his hand gripping the arm of a chair as he stood, 'more of an obsession, really. A search for answers.'

Alfred Trowton was ancient but immaculate. The old man's five-foot stature was deceptive; he had clearly once been much taller. His spine bulged backwards from his waist, shoulders hunched and neck hovering, horizontal, like a tortoise – which was apt, as everything about Alfred Trowton was slow. Yet while his face was thin and gaunt, and his eyes sunken in their sockets, they were bright and alert, while his cotton-like white hair was combed neatly to the side.

He gestured for me to sit but then stood, just for a second,

211

scanning the back garden through the bungalow's tall bay window. I watched as his eyes drifted up to the sky. Then, with shaking thumbs and forefingers, he pinched his slacks above the knee, gently raising their hems from his slippers, before sinking carefully into his chair. A mug of tea was presented to me, chesslike, across the table by a spotted hand.

'That's yours, young man. Best not get them mixed up. I think four sugars might finish me off!'

I picked it up and took a sip. 'Thank you. I'm on my third already today, so I don't think it's having the desired effect anymore.'

'Goodness. A real teabelly,' he said in his soft Yorkshire accent, before focusing on lifting his mug. His mouth puckered in anticipation.

'Well, I finished at the base early, so I've been sitting in a coffee shop round the corner for a couple of hours. Didn't want to disturb you too early.'

He looked at me over the brim of the mug. 'Oh, yes well, you needn't have bothered. At my age you barely sleep. Don't need to. Anyway, I'll sleep when I'm in my box, that's what I always say!'

'Do you mind if I ask how old you are?'

'Why would I mind? I am ninety-nine years old. Six months off that bloody birthday card from Her Majesty.'

'And you live here alone?'

The mug descended unsteadily to the tabletop. 'Yes, just me. My wife, Dulcie, died ten years ago. But I manage. People expect you to go into a home, to be looked after. Balls to that.'

I sniggered into my tea. I liked Alfred. 'You know, you're not quite the archetype of the World War II RAF man.'

'Oh, yes? What did you expect? Someone a bit posher? A bit of "*Pip pip, what-ho, old chap*"?' He shook his head. 'I'll let you into a secret. We weren't like that at all. The only reason you expect us to be posh types is the actors who played us in those old films were all posh. It's all balls, sunshine.'

'When did you retire?'

'Well, I left the RAF in 1955 – retired, I should say – but I kept my hand in by helping to set up the museum, and then run it as curator. Of course, I never really was a historian, but the trustees thought it would be nice for me to be involved somehow. So, I did that until... oh, 1970, then retired properly, to be with Dulcie. But the trustees still look in on me from time to time, make sure I'm still breathing.'

'Captain Fairfax said his father ran the base after you – did you serve with him during the war?'

Alfred raised an eyebrow. 'Fairfax? Yes, after a fashion. He was at Binton alright, but in what you might call a more auxiliary role. In charge of refuelling the men. Vital for morale, or so he told everyone.'

'Refuelling the men?'

'He was the cook.' Alfred gave a wry smile, then turned his gaze to the window and the sky.

I watched, in the silence of the morning light, as his mind drifted, his eyes stirring as old conversations and faces waltzed by. Then, as if re-entering the room, the old man blinked and looked at me again.

'I'm terribly sorry, happens all the time these days – I just drift off.'

He sat back, his hands in his lap. 'Do you know that the American Navaho believe that when a baby is born that it does not have a soul? It has to wait until one finds its way in – they call it a "wind" – and that when the baby first laughs, *that's* when you know a soul has taken up residence.'

'Is that right?' I said, surprised at the tangent the conversation had suddenly taken.

'Bear with me,' he said. 'They also believe that the older a person gets – and the closer to death – the more detached the soul becomes from the body. Sort of getting ready to move out, I suppose. I feel a bit detached these days.'

213

'Fascinating. Is that from one of your books? Our shared interest?'

'Yes, that's right. My eyes aren't good enough to read these days, but it's all up here.' He tapped his forehead softly. 'So, tell me, how did you get on last night? I'm very interested. One of the trustees told me about your request to stay over to do a… séance?'

'A vigil. I'm a journalist, not a medium or anything like that.'

'And?'

I shrugged. 'Nothing. I saw nothing at all to suggest that RAF Binton is haunted.'

My words seemed to hang in the air. Alfred lifted his chin, lips pursed, his old eyes studying me. Then, with the subtlest of nods, he made a decision.

'That's not surprising,' he said, 'it's not haunted. I am.'

⋆

'That's the one,' he said, pointing to a large wooden box on top of the wardrobe. I lifted it down and carried it from the bedroom into the living room. Alfred sank back into his chair as I set it on the table. The old man looked at it with trepidation, then, with shaking hands, lifted the lid. A musty smell drifted lazily upwards. He nervously scanned the contents: inky type-written documents attached to blue carbon paper, old photographs and tissue paper parcels bound with string. The Wedgewood blue of a carefully folded uniform peeked out from beneath.

Alfred stared into the box. He swallowed, then turned his gaze to the window, then to the sky. Finally, he looked at me.

'I haven't opened this box in forty-five years,' he said. He was clearly nervous.

'Why? Were you frightened to open it?'

'No, no. Ashamed. Believe me, if it was just a question of fear, I would have thrown it out decades ago. This box is a reminder.'

'A reminder of what?'

214

He reached hesitantly inside, retrieving a large black and white photograph. He passed it to me with a look of resignation.

'Of them.'

A group of young men, smiling, laughing, arms outstretched and interlocked, posed in flight suits in front of the *So Long Betty*. Alfred, tall and impossibly young, stood at the centre of the line, his strong shoulders almost appearing to hold his crewmates up. He pointed to the small man at the end – blond and freckled, a gap-toothed smile dimpling his face. His suit, which ballooned out with heavy padding, made him look child-like.

'That's Eric. Eric Tanner. He was the youngest of all of us. Just a boy, really. Just a boy.' The old man's eyes moved to the window again, then back to the photograph.

'Eric died more than seventy years ago. Nearly eighty years – a lifetime. But I have seen him practically every day since.'

'He's haunting you? Why?'

'He's tormenting me, young man. And rightly so, considering. I let him down, and then… well, he had every right to want to ruin my life.'

'And this has been going on since World War II?'

'Since May 1943. The day after Easter Sunday, to be precise.'

I looked at the young, carefree face in the picture. 'Have you seen him today?'

Alfred sat back. 'Before I answer that – and I will, I assure you – I think it would be better if I told you the full story, right from the start.' He waved limply at the chair opposite. I sat and watched as he gathered his words.

'Your first thoughts,' the old man said, 'and perhaps your last after I've finished my story, may well be that I'm mad, or traumatised, or suffering from some grand delusion. Believe me, that was my first thought as well and, after a while, my hope too. I think my situation would be much easier to cope with if it were classified as mental illness. But this isn't PTSD, and it's not dementia.'

His eyes scanned the bookshelves. 'I've spent decades trying to understand, to cope, to... redeem myself. Seventy years looking for answers which I probably knew from the start I would never find. How could I? My poor wife, Dulcie, lived with this obsession. She took me for my word when I told her, truthfully, what was happening to me. And yet she never saw him, not once – but she trusted me, because she believed I was being completely honest with her. But I wasn't. I couldn't be. All those years. She died not knowing.'

'Not knowing what?'

'Who he was. I never told her who he was.' Again, Alfred turned his eyes to the window.

'Why didn't you tell her that?'

He reached across, gently took the picture from me and studied it, his fingers running across its front. 'I couldn't. I just couldn't.'

His old eyes fell on me. He spoke in a whisper.

'Young man, if I could tell you one thing, if I could pass on one piece of advice it would be to find someone to love and cherish them. Find someone to put in a picture frame.'

The room fell quiet.

I took out my phone and placed it on the table. 'Alfred, would you like to tell me about it? From the beginning, like you said?'

His eyes drifted up. 'For your book?' His voice was distant. 'Perhaps it's right that I should be in a book, to help someone else like me.'

'I promise to do you justice, to tell your story responsibly.'

His old face creased into a soft smile. 'I know, young man, of course. I sense I can trust you. I know a fellow traveller when I meet one.' His gaze returned to the books. 'You can have these, all of these, when I'm gone. Carry on the journey.'

'I thought you wanted that birthday card from the Queen.'

He gave a weary chuckle. 'I think I've had enough birthday cards. It's time to set the record straight.'

We sat in silence, for perhaps five minutes, as Alfred studied the picture. Eventually, he spoke in a whisper, as if to himself.

'You know, these were the closest friends I ever had, yet I didn't really know them at all. We never met before the war; we were strangers. We were just sort of thrown together – all the bomber crews were. Actually, we picked each other – the top brass told us to sort ourselves into crews. So, the only thing we had in common was youth, and the kind of blind, dumb courage that comes with it. But we looked out for each other.'

He rested the photograph in his lap. 'We had our own corner at the Otter – the little pub near the base – where we used to drink the night before raids. The barmaid was called Betty; she was brassy and funny and just what everyone needed. She kept us all in line, made us laugh, helped us forget the war. Every single man on the base adored her – but she only had eyes for Eric. They were quite the couple. He called her "my Betty" whenever anyone got too pally with her. We used to tease her, on the eve of a mission, when closing time came. Gallows humour, I'm afraid. She would tell us all to come back in one piece, and we would all chorus "*So long, Betty – see you on the other side*". We said she was our lucky charm.'

He looked up at me. 'Tell me, did you go onboard the *So Long Betty*?'

'No. I never thought to ask.'

'Shame. I think you would have been surprised. Lancasters are big planes, but on the inside, they're cramped and compact – claustrophobic even. There's so much equipment there's barely room for the crew. Seven men, each with a job: pilot, engineer, bomb aimer, navigator, the wireless man and the two gunners on the top and at the rear, each squeezed in, jammed between all the wires and gizmos and gadgets. Sometimes, when we were in the air, and all in our places, and the whole plane was throbbing with the engines, it felt like we were her internal organs, actually part of her – we were her brain, her eyes, her ears, her teeth, her claws. That's what it was like on that night in 1943. More than a hundred Lancasters in the sky, a great armada of bombers, but all that mattered was what was happening inside your own plane, with your people.'

Outside, the morning sun had shifted to cast shadows across the room. Alfred wet his lips and went on.

'We took off at night, heading for Duisburg in the Ruhr. Industrial targets, this time. We had a little escort from some Hurricanes over the Channel, but then when we reached land we were on our own, flying over occupied Europe. I remember the moon was surprisingly bright, and we all prayed for cloud cover. We were going to be in the air for six hours there and back, most of which you spent with your eyes peeled looking for enemy fighters, so moonlight made you feel like a sitting duck.

'Everyone was on edge, trying to concentrate on their job. But it was so cold, I remember that. At 25,000 feet the temperature can drop to as low as -40. It can give you frostbite, freeze your fingers, burn the cheeks on your face. But that night seemed even colder than usual.

'Eric, as the rear gunner, had the worst of that. The rear gun position is pretty much outside the plane – the gunner sits in a glass bubble with a steel blast door behind his back – so any small protection from the cold that the rest of us got, or warmth from equipment, never reached him. Eric wore a thick, heated electric suit, which plugged into the plane, but even that struggled to keep you warm at that altitude. You know, he used to smear his face with goose fat to stop it from freezing up? It was a lonely job. So, one of the things I did was talk to him all the time, over the comms, to keep him alert and remind him that the rest of us were still with him.'

The old man shifted on his chair.

'We were around two hours into the mission when it happened. Billy Elkes, the top gunner, spotted the German fighters. Messerschmitts. I remember there was real fright in his voice because there were so many of them, they just appeared out of nowhere. And they just come tearing into us. Billy and Eric opened up their guns, three-second bursts, trying not to waste rounds, but these fighters were everywhere, and so quick, so nimble compared to a Lancaster. I remember thinking that I knew what an animal feels like when it's set upon by a pack of wolves or lions – all we could do was keep going, keep lumbering on, and hope the gunners would see them off, be our teeth, be our claws… but… we didn't know that these were new Messerschmitts, with a new weapon. An upward-firing canon.'

Alfred swallowed. His hand gently gripped the side of the box in front of him. He closed his eyes.

'One of them got underneath us, where we were unprotected. He opened up this canon. It was brutal, so fast, so loud. Suddenly bullets just erupted from our feet, ripping everything, bouncing everywhere. I looked to my right and the engineer, Harry, who usually knelt at my side to watch his instruments, he'd taken one from below and it had come out of his shoulder, his neck. He was dead. Behind him Hamish, the navigator, was squirming with one in his belly and he had blood running down his face; Dick Simmons, the wireless operator, was behind me and was unhurt, but I could hear him screaming, panicking, and kicking about… but our guns were still firing, so I knew Eric and Billy were still alive and fighting on, giving it all they had. Claws and teeth. The whole plane was rocking from side to side, and filled with the smell of burning, of hot metal, and I knew the German fighters would be banking to come back at us again.'

The old man gulped.

'Then I heard a dreadful gurgling from my feet, from poor Charlie Draycott. Charlie was the bomb aimer, and his position was underneath the nose, lying on his belly, but I needed – we needed – him to climb up and man the front guns, the big Nash and Thompsons but… well, I leant forward and I strained my neck to look down to him, but I could just see… just see blood on the inside of the glass, so much blood, and the sound of Charlie gurgling softly… he was saying something, pleading or praying or… then there was a deafening roar and a Messerschmitt screamed up in front of my cockpit, all its guns firing, its wings spread out like a bloody great crucifix, and rounds ripped through us again, but this time across, Dick screaming his lungs out, thrashing about. I remember Harry's body fell forward onto the throttles and then… then… the plane started to go. I saw the needles on three of the four engine dials just slowly glide from right to left, from alive to dead, and looked out to see the props splutter and stall as smoke poured out. Harry's position, where all the engine controls were, was smashed to bits. And then her nose just lurched downwards, as if we had been grabbed by a great hook, pulled towards the ground. We went down so fast, so heavy, like a lead weight. I looked up and I could see the other planes moving away above, like boats on the surface of a lake and we're sinking, diving, falling and then there was the ground, a million trees racing up at us.'

He looked at me. 'I don't know how I did it, really, I don't. I was never considered a particularly good pilot, just run of the mill, one of the crowd… I think it was just instinct, self-preservation.'

Alfred's old hands curled around an invisible wheel.

'I pulled back on the con column, just pulled and pulled, and I pushed the one engine we still had – that bloody beautiful Merlin – and somehow, somehow I pulled her up from the dive.'

Alfred exhaled slowly. He shook his head. 'I loathe the term "Miracle Mission" but if there was a miracle that night it wasn't that we made it home, it was that we didn't crash.'

I realised I was staring, my mouth hanging open. 'I can't even imagine what it must have been like. I saw the holes in the plane.'

'She was like a colander,' he said, 'in shreds, really, and she was rattling and flapping, everything shaken loose by the dive. The guns were spent, Eric and Billy had fired every round we had. Billy climbed down and saw Harry lying there. Then he checked on Charlie below, but he was dead, shot to pieces. Dick had quietened down but was curled up on his seat, mumbling to himself, completely out of it, and Hamish, the navigator, was holding his stomach now, breathing heavily. We agreed that we should grab the parachutes from the back of the fuselage and bail out.'

Alfred's eyes rested on the box.

'Then there was this dull bang, a thud, from the back of the plane. From the rear turret. From the blast door. From Eric. We had forgotten about Eric. I pulled my mask across my face and spoke to him. I said:

'"*Eric, Eric, are you alright?*"

'There was no reply, just static in my headgear… then another dull thud against the other side of the blast door.

'"*Eric, are you hit? Can you hear me?*"

'Billy moved to the rear and tried to open the door. He said, "*It's stuck fast, looks like it's been shot up.*"

'Somehow, the *Betty*'s fuselage had bent around the door – maybe it was German bullets, maybe it was the velocity of the dive or the G-force as we pulled up, but the frame of the door was warped, twisted. It wouldn't open. Billy grabbed tools from Harry's engineer position and started work. I tried again.

'"*Eric, can you hear me?*"

'This time, I heard him, weak and quiet.

'"*I'm here, Alfie old chum,*" he said.

'"*Eric, are you hit? We're trying to open the door.*"

'"*Waste of time, I'm afraid. It's a gonner. All bent out of shape on this side.*" He sounded breathless.

'"*Are you hit, Eric?*"

'More static.

'"*No, no, not me. But the glass is all smashed. Bit nippy back here, old chum.*"

'"*Billy's working on the door, Eric, we're going to get to you.*"

'"*Jolly good,*" he said. "*Jolly good.*"

'"*As soon as Billy gets through that door we're going to have to bail out, Eric. We'll get a parachute to you.*"

'"*Good old Billy. What about the others?*"

'"*I'm afraid Harry and Charlie bought it.*"

'"*Oh… and Dick, Hamish?*"

'"*They're still with us.*"

'"*Good-o,*" he said. "*Jolly good.*"

'Static flared up in my ears, and the lights flickered.

'"*Eric, are you still there?*"

'Silence.

'Then he said, "*I am. Still here. Bit chilly, old chum. Suit's not working. No power.*"

'I pulled the mask away and shouted back, "*Billy, how's that door? Will it open?*"

'A tool clanked across the floor. "*No good. Stuck fast. Won't budge.*"

'I told Eric.

'"*I know, that's what I was trying to tell you,*" he said, "*it's a goner. It's worse on this side.*"

'Hamish and I looked at each other. There was no way to get to Eric. Billy reappeared, shaking his head, clutching parachutes. Thank God for Hamish. He was from Aberdeen and used to tell us he was made of granite. He was that night. He really was.

'Without a word, he took a parachute from Billy, pulled it open and tore away a strip of silk – then started to bind the wound in his gut, tighter and tighter. The decision went unspoken. We weren't going to bail out and leave Eric to go down on his own, not while the *Betty* was still flying.

'Then, Hamish began plotting a route home, getting us to the Channel as quickly as possible but trying to avoid populated areas. We would have to fly low, you see, because we couldn't risk climbing on one engine and we were slow too and noisy as hell. But Billy, Hamish and I knew what we had to do.

'I spoke to Eric again: "*Eric, Hamish has a plan. We're going home.*"

'"*Not bailing out?*"

222

'"*No. We're going home.*"

'"*I think you're all mad.*"

'"*I think you're right – but that's the plan. We'll try to get the power back to your suit.*"

'There was a pause, then he said, "*No good, old chum. Circuit's broken on this side. I can see it. The wire's gone, clean through.*"

'"*Well, we're heading home, so you'll just have to hang on.*"

'"*I don't think I've got much choice, old chum.*"

'So, Billy stowed poor Harry's body down below with Charlie, and I turned the *Betty* round to head home.

'After a while, Eric said, "*Do me a favour, Alfie, talk to me. It's frightfully cold. Never been this cold. Would take my mind off it.*"

'So, I talked to Eric. I just talked at him, really, for the entire flight. I told him about what we would do when we got back, about the reception that would be waiting for us, how we would go for a pint, into Grimsby to a dance, about how Betty was waiting for him, about the motorcycle I wanted to buy, how I'd let him have a go on it… and all the time he'd just reply quietly, "*That's nice, jolly good.*"

'Then, just as we could see the moon on the Channel ahead, he suddenly said, "*It's no good, Alfie. Think I've had it. It's so very cold back here. Can't think.*"

'I said, "*Come on now, Eric.*"

'"*I want you to promise to look after Betty,*" he said.

'I'm afraid I lost my temper with him. I said, "*Now look here, that's enough of that, you stupid bastard! We're nearly there, we're at the water, just hold on and keep talking. We've got our whole lives ahead of us, and I'm blasted if I'm going to spend mine without you. You're my friend and that's the way it's going to be, so I don't want to hear any more of this rot.*"

'Eric went quiet. Then he said, "*What will our lives be like, Alfie, after all this? Tell me about that.*"

'So, I carried on talking to him. I told him how he'd marry Betty and I'd find a sweetheart too, we'd celebrate the end of the war together with a huge party, then how we'd find jobs together, maybe start a business, buy homes near one another, send our children to the same school, spend Christmases, holidays together; and he listened and said things like: "*Yes, I like that*" and "*Sounds wonderful.*" That wasn't enough, though, I wanted to keep him talking. I promised we'd be friends always and I made him promise me back.

'By now I knew we weren't far from home and the sun would soon come up.

'Then Hamish, who had been quiet for a while, said, "*Alfred, there's something we need to do. We need to get rid of the bombs, we can't land like this with them beneath us. I think we can make it to Binton, but for all we know the landing gear's shot and we could blow up the entire base if we still have this lot in the bay.*"

'I turned around and he was as white as a sheet, with a big red stain on his belly. Billy was next to him, grim-faced. I knew he was right, of course, I should have thought about it earlier – but the problem was, while I could open the doors to the bomb bay, the release button was down in the nose of the *Betty*, under my feet, where poor Charlie and Harry were. Someone would have to go down there and press it.

'Hamish held up a blood-soaked hand and said, "*I'm afraid I'm no use, now. Sorry.*"

'Then this voice came from behind me: "*I'll do it.*" It was Dick.

'I said to him, "*Are you sure, Dickie, do you know what to do?*"

'He squeezed past me and crouched at the entry to the turret. He said, "*I've been listening to you talking to Eric. Sorry I lost it, boys. I'll do it – but you'll need to climb a little first. We're too low to drop the bombs.*"

'He was right. We were flying very low now over the Channel – and dropping the bombs onto water from that speed would have been like dropping them onto concrete anyway. So, we'd have to risk the strain on the engine to get a little higher. Hamish and Billy nodded in agreement.

224

'I spoke to Eric. I said, "*Eric old chum, I'm going to go quiet for a short while because we've got to get rid of these bombs, and we're going to have to climb a bit, so you may want to hold on. It'll get a little colder, I'm afraid. Then we'll be home and dry.*"

'In a very faint voice, he said, "*I understand.*"

'So, we went for it. I pulled the *Betty* up as high as I could, with the Merlin screaming all the way, and managed to level her off at about 2,000 feet. She was shaking apart. Dick crawled down into the bomb aimer's position, climbing past Harry and Charlie, and then he shouted, "*Open bomb doors!*" I pulled the lever; he pressed the button and we ditched all of the bombs into the Channel. There was an almighty bang, but the *Betty* was instantly more stable, lighter. I eased her down low to the water again and closed the bomb doors, as Dickie climbed back up. I remember he put a hand on Hamish's shoulder as he took his seat – and then the sun's rays suddenly streamed into the cockpit, colouring everything yellow. Everything warm. I put my mask back on.

'I said, "*Eric old chum. The sun's up. The sun's up!*"

Gently, the old man raised his hands to his head.

'There was no answer,' he said. 'Just static. Just static.'

He looked across the living room to the window, to the sky.

'We flew the rest of the way in silence, Dick and Billy with their arms around Hamish. The *Betty* got us to Binton, as Hamish had predicted, and when we landed there was a great rush of men and vehicles to us at the end of the field. I was in a daze, exhausted. I remember the ladders came up and then there were men on the wings, silhouettes in the morning sun, pulling the glass back, helping us out, talking to us, lifting Hamish up. Then I started to climb down a ladder and looked out across at this mass of people running about – and my heart almost burst. There he was. Eric. Among the ground crew, my friend Eric standing perfectly still in the sunlight, looking up at me. Relief washed over me. *He made it*, I thought, *he made it*. I raised my hand to wave. But then there were shouts below, frantic activity, and a group of men scurried out from under the tail. They were carrying a body. It was Eric, frozen. Dead. I looked to where he had been standing. Of course, he wasn't there. That was the first time.'

*

'The next morning, I woke and dressed. Billy, Dick and I were due for a debrief with Group Captain Winters. I went down the stairs from my digs and out onto the airfield, which was deserted. It was a bright day and there wasn't a cloud in the sky. More Lancasters had come in during the night and were lined up outside the hangar. In the far distance, at the end of the field, the *Betty* was in the long grass, with ladders still up to her wings. I remember sucking in the air deeply, as I looked across at the low hills beyond, towards the sea, then… I saw a figure. Distant. Still. He was black against the sky. I knew he was looking at me. I blinked, rubbed my eyes. Still there. Standing in an awkward, stooped stance, like a scarecrow. It was Eric, I knew it was Eric. I felt panic rise in me.

'I rushed across the road and into the main offices, and into the waiting room outside Captain Winters' office. Billy and Dick were already there, smoking their pipes, chatting quietly. His secretary was making a tray of tea for the meeting. The boys saw, straight away, how agitated I was, and they were on their feet, calming me down, talking to me. I didn't tell them. I wasn't even sure if I was awake.

'We were called in. I sat in a daze at the back of the office, as Winters questioned us about the mission. The other two chaps did all the talking. I couldn't think straight. Then my eyes wandered to the window. Across the road. He was there. Eric. Looking in, looking at me. I felt panic rising again. I must have shut my eyes. I heard Winters say, "*Are you alright, Trowton?*" He, and Billy and Dick, were staring at me too now, with real concern. I stood, shakily, and said, "*Sorry, sir, I feel a little peculiar,*" and then I

226

lunged for the door, grabbing at it clumsily, rattling it, pulling it to get out to run, to breathe, pulling and pulling and pulling but it wouldn't budge... then suddenly the handle slipped from my hand, it swung away from me, opening – and Winters' secretary was there, white-faced, a tray of tea in her hands. She bit her lip. I gawped into her confused face, then away in embarrassment. Over her shoulder Eric stared at me with dead eyes. I screamed. The tray fell to the floor.'

Alfred shook his head, slowly. He said, 'That was just the start. Every time I see him, it feels like part of me dies. My skin bristles, the pit of my stomach falls away, I catch my breath. Something inside me crumbles... and I'm reminded of what I did.'

Alfred put the photograph back in the box and replaced the lid.

I asked, 'And you kept seeing him?'

'Every day. At first, I thought I was going mad. I saw him everywhere. At Harry and Charlie's funerals. At the graveside. As their coffins were lowered into the ground, his gaze never shifted from me. I saw him on the base, on the road to the village – everywhere. Sometimes just yards away, sometimes a distant figure; always recognisable. When the men from Pathé News were filming us all in front of the *Betty*, Eric was standing behind the camera. Watching me. Judging me.'

'And you told no one?'

'Goodness no. Back then, the medics would add "LMF" to a patient's file. Lack of Moral Fibre – that's how they would explain an airman losing his nerve. They put my reaction in Winters' office down to exhaustion. There was no way I was going to tell anyone what was really happening. It would have been straight off to the funny farm. I had to live with it.

'Then, inevitably, people started to talk about my erratic behaviour. I was taken off active service, but all the publicity surrounding the mission meant they couldn't put me out to pasture. I found myself on flight training. Only Dick and

227

Billy ever flew on bombing raids again. Hamish was too badly wounded.'

'And did anyone else ever see Eric?'

'Yes, thankfully, but rarely. That's what made me accept I wasn't going ga-ga. Sometimes in the hangar, people would spot him, and always when I was there. But while I could see him as bold as day, I realised that they would just catch him, for just a moment, like a blur, in the corner of their eye. No one else ever recognised who he was. So, we ended up with ghost stories at the base. But it wasn't the base. It was me. He wanted me.'

I leant forward. 'I don't understand why you believe this is about revenge. You could have bailed out. You all risked your lives to get him home alive.'

'Yes, but we didn't, did we?' he said quietly. 'And he was my responsibility. I was in command. That's why he left Dick, Hamish and Billy alone. There were so many mistakes that night – my mistakes. I allowed us to stray too far from the rest of the squadron, to fall behind, so we could be picked off. After we turned for home, I should have thought about ditching the bombs and I should have known that last climb would... *I should have known*. Most of all, I should have kept talking to Eric – I promised I would keep talking. All I needed to do was keep talking. I have spent seventy years going over that night, over and over again. I know I let him down.'

He pushed the box away, wearily. 'But it's worse than that. Much worse. First of all, there was all the coverage, the news stories, all that rot about us being heroes. It was deeply shameful. We cocked up. I cocked up. They called me a hero, and I never corrected them. The truth was very different: I was a bomber pilot who got half his crew killed, turned back and dropped his bombs in the sea... But even that pales next to my real betrayal of Eric.'

The old man straightened a little in his chair, his eyes sweeping the bookshelves. He composed himself.

'Tell me, Joe, are you familiar with the Chinese concept of Yin Yang? In Japan, they call it *in-yō*.'

'No, please... tell me about it.'

'Well, Yin Yang is a very ancient way of looking at life, at balance. It's about aligning earth and heaven, good and bad, dark and light, male and female, calm and anger, death and life – you get the picture.'

I nodded. He went on. 'Like a lot of very old philosophy, you can find echoes of it in science – Newton's Third Law, for example: For every action, there is an equal and opposite reaction. Or matter and dark matter. Practically everything in the universe has an opposite and, for the most part, they seek balance. But life never finds that balance, that is the nature of being. I think that, on that night, my life struck an unnatural balance – it touched two opposing points – and I have been paying for it ever since.'

'What do you mean?'

'Eric's death was simultaneously the worst thing that ever happened to me and the best thing that ever happened to me.'

Slowly, Alfred stood and reached to the nearest bookshelf. He selected a framed picture of Dulcie, which he inspected tenderly before handing to me. He sank back into the chair as I looked at her young face.

'I became something of a recluse after the mission,' he said. 'I rarely left the base, stayed away from the village, never ventured into Grimsby and I just couldn't face the Otter. I couldn't bear the thought of seeing Betty, with *him* staring at me over her shoulder. Then, through Dick, Betty sent me a message. Said she wanted to see me. So, I plucked up the courage to go to the pub, and we sat outside on a bench. Eric didn't put in an appearance. Betty told me that she was worried about me, that she had heard people talking about how I'd changed after the mission.'

He smiled to himself. 'She was her usual, brilliant, bossy self. She told me that I was lucky to be alive, and that I was wasting the opportunity that I had been given. She said that it was time to start living again. Then she looked me straight in the eyes and told me that we were going to Grimsby, to the pictures, for a night out. She had arranged for one of her friends to meet us there and that we would have a laugh and forget about everything. She wouldn't take "no" for an answer. In the end, I agreed, as long as we wouldn't see some awful war film. She said we would go to see *Meet Me in St Louis*, with Judy Garland, all colour and songs and pretty girls.

'That night, Billy drove us to Grimsby and left us outside the Odeon waiting for Betty's friend to arrive. I had never been so nervous; it was worse than before a raid. We waited and waited, and it started to rain, but she didn't show up. So, we went to the box office, but we had missed the start of *Meet Me in St Louis*, and the only other thing showing was *Arsenic and Old Lace*, with Carry Grant – which was the exact opposite of a Judy Garland picture! A silly, black and white farce about murderous old ladies. She said, "That'll do!" and bought the tickets before I could protest.'

Alfred wiped his eyes. 'It was wonderful. Riotous. We laughed and laughed. Do you know it?'

'I do,' I said. 'Frank Capra. It must have been just what you needed.'

'It was – for both of us. All the way through the movie, Grant calls everyone "darling", in that ridiculous transatlantic accent of his. It made us roar. We came out calling each other "darling", calling the usherette "darling", the bus driver. It became a bit of a private joke between us.'

He reached out and took the picture from me, cupping it in both hands as he spoke. 'But more passed between us that night, a realisation, a connection. I had always loved Betty – just like everyone who went into the Otter – but as we sat, laughing in the dark in that cinema, I fell *in love* with Betty. It came across me almost like a breeze. I felt it happening. As we climbed onto the bus across the road from the Odeon, I saw him – Eric –

230

silhouetted, standing by the cinema doors, watching us. But it was too late because she felt it too. We both knew. I sat up the whole night thinking about her.'

He carefully placed the frame on the table. 'The next day I went to her, and I proposed. She knew that what had happened to Eric had affected me deeply – more than Harry and Charlie – and asked if that would have a bearing on us if we married. She had been *his* girl. *His* Betty. I told her I had two questions for her, both difficult to answer: "Do you want to marry me, and will you use your middle name, Dulcie, from now?"'

He blinked lovingly at the photograph. 'She thought for a second and said, "*Alfie, I do, and I will. But you can always call me Darling.*"'

The memory seemed to make Alfred glow with happiness. Abruptly, his mood darkened. 'So you see, he has every reason to want to punish me. I caused his death, then I took his girl. I stole his life. I married Dulcie – I never called her Betty again – two months later. At the church, as we came out after the ceremony, he was there, among the gravestones, watching. From that day to this, I have seen him constantly. Seven decades. Any happy occasion – parties, Christmases, reunions – he would be there, torturing me.'

'And you told her about him?'

'Yes, but not who he was, for obvious reasons. I don't think she really believed me at first, but she came to believe it, and she helped me deal with it. I owe my life to her. Because of her I learned how to get on with things, to get back on track. There were three people in our marriage – one of whom was dead – but we had a good life. I have Dulcie to thank for that.'

I looked at the bookshelves. 'And all this was to try to make sense of it?'

'Yes, and to try to resolve it. To talk to him. I tried everything, all manner of nonsense and rituals. In all these years he has never averted his eyes from me, never changed his expression. Never uttered a word.'

The room had grown darker now, the sun slipping behind clouds. Alfred knitted his fingers together.

'So, young man, what do you think? Am I a mad old fool?'

I reached and stopped the recorder on my phone. 'It's an incredible story, Alfred, and I believe you. It's funny... *Arsenic and Old Lace*... what would you say the theme of that film is?'

He looked puzzled. 'I haven't the faintest idea,' he said. 'Madness and murder?'

'I would say that it's "even the nicest people have the darkest secrets".'

He chuckled. 'Have you any more questions?'

'Just one. Have you seen him today? You said you would tell me.'

'Ah yes,' he said, struggling to his feet. He reached out and gently took my hand, then led me towards the big bay window. 'Eric has been standing, looking through this window the entire time you have been here – in fact for a couple of hours beforehand too.'

As we arrived at the window, Alfred waved his arm broadly. 'Joe, this is Eric.'

There was no one there. I turned to the old man. 'So where exactly...'

Alfred was frozen, his eyes wide, his mouth open. '*Holy Christ!*' he muttered.

'What is it? What's wrong?'

His old face turned in the sunlight. 'He's looking... at you!'

*

Alfred Trowton stood, transfixed.

I said, 'Alfred? What's he doing? Where is he?'

The old man's gaze jerked towards me. 'What? What? Oh, he's here – right in front of me, but...' his head tilted in amazement, 'he's looking at you. Not me. He's never done that before! Never!' He whispered, 'Eric? Eric – can you hear me?'

I watched as his eyes wandered down the window – and then widened. Instinctively, he gripped my arm, unsteady on his feet. He croaked, '*Holy Christ.*'

'What? What? What's happening?'

'His arm is moving. He's moving his arm!'

'What's he doing with...'

'He's reaching – he's reaching across to you.' Alfred's finger hovered, following the movement of the invisible hand, as he squeezed my arm harder.

'To me? What does he want?'

'I don't know... I don't know...'

Thut.

The soft sound of a palm padded against the glass.

Alfred's drawn face turned to me. 'It's there,' he said, his trembling fingertips almost touching the window directly in front of me. 'His hand is there. Against the glass. He's still looking at you. Joe, this is incredible!'

'What does he want?'

'I don't know. I think he wants you, Joe.'

Patience's words came back to me: '*You need to be careful who you let in.*'

'What shall I do?'

'I don't know, I don't know! Can you respond?'

'You mean touch him?'

'Yes! Anything!'

'I don't think that's wise...'

'Please, Joe! Please!' He grabbed my arm with both hands. 'Seventy years! Seventy years!'

I looked at the glass in front of me and slowly raised my hand. Alfred's shaking fingers stretched out, guiding me as I reached forward.

'There,' he whispered. 'Just there.'

I felt the coolness of the glass touch under my fingertips – one, two, three, four – then nervously looked at Alfred.

He bit his lip, then nodded.

I pressed my palm down.

The air crackled. Across the surface of the glass, from my wrist, a sheen of speckled light spread out, as if a great breath had been expelled on it, expanding and rippling and refracting like water on ice, revealing a different daylight beyond, a greyer sky, a darker world. And there he was, his hand outstretched to mine, his unblinking eyes looking through me, his shoulders hunched. Eric Tanner was frozen solid, his mouth open and lip slack, his perfect teeth dull like stones, his great stuffed flight suit stiff and solid. He didn't move.

'I… I… I can see him,' I stammered.

'Holy Christ,' Alfred said.

Suddenly, from above our heads, came the sound of white noise, of hissing, buzzing electricity, of static dancing in the ether. I felt Alfred squeeze my arm again.

The sound fizzed and spluttered, phasing in and out as if moving across bandwidths. Then, like a dial had been turned up, a voice surfaced, thin and scratchy, crackling through a metallic mouthpiece. It said, '*Hello? Hello? Hello?*'

I looked at the lifeless face. His lips were not moving. He stared back.

The voice came again: '*Hello? Hello?*'

I swallowed and spoke: 'Hello?'

The static fizzed, as if stabbed by my words.

'*Who's that?*' The voice was youthful, assertive.

'I'm Joe. Joe Baxter. Is that Eric?'

'*That's not right,*' the voice said. '*No, that's not right. Where is he? Is he there?*'

Alfred's eyes were searching the air above his head. His chin dropped as he looked back to the window. 'I'm here, Eric. I'm here.'

Slowly, as if he were underwater, the young pilot's expressionless stare detached from me, then slid down, down, down to rest on the old man's face.

'I'm here,' Alfred repeated.

Suddenly, the temperature plummeted, ice cutting through the air, biting at my skin. The cloud of static above us moved and shifted, bloating and contracting as Alfred's words soaked into it. I could feel him trembling now, his frail shoulders rising and falling as his breath puffed out in clouds of white mist. The noise dipped to a muted hum, as if considering its response, choosing its words. We both waited.

'Hello, old chum,' the voice said. '*Sorry about the radio silence. Can you hear me?*'

Alfred threw his hands onto the glass. 'Oh, Eric, I'm sorry, I'm so sorry!' he said. The static above us fizzed with emotion.

The voice came back quiet and distant: '*Quite alright, old chum. Quite alright. What went wrong?*'

Alfred began to weep. 'What went wrong? It was all my fault, Eric, all my fault.'

The static danced. '*Not at all. You did your best, I'd say... we all did. The others agree.*'

He wiped his eyes. 'Others?'

'*Harry, Charlie, Hamish, Dickie, Billy. They all agree. Did your best. We were just boys, old chum.*'

'But... but... where are you? Are you with them?'

'*Not sure, really. Can't really say. But I kept my promise, didn't I?*'

'Promise?'

'*To stay with you... to share our lives...*' The room crackled loudly, as if injected with new energy.

'But I thought you were angry!'

'*No, old chum, just can't seem to do anything else. Sort of... stuck. Like that bloody door. It's still stuck, you know. Still stuck...*'

'But why didn't you tell me?'

'*Couldn't speak. Too far away. Or too close. Frozen. It's frightfully cold here, old chum. Bloody suit.*'

'I'm so sorry, Eric, so sorry...'

'*What for?*'

Alfred pounded his fist feebly on the glass.

'Such a waste of life,' he said. 'I stole your life.'

'*No,*' the voice came back. '*You shared your life with me. It was a good life.*'

The old man nodded. 'It was. It was. A good life.'

Then he looked up into his friend's cold face. 'I didn't know, Eric, I didn't know. It's all been a misunderstanding.'

'*Crossed wires?*'

'Yes, crossed wires… but now I think I understand. I should have trusted you. Don't leave me now, Eric, stay with me, it won't be for long.'

'*Of course, old chum. A promise is a promise…*' the voice said, '*and you kept yours too.*'

'My promise? What promise?'

'*To look after Betty, my Betty. Our Betty. I'm very grateful.*'

Alfred looked at me, his ancient eyes red and alive with realisation.

'Betty? Is she there? Can I see her? Can I speak to her? Dulcie?'

Eric's voice came back softly: '*That's not how it works, old chum.*'

The old pilot nodded.

'*But she does have a message for you. She says, "So long, Darling – see you on the other side."*'

Slowly, the hand slipped from the glass.

*

I left Alfred Trowton that night, in good spirits. After the drama of the day, he told me he fancied a pint at the Tame Otter. He hoped to see an old friend there.

TWENTY-ONE

Memento Mori

As the dead watched down from their gallery above, his fat, wet fingers, their ends glistening smooth with charcoal, pushed aside another face. It slid silently from the table to the floor. He blindly reached for another sheet – more to do, always more to do – but he groped at air.

Remember me. Remember me.

The paper was gone. There would be no more until the morning. But he had not finished! Now his fingers were on his cheeks, dragging downwards, trailing black stripes that weaved into his thick beard. He must continue; they were not quiet. The voices pleaded.

Remember me.

Now he heaved his huge body from the plastic chair, shoulders piercing the ring of lamplight that surrounded the table. Moving to the bed, he dropped clumsily to his knees. A furtive glance to the locked door. Then he reached behind the hanging sheets and slid the cardboard box from its hiding place. Quickly, the lid was up; he clutched paper, precious paper. The box was shoved back into the dark. The old documents tight in his fists, his wet lips let out a sigh of relief. It didn't matter that the paper had writing on it. He could continue.

Again, they pleaded.

Remember me. *Remember me.* Remember me.

'I will, will,' he muttered as he returned to the table, sinking with a thump into the chair and reaching for charcoal. He stacked the typewritten papers to one side, and slid the top sheet onto the table, hand poised to draw, to remember.

Now the voices fell, a shower of mournful pleas pouring onto him, imploring him as he waited for a face to emerge, waited to remember. The inky typewritten sheet stared up at him. His eyes scanned the first line.

The voices stopped.

*

Monday, June 5th, 1989

CONFIDENTIAL: Interim report on Joseph Baxter, aged 15, by Dr Leonard Quantrill (LQ), Psychiatric Consultant, Westcroft.

CC: Det Insp Matt Kenny, West Midlands Police; Nicola Robinson, Birmingham Social Services; Dr Esra Sabapathy.

This report has been compiled at the request of West Mids Police, with regards to the incident at Warstone Lane Cemetery, based on discussions with Joseph Baxter, a minor currently in the care of the acute unit at Westcroft.

While the discussions held were primarily to ascertain the mental state of Joseph, and to help guide his treatment (and as such are covered by patient confidentiality) we have agreed to share those elements with the WM Police that may help in their investigation of the incident. Joseph's own psychiatrist, Dr Esra Sabapathy, and his mother, Jeanette Baxter, have consented to this, in the interests of openness.

Note: Joseph was in an extreme manic state when he was found but became withdrawn directly after the incident. This gave way to night terrors and panic attacks in the days that followed, as well as bouts of uncontrollable weeping. Dr Sabapathy's input has also helped us understand that this crying is part of Joseph's emotional make-up; he is a very empathetic child whose emotions are never far from the surface.

He has now begun to respond to the approaches of staff at Westcroft and is starting to open up about the circumstances that led to the event.

While much of what he says is straightforward and has been corroborated by others who were present, I would stress, however, that his explanation of the reasons for his actions that led to the search for Child A (referred to by Joseph only as 'Nipper') are clearly delusional. For the record, on initial analysis, I do not believe he is making this up, rather that he genuinely believes it happened, and that it was a hallucination generated by his subconscious as a result of extreme stress.

Dr Sabapathy has informed us of Joseph's previous fascination with mortality and the occult, although he believes this does not venture any further than fads experienced by many teenagers.

Joseph has also, arguably, displayed some symptoms of what could be ascribed to schizophrenia – he has described hearing voices – but a diagnosis at such a young age is difficult, as other explanations are more likely, not least an overactive imagination or a need for attention.

Most importantly, Dr Sabapathy believes categorically that Joseph's current state of mind is a direct result of the suicide of his father when he was a young boy. This obviously had a tremendous impact on him, and I expect, as his court-appointed clinician, the police to take this into account when dealing with the incident in question. Birmingham Child Services are in full agreement with me on this.

However, for the benefit of the police investigation, I will provide a brief overview of Joseph's explanation of how the children came to be in the catacombs. For the sake of clarity, I will also include a brief excerpt from the transcript of my conversation with him, so you can see the nature of his explanation of what happened to Child A. Be warned: this is the testimony of a child who was clearly very disturbed. I trust this will leave you in no doubt that this is a young man who requires support and understanding, rather than accusations of criminality.

Dr Leonard Quantrill

*

Preceding events:
Joseph explains that he and the three other children involved (Child A, Malcolm Perch and Louise Beestone) had been meeting at the cemetery each Sunday. They were not initially friends, but bonded over shared interests in music and fashion, which was reflected in their choice of meeting place. Child A was the junior of the group by some years.

Joseph explains that while hanging around near the Birmingham catacombs, they discovered a metal service door was open. Their natural inquisitiveness led them inside, however, they found that another internal door – the much older Victorian entrance to the actual burial chambers – was tightly locked. He explains that they then decided to return each weekend to work away at the rotten wood around the lock in an attempt to open the door. All four of the children did this.

He says that on Sunday, after 'chipping away' at the wood all afternoon, they finally gained access to the vaults in the early evening. He, Malcolm Perch and Child A went inside, while Louise Beestone opted to remain outside.

He said inside was a 'very dark and long' corridor, where the left-hand wall was lined with sealed burial vaults, and the other with coffins in niches. He said he was not frightened to be in there. They made their way along the corridor, with Child A leading the way, when they came upon a doorway to a vault where the brickwork had crumbled away, revealing 'hundreds of coffins inside'.

At this point I will defer to a transcript of the conversation.

*

Joseph: Then I heard this noise from the end of the corridor. In the darkness. Past where Nipper was standing.

LQ: What did you hear?

Joseph: It was a moan. Like a deep moan.

LQ: You heard a moan? Did the others?

Joseph: No, Perch said he couldn't hear anything. He was standing behind me – hiding behind me – and Nipper was in front of me, at the doorway to this vault, which was all broken down. Then Perch dared Nipper to go through the hole – into the vault. He was little enough to go through it, you see. But then I heard... I heard the moan again at the end of the corridor, and it sounded closer, it was very clear... but Perch still didn't hear anything. I couldn't understand it. I said we should leave, we should get out, but Perch dared Nipper again, told him to do it, told him he was a chicken, then Nipper said he wasn't and started to climb through the hole and I felt Perch's hand grab

241

my jacket, from behind – he pulled me back, away from the vault... I think he was going to play a trick on Nipper, pretend to leave him there, I don't know. Then I heard the moan again. Really loud this time. From the end of the corridor. But they didn't hear it! They still didn't hear it. I started to get scared, then I saw that Nipper had climbed into the vault through the doorway and gone inside. I shook Perch's hand off my back and shouted, because I knew it wasn't safe, and Nipper stuck his head back through the hole and then...

LQ: Go on, Joseph, go on.

Joseph: Then I saw...

LQ: What did you see?

Joseph: There was a figure. In the dark.

LQ: Where?

Joseph: At the end of the corridor. Past where Nipper was.

LQ: I see. Tell me about it. The figure.

Joseph: Well...

LQ: It's OK, go on.

Joseph: He was big, very tall, and it was a man – but it wasn't a man – he was white, white and smooth all over like stone. Like marble. He was wearing a hood and that was white too. His face was... like it was chiselled, like a statue. His eyes were white, all white, no pupils but I could tell he was looking straight at me... but... it felt like an animal was looking at me, not a man – I can't explain it. I knew then that we shouldn't be there, I knew it. It was like we had woken him up. He moaned again, then he saw Nipper in the doorway between us, and this thing... he growled. He growled like a... God, that sound!

LQ: What did it sound like?

Joseph: Like a... like a beast. I can't explain it any other way. The sound went right through me. The growl. I was so scared. And then he just started to... glide... to glide towards Nipper, with his hands out.... Nipper was looking at me saying 'Where are you going?' – and I heard Perch running away behind me – he was laughing – but I couldn't take my eyes off this thing and it was sliding towards Nipper, so I... so I...

LQ: What did you do, Joseph?

Joseph: I shouted 'It's coming!' and I ran to Nipper and pushed him back into the hole, back into the vault, to protect him, to get him away from this thing, but...

LQ: But?

Joseph: Nipper didn't understand, he looked terrified as I pushed him, and he held onto the doorway and it... it collapsed, the whole wall just gave way, and the roof fell in. Nipper was inside, trapped inside with all those coffins, and there were bricks everywhere. And then I looked up and... it was there. This thing was there – right there, in front of me in the dark, looking at me, as if it was... inspecting me.

LQ: Inspecting you? How do you mean?

Joseph: Like it didn't know what I was. It sniffed the air around me. Then I heard Nipper shouting and screaming from the other side of the wall and then this thing reached out and it touched me, with its finger, and I just flew back along the corridor, like I'd been shoved hard. I landed on my back. When I sat up it was gone.

LQ: What did you do then?

Joseph: I ran back to where Nipper had been and tried to get him out, lifting bricks and stones, digging and digging but it just kept causing more rubble, more collapses.

LQ: And you couldn't find him?

Joseph: No, I looked and looked but I couldn't get through. I looked and I looked, and I was screaming for him and I could hear him crying. I could hear him crying somewhere.

★

Joseph became extremely agitated at this stage, and the conversation was ended.

I am recommending that no further questions are put to him on this matter for at least a week, while he acclimatises to life at Westcroft. I will then reassess the situation with regards to any further questions you may have.

Dr Leonard Quantrill

*

Tuesday, July 4th, 1989

CONFIDENTIAL: Further report on Joseph Baxter, aged 15, by Dr Leonard Quantrill (LQ), Psychiatric Consultant, Westcroft.

CC: Det Insp Matt Kenny, West Midlands Police; Nicola Robinson, Birmingham Social Services; Dr Esra Sabapathy.

Following an enquiry for further information from WM Police, I have held another assessment with Joseph Baxter, as requested.

After one month here, Joseph is settling in satisfactorily at Westcroft, and is experiencing fewer episodes of panic, which occur mainly at night. He is also crying less. I do not, however, believe he is ready to be interviewed by police.

Joseph is adamant that his account of what happened inside the catacombs is entirely accurate – evidence that the delusion is more deeply seated than at first thought. Joseph is an extremely intelligent child, however, and I believe at heart he realises how implausible his story sounds. For that reason, I believe his eventual acceptance that the figure he saw was a hallucination, brought on by extreme stress, will ultimately provide evidence of his improving mental health. The clinical team has identified this as a goal to progress towards through treatment. To put it simply, when he accepts it didn't happen, I believe he will be on the road to recovery.

One interesting development: He has asked on a number of occasions about the wellbeing of Child A, and what happened to him. Having discussed it with his mother and his psychiatrist, we thought it best to be open and frank.

I explained to Joseph that, after the collapse, Child A was lost in the catacombs for five hours, after which he was recovered by emergency workers, and that he is now being cared for. Joseph exhibited great relief to be told this, but soon dissolved into another prolonged period of crying, which I believe was out of sympathy for Child A's predicament.

*

Monday, July 31st, 1989

CONFIDENTIAL: Further update on Joseph Baxter, aged 15, by Dr Leonard Quantrill (LQ), Psychiatric Consultant, Westcroft.

CC: Det Insp Matt Kenny, West Midlands Police; Nicola Robinson, Birmingham Social Services; Dr Esra Sabapathy.

I was pleased to be informed that the Crown Prosecution Service has confirmed that Joseph Baxter will not face criminal charges following the incident at Warstone Lane Cemetery. I understand, however, that part of the discussion that led to that decision was an undertaking by Birmingham Child Services to monitor Joseph's progress here at Westcroft.

Having discussed this with his mother and psychiatrist, I am happy to share updates during his time with us, which I hope will be brief.

Joseph has now been at Westcroft for eight weeks and is settled into a daily routine which has helped him overcome much of the anxiety that he was experiencing when he first arrived.

In terms of his recovery, I can report two major steps forward: he is no longer claiming to hear voices – and now accepts that he most likely never did – and he has expressed deep regret for his behaviour in recent years. I believe he is genuine in that regret.

However, one key target of his treatment has yet to be satisfactorily met. He still insists that his account of what happened in the incident is entirely accurate and was not a hallucination. I will update you further in my next report.

Dr Leonard Quantrill

*

Monday, September 28th, 1989

CONFIDENTIAL: Further update on Joseph Baxter, aged 15, by Dr Leonard Quantrill (LQ), Psychiatric Consultant, Westcroft.

CC: Nicola Robinson, Birmingham Social Services; Dr Esra Sabapathy.

I am pleased to report that Joseph Baxter is making very good progress in his recovery and is now in a considerably better place in terms of his mental health. He no longer suffers from night terrors or claims to hear voices. He is engaged fully with his treatment. He has expressed a wish to go home.

He has also taken up writing while here and had

spoken about his ambition to follow it as a career, perhaps in newspapers.

One hurdle remains: his refusal to acknowledge that his version of events at Warstone Lane Cemetery cannot be accurate. This is a concern, as it calls into question his willingness to fully accept responsibility for his actions, and therefore provides a barrier for his release from Westcroft.

Some on the clinical team have suggested that Joseph now feels unable to admit the truth, out of a misplaced sense of teenage pride.

Having spoken to Dr Sabapathy, it has been decided that we should spell the situation out to Joseph – and tell him that until he accepts that it did not occur as he has described, he will be unable to go home.

A softly, softly approach is best in these circumstances: his mother and a family friend, Mr Fergus Harper, will communicate this to Joseph.

Dr Leonard Quantrill

*

Monday, November 20th, 1989

CONFIDENTIAL: Further update on Joseph Baxter, aged 15, by Dr Leonard Quantrill (LQ), Psychiatric Consultant, Westcroft.

CC: Nicola Robinson, Birmingham Social Services; Dr Esra Sabapathy; Mr Fergus Harper.

I am pleased to say that Joseph Baxter has now left Westcroft, having completed his treatment. Over his six months with us he has grown up a great deal and has now returned home to his mother.

In his final assessment, Joseph went to great

lengths to stress that he no longer believed his initial explanation of the events of six months ago and is embarrassed that he stuck to the story for so long. This was a crucial breakthrough.

Mr Fergus Harper has agreed to be a sponsor for Joseph over the next year and has also arranged for him to do work experience at the *Midland Echo*, which is where his father worked.

I like Joe, who is an intelligent and extremely sensitive and empathetic young man. He has become very popular with the staff here. I am confident that, if he is mindful of his own mental wellbeing and avoids the triggers that led him down the wrong path, he can look forward with confidence.

This will be my final update on Joe's case.

Dr Leonard Quantrill

*

The charcoal still hung over the paper. The dead were quiet. Slowly, and methodically, he began to read the document again, looking for the truth. With shaking hands, he crossed out the lies.

TWENTY-TWO

Deadman's Wood

The Ninth Vigil

I didn't notice at first. The little concrete room was so blank, so empty, so quiet. This had been a long vigil. Sitting in the gloom, my eyes were focused only on the white stone slab, which rose from the centre of the floor on ornate pillars.

As the hours limped by, I had inspected every inch of it: the smooth, bevelled edge, the carved feet, the blue veins in the marble, and the rippled dunes of red dust that lay an inch thick along its length.

That's when I noticed. The dust was only on the slab. There was none anywhere else in the room.

Throughout the rest of the Evergreen building, everything was dusted with a thin coat of it. The floors, the walls, every ledge, every step, everything. But in here, hermetically sealed by the concrete ruin's only surviving door, the dust lay only on the slab. It was like it had all been scooped up and carefully laid there, sprinkled along its length to form a soft, red bed. I squinted and looked closely at its ripples.

The slab wanted to be looked at. How many shoulders had sagged as the sheet was pulled back from it, revealing a loved one laid out, cold and dead, their face made up with living colour, their hair washed and set?

The rusty metal chair creaked softly as I sat further forward to inspect the dust. As I did, a wisp of breeze curled around the back of my neck, lifting hairs and brushing my ear. Air movement. Was that me? My eyes flicked to the heavy door. It was still shut.

Another gentle waft circled my wrist, and again around my collar. Something was happening. I felt fear climb my spine. The air *was* moving.

I looked again at the cushion of dust on the slab. My eyes widened.

Dancing. The fine red grains were dancing, beginning to lift in the moving air, blown swirling in little spirals, rising then falling as the surface shifted and flattened out. Then, with a quiet thud, depressions began to sink into the dust, distinct edges dropping into rounded forms: two smooth, long furrows at the far end of the slab, a circular dent near me, a broad hollow in the centre.

Suddenly, the wind whipped and whistled around the little room, circling the slab. I sat upright as I watched the imprint of a human body take form in the dust.

*

'All woods are haunted. For a very good reason, too... that's how they keep children from getting lost in them,' Martha Craddock said as we weaved between the trees. 'Ghost stories keep them away. The only problem is that for a few kids – and I was one of them – it has the opposite effect. Makes you determined to have a look. To go deeper.'

I said, 'It certainly wouldn't have worked on me.'

The late afternoon sun cut through the forest as we walked, glowing on the silver bark of the young saplings, and wrapping horseshoe haloes around the thick trunks of the old oaks. Despite the cold, it was beautiful. Beneath the long, wet grass the ground felt spongy and uneven.

High above, a crow caw-cawed.

A few paces away Martha, her short grey hair peeking from under the hood of a zipped-up anorak, stepped confidently, delicate old hands occasionally drifting out to steady herself. The only sound was a gentle, pendulous *swish-swish* as her waterproof trousers rubbed together as she strode.

'All of this used to be immaculate,' she said. 'It was all lawns and benches and fountains and trees. I think I prefer it now that it's wild again.'

She stopped and ran her hand down one of the thin saplings. 'These are all new, they've sprung up since the place was abandoned. Taken root with no gardeners about.'

She looked at me as I rested my bag on a clump of thick turf, then tipped her brow towards a distant ridge rising from the forest floor. 'It's not too far now,' she said. 'That's what's left of the wall that surrounded the main building. Completely grown over.'

We began moving again, the bottom of my bag ploughing through the undergrowth.

'It must have been an idyllic place to live,' I said.

'That was the idea. All the way out here, miles from the rat race – retire to the great outdoors they said, spend your autumn years with Mother Nature. Getting back to nature was all the rage at the time. The company was based in California – but this was the first in England. And the last.'

'My friend at the *Mercury* said you worked there when it opened.'

'Until 1975,' she said, squinting into the light. 'I was a nurse. Not an actual nurse, you understand, that's just what we were called back then. I suppose these days I'd be called a care assistant. I was twenty-two years old, a bit of a hippy, and I thought it would be a nice place to work. I grew up around here, on one of the farms on the other side of the valley, so it was local for me, too.'

This didn't surprise me. Martha's well-spoken but matter-of-fact tone had the ring of a rural childhood – all early morning rises and dinner table debates. Even the way she strode through the long grass betrayed her roots. For me, every step was a clumsily planted hazard. The grass seemed to yield for her feet, as if it were propelling her along.

'Anyway,' she went on, 'I thought it would be nice… out in the woods, serving the old folks their tea, listening to their stories. But the place turned bad. I was glad when it was over.'

The sun was sinking lower.

Ahead of us, the twisted iron frame of a bench jutted upwards from a dense bush. Martha approached and gripped the rusting metal in her hand, her eyes inspecting it closely.

'Funny to think I might have sat on this to eat my lunch,' she said.

'It sounds more like a holiday camp than a retirement home,' I said. 'Or a commune.'

'It was an impressive place, very expensive. The main building was one of those modernist things they went crazy for in the 70s, like a big glass box with all pine panelling and thick carpets inside. It was cosy and warm – and there were huge windows everywhere, so you could always see the woods. That was great during the day, but… I don't think the designers thought it through.'

I looked at the trees ahead. They were growing denser and taller. For the first time since we began our trek, I felt a little disorientated.

Martha sniffed the clean air then frowned. 'As beautiful as the forest is now, when the sun goes down… it's a different place. Your eyes play tricks. And the gaps, the gaps between the trees… they're so black, so dark, so… deep… you just can't tell what's in there. We all felt it. Like we were being watched at night.'

'Watched by whom?'

'By the woods, by nature. We were out here in this... glass bubble, like a spaceship that had landed on a different planet. The head gardener said it was like we were an infection.'

'An infection?'

Above, the crow interrupted again.

'Oh, I understood what he meant. This is ancient woodland – some of these trees are centuries old – and the forest is like a living organism. You know, there's a saying round here – that the "woods remember". Like they're alive.'

'The woods remember. What does that mean?'

Martha shrugged. 'Sayings like that are part of country life; nobody really knows where they come from. There are lots of stories attached to this place. As many stories as there are trees, that's what they say. According to folklore there was a battle here, in the distant past, a terrible long-forgotten battle that turned the soil red. Supposedly the dead were buried among the trees and their spirits wandered off into the woods – and they're still there. Lost. Another legend says that this is where they would hang criminals in the old days, from the big oaks. They used to say you could see rope burns worn into the branches. That's why it's called The Lichwood on old maps. *Lich* is an old English word for corpse – so this is Deadman's Wood.'

Martha looked at me, smiled apologetically, and let go of the rusting metal. 'Like I said... stories for kids.'

We began walking again.

'So, what went wrong? With Evergreen?' I asked.

Martha's eyes stayed fixed on the thick undergrowth as she walked.

'It started at night,' she said, 'with the residents.

'First the old folks stopped sleeping. All of them. You would just find them, wandering the corridors in their pyjamas in the middle of the night, their faces blank. Next, they just stopped talking. Then, they stopped moving.'

'They stopped moving?'

Martha paused again, pulled her hood back and placed her hands on her hips.

'We had these chairs – we called them the comfy chairs – that had the best view out of the main window. At first, the old folks would sit in them and read or chat, laughing with each other. They all had their favourite chair. But then they just... changed. These had been energetic older people, attracted by outdoor living, but within months of moving in it was like the life was seeping out of them, day by day. Their personalities just crumbled. They stopped telling stories, stopped sharing memories. The old married couples even stopped holding hands. They just sat there in silence. Day and night, staring at the trees. The only time they would move would be to go to the hatch to get their meds, and then they'd shuffle back, sit down, and watch the trees. Always watching the trees.'

She looked at her watch, then blinked into the lowering light. 'We better press on, because it'll be dark soon and I might not find my way back to the car.'

'Sounds like it was dementia,' I said as we headed for the ridge.

'Well, yes, that would be the natural conclusion, but all of them at the same time? That wasn't right. It was like they were dying a little each day. Fading away.'

Martha began to walk more quickly.

'And then it started. They started to die. Maybe two each week at first, but then more and more. You expect residents to die in retirement homes, but... Evergreen had a little chapel of rest, where we would lay them out, for when relatives came to view and collect the body. It was my job to wash them and lay them out nice. I didn't mind; growing up on a farm it didn't bother me at all, but – suddenly, there was a new body to wash every day. Sometimes the little morgue we had was full of them, on ice, two or three to a drawer. There were 150 residents when it opened, and in the space of one month more than forty died. All marked down to natural causes. But the worst thing was you could predict it. You could tell who was going to die. You could tell.'

'How could you tell?'

'From their eyes. The day before. You could tell when they'd reached the end. Suddenly, one day, they were an empty husk, sitting in their chair, staring at the woods. Next morning, without fail, you'd find them dead in their beds... but it was like they had already checked out. Some of us were really concerned but others, other staff – well, they changed too. They were cruel.'

We were approaching the ridge in the forest floor now – a steep embankment that dropped away on the other side. Martha spoke breathily as she began to climb the slope.

'It was shocking. Out here in the woods, Evergreen was... cut off. It brought out the worst in some people – how they treated the old folks. There was no patience, no kindness, no dignity. And then we found out about the meds.'

'What about them?'

'They were being given all sorts of drugs. Every time they went to the meds hatch, they came away with more and more pills. I think the isolation got to the medical team. No one was sleeping. Everyone was paranoid. It got out of hand.'

'And you thought this had something to do with the deaths?'

'Hard to tell. That's why we went to the *Mercury*, me and two other nurses. A reporter looked into it – your friend at the paper knew him, he's gone now – but he showed up out here, with his notepad, asking questions. Frightened the life out of the management. The owners panicked and pulled the plug. Evergreen closed within a month. They moved all the remaining residents out. They would have sacked us, but they didn't get a chance to, it was that fast. They just abandoned it out here, abandoned it to the forest.'

We reached the top of the slope and Martha pointed to her feet.

Broad, raised letters pressed up through thick moss from a brick surface beneath: '*Evergreen Retirement Community*'.

'It's not far from here, just keep going that way,' she said. 'Mind your step and try to stay dry. I think you're mad staying out at this time of year.'

'You're not coming any further?'

She shook her head. 'I've no interest in going back there. There's nothing left of it, anyway. You'll see that. I hope you've got plenty in that bag to keep you warm, you'll need it.'

'I think I'm quite well prepared.'

'Well, be warned – it's open to the elements. I need to get back to my car.'

I dropped my bag. 'Of course, thank you. Can I just ask you one more question? Have you ever seen anything unusual there? Personally?'

She raised an eyebrow. 'No, but I know plenty of people who have. Put it this way – nothing would surprise me in these woods.'

As she turned to walk away, I said, 'So, no final advice?'

'Just stay warm,' she said, striding away down the slope. 'I'll come back for you tomorrow. As far as I know there are no windows left there at all, and there's only one room with a door in the whole building. I think you'll need to hunker down in there because it's going to get really cold.'

'Where will I find that?'

'Right in the middle, you can't miss it. Chapel of rest.'

I blinked into the sun's rays.

*

The metal rim of the tin hoop clatters and bounces off the cobblestones as I race after it, young cheeks scarlet and hot with excitement and lungs bursting, busting, breaking and baking in the midday heat, as my little fingers – their nails soot black – clutch tight to the stick, urging my hoop on and on, the best game ever, it's the best, I'm the best, bombing along the narrow stone street, heavy little boots slapping down and down and down but then a jolt – I'm caught, caught, tripped over and over I go, knees skimmed, the hoop sliding away beneath a cart as grit stings into the soft flesh of my palms…

*

The crow caw-cawed.

I blinked and looked around, my eyes slipping back into focus, the edges of trees pulling into line with the shadows beyond.

What was that? Martha was gone.

Instinctively, I looked at my palms.

What was that? I shook my head. I was alone. Exposed.

Time had passed. The trees stood to attention, looming around me in the hazy light. Between them, shadows lingered and watched. Deeper, blacker. Night was coming. Must press on. Find shelter.

Dazed, I hopped down from the other side of the embankment and walked with intent down a small incline into the old Evergreen site, my bag dragging at my side. The grass was still long, but the ground firmer underfoot. I realised that somewhere beneath lay a car park, devoured by the forest; asphalt absorbed like a seam of manmade sediment.

The trees, though, were everywhere, filling my vision, arranged in neat rows and scattered randomly, thick and tall, young and slender; a patchwork of black-edged lines and rounded limbs, wrapped in swirling, grainy thumbprints or smooth silver-paper bark.

My eyes searched for any sign of the building. And then suddenly, like the dried bones of a great beast lying among the foliage, there it was.

Martha had not exaggerated. All that was left of the Evergreen building was a huge weather-beaten concrete shell, every square inch of which seemed to be daubed in brightly coloured graffiti.

Its three storeys stretched between the trees – angular edges, cracked grey boxes and red and blue paint hiding amid a sea of organic green.

It was hard to believe this had once contained luxury of any kind. Martha had described it as a spaceship. The forest, slowly but surely, had brought it down to earth.

I ventured inside, aware of the need to find a place to set up my vigil. It was vast. While the great box still had a roof, the gaps where glass had once provided sleek walls now yawned emptily into the damp forest air.

A fine layer of reddish dust coated the floor, the walls, everything. My steps echoed as I explored, tripping down wide corridors past bare doorways and cell-like rooms, the occasional rusting bedstead their only occupant. Then, the space opened out to reveal an atrium that reached high up to the roof and extended half the length of the building – with a panoramic view of the woods beyond – unbroken, deep green and illuminated by the day's dying light like a projected image. And all along the edge of this vantage point, dozens of crooked and broken shapes leant against each other, their silhouettes dwarfed by the soaring trees. The old folks' comfy chairs were still keeping watch. A view to die for.

I walked to the edge. The chairs were a motley collection, their arms gnarled and cracked, their discoloured seats sagging beneath black, rotting leaves.

At the rear of the atrium sat a small concrete kiosk, little bigger than a bus stop. As I approached it, something glinted dully at its front. It was a sliding window, set behind a narrow counter – apparently the only glass in the entire building to survive. Inside, a bent metal chair lay on its side.

My fingers tapped on the counter. The meds hatch. This was the place where the old folks had queued, in silent lines, to grasp paper cups of pills before returning to their chairs and the woods.

Tiredness washed over me. I rubbed my face, my vision swamped by the dull red of my eye lids.

*

The water in the fountain is cold as it splashes up my calves, the hem of my dress clinging to my legs as we sing and we dance and his strong arm is around my shoulders and then his hand is on my waist and his sailor's hat, with its stiff felt brim, is on my head, tilted back as we kick our legs up, hundreds of legs, splashing the water, singing and shouting as the flags wave and I laugh as a bus tries to get through the crowd, across the square, but it can't because of all the people and the driver is laughing and the passengers are laughing too and banging on the windows as the bells ring out from St Paul's, from St Martin's, from everywhere and the fat lady shouts, 'God Save the King, it's over!', and I feel his hand tighten on my waist and slip higher and his finger touches my breast and my face flushes but I don't care, because it's over and it's life again and I'm alive, I made it. Everyone here made it.

*

'*Loose bitch. Lots of loose ones here, loose ladies, loose men.*'

Wilko's voice rasped close to my ear, jarring me back, tightening my retinas, pulling my eyes from the trees.

'*All loose, nowhere to go. Lost. Lost their skin, they have. Wilko?*'

I gripped the soft arm rest, squeezing out cold rainwater, black and fetid. Confused, my head turned to inspect my wet fingers.

What was that?

I was sitting in one of the old chairs, my toes inches from the edge of the great gaping window. How did I get here?

Night had arrived. The forest was dark, the sky above dotted with stars. It was cold. *Cold.* What was happening? This was new, I didn't like this. Wilko was silent again.

That fountain. The crowds. That wasn't a voice. That was...
inside of me.

SLAM! From behind me a loud bang echoed through the
dark shell of Evergreen. I stood with a start and glared into the
black corridors.

'Hello? Is there someone there?'

Deep in the bowels of the abandoned building I heard voices
shout. My bag lay on the floor across the room, near the hatch,
near the counter.

How did I get here? Get yourself together, Joe!

I picked my way around the old chairs and crossed to the bag,
took out my torch and flipped it on. Graffiti danced in the beam.
The voices echoed again, distant and muffled.

My breath held, I peered into the void. The shouts came again.
And... music? People? Were there people? I edged my way along.
A light flickered. A smell cut through the damp.

Sweet. Sickly. Weed.

The three teenagers, their backs to me, were oblivious to my
approach. A lamp, hooked to a car battery, illuminated their tall
frames in a pool of yellow. Evidently, the uniform was the same
in the countryside as in the city: tracksuit bottoms hung low from
the waist, a thick jacket with its hood pulled high over a baseball
cap. I watched as their hands moved quickly, plumes of spray
paint arcing and zigzagging in front of them. Rap spat from a
tinny Bluetooth speaker on the floor, next to a canvas bag that
groaned with spray cans. I could hear them murmuring intently
to each other, their deep voices edged with a tough-guy Jamaican
lilt.

I cleared my throat. They froze. A hand deftly dropped a joint
into the darkness.

Silence.

Then the one in the middle – the biggest one – said over his
shoulder, 'Officer, like... obviously... we ain't doin' no harm. Ya
get me?'

I waited. 'I'm not a policeman.'

Slowly, they turned round to inspect me. Three pale white faces, ginger hair sprouting from beneath their caps, squinted into my torch light.

'You a pervert, then, innit?' another said, his eyes bleary and wet. 'You a paedo? What you doin' out here?'

'I could ask you the same thing.'

The big one waved a spray can at the wall. 'We're doin' our art, expressing ourselves, ya get me? Now let me arks you again – you a perv?'

The other two sniggered. They weren't frightened anymore. I smiled. 'No. I'm not a pervert. I'm… exploring.'

'Well, you're not exploring me, bruv,' the second one said. More sniggers.

The third teenager's gangsta accent was less convincing. He seemed younger.

'That's well suss, though, innit?' he squeaked. 'What you exploring?'

'This place.'

'Why?'

'For a book I'm writing.' I turned the torch on my face. 'My name's Joe. Didn't mean to sneak up on you. Sorry.'

The biggest one studied me for a second then looked at my bag. 'What you got in there?'

'Sandwiches, a flask of tea, chocolate, sweets.'

'Sweeties? You got sweeties in there?' the second one said. 'You defo sound like a paedo to me, bruv.'

The other two laughed.

'Give us some chocolate, bruv,' the youngest one said, 'I missed my tea, innit.'

*

261

We sat on cardboard in one of the small concrete rooms. Their wet bikes, leant against the graffitied wall, laced the air with a smell of mud.

The oldest boy sat playing with my torch, and eyeing me with nonchalant suspicion, as the younger one hungrily demolished a bar of Cadbury's Dairy Milk. Their bleary-eyed friend stared blankly into the darkness.

I sipped tea from the cap of my flask.

'So, I take it all this is your work?' I asked. 'You must have been coming out here for a while.'

The oldest shone the torch beam lazily against the wall as he spoke. 'Long enough. Not much else to do round here. The good stuff is ours, we don't tag, ya get me?'

'How do you not get lost in the woods?'

'We know the Lich like the back of our hands, bruv,' the bleary-eyed one said. 'Grew up round here, innit.'

I had chanced upon the latest generation of Martha's fellow feral kids.

The youngest looked up from his chocolate bar. 'There's a bike trail brings you right here. Everyone knows about this place, but everyone else is too frit to come out here.'

'Frit?'

'Frit. Frightened. Scared,' the biggest interjected, quietly.

'Scared of what?'

'This place. The Dust Devil, man.'

They looked at each other.

'Have you seen it?'

'Jacob has,' said the youngest, throwing away the wrapper.

The biggest kid glared at him. 'Might have,' he said.

'That's your name... Jacob?' I asked.

'I'm Jacob, this is my cousin, Caleb, and my little brother Izzie.'

'Isiah,' the youngest corrected him.

I took another sip of tea. 'So – the Dust Devil – do you know what it is?'

Caleb wiped his wet eyes. 'Depends which story you believe. What you think this place used to be.'

'What do you think?'

He crossed his arms. 'Everyone knows. It's a mansion that was never finished. A millionaire wanted it built out here.'

'And why wasn't it finished?'

He tilted his head, considering his next answer. Then he dipped into a pocket, pulled out a joint and lit it. 'What I heard is that the builders went mad out here in the woods, turned on each other, killed each other.'

'How do you know that?' I noticed young Izzie was shaking his head.

Caleb shrugged and blew out a cloud of smoke. 'One of them survived. He staggered out of the woods, been lost for days. He said the dust came out of the trees and sent them all mad.'

'That's bullshit innit,' Izzie said.

'What do you think then?' I asked. As many stories as there are trees.

He smiled. 'This used to be a juvie, bruv.'

'A juvie?'

'Yeah, a *juvie*. You know, for young offenders. I heard there was a riot, and they burned it down, man, but some of them died in it. The dust is their ghosts, man, still serving time, ya get me.'

Caleb sucked in another lungful of weed. 'This ain't no juvie, bruv – man, a juvie would have bars on the windows and shit to keep you in. This place ain't even got any walls, there's no way this was a juvie, you're talking bare shit, man.'

'Like I said, bruv, it burned down, destroyed and that.'

'Bullshit, bruv, it was a mansion – you can tell it wasn't finished.'

'You're both wrong.' Jacob was staring into the torch beam. 'I seen it. Don't know what this place was, doesn't matter, but I seen it. I was walking through and it was just there, in one of the rooms, like a… what do ya call it… a whirlwind. Just spinning in the air.'

'What do you think it is?' I asked.

He looked at me for a second, then returned to the torch. 'Don't know,' he said quietly. 'It felt proper angry... like... confused, and angry. It knew I was there, though, I know that. It messed with my head.'

'How did it mess with your head?'

He wrinkled his nose. 'It scrambled me for a minute, couldn't think straight. I saw all these things, places... I don't know. But I wasn't scared of it. I ain't frit of nothin'.'

The little cell fell quiet for a second.

'Show him the video, bruv,' Izzie said.

Jacob's phone was passed to me. On the screen a blur of sandy dust spun violently inside a room, contained entirely within the open doorway.

'Where was this? Can you show me?'

'I can show you. It's the only room with a door. The only one we won't paint.' He stood and waved the others to their feet, Caleb obediently stubbing out his joint.

'But then we gotta go,' he added. 'It's a school night, innit.'

＊

The deep, crystallised snow bites at my fingers as I dig at the wheel of the truck, the old shovel hitting the road beneath with a loud PANG as I hug myself to keep warm, slapping my sides, stamping my solid feet, breathing hot air into my cupped hands and then POP! A bottle in the back of the truck fires open like a fizzy firework...

＊

Again. It happened again. I shook my head. Where am I? The wind whipped around me, the dust carried on the air now, rolling in a growing vortex around the slab. The slab. I'm in the chapel.

The wind whistled around my ears. I looked again at the bed of red dust on the slab. The clear shape of a human being was pressed deeply into it. I felt the metal chair rock as the swirling air rushed underneath it, lifting it. I stood, suddenly shaky on my feet, bracing myself against the growing wind. The humming walls of the whirlwind lifted around me.

*

The cruel teacher glares down at me, his nostrils flaring with anger as I hold out my upturned palm. He raises the cane then down, a blur, and it stings, it cuts, it burns and my tears swell but his eyes are alive, gleaming...

*

Again. I slipped my stinging hand under my arm. What was happening to me?

I was deep inside the whirlwind now, the air shrieking past my ears, the slab barely visible as the flying dust seemed to multiply and grow, pushing me and pulling me as the air thickened with red particles, deafening, filling the room, fogging my vision – a gust pushed me from behind and I toppled blindly forward into the maelstrom, into the slab – but it wasn't there. Where was it? The room was gone! I stumbled on, moving blindly into the twisting air currents.

Now I was walking in the red sandstorm, through it, buffeted by the wind, eyes pulled into slits, my hands over my ears then outstretched, lost in the churning air as a silhouetted figure loomed somewhere in the redness, standing perfectly still, its back hunched and arms at the sides. I lurched towards it. An old woman emerged, naked, her grey face expressionless, standing lifeless in the red fog.

*

I slap his face and he recoils; his hand pulls from my knee and his teacup falls to the ground with a crack. You're not my husband, what kind of girl do you...

*

Stop. Stop this! I staggered on into the red wind, past her glassy stare, and on into the cloud, into the billowing red air, toward another cadaverous shape: a round, naked figure standing amid the flying silt – an elderly man, yellow-skinned, so old, his mouth hanging open, his eyes unblinking.

*

The turkey is moist and soft as I carve into it, the tissue paper crown on my head slipping backwards as the family watch on...

*

No! No more! Reeling past him, I felt the wind push me on again into the swirling dust as another figure loomed, then another, then another, then dozens of them – naked, empty and dead, a forest of corpses standing limp and vacant as the red air span around them. And carried on each eddy was another memory, amputated and removed from its source; lost moments looking for a home in the dark, for a head, for a soul, for connection, for release, for an open door.

The wind wailed as blue light cut through the redness, ethereal and flickering. I stood now in the centre of this forest of the dead, spinning on the spot, looking for a way out, for gaps between the clean-washed cadavers. Blue glinted on their smooth shoulders. I looked up.

Above, the neon shape fizzed and buzzed in the churning red

mist – a swirling figure of eight, scratched into the air.

Then slowly, as one, the cadavers began to turn, shuffling their lifeless legs to face me, to surround me, then with dragged steps they started to lurch forward, a wall of grey skin closing in, closing the red gaps between their sagging shoulders, closing in on me. I sank to my knees and shut my eyes.

Silence.

With a soft *WHUMP*, I felt the dust stop and fall.

I looked. I was back in the chapel, crouched next to the upturned metal chair. My eyes climbed the ornate legs of the slab, to the soft cushion of dust still along its length. A body lay on it, its toes peeking over the bevelled marble edge. Slowly, I stood.

The pale body was male, naked, clean, washed. I looked at the face. It was blank – just flat smooth skin. An empty vessel.

Then, like ink expanding on water, I watched as deep scars crept up and over its shoulders, and a raw rope burn twisted snake-like around its neck. With a shimmer, my father's features appeared on the smooth skin.

His eyes flicked open and his face, serene and calm, turned to regard me.

A hoarse, gentle whisper escaped his lips: '*The doors. Find the doors.*'

I felt emotion rise. 'Dad, what do you mean? Dad, can you hear me?'

Suddenly, his face twisted with rage, his mouth contorting into a snarl. Wilko's voice screamed out.

'*No! No! Get out! Get out!*'

I ran. Out of the chapel, down the black corridors, bouncing off walls and then out into the atrium, the same blue light glinting high off the concrete ceiling as I ran towards the chairs, towards the great open window and the trees, all the time Wilko's rasping words driving me to the edge.

I leapt. Now into the woods, falling into the dark, pushing aside branches, my feet sinking in the soft grass.

As I stumbled on through the forest, I looked up to see the naked torsos of the old folks, standing in the inky dark gaps between the trees, their memories cast into the ether by drugs only to be drunk up by the forest's roots, trapped in the rings – more souls caught in the ancient Lichwood. The woods may remember, but they could not.

When I came across the boys' cycle track, I knew that, unlike the residents of Evergreen, I could find my way out of the woods.

TWENTY-THREE

The Right Place

I only knew roughly where Westcroft was. In my years as a reporter, it was one of the few local landmarks I hadn't visited. Police and fire stations, schools, hospitals, churches, town halls – I was familiar with most. But I had avoided Westcroft. I made excuses, for obvious reasons.

Even the sight of road signs pointing to the place had been enough to turn my stomach and send me in a different direction; anywhere other than there.

But the route I was now taking to the hospital was guided by those signs, coloured by half-remembered snapshots from decades ago. But I had to go back. I had to see Kate.

I turned Mom's VW left then right then left, heading out of the town's quiet streets and into the surrounding hills, trees rising in banks at the side of a curling, empty road that became more familiar the further I ventured along it.

The smell of the Lichwood was still on my clothes, my shoes still wet. It was here somewhere; I knew it was. I plucked a piece of fern from my lapel and drove on.

I stopped as the treeline rolled back, and metal gates slid into view; I knew them. I got out, the engine still running. Yes, I knew these old gates, only now they were chained shut and had long surrendered to a curtain of climbing ivy.

In my pocket, my phone buzzed. *02135652108.*

'Hello?'

The little boy's voice prickled with fear: 'I'm hiding,' he whispered.

'Hello? Are you OK?'

Silence, then: 'He's looking for me. I'm hiding. Please be quiet. He's looking for me.'

My voice dropped. 'Do you need help? Where are you hiding?'

'My place. Under the stairs. It's dark.'

'Don't worry. Tell me where you are and I'll come and get you, I'll help you.'

'You can't,' he whispered weakly, 'he's…'

Suddenly loud banging hammered out. *Click.* The line was dead.

Frustration coursed through me. I squeezed the phone between my hands. Kate. I needed to find Kate.

The gates. Nearby was an exposed patch of brickwork, its corners crumbling with holes that had once held a sign. In its place a laminated sheet of paper fluttered on yellowing tape: 'Westcroft hospital next right'.

The VW's wheels span as I pulled back onto the road.

A hundred yards on I turned into a sweeping driveway that meandered through open lawns that sparkled with winter dew. Across the grounds, a low white building reflected the early morning sun, while a distant crane moved slowly across the sky beyond.

This was new. All new. I felt a wave of relief sweep over me as the Westcroft of my youth receded in my mind. I must find Kate.

I pulled into a parking space near the new building and made my way to the front door, which opened with an electric *swish* as

I approached. Inside, a young woman looked up behind her glass-fronted counter and tried to hide her wide-eyed reaction to my bedraggled appearance.

I stepped forward, my shoes squelching on the grey tiled floor.

'Can I help you?'

'Can I speak to Kate Hart? She's on the nursing staff.'

She looked me up and down, her training evidently kicking in. 'I'm not sure she's immediately available – can I help you at all?'

'No – no thank you – it's Kate I need to speak to. Straight away, if possible.'

I was aware that my voice was carrying across the open reception area. Two burly, blue-coated men, orderlies busily talking as they dismantled a gurney, fell silent and looked across at me.

Instinctively, I ran my hand through my hair. A small leaf tumbled out.

She lifted a pen. 'Can I ask what your name is, please?'

'Joe Baxter. I'm a friend of Kate's. An old friend.'

She offered an unconvincing smile. 'I'll just see if I can find her on the rota. Kate…?'

'Kate Hart. Maybe Katherine Hart?'

She tapped at her keyboard, waited, then inspected the screen. Her gaze moved to me momentarily then she said crisply, 'Would you give me just a moment, please, Mr Baxter?'

Moving to the back of the room, she tapped on an office door and a grey-haired doctor appeared. They spoke into their chests as his eyes drifted to me.

I leant forward and looked at her screen. My teenage mugshot stared back. Now the doctor was striding towards me, his face radiating an all-too-familiar look of sympathy.

'Can I help you, sir? Mr Baxter, is it?' His voice was calm.

'Yes, I need to speak to a nurse who works here, Kate Hart. I'm a friend.'

His eyes sank to my sodden shoes. 'And may I ask what it's about?'

'It's a personal matter, that's all.' I felt my voice rising. 'Look, I'm a visitor. Is this how you treat visitors these days?'

I saw him glance at the screen. 'Well, we always have to be careful, you understand. Could I possibly take a message for Nurse Hart? I'm not entirely sure she's on duty today.'

'He's a lying fucker. White-coated bone-sawing fucker. Wilko?'

A sickening chuckle brushed my neck. As the doctor's kind eyes waited for a response, I felt anger bubble. My hands balled into fists at my side.

'Look, it's a simple request. I don't want to leave a message, I can leave a message at her house, I know where she lives – I need to speak to her now.'

'Joe?'

I span round. Standing in the doorway, her blue scrubs backlit by the morning sun, was Kate. The clipboard in her hand dropped to her side as her eyes took in my sorry state.

'Joe, what are you doing here?'

'Sorry, Kate, I need to speak to you. I need to tell you something.'

The doctor interrupted. 'Is everything alright, Nurse Hart?'

'Yes, Doctor, I'm sure everything's fine. Could I just have a couple of minutes to talk to Joe?'

He considered the request. 'Of course. You can use the family room at the end of the corridor.' He turned to the orderlies. 'Gentlemen, could you open up the family room?'

*

A suspicious slick of beige oil floated on the surface of the tea, rising on one side to stick to the Styrofoam cup. I planted my elbows on the table as Kate waited for her coffee, tapping her foot impatiently with her thumb pointlessly pressed to the vending machine button.

Through a round window in the door, I could see the orderlies skulking conspicuously.

Then she was there, sitting in front of me, and holding her drink in both hands below an amused expression.

'You look like you need that,' she said.

'I do, I do.' I took a sip. Not enough sugar. 'I really do.'

Kate placed her coffee down and crossed her arms.

'So, what's up, rib boy?'

'I wanted to see you.'

'Yes, we've established that. What about?'

'I wanted to tell you something.'

'What?'

'This is going to sound mad.'

Her eyes wheeled around the room. 'Well, you've come to the right place.'

'I suppose I have. Couldn't find it at first. It really has changed.'

'Yes, we've had this conversation… what did you want to tell me?'

I shifted on the seat. 'Well, two things.'

'OK.'

'First, I want to be honest with you about what I'm doing.'

'What you're doing?'

'The book.'

'Oh, OK. The book.' She was either humouring me or enjoying watching me squirm. 'Go on.'

'So, you know roughly what I've been doing. Haunted places. Spending the night.'

'Right.'

'I need to tell you what's happened to me.'

'Joe, just say it.'

I took a deep breath. 'It's all true.'

'What is?'

'All the stories. The hauntings. I've seen them, seen them all. I don't expect you to believe me…'

She paused, then said, 'Why did you need to tell me that?'

'Because I want to be honest with you. I wouldn't tell anyone else, because… well, it's messing with my head. I think I'm going mad. Again.'

'D'you think?'

I ran my fingers across my face. 'I can't believe I've actually come here of all places… and started talking like this. They'll lock me up.'

'Well…' Kate took a swig from her coffee, 'I'm not so sure, kiddo. If we locked up everyone who said they'd seen a ghost it would be standing room only round here. Besides…' a casual shrug, 'I believe you.'

'You do?'

'Sure, why not?'

'Because it's mad, that's why.'

'Perhaps this place is rubbing off on me.'

I stared into the tepid tea. 'I've seen things, Kate, seen things you wouldn't believe. When I think about it, I'm not sure I believe it myself.'

'Well, there's two things I am sure of,' she said.

'What's that?'

'Firstly, that you haven't been getting enough sleep, and secondly that if these big nights out of yours are having this kind of effect on you, you really ought to stop doing them. Look at the state of you. You're not mad, Joe, you're exhausted. I know what that's like.'

'I can't stop. Not yet. I can't explain why. It feels like I'm getting somewhere. It feels important.'

'More important than your sanity? Because, as the old saying goes, doing the same thing over and over again and expecting a different outcome is the *definition* of insanity. You've got to stop.'

I nodded. 'I've got two more arranged – one tomorrow. I'm going to do them. I was taught a long time ago never to miss an appointment. It's one of "The Rules".'

'The rules?'

'Journo stuff. Ask Helena. But you're right. They'll be the last. I wanted to do thirteen, but...'

'So, what happened last night? You look like hell.'

I looked down at my wet shoes. 'I spent the night running through a forest. I was lost.'

Kate laughed. 'You're a real catch, aren't you, Joe Baxter?'

I had to smile. 'That's the other thing I wanted to say. That I have to say.'

'That you have no sense of direction?'

'Seriously, Kate...'

'Go on.'

'Last night I saw things... and felt things... that I can't shake off.'

'I don't understand. Tell me what you saw.'

'No, that's not important, it doesn't matter. It's what I felt when I saw them. It made me realise something. It's all I could think of when I was in the trees, in the forest.'

'What's that?'

I swallowed and looked at her. 'That I'm lonely, Kate. That I've built this solitary life for myself, for whatever stupid reason, gone down this path, and I'm lonely and I spend all my time pretending I'm not. I should be making memories – memories that I can share with someone, living life while I can, because it's over before you know it. And then...'

I sat back.

'And then what?' she said.

'And then you.'

'Me?'

'You.'

'What about me?'

'You reminded me of what it was like before I took that path. What it was like when I didn't care what people thought, when I wasn't scared of messing up.'

'I did that?'

'You did. That's what I realised last night. These last few weeks, the places I've been – the risks I've taken – all the things I've seen. I've been surrounded by all this… macabre… stuff, all this death, and I've never felt so alive. I thought it was the excitement, the fear. But it wasn't. It isn't. It's you.'

'I see.' She was blushing. 'Yep… this was not the way I expected this conversation to go.'

Now she was squirming.

I said, 'So, what do you think?'

'What do I think?'

'Yes. What do you think?'

She puffed her cheeks. 'I think you've definitely gone fucking mad.'

I laughed out loud. 'Well, I feel better for telling you anyway.'

The orderlies peered at us through the round window. I waved at them, and Kate giggled, pulling my arm to the table.

Her hand came to rest on top of mine.

'I'm glad you told me, Joe… I think. And I can't wait to tell Helena how you feel. She'll be delighted.'

'Now that's something to look forward to,' I nodded. 'How's she doing?'

'Good. She's started the data journalism course. She seems happy, if a little distracted.'

I sat forward and took out my phone. 'Actually, there's something she could look into for me. Would you ask her?'

'Sure. What is it?'

I scribbled in my pad, tore out the page and passed it to her. 'See if she can find out whose number this is. I keep getting crank calls. At least I think they're crank calls. I can't figure out the dialling code.'

She inspected the number. 'OK. I'll ask her.'

Suddenly a high-pitched electronic alarm echoed through the building. The orderlies turned on their heels and sprinted down the nearest corridor. Kate was on her feet.

'Wait here,' she said. 'Nothing to worry about, just don't move. OK?'

'Fire alarm?'

'No, no. It's a staff alarm. I should go. Wait here, OK?'

She tapped the table. I nodded obediently. Then she was gone, leaving the door open.

I sat for a moment, digging my fingernails into the soft cup, inspecting the thickening skin on the tea. The alarm stopped. As its echoes died away, I could hear the squeaks of shoes running on polished floors somewhere deep in the complex, and distant shouts. A door slammed. Then it was quiet, the only noise the humming of the vending machine.

Through the door, a sound reached in – tinny and stilted, but familiar.

The mournful guitar of 'Iron Man' drifted into the room.

I rose and peered into the corridor. The strip lights reflected dully on the polished floor. The doors were all shut. Black Sabbath curled around a far-off corner. I followed.

Around the turn, another long corridor stretched, with a dozen identical closed doors on each side. At the end, one door was open, the room inside dark. The music drifted out of it. I stood for a second, unsure what to do.

Then a huge figure filled the distant door frame, the silhouette's broad shoulders rising into a wild crown of hair. Slowly, it raised an arm to me, beckoning, then disappeared back into the dark. I had to follow.

The bedroom was big but almost completely empty. A desk, piled high with paper and lit by a dim lamp, stood in its centre. A battered cassette player whirred in the yellow light, the music disappearing into the room's dark corners. A small unkempt bed sagged under the weight of the man, whose thick legs stretched out onto more papers scattered on the floor.

As I stood in the doorway, I became aware of faces, hundreds of faces, hovering in the gloom. I looked up. The walls were covered in drawings, etched in black and white, rows of scratched charcoal faces, their eyes closed, their mouths limp and expressionless; each one different, luminous. Asleep. They hung over the silent man like an expectant audience. In his lap, his fat fingers clutched a document. I could hear his laboured breathing.

'H-h-hello, Joe,' he said from beneath a thick brown fringe. His deep voice was weak and dry.

I stepped forward. 'Do I know you?'

His face turned up to me, bloated and wrinkled above a thick beard. Impossibly tired blue eyes rested on me. With a heavy sigh he raised a hand and swept back his hair. The red wine stain birthmark. He smiled gently at me.

'Nipper? Nipper... is it you?'

'N-N-Nipper. Not heard that for a while. A-Andrew here. Always Andrew.'

'How long have you been here?'

He exhaled. 'All night,' he said. 'All night.'

'You look so different,' I said.

'Do I?'

Somewhere, the alarm went off briefly before falling silent again. He smiled. 'A Kit Kat can b-buy you a lot in this place. I wanted to speak t-to you.'

'How did you know I was going to be here?'

Wearily, his eyes rose to sweep across the faces above. 'I am going to tell him. I should tell him.'

'Tell me what?'

'Don't tell anyone else.'

'OK, I won't. Tell me what?'

He waved the document limply. 'What they t-told you. About what happened. You didn't imagine it. I saw it too. I still see it. They still see it.'

'What do you mean?' I reached out to take the document. He snatched it away.

278

'In the catacombs, J-Joe. You know it was real. They told you it wasn't. Well, I saw it too. They w-wanted me to change my mind, but I wouldn't. I saw it. You saved m-me.'

He looked up at the walls again. 'And then they saved me.'

'Who are they?'

'The people it holds back.'

'It?'

He closed his eyes. 'They are people. It is not people. It won't let them sleep. It belongs somewhere else. It's not in the right place. It's not alive. But they don't deserve it. They deserve their rest.'

'I don't understand.'

Slowly, Nipper lifted his heavy legs onto the bed and rolled away from me.

'All they w-want is to be remembered,' he whispered over his shoulder. 'Then they can sleep. I remember them, every n-night. Now I need to sleep.'

The cassette player clicked off. The room fell silent. A shadow fell over the open door. I turned to see Kate beckoning me urgently.

As we walked back along the corridor she said, 'Jesus, Joe – what were you doing in there?'

'I heard the music – sorry, I should have stayed put.'

'Yes, you should. I should have locked you in.'

She stopped. 'Were you speaking to him?'

'I just wanted to make sure he was alright.'

She shook her head and started walking again. 'You're wasting your time with Andrew. He hasn't said anything in nearly thirty years.'

TWENTY-FOUR

Knock for Jossie

The Tenth Vigil

One-two.

One-two.

As the train raced through the countryside, the wheels clattered across the points, drumming an insistent rhythm. My senses still dulled from the long night in the forest, I stared at blurred trees, my tired reflection merging with Nipper's haunted face.

Nipper. I thought the old Westcroft had been swept away, but it had just retreated to his room, hiding like a wounded animal. It had been there all along. He had been there all along.

One-two.

One-two.

And while Kate – unflappable Kate – lived and walked the gentle humanity of the new hospital, Nipper's revelation about that day in the catacombs had jabbed awake memories of my treatment – and a dead-eyed doctor called Quantrill. He had bullied me into believing that what I had seen was a figment of my imagination.

One-two, one-two, one-two – the train rattled and rocked into a tunnel, dim lights flickering into life, my reflection now a yellow hue against the black glass. Something was coming. I felt it. In the dark, I felt it.

And I also now knew what I had seen all those years ago – what *we* had seen. Patience had told me. An elemental. It was almost as if she had known. I rubbed my face. How I could use her wisdom now!

The carriage swayed as we burst back into the light, pushing on – *one-two, one-two, one-two* – faster and faster towards the North East. For the first time since Nottingham, since London, I was about to venture below ground again. It filled me with dread.

*

It was closing time as I entered the Wall End Living Mine Experience.

I found myself wading knee-deep against a tide of excited schoolchildren, toy miners' helmets bobbing on their heads, as they jostled their way to coaches waiting outside. Their little pink knuckles rapped playful *knock-knocks* on each other's plastic hats, provoking giggling retaliations from classmates and gentle remonstrations from tired-looking teachers.

Ahead, a moon-faced teenage girl and an elderly woman in a wheelchair, both in long skirt and high-necked blouse, watched as the kids streamed through an ancient iron turnstile. Its dull *clunk-clank* echoed off the cobbled yard beyond.

The girl's hand rested gently on the shoulder of the old lady as they watched the children leave with soft, faraway smiles. Their faces turned to surprise as I emerged from the retreating shoulders and heads.

'They look like they've had a good day,' I said wearily, dropping my bag to the floor.

The young girl offered a curious look and said, 'Yes… I think some of them are just glad to get back up from the pit, to be honest.'

Then she looked me up and down and said, 'Sorry, sir, but we're closing up. No one else going down today.'

'Oh, sorry… I'm here to see… Mei Liu? I'm staying the night.'

The old lady, who had been staring blankly after the children, seemed to wake up. Her face cocked to the side. 'Staying the night? Where?'

Her voice was weak, slurred.

'Down the mine,' I said. 'It's all been arranged. With Mei.'

A little shake of the head. 'Oh, I don't think that's a good idea,' she said. 'What would y'want to do that for?'

'For a book I'm writing. It's all agreed. Is Mei around?'

'Yes, she is,' she said, confused. She waved a limp hand and the young girl stepped behind a desk. She punched two digits into a phone, spoke quietly, then returned to stand in front of the turnstile. Her hand rested back on the old lady's shoulder.

A moment later a trim middle-aged woman, her elegant features accented by subtle make-up, appeared beyond the barrier, straightening her smart business suit.

'Mr Baxter? I'm Mei. Jenna, could you open the barrier, please?'

The young girl did as she was told. The old lady watched as Mei Liu walked through with an outstretched hand.

'I'm the CEO of the museum – sorry, *experience* – how was your trip up?'

'Fine thank you. I caught the train.'

The old lady interrupted. 'Mei, he says he's spending the night down the mine. That's not right is it, Mei?' She seemed to force the words out.

'Yes, that's correct, Winnie.' She waved me through. 'Let's get you kitted out for the night, shall we?'

'But what would y'want to do that for?' she called after us. 'S'not right.'

'Take no notice of Winnie,' Mei said as she marched me towards a Victorian building topped with a bell tower. 'She's a volunteer now, but she used to run the canteen here. Sometimes she thinks she's still in charge. She's only allowed to come in now if her granddaughter helps her. Motor Neurone or MS or something. I'm trying to find a vintage wheelchair for her, because it spoils the immersive effect somewhat – don't you think?'

I looked back. Jenna and Winnie were watching us.

'I can't say I noticed. What did you mean by "kitted out"?'

'Well, health and safety have signed off but with a number of provisos,' Mei said, holding open the heavy wooden door. 'That means the right safety boots, headgear – and there's rules on where you can go when you're down there. And, of course, there are disclaimers for you to sign.'

Inside, it smelled of disinfectant. Mei picked through a large set of keys. An inscribed sandstone block loomed over a locked door.

'Wall End Sunday School, dedicated January 7th 1900. Funded through the kind benevolence of the Colliery board for the spiritual edification of miners' children'.

The door finally unlocked, she led me into a room where a large TV hung in front of pew-like benches. Hard hats covered the walls. Plastic tubs overflowed with boots.

Mei Liu drew my attention, impatiently *tap-tapping* one of her expensive-looking shoes.

'So... as the interim CEO, I have been sent up here to identify new revenue streams. That means monetising the resources that we have. I want to broaden the visitor experience with a full calendar of events... and a Halloween scare festival next year is a strong option. The concept works well at similar attractions.

So, your request fits in with that strategy, in terms of raising awareness. However, you will have to go through the same safety induction process as all visitors.'

She moved to the wall and turned a switch, dimming the lights. The TV screen flickered on. 'I'll be back in twenty minutes to pick out your kit.'

*

The elevator cage shuddered to a halt at the bottom of the shaft as the great sheave wheel above froze. With a jarring rattle, Mei retracted the door. I stepped down into the brightly lit chamber, my heavy steel-capped boots clumping onto the black floor in little clouds of soot.

Instinctively, I listened.

After so many long vigils, I now had a sense of the true spectrum of silence – its little deceptions, its changing shape, the viscous way it can cling to a space. Here, the cold, sulphurous air hung in a claustrophobic hush, deadened by the layers of rock above – but the chamber seemed to almost vibrate with an oppressive, soundless hum. Like a pulse.

Mei, having opted for her heels instead of safety boots, remained in the elevator. She gave another *tap-tap*.

'You'll have to stay in this part of the mine all night, it's not safe for you to wander around without a guide,' she said. 'All the doors are locked, so I wouldn't waste your time trying to explore further.'

The chamber was big – about 20 metres across – and appeared to be entirely chiselled out of coal and rock. Its walls, ceiling and floor were jet black, and glistened slightly under lamps that shone from industrial tripods. Padlocks hung on four grey metal doors. Crates and barrels were scattered around – stage dressing to make it look like a working mine.

I ran a hand down the wall, my fingertips bumping gently

across subtle grooves and gouges. I inspected the coaldust that rubbed off, ingrained into the ridges of my skin.

'Amazing to think this was carved out by hand,' I said. 'It must have been back-breaking work.'

She looked at me with disinterest. 'Yes, well, it's a shame more people don't share your fascination. If we want to achieve the kind of profit targets I've been set, this will need to become much more than a walk-through attraction. It will need to be more... interactive.'

'The kids I saw seemed to have enjoyed their visit today.'

She cast her eye across the chamber from the cage. 'Did they? School visits are a long-standing part of our offer, but... they're not attached to significant revenue. We need sponsors, we need corporate, and we need timetabled calendar events throughout the quieter months. The new owners are clear: this is a business, not a classroom.'

A chair and table had been set up for me in the middle of the chamber, with a pile of blankets and a six-pack of bottled water stacked at one end. I put my bag down.

'Tell me, what did you make of the stories in last week's *Chronicle*, about the schoolkids?'

She crossed her arms. 'Legacy media coverage is useful, but it's social that we need to build a real profile on. But it all helps raise awareness.'

'No, I mean... did you believe them?'

She gave me a rueful look. 'Do you mean do I believe that those little... darlings... were kicked by Old Jossie? Like I said... it all helps raise awareness.'

'So, you didn't believe them? Their parents did.'

'Let me put it this way... that party was from the primary school around the corner. It's a sink estate, low aspiration; all the old miners' housing. Those kids have been brought up on stories about the mine. There's always going to be a couple of kids who misbehave.'

'One of the kids had a bruise on his back.'

'Yes, well, the less said about that the better. Did you see his father?'

I let her last statement hang in the cold air for a moment, then said, 'No, I didn't. So, you're not a believer.'

She put her hand on the door lever. 'I believe in the bottom line, Mr Baxter. Have you got any questions?'

'Just one – what's that sound I can hear? Like a hum... a throb?'

She listened for a second, *tap-tapped* her toe again and shook her head. 'I can't hear anything. Stay safe. I'll see you tomorrow.'

With that the door rattled shut and she was gone. The cage slowly climbed away.

*

Time to begin. I found the switch box for the lighting and turned it off. The chamber plunged into darkness. Then I stood with my eyes tightly shut, draining any remaining colour from them, and listening. The silence seemed almost solid – a block of soundless air edged in by the rock walls. But beneath it, the hum continued its dull beat.

I opened my eyes.

It was apparent immediately: this was the darkest place I had been. It was as if my eyes were still shut. Even so, the vaguest lowlights began to slowly emerge from the blackness: the sheen of the tabletop, floating like an abstract shape in the void, and a cloud-like bloom of light at the foot of the elevator shaft, gathered like luminescent algae on the seafloor.

Slowly, I worked my way through the dark back to the table, my hand groping for the chair, then sat down. I unzipped my bag and blindly felt the contents inside: my sandwiches, the pad... and a new torch, sleeping bag and flask to replace the ones that were now gathering dust in the shell of Evergreen.

Time to wait.

The black chamber hummed its quiet pulse. An hour passed.

'All alone. Not alone. You and me. Wilko?'

I felt my shoulders drop. I had to ignore him.

'Want to leave? Want to go? So do they. But not all. He's a stayer. Like me.'

In the dark, in the silence, his voice was louder than ever.

'Waiting for the last load. Still waiting. Wait forever they will. Wilko?'

Ignore him! I leant forward and retrieved the sandwiches, unwrapping the aluminium foil noisily, so its tinny sound shattered the silence, crinkling and cracking. I bit into the bread in the dark and chewed, listening to my breath as my jaw worked. Ignore him. Ignore him.

Now, he was silent. I tossed the sandwich on the table as the dark chamber fell quiet again.

Suddenly, a mechanical scream filled the air. The cage. The cage was descending.

I rose to my feet, staring into the blackness towards the dim light at the foot of the shaft.

Pullies turned. Wheels rolled. The bottom of the cage appeared, a thick black line sinking slowly to the ground, followed by the mesh of bars and struts that formed its sliding door. And standing inside I could just see, tall and upright, a thin man: a dim silhouette in ill-fitting clothes, boots tied high around the shins, bulbous round toecaps and a circular cyclops eye glinting dully above broad shoulders. He was wearing an old miner's helmet.

The cage stopped. Slowly, a thin hand rose, and the little lamp flicked on, emitting a weak, yellow light into the chamber. I heard the door rattle open.

'If you're still down 'ere, turn the lights on y'bloody idiot!'

Winnie's exasperated voice called out across the chamber. She appeared from behind the silhouetted figure, her wheelchair pushed by Jenna.

*

The lights were back on. Jenna placed a small bottle of whisky on the table as the old man dragged crates to sit on.

'This is my brother, Ted,' Winnie said slowly. 'He brought you something to keep the cold out.'

Ted's long hand brushed lovingly across her shoulder as he sat down. 'That's enough, pet. I'll do the talking.'

He pushed the bottle towards me.

'Thanks, but I don't drink when I'm working – I've got a flask of tea.'

'Well then,' he winked, 'put a drop in y'tea. You're going to need it, I reckon. Dutch courage.'

Jenna perched nervously on a crate between them.

I inspected my sandwiches. A thin layer of soot glistened on the bread. I wrapped them up and put them back in the bag.

'Why have you come down here? Did Mei send you?'

Winnie let out a loud 'tut'.

Ted unscrewed the top of the whisky bottle and took a swig. 'Mei Liu? God no. She'd do her nut if she knew. We've come to help.'

'Help? How?'

'By letting you know what you're dealing with. Seems to us that, if you're hell-bent on being down here, you might as well know what went on. And besides, even if nothing happens to you tonight, we want the real story written up. But we're not stopping, y'understand? We're not stopping.'

Jenna nodded.

'OK, I always want the real story. Thank you.'

My phone came out and I hit record. Ted leant across and gently pressed stop.

'I would prefer not to be recorded,' he said.

Winnie took a deep breath and said, 'Just listen.'

'OK.'

Ted removed his helmet, set it gently on the table and ran a hand through his thick sandy hair. 'So... what do you know about all this?'

'Just what I was told by my friend at the *Chronicle*.'

'And what's that?'

'That... there's supposed to be a ghost down here – he's called Old Jossie – and he's the ghost of a miner. They say that if you knock, then he comes. And... he's lonely. That's why he likes children... or is drawn to children. I thought you were him when I saw your old helmet.'

He smiled. Winnie shifted uneasily in her wheelchair. 'No, no. Not him. Wrong clothes.'

Ted raised a calm hand.

'See, what you have there, young man, are bare bones. It's all that's left for most. But I know the whole story. I'm going to put meat on the bones for you, OK?'

'OK.'

Ted placed his palm on Jenna's knee. 'Don't be frightened, sweetheart, he won't hurt you. He's not interested in you.'

Then he slid his large hand out across the tabletop, curled it into a fist... and knocked angrily on the wood, sending a loud *RAP-RAP* into the still air. Winnie shut her eyes.

Then her brother lifted his old chin and boomed into the silence: 'And I'm not frightened of you. I'm not frightened! You hear me?'

His eyes dropped to me, defiant. I took out my pad. 'Do you mind if I take notes?'

Ted considered, took another swig of whisky, then nodded his approval.

'There's three things you need to get right about Old Jossie,' the old man began. 'He wasn't a miner; he didn't die alone – and, as for him liking children, well, that's the sickest joke of them all.'

'Go on,' I said, my pen poised.

He thought for a second, wetting his lips. The silence pulsed expectantly.

'*June 6th.*' Ted tapped the table. '*1910.*' Another tap.

'You can look it all up in the papers, it was all reported. The mine was full, all the seams were being worked. Normal day.'

He pointed to the four locked doors. 'Behind those there's a maze of tunnels that stretches six miles underground, like veins branching off from here, from the heart of the mine. Some of the tunnels are lost now, some dangerous, some collapsed. Some are big enough to walk a cuddy down – that's a pony – some of them just a few feet high. On that day, in 1910, there were miners in all of those tunnels, stripped to the waist and working, digging, cutting. Some on their knees, some on their backs, all spread out across the network. Then a message gets passed round. Something no miner wants to hear.'

He looked at Winnie, who was listening intently while staring at her lap.

'Fire,' the old man said. 'It goes round that there's a fire. Underground. Now this is very bad news in a mine, because of the firedamp.'

'What's firedamp?'

'Gas that collects in mines. Very dangerous. Very flammable. And there had been explosions at other collieries in the months before this, all caused by fire, with hundreds dead. Hundreds. So, everyone down here was already nervous. They were almost waiting for it to happen. So, they raised the alarm... fire... fire... they beat out the message.'

'Beat out the message?'

'Through their tools,' Ted said. 'That's how it worked. If you discovered a fire, you'd hammer two short bangs and then repeat it. Over and over again. If men in the next tunnel heard this, they'd join in. Beat out the message. Everyone did. It would echo right through. That way it reached the far end of the seams quickly, spread through six miles of tunnels in minutes. Better than bells, quicker than runners.'

'Just yakka,' Winnie said.

'Yakka?'

'Pitmatical – like a miners' language,' Ted explained. 'It was how men down here communicated... we called it yakka. It worked that day. They were ready. They beat the message out. Fire. Fire! Get out! Then, the miners all dropped their tools and headed here, streaming through the tunnels together, to the shaft, so they could get out, get up top, get safe.'

He looked at the cage. 'They all came here, hundreds of them, frightened and packed into this space. This chamber was full of them, shoulder to shoulder. They put out their lights, for safety, and then they waited in the dark for the cage to come down. That's when, well... things started to unravel.'

'What do you mean?'

Ted's watery old eyes rested on me. 'Mining was different back then. It's hard to imagine now. It were dangerous enough in my day, but... People round here were poor. The whole family had to earn. There were more than 200 men down here... but... the thing is... there were children down here too, dozens and dozens of young boys who worked next to their fathers, their uncles, their big brothers.'

'Children?'

He nodded, grim-faced. 'Yes. It was the same at all the mines. Just boys – as young as ten. And... it got too much for them, standing there, as they waited. It were dark. They were just frightened little boys ... and they started to cry. Just one at first, then all of them.'

He took another big mouthful of whisky, swallowed, and wiped his mouth. 'It's all there in the newspapers. Imagine being down here in the pitch black and hearing those children crying. It would break your heart. Of course, the men reached out to the boys, they found them in the dark and picked them up, held them, cuddled them, tried to comfort them, but a lot of the men were overcome with emotion too. Some men started to cry. They really thought they were going to die, you see. All of them. The atmosphere was charged with emotion. Then the cage arrives. Then all hell breaks loose.'

'Did they panic?'

Indignation flashed across his eyes. 'Panic? God no. These were professional men. Men who went underground every day. They didn't panic. But *he* did. *He* panicked.'

'Old Jossie?'

Ted raised a thin finger and fixed me with a hard stare.

'Here's more meat for your bones. His name was Josiah Alexander Rowlett the Second – and he was not a miner. He was the son of Sir Josiah Rowlett, the owner of the mine.'

Ted let out a sarcastic chuckle. 'You know, they say he was down here dressed to the nines – in a bloody tailcoat. He was going off to the races but had come storming down here to confront men who had the audacity to complain about safety. That's the only reason he was down here that day. The men were refusing to load coal. He wasn't a miner. He didn't care about what or who was down here. He just counted the money.'

Winnie spoke up: 'Just like her... Mei bloody Liu.'

Ted raised his hand again. 'Well, Rowlett suddenly found himself standing there in all his finery surrounded by hundreds of miners, in their tattered working clothes and with their blackened faces. He'd spent years arguing against safety improvements and now he was right in the middle of a disaster. There wasn't even a fire engine at the mine. He refused to buy one.'

'So, what happened when the cage came down?'

'Well, the cage were smaller back then – not like that one. That's modern, from my day. Back then, it could only carry so many people. Everyone knew that.'

Ted exhaled.

'But, of course, *Josiah Alexander Rowlett the Second* demands to go up on the first load, he pushes his way to the front. He barged past men who were holding their crying children.'

'And?'

Ted shook his head. 'When you're about to meet your maker, it doesn't matter how much you've got in the bank, or who your father is. There was uproar. The men dragged him out of the cage and told him that the children had to go up first. It were only right. So, Rowlett says he'll go up with them, go up with the boys.'

'No,' Winnie interjected, shaking her head gravely. 'No.'

Ted nodded in agreement. 'That wasn't going to happen. No way. So, then Rowlett climbs on a crate and threatens to sack the lot of them when they get up top, evict them from their homes – he says they'll starve.'

He looked at Winnie. Pride gleamed in his eyes. 'That's when the senior foreman – our great-grandfather – steps forward and tells Rowlett to shut up. He tells him in no uncertain terms what he thinks of him, that he can sack him if he dares, and that he can wait his bloody turn – in fact he can share the cage with him on the last load up. The men all cheered.'

Winnie said, 'The whole village was waiting at the top of the shaft. They heard the cheer.'

Ted nodded at the cage. 'So, the little boys went up first, and then it took four more loads to get almost everyone up, while the smell of smoke drifted about down here in the dark. When the fourth load went up, it left just the four foremen and Rowlett behind.'

He thought about taking another shot of whisky but pushed the bottle away. Then he spoke quietly, his eyes drifting around the black walls.

'As it went back down to get them there was a flash. Firedamp had ignited. All five of them were killed.'

Jenna's frightened eyes rolled around the chamber.

Ted placed his hand on her knee. He went on.

'In the weeks afterwards, Sir Josiah Rowlett used all his influence to control the story, to protect his son's reputation. The world was told how he had been a God-fearing man who gave to charity, who volunteered to teach at the Sunday school that the family built, who adored children. They even said he had *insisted* on staying down here until the last cage... the paper reported that was why the men cheered! But everyone in the village knew the truth. Over the years, the truth has been reduced to a fairy story. A fairy story about Old bloody Jossie.'

Winnie leant forward and tapped Jenna softly on the elbow. 'Tell Mr Baxter about what you saw, pet.'

'I didn't *see* anything,' she said quietly, 'but I heard him, and I saw what he did.'

'What did he do?' I asked. 'When was this?'

'When I was at school.'

She looked nervously at Winnie, who gave an encouraging look.

'We came down here on a trip. We all knew about Old Jossie, although I didn't know all this then.'

'You were too young, pet,' Ted said, 'too little.'

She bit her lip, then said, 'They always said you had to knock to get his attention – to make him come out to play. So, some of the boys did it. I heard them say the rhyme.'

'What's the rhyme?'

Again, Jenna looked to her grandmother for encouragement. She swallowed.

'Knock for Jossie once... knock for Jossie twice... if old Jossie knocks back... pray that he'll be nice.'

Ted leant across to her. 'And the rest,' he said softly.

She shook her head. 'I don't remember the rest.'

The old man nodded kindly, then winked at me.

'And then what happened?' I asked.

She took a deep breath. 'You're supposed to say the rhyme, then you knock twice... and listen for Jossie to knock back. If he does, then... then he's there.'

'And did he knock?'

'No, I didn't hear him knock… but I saw the boys knock, on a wooden crate, and then… one of them just went flying, like he had been shoved, pushed really hard from behind. I saw it. He went right across the room. But there was nobody there. I saw it happen… and then I heard him. I heard him laughing. Old Jossie.'

'What did he sound like?'

She looked at her feet. 'He sounded slowed down. Deep, like a voice that has been slowed down.'

'Did he do anything else?'

'Afterwards, some other boys said they were pinched, and others said… well… I don't know… but it was just the boys, not the girls.'

'That's right.' Winnie's voice was slurred. She looked exhausted. 'He was only ever interested in little boys.'

'We know that for a fact,' Ted said. 'For a fact.'

'How?'

'We know from the horse's mouth. Y'see, our great-grandad might have died down here with him, but his son – our grandad – was one of those little boys on that first cage to come up. He was only ten years old, and he was always proud to admit he was one of the boys who was there – one of the boys who cried. But he always said the boys weren't just frightened of the fire. He said they were frightened of the man in the top hat.'

*

I was alone again. Time to start over. The lights off, the chamber was plunged back into darkness. I lifted my bag from the table, placing it on the floor, then settled into the chair. The silence throbbed.

I waited for around an hour, motionless, listening, breathing, watching the pool of dull light at the foot of the shaft.

Then, slowly, I slid my hand out across the tabletop and curled it tightly into a fist.

I cleared my throat.

'Knock for Jossie once...' I whispered, 'knock for Jossie twice... if old Jossie knocks back... pray that he'll be nice.'

Then I raised my hand and brought it down hard on the wood, my knuckles firing a loud *RAP-RAP* into the blackness.

The sound echoed around the chamber. I waited. I listened.

In the silence, the dull throb ceased.

I waited.

DINK! A sound, metallic and abrupt, cut through the void. I caught my breath.

Then another.

DINK!

The same again – metallic, sharp, like steel on stone. Two knocks?

My mouth was dry.

'Hello?'

From across the chamber, the sounds came again. Closer. Together.

DINK... DINK...

I sat forward. Definitely two knocks. Was there somebody there?

DINK-DINK. DINK-DINK. Louder now. More certain.

Then, further off in the blackness, another joined. Dink-dink... dink-dink.

Further away. Another. Beyond the doors. Dink-dink, dink-dink, dink-dink. A rhythm. Tools working.

My hands gripped the table in the dark. The doors. The doors were open. *Dink-dink, dink-dink.*

Now more joined, then more, then more, *dink-dink, dink-dink*, the black void filling with metallic pounding, pealing like bells, rippling off into the distance, through the tunnels, down distant galleries, growing in number, pulsing the air, beating out the message, ringing in my ears – *dink-dink, dink-dink*, fire-fire, fire-fire!

At once, the tools stopped. The air seemed to pause, to hang suspended for a moment.

Then, like a great lungful of ancient breath, air rushed into the chamber, hissing in the dark through the doorways, pushed by movement far beyond, somewhere deep in the mine. Now came another sound – rumbling, growing and approaching. Footsteps, feet pounding in close quarters, hundreds of them, running, a distant, muffled stampede, streaming towards me in the dark.

I stood on shaky legs, gripping the table as the sound of the approaching men reached the unseen doorways.

I gawped blindly into the black, eyes peeled wide against the cold air, ears straining.

A flurry of boots. They poured through the doors, toes catching heels, jostling and stumbling, palms braced against backs, staggering, halting, falling over each other, surrounding me, breathing heavily, coughing, whispering prayers and curses, hundreds of men, shoulder to shoulder, filling the chamber, seething and swaying as one – and with them came an electricity, a charge in the air that seemed to climb the walls and hang like a pregnant cloud above. Desperation. I could hear the panic in their shallow breaths as they milled in the dark. They waited. I waited.

I felt it in my stomach before I heard it. In my chest. In my heart.

The gentle sob drifted up from the floor – a pitiful, primal whine cracked by stilted gulps of air. The little boy's fear cut through the darkness. Stripped of all comfort, his fragility reached out. A few feet away in the blackness, another boy began to whimper. I felt emotion surge through me like never before, my eyes brimming, my chest rising.

Bite down on it, Joe, Jesus Christ bite down on it!

Too late. Too late. As one, the boys wept – dozens of frightened little voices rising in waves through the dark. The cloud burst. Despair drenched the chamber. Hot tears streamed down my cheeks.

I heard the men reach out, to find, to hold, to pray; whispering words of comfort in voices edged with terror. Slowly, the chamber fell quiet again.

FLASH! The air screamed. A shock of blinding blue. Wheels rolled and pulleys rumbled as light flooded in, ethereal and bright, pouring down the shaft like icy fog. I forced my stinging eyes open. The chamber, bathed in blue, was empty, the men gone, but the cage... the cage was descending! Slowly, it crawled into view – somehow older and smaller – suspended in a column of flickering light. It cast a web of shadows which swam across the glistening black walls.

I stumbled forward, hands shielding my stinging eyes from the dazzling light. The cage came to rest. Its crooked old door rattled aside violently. I stared into the empty space within.

From behind me came a gentle KNOCK.

The deep voice was playful.

'Going up?' it said.

I span. The little man lounged against the doorframe in the flickering blue light, watching me with nonchalant amusement. A smile spread across his face as I took him in.

Josiah Alexander Rowlett the Second was dressed from top to toe in sparkling white perfection. His white shoes gleamed below pressed high-buttoned trousers. His elegant white tailcoat hung unbuttoned to reveal a white waistcoat and spotless collar. His white-gloved hands delicately clutched a white silk top hat. And above his crisp white bowtie, sat a pinched face of alabaster white skin. But his eyes were black. As black as coal.

He pushed himself away from the doorframe with a little skip and placed the hat on his snowy hair. Then he daintily tilted it before holding his hands aloft.

'How do I look?' His deep voice was hollow and detached. 'Quite remarkable, isn't it? Look at me, Mr Joseph Baxter... just look at me.'

He executed a little twirl, then took a step forward. 'I said...

remarkable, isn't it? By my reckoning, I've been down here for at least a century and... just look at me. I'm more real than you!'

He took two quick steps towards me and stuck out a tailored elbow. I recoiled. He presented it again, with a black-eyed smile. *'You can touch me if you wish, go on! I'm quite real, I assure you.'*

I was speechless, frozen.

'Sorry if I boast, but... it's nice to be seen. No? Cat got your tongue?' His white lip jutted in feigned disappointment, then he inspected my tear-stained face. *'My dear boy! Why so sad? It's good to weep, you know – it releases all that pent-up energy. Better out than in!'*

He reached out to touch me, but then pulled his hand back. *'Oh... I can see someone's already got their claws into you... shame.'*

Then he turned and paced across the chamber, sat on the chair, and crossed his legs, primly.

'Yes, I'm as fit as a butcher's dog, Mr Joseph Baxter. That's not surprising, though, I must say. I like it down here. It's... cosy.' He looked around the walls. *'Lots to do, plenty to meet. Lots of little visitors. It's wonderful. What a playground! So much life! Why would I leave?'*

The little man leant forward, as if to coax a response from me. I was still frozen in fear.

'Really?' he said. *'Nothing? Come on, Mr Baxter – it would be nice to have a conversation with an adult!'* He sighed and brushed his knee.

'I heard you saying my little rhyme. That was good. They like that, my little darlings... although I'm not so keen on all of it, I have to say. Tell me, Joseph, what's it like up there?'

Get a grip, Joe.

'W-what's it like?'

He clasped his gloved hands. *'That's better! Yes, what's it like? Tell me – is my lovely school still open? Still saving little souls?'*

'No. No. It's offices now.'

He looked crestfallen. *'Oh, that is a shame. I had such wonderful times there. I made so many little friends. Bible studies* can be so dry – don't you think? But there's nothing quite like personal tutoring, that's what I always told them. My speciality, you might say. Just me. And a boy. Undisturbed. Learning about love.'

His black eyes glinted mischievously in the flickering light.

'Oh!' He raised a gloved finger, then produced a pearl-white pocket watch. 'Would you excuse me for just one moment?'

Rowlett stood and marched purposefully towards me, then ushered me aside with a polite 'Would you mind…?'

I stepped to the wall and watched as he took up position at the entrance to the cage. Then he turned and faced the four open doors, glancing again at his watch.

'Gentlemen!' he exclaimed. 'Right on time, as always!'

In each of the four doorways stood a burly-looking man. They were stripped to the waist, sweat shining on their soot-smeared skin. One stroked his large sandy-coloured moustache as he studied the little man in white. Determined eyes stared from their blackened faces.

Rowlett put away his watch. 'Shall we begin?'

The light behind him began to pulse, the mesh of shadows cast by the cage strobing across the walls. The four men gripped the doorframes with strong arms, their heavy work boots teetering on the threshold of the chamber, their eyes looking warily at the floor.

'Come along, come along,' he said impatiently, 'you know how this works!'

In unison they stepped into the room, but just as their heavy boots stamped down into the dust, they seemed to falter, to fold in on themselves. Instantly, the chamber was filled with searing heat. All four men fell to their knees as their bodies seemed to contract, to crack and dry as if burned by an unseen flame. Rowlett stood ahead of them, the shimmering cage behind him, his jet eyes watching impassively. Now the four men staggered forward on their knees, beckoned by the glowing cage, but their bodies corrupted again, breaking down, the skin shrinking around their bones, hardening, blackening, their clothes twisting and crumbling into black, singed fibres. I felt my face flush as the temperature climbed higher. Now they were on their hands and knees, crawling desperately towards the light, as deep fissures appeared in their flesh, as it turned to charcoal, as their eyes collapsed into their skulls, their hands grasping at the ground as their flesh retracted to form skeletal cinder-stick fingers. The man in white loomed above them as the first of the miners collapsed onto his exposed ribcage, before crumbling into a mound of ash. But the others still dragged themselves onward, black, blind eye sockets searching for the light, knotted fingers scraping the floor, clawing the soot near his perfect white shoes. With a sigh, two of them disintegrated away in dust. Hotter still. The hairs on my neck spiked as the temperature soared, my lungs aching as they gulped at burning air. The last of the miners, now little more than a blackened skeleton, dragged himself forward still, the remains of his sandy moustache pressed into the dirt as he stretched out a hand, extending between those immaculate shoes, edging towards the cage, reaching towards that light, but he could not, he could not. His hand fell to the ground an inch short of the pulsing blue glow. The air in the chamber boiled.

Rowlett looked down with contempt at the pathetic remains at his feet and watched as the cremated fingers trembled in one last attempt to reach their goal.

'*I think not,*' he said, and brought his heel down hard on the miner's paper-like skull. The figure vanished in a cloud of inky black ash.

I felt my knees sway, my eyes drying up, my nostrils burning.

The little man buttoned his tailcoat stiffly. '*As I have stressed before, gentlemen,*' he announced to the chamber, '*I'm afraid you will have to wait until the last load to leave.*'

Shimmering in the heat haze, Josiah Alexander Rowlett the Second cast a pitiful glance at me. I felt my legs give way.

*

Knock-knock.

Sunlight blurred as I struggled to sit upright. Wood polish.

Knock-knock.

I heard it again, and then the soft creak of a heavy wooden door opening slowly.

Jenna stood over the sofa, a look of concern on her face.

'Are you OK?' she said.

'Where am I?'

'In Mei's office, in the old school. They found you this morning passed out. Are you OK?'

'I think so.' I rubbed my face. Light was pouring into the little oak-panelled room through a stained-glass window, falling onto antique bookcases and a leather-topped desk.

'Grandma said I should tell you to go, to leave, before Mei comes back,' she said.

I swung my legs round onto the floor.

'Why?'

'She's on the warpath, on the phone to her lawyers. Says she won't be blamed for whatever happened to you. Says we need to control the story.'

I shook my head. 'That won't happen,' I said.

'What did happen to you?' Jenna asked.

'I'm not sure you'd believe me.'

She thought for a second, then pulled open the door again. 'I'm not sure I want to know anyway.'

'Jenna,' I said as she turned away, 'what happened to the other kids on your trip? Did he... touch them?'

She looked at me then nodded. 'Just the boys.'

'And what's the rest of the rhyme?'

She shut the door again. Her broad face looked up at the window, caught in a yellow shaft.

'Knock for Jossie once,' she said, 'knock for Jossie twice, if old

Jossie knocks back, pray that he'll be nice.'

She took a breath.

'He might give you a kick, he might give you a kiss, but let old Jossie have his way to keep him down the pit.'

She opened the door. 'I'd get out of here if I were you,' she said, then disappeared down the stairs.

I sat for a moment, the events down the mine running through my mind. The children crying in the dark. His black eyes. He had spoken to me. *He knew my name.*

Patience's words came back to me: 'If they are talking to you, then they are connecting to you.'

I needed her. I needed her advice.

I gathered my things. As I closed the door quietly behind me, I saw an engraved brass plaque, deeply scratched and barely legible.

'*Headteacher's office. Private. During Bible lessons, please knock three times and wait to be admitted*'.

TWENTY-FIVE

Losing My Patience

It took me a while to get my bearings. The high-rise estate had been almost entirely demolished now, leaving behind a vast, flat expanse of earth, gravel and twisted steel wire. As I drove the VW down the hill towards the huge building site, it looked like a wound, gouged into the heart of Grimsby. The workmen, the trucks, the portacabins and the corralled, sleeping diggers were also gone. Even the roads had been torn up and flattened – all except one.

The last remaining piece of tarmac cut directly through the wasteland to stop at the foot of Mulvaney Tower, which looked even more sorry than on my last visit to Humberside. As I parked, I peered up, looking for Mo and Ellie's flat. Nearly all of the windows in the tower block were smashed. Ragged curtains fluttered like sails in the breeze.

But there, three quarters of the way up, three intact windows glowed from behind closed blinds.

I turned the engine off, sat back and puffed out my cheeks as another wave of exhaustion swept over me. Mom's car felt clean and quiet after the horrors of the mine.

The boys. Crying in the dark. The office. My God, that office! And the little man's deep, hollow voice. How did he know me? How did he know my *name*? I needed help. I needed Patience.

I trudged across what remained of the car park and into the lobby of the tower block, heading for the lift. There, sitting despondently on a large old suitcase, was Mo Spooner, his sizeable chin resting in his palms.

He sat up, an initial look of friendly recognition evaporating as he crossed his tattooed arms.

'Look who it is, it's Mr Journalist.'

'Hi, Mo, sorry to bother you. I need your help.'

His eyebrows lifted. 'Need my help? That's rich. Don't need your help, not after last time.'

I was finding it hard to concentrate. The miles covered were taking their toll.

'Sorry, I don't understand.' I pointed at the battered suitcase. 'Have they finally managed to kick you and Ellie out?'

He stood up, then yanked up his black jeans by the belt loops. 'No, no, this isn't mine. It's for Ellie, she's coming to get her stuff.'

I shook my head, bemused.

'I've still got the flat, I haven't lost that. Won't lose that. I've lost her – she run off with that Adam Zacharanda bloke!'

'Oh… I'm really sorry to hear that…'

'He bamboozled her with all this medium stuff. Told her she had a gift.' His eyes drifted to the dirty floor. 'She's his groupie now.'

I stared at him blankly.

'It all went bad after that night,' he muttered.

'Shit,' I said. 'That's shit. Sorry, Mo.'

I sat down on the floor. He considered this.

'You alright, mate? You look knackered.'

'I am. Losing it a bit. Didn't sleep at all last night. Got a train from Durham to Birmingham, then drove straight here. Not sure why. I need your help.'

We both turned at the squeak of soft footsteps in the doorway. Ellie, in a bright yellow T-shirt, slipped her fingertips awkwardly into the pockets of her tight blue jeans. She looked like she had lost weight.

'What's going on here, then? You selling your story, Mo?'

His face melted. 'Hello... Elvira my love, how are you? How have you been?'

She smiled kindly. 'It's just Ellie, Mo, just Ellie now. That my stuff?'

He passed the suitcase. 'Yes, all here, babe. I can bag up all your soft toys for you too...'

'No, that's alright, Mo, you can keep them, they're not really...'

'No, I want you to have them. For the memories, you know...'

'Thanks, but...' She looked at me, sitting cross-legged between them. 'Sorry, what's he doing here?'

'Says he wants my help.'

'*You alright, mate?*' Ellie said. She looked concerned.

I stood up and dusted off my backside.

'Er, yes, I'm alright. I just need to find Patience.'

They looked at each other.

'Who's Patience?' Mo said.

'Patience. The lady who was here when we all came to look at the stain.'

They looked at me blankly. I felt a jab of panic.

'Patience. Black lady. In a green coat. She was in the kitchen with me.'

They exchanged looks again. Mo shook his head.

'Sorry, mate, no idea what you're on about. We never invited a black lady. What was her name?'

'Patience. Patience... Dubois. She was playing cards at the kitchen table.'

Mo thought for a second. Then his black polished fingernails slapped gently against his cheek.

'Dubois? A black lady?'

'That's right. From St Lucia.'

He looked wide-eyed at Ellie.

'What?'

'You remember when my mam lived here, when we first met?'

She nodded.

'Mrs Dubois lived in the flat next door. She used to keep her company – she taught her Solitaire. When she was really poorly, she used to carry her laundry to the hatch, the chute in the corridor. She was... West Indian?'

Flick, flick, flick.

'That's her!' I said. 'West Indian... St Lucia...'

He shook his head again.

'Mate... she's been dead twenty years.'

I felt the world stop.

Flick, flick, flick.

Somewhere inside, Patience's warm voice surfaced: '*Some folks are between two places. That's me.*'

Mo and Ellie stared.

Flick, flick, flick.

Her soft brown hands gathered the cards. She started again.

I saw young Cameron's sheepish face, his eyes on me only, as he propped open the kitchen door.

Her kindly voice came again: '*Life goes wrong all the time – and sometimes death goes wrong too.*'

I heard the confused bus driver outside RAF Binton: 'You getting on or what?'

I watched as he rolled his eyes at me, unaware that Patience had taken her seat.

Flick, flick, flick.

The cards danced as she placed them on the table.

'*They can follow people, walk in your shadow,*' she said.

Now I felt Mo's hand on my shoulder. He was speaking. I couldn't hear him.

Patience smiled. '*Sometimes they just look completely normal.*'

307

The cards moved faster and faster, bewildering, a blur of white.

Flick, flick, flick.

'Blank,' I said. 'Blank.'

Ellie blinked. 'What?'

'The cards were blank.'

'The rules are different where I come from,' I heard Patience say.

TWENTY-SIX

The Bitter End

The Eleventh Vigil

Blue lights circled. The German Shepherd lunged at the protester chained to the post box, its teeth flashing white as the leash pulled taut. The dog's muzzle snapped and spat, billowing breath that mingled in the bitter evening air with oil and diesel fumes. With a sharp tug, the handler yanked the animal back. The long-haired youth shouted angrily at the policeman.

I watched, blinking, from the other side of the crossroads, my collar turned up against the December chill. Aggression charged the air. I felt on edge. What day was it?

Now a muscular officer was stomping his way along the protesters, snatching placards as he went. A thin dreadlocked youth struggled to keep hold of a crudely painted sign, then surrendered it with a scowl.

The tall man next to me on the kerb chuckled to himself.

'In my day, that dog would have been off the lead by now,' he said in a gruff Cockney drawl.

All around the junction, engines growled, lines of vehicles held at bay in all four directions. A van driver jabbed angrily at his horn, provoking another volley of barks from the police dog.

'That's where it happens,' he said, 'in front of those old doors. Right behind that idiot chained up on the kerb.'

He pointed at the dark boarded-up building across the road, its brickwork cast in revolving whirls of blue and yellow.

'Back in the day, that pub was right at the heart of East End crime. All the villains knew it, most of them used it. We knew all about it too. It was neutral territory, you see. Like a kind of Checkpoint Charlie. Every now and then they'd meet up for a parlay in it, have a bit of a sit down, to clear the air between the gangs, sort out their grievances.'

He watched as a policeman used bolt cutters to release the shouting man from the post box.

'I'm not sure what they would have made of this lot,' he muttered.

'Do you think they would have disapproved?' I asked.

'I think they would have beaten the living daylights out of them,' he said, matter-of-factly.

Something, somewhere, creaked coldly in the breeze. I felt irritation stir. 'What are they protesting about, anyway?' I found myself asking.

He shrugged. 'Climate change. Immigration. Gentrification. Urban decay? If you ask me, there's a lot more decaying around here than old buildings. There's no community anymore. I mean, who are these people? They're not from around here. They think they're making a difference, but all I know is they're stopping this lot from getting home.'

The van driver's horn split the air again.

I looked at Mickey White. He was every inch the retired detective. He was in impressive shape for a man of his age – fit and lean. His smart blue blazer was unbuttoned to reveal a crisp white shirt, which despite the cold gaped open at the collar, a gold chain glinting on tanned skin beneath. His eyes seemed caught in a permanent squint above a flat, boxers' nose. He looked like he was made of oak.

He returned my gaze, lingering a little on my tired eyes. 'You look knackered, sunshine – you sure you want to do this tonight? It's bleeding cold. I wouldn't.'

Another thin creak carried on the breeze. I looked for the source. 'Yes. Sorry I brought it forward, but it's the last one of these I'm going to do. I just want to get it out of the way. I've had enough. Sorry for the late change of plan... I won't keep you long.'

'Makes no odds to me, sunshine, no skin off my nose. I'm out doing these tours most nights now. Supplements the pension.'

'The reporter at the *Standard* said she'd done one of your tours. Said it was eye-opening.'

Mickey put his hands in his pockets. 'Mind out,' he said, 'here comes the meat wagon.'

With a piercing blare of siren, a police van shunted its way awkwardly through the rows of traffic to stop outside the old pub as the protesters jeered.

'Yeah, I call it my Gangland Crime Beat – walking tours of London's mean streets,' he said, watching as more officers clambered out. 'The tourists love it. And women too – women love a bit of true crime. It's their football, I reckon. I leave in all the grisly details, that's what they like. Inside knowledge, you see. It takes about an hour, and I walk them around the hangouts of the old 60s gangsters, scenes of crime, murders, stabbings... some of the old red light district. It's nearly all gone now, of course, but when it gets dark you still get a feel for it.'

It was getting darker now, and colder. Herded by half a dozen policemen, the protesters were trooping noisily into the van, as the dog handler inspected the chain coiled around the old post box. The German Shepherd was sitting quietly, staring intently at the old doors. I couldn't see what it was looking at.

'And do you include the ghost in your tour?' I asked.

'Well, I mention that sort of thing sometimes but it's not really a ghost tour – that's someone else's game,' he said. 'I bring 'em here cos of the pub, but like I say, I mention it. Well, there's not a lot going on here otherwise. The place has been shut for twenty-odd years. So, I tell 'em about Donnie Devlin.'

'That's his name?'

'That's his name. And that was where he died – right there – outside his pub.'

'And you've seen him?'

He shook his head. 'No, but I've heard him alright. In fact – and this is where my inside knowledge comes in again – I've heard them. *Them.*'

Mickey White flashed a satisfied smile, then waved to the driver of the police van as it pulled away, its occupants banging noisily in the back. Then he picked up my bag, handed it to me, and led me by the elbow into the road. 'Come on, let's get across before they open it up.'

Motorists glared from behind their steering wheels as we walked through their headlights. An older copper greeted Mickey with a weary 'Alright, Chalky!', eliciting a pat on the shoulder.

We reached the other kerb just as, with a triumphant blast of horns, the traffic started to move, wheels arcing dirty water into the gutters. Within seconds the crossroads had roared into a noisy blur of motion and lights. The police moved off too; only the dog van remained, parked on the pavement outside the pub, as the handler struggled to untangle the grimy chain. Mickey bent to help.

I watched the dog. Sitting bolt upright, it stared into space, its head slowly tilting one way, then the other. When the handler came to lead it away, it resisted for a second, then relented and padded off to climb into the van. Mickey thumped the roof as it drove off the pavement.

This was a dingy, dark little corner of London. Decades of exhaust fumes had stained the pub's walls a grimy grey and blackened the wooden sheets that covered its windows. The tall, thin double doors were nailed shut, criss-crossed by half a dozen knotted planks. A litter-strewn bench lurked forgotten under a flickering streetlamp. Only the post box, painted in vivid red, escaped the sense of decline.

Above the doors, painted directly onto the brickwork, was a barely legible old advertisement, its faded letters spelling out 'Drink Best Bitter – the taste of courage'.

Mickey appeared at my shoulder, wiping his hands with a handkerchief.

'That's apt,' I said. 'They call those ghost signs.'

His squint tightened as he read the vague lettering. 'Lots of them round here, sunshine,' he replied. 'They're one of the few things that the council won't let you get rid of. Kind of sad, aren't they?'

I nodded. 'Them. You said them – so there's more than one ghost?'

'Yep, I reckon. It's Donnie alright, but I think it's Tommy Devlin too. They were brothers. Twins.'

'Twins? That's a bit of a cliché, isn't it? Sounds like the Krays.'

It was Mickey's turn to display a flash of irritation.

'The Krays. Everyone wants to know about the bleeding Krays. The Krays only stood out because they liked having their picture taken, liked being in the papers. But it wasn't unusual that they were brothers. There were loads of brothers – the whole thing was built on family, every gang was. There was the Krays and the Richardsons at the top, but there were brothers in all the smaller outfits as well. The Devlin twins were small fry – but they ran this pub together, which gave them a little bit more clout.'

'And you reckon it's both brothers here?'

Mickey grinned. 'That's what it sounded like to me.'

'You know, for a policeman you seem to accept all this quite easily.'

Another irritated flash. 'And that surprises you? Why?'

'I don't know. I thought you'd be more sceptical, I suppose. Evidence and all that.'

Mickey ran his palm around the back of his tanned neck. 'Well, what more evidence do you need than your own ears? Or your own eyes?'

'I thought you didn't see anything?'

I bristled slightly as I felt him take me by the elbow again. 'Let's me and you have a squat, sunshine,' he said.

Mickey used his handkerchief to brush off the bench.

'As a copper, you see a lot of things,' he said, scanning the buildings opposite as he settled next to me. 'And you hear about a lot of things too, from people who you trust. I knew one fella who was with the transport police, and he swore blind that people saw ghosts regularly on the Underground. He told me it was almost a monthly thing, just part of the job.'

He crossed his arms and stretched his legs out. Mickey White made himself comfortable.

'Let me tell you a story,' he said, as the streetlamp flickered above.

'On my first week in the job, when I was a young uniform, I was working out of Penge – which is the oldest police station in London. Lovely old building, like a great big house really, but a tough beat at the time because there were so many pubs in the area. Anyway, at the end of my first week I was due to go out on an evening patrol round the boozers with one of the old-school constables, who'd taken me under his wing. It was raining cats and dogs outside, but I still hadn't been issued with an overcoat, because I was new, you know. So, he tells me to go down to the basement – where all the old cells are – and get an old overcoat from the surplus room. I do as I'm told. The basement was only really used for storage by then, and I remember the stairs going down were narrow, and all cluttered with boxes of files and junk. But I went down and turned the lights on.'

Mickey's brow knotted. 'The moment I put the lights on I

hear someone call, "Hey, you!", from down one of the corridors. Bear in mind this is like a warren of empty rooms and offices, all stacked with boxes and filing cabinets and old desks and all sorts of rubbish. The whole basement has got a very low ceiling, and it's not used at all. Then I hear it again – someone calling, "Hey, you!" So, I call back, "You alright?" It goes quiet, then again, I hear "Hey, you!" And it's coming from where the old cells are, right at the far end of the basement. Anyway, I don't hang about, I go to the surplus room, and find an overcoat and I'm just about to go back to the stairs when – "Hey, you!" – there it is again, louder this time. I thought maybe someone's pulling my leg, having a laugh with the new lad, so I shout back, "You're not funny, you know!" It goes quiet, then – "Hey, you!" – it comes again. Then he calls out, "Hey, you! *Come here!*"'

Mickey looked at me and smiled. 'I was shitting myself; I'm not going to lie. I didn't want to go and have a look, but I thought, *I'm in a new job, what if it's a* test, *what if I get in trouble for ignoring him?* So, I tuck the overcoat under my arm and start picking my way towards the old cells. It's dark down there at the back because the lights haven't worked in years. When I get to them there's this little passageway, with cell doors closed on either side, and one at the end. They're proper old cells, with big iron doors and a little barred window, and they're really small – like something from the Middle Ages, really. Anyway, in the one at the end, I can see a light – but it's flickering, like a candle. And then the voice comes again – from this cell at the end: "*Hey, you! Come here!*"'

I felt him shiver. He closed his blazer and took a deep breath.

'So, I makes my way to the door at the end. I get on my tiptoes, and I try to look through the window... but I can't quite see the whole cell. Then the voice comes again, from inside: "Hey, you. Hey, you, *come in!*" I whisper, "Who's in there?" – but it goes quiet. So, I think... *Sod it!* and I grab the door handle and turn it but the door won't budge, 'cos it's so old, so I give it a yank and it moves a little then, so I pull again and it moves a bit more and then I dig my heels in, grab the handle with both hands and get ready to give it a right good heave when "*Oi!*" – this angry voice comes from behind me. I jump about two feet in the air with fright and turn round and there's this bloody massive copper stood at the end of the passageway, like a silhouette, with this tall helmet on and his hands on his hips. "What the bleedin' hell do you think you're doing?" he yells at me. "You shouldn't be down here!" So, I say, "Sorry, sir!" as I scurry back towards him, and he shouts, "Sorry, *Sergeant*" as I get close to him. As I go past him, he growls, "Nothing for you to see in there", and I look up... just for a second and... and... his skin is as white as a sheet... powdery, like snow... and he's got this big bushy grey moustache... and his uniform... it's like it's Victorian ... blue, not black, and it's got a row of big brass buttons down the front and a bleeding cape on the shoulders. A bleeding cape! But I don't stop, I just mutter about getting an overcoat and stumble all the way back to the stairs. My heart's pounding away and it's only as I'm nearly at the steps that I think about what I've just seen – his face, his uniform – and I think about his eyes...'

'What about them?'

He thought for a moment. 'They were stitched up.'

Mickey looked at me, gauging my reaction. 'I swear. Sewn shut. That was enough for me. I rocketed up the stairs, clambering over all the junk. When I get to the top the old PC's waiting for me. He takes one look at me and he says, "I see you met the sergeant, then!" That was my first week.'

He exhaled and looked at his shoes.

'So, you see I'm quite open to all this stuff. I think most coppers are. Like I said, you see things, you hear things.'

'And what did you hear here?'

He looked over to the doors. 'I heard the fight. Clear as day. Proper nasty it was, you could feel the aggression. So did some of the tourists – freaked some of them out. I think they put it on social media, which is how the *Standard* picked it up.'

It was dark now. The traffic was starting to die down, with passing headlights shining off the wet road to sweep blankly over shop windows. Mickey sighed.

'It's all changed round here. Not just the place, the people. This used to be like a little country, you know, with its own language, its own rules, its own laws. Life was tough, but that's because the people were fighters, they had to be. They all fought to do better for themselves – all of them – to make a better life. I look at those weirdos who were here earlier, making a nuisance of themselves, and I think, *They don't know how lucky they are.* They're here fighting over some grand issue, some bleeding flavour of the month campaign or protest, and they've no idea. They blame the older generations for creating all these so-called issues, but they don't realise that we were too busy fighting to put food on the table, to heat our homes, to fix the roof, to put shoes on our children. They think they're making a difference – and maybe they are – but it's a luxury. They think they're fighting, but it's a luxury.'

'And the Devlins were fighters?'

'Yep – literally, as a matter of fact. They were boxers. They were right handy too. There was a boxing club above the pub for a while. When they were little boys their dad, Reg, got them into it. I grew up round here, and I remember them – I was bit younger, like – but I remember the family. Dirt poor. Dirt poor.'

'Did you ever see them fight?'

'You could say that. Everyone did – all the time. Reg, you see, well he was a nasty piece of work. He was a drinker, and he used to knock them about. Never had a job in his life, and never had two pennies to rub together. When Donnie and Tommy were little, he used to make them box each other in the street and he would take bets. I remember it really clearly – all the kids used to come out and watch. Reg would put this tatty old dining chair in the middle of the street, and he'd sit there, in his dirty vest, and he'd referee the fight. It was hard to watch. "To the bitter end" he would say to them, "to the bitter end". The neighbours had to break them apart. The fights used to go on forever.'

He turned to me. 'It was like they couldn't feel the punches. And, of course, while they were boxing, Reg couldn't hit them. It was like they were fighting each other and protecting each other at the same time. Turned them into right little hard bastards, it did.'

'So, how did they end up running this place?'

'Well, I remember when they were called up for National Service in the 1950s, like all young men were back then – they did eighteen months in the Fusiliers. It was the first time they had three square meals a day, and they met a lot of other East End wide boys in the army, who were impressed by their boxing. They were both Regimental Champion, you see. Just kept passing the title back and forth between them. No one else could beat 'em. They were never happier than when they were knocking seven bells out of each other. They were always going to fall into this kind of life. But the pub was supposed to be their way out.'

'Their way out?'

'Like a retirement plan. After the army, they ran a little gang together for a few years, providing muscle for some of the bigger faces, protection rackets on local businesses, bit of pimping, card games... but they were cleverer than that. So, they bought this pub, and set it up as neutral ground for all the gangs. That way they kept their profile but didn't have to get their hands dirty anymore. And no one would mess with the Devlins, partly because all of the major faces bought into their idea of a neutral pub, but mainly because the brothers were as hard as nails.'

I was beginning to realise why Mickey's tours were so popular. He told a good story.

'So, what happened? How did Donnie end up dead?'

'What do you think? Another fight! The story that went round was that they had fallen out – again – and Tommy had arranged for him to be done in by a hitman as he locked up one night.

Donnie was stabbed – just a single, fatal stab – right there outside the doors. Tommy disappeared afterwards. He hasn't been seen to this day. But... that's not what happened. I know what happened. I found it. In the files.'

He looked at me, waiting for the question.

Somewhere, the creak lifted on the wind. I felt another jab of irritation.

'Inside knowledge?' I asked.

'Donnie was on the take. He was a police informant; it's all there in the old CID files. He was listening in on the gangs when they came to parlay in the pub and then feeding it to us. He was using that post box to get it to us. We had it set up with the post office, they knew what to look out for.'

'Why would he do that?'

'No idea. Maybe we had something on him. Maybe he had a problem with the horses, or drugs. Could have been any number of reasons – but it's true. And that's not all. It wasn't a hitman.'

'Who killed him, then?'

'Tommy, of course. That's what I reckon anyway. One last fight. I think they found out about Donnie and ordered Tommy to sort his brother out.'

'And then he disappeared?'

Mickey shook his head. Another creak.

'I reckon they both died. That night.' He looked across at the doors. 'That's why they're both still here.'

'Is that in the files too?'

'No, but it makes sense. When they found Donnie's body there was blood everywhere. *Everywhere.* All of this pavement was soaked red, so they assumed it was Donnie's blood. There was nothing like DNA back then, of course, but they could check that – against his army records. And it was his blood type, so it made sense. But here's the thing – Donnie's wound wasn't a bleeder. I saw that as soon as I read the report. Straight stab to the heart – almost instant death. So, the blood came from someone else. I reckon Donnie managed to stab Tommy in the fight too, maybe caught an artery. My theory is: Tommy goes staggering back into the pub. They get him to one of their doctors, but it was too late. Lost too much blood. Basically, what happened here killed both brothers.'

'And what about Tommy's body?'

'Oh, well, you've got lots to choose from there – the bottom of the Thames, fed to the pigs on some farm, cremated by a friendly undertaker, crushed in an old car, shoved in the same coffin as some other poor sod. That's straightforward – but the main point is he died. He must have. Never seen again! Never heard of again! He just vanished. The next day, there was someone else behind the bar, someone else running the pub. That's the end of the Devlins.'

Dry leaves and litter were swirling around the old doors now.

'So why did it close down?'

'Oh… it lost its licence. This was years after the Devlins, though.'

'Why did it lose its licence?'

'Violence. Just fights… fights every weekend, right outside those bloody doors. Worst spot in the whole East End for brawls. Something just comes over people here. Eventually the magistrates had enough and just shut the place down.'

Mickey looked at his watch and stood up. 'I've got to go, sunshine, got a tour to do later. You sure you want to do this tonight? It's bleeding cold and this ain't a nice place to sleep, out on the street. Some unsavoury characters around here. You up to it?'

I was getting a little tired of Mickey's tough guy act.

'I'll be fine,' I said. 'I won't be sleeping.' I patted the bag on the bench next to me. 'I've got all I need. Anyway, I'll be busy making notes if my fingers don't freeze.'

'Just be careful, yeah?' he said. 'This has always been a violent spot.'

'Understood… One more question: what was the pub called?'

He eyed me coolly for a moment. 'Like I said, it was a retirement plan, their way of stepping out of the ring,' He gestured above the doors, then hurried away across the junction.

High on the blackened wall, the old pub sign creaked as it swung in the wind, its painted front cracked and flaking. Two plump red boxing gloves met over curling letters: 'The Bitter End'.

⋆

It wasn't the cold that stopped me making notes, it was the flickering streetlight above, which blinked and clicked and flashed, making it impossible for me to write anything, anything at all. In the end I slapped the pad back into the bag in frustration and took out my flask, then poured hot tea into its thin, round cup, balancing it awkwardly on the warped wood of the old bench. With numb, frozen fingers I lifted it to my mouth but recoiled; the tea tasted of plastic. My sandwiches were stale and were returned half eaten to my bag, wrapped in a crumpled parcel of tin foil.

At around midnight I had watched as Mickey returned with a tour group in tow, telling them the story of the Devlins from across the road. I just wanted them to leave; it felt like they were intruding. I ignored his wave.

By 1am the junction was quiet, but still the incessant creak of the pub sign echoed around the closed shops. This was my first outdoor vigil, and it was impossible to get comfortable in any way on the hard bench. What was I doing here? I tried sitting on my sleeping bag, but it kept sliding forward. I tried putting my feet on the bag, but my legs began to cramp up in the cold.

In the end I zipped my sleeping bag up to my waist and sat with my arms crossed, my head tipped sideways onto the back of the bench, my eyes fixed on the old doors.

My shoulders sagged as the light blinked... blinked... blinked... the long shadow of the post box unfolding then retracting on the greasy pavement, swinging like a pendulum as the sign above creaked back and forth. I closed my eyes. I felt the day slip away.

I didn't completely fall asleep, but I know I didn't dream either, the long hours, the travel and the exhausting experiences of the last few days dragging me slowly down and down and down but the charged ether of the junction above pulling me back to the surface – to the blinking light, the cold warped wood, to the creaking sign, the wind, the wet road, the protestors, the irritation of it all, of this *place*. It had a hook in me, in my skin, and it was holding me between the waking world and the sleep that waited somewhere, as I fitfully balanced on the edge of rest. But how could I rest? This place. *This place.* I felt resentment wrap around me like a stiff blanket, itchy and coarse and too close, and there was rage trapped beneath its material, rage that needed to be let out, to strike out. The sign creaked and the light flickered and the hands... the hands moved across me, their filthy brown nails protruding from the sodden wool of thick fingerless gloves, the hooded head turning to my feet, and the sign creaked again as the zip on my bag slid slowly open and out! The rage burst out, the anger and the aggression boiling in me, my teeth clenched and my fists tightening under my folded arms.

I opened my eyes.

The dark figure stooped at my feet, his arms moving slowly, silently.

I screamed at him. I screamed, 'What are you doing? What are you doing?' and hurled myself at the crouched figure, clawing at his back, my legs still bound in the sleeping bag, toppling onto his thin, skeletal body, my fingers digging into his stinking clothes, yanking him away from the bag and turning him, spinning him as I screamed, 'Get away from me! Get away from me!'

The terrified face of the homeless man stared up. The stale sandwiches dropped to the pavement.

My shaking hands let go of him, the aggression evaporating into the cold air.

'I'm… I'm sorry,' I said. He rolled away from me and ran off into the night.

I sat back onto the bench, staring at my hands.

'Temper, temper.'

Wilko's voice prickled with excitement. I was alone.

'Where is she now? Where's Lady Solitaire? She'd know what to do. Left you all alone. All alone.'

In a daze, I kicked off the sleeping bag. Ignore him. Ignore him.

'Blood. Blood is thicker than water. Family first. Always here for you, I am.'

My eyes wandered to the doors as his voice wheezed in my ear.

I felt cold air whip across the pavement, litter swirling around my ankles. The sign stopped creaking. The junction was silent.

'Family matters. Families stay together. Together forever. You know that. I know that.'

Across the pavement, a dim light moved on the doors. I looked again at my hands. Aggression pulsed dimly in my fingers, like a spark circling a circuit board.

'Feel that? Life. Life in your hands. There for the taking.'

I stood and stepped away from the bench.

'Shut up!' I hissed. 'Leave me alone!'

The old doors loomed over me, suddenly impossibly thin, impossibly tall. I felt my body tense and tighten, my chest rise, my shoulders pull forward. Fists curled under my wrists.

Dull, dappled light danced on the old wood. It was coming from somewhere else. I turned.

A vivid blue block of light flickered from the slot of the post box, projecting sharp edges into the night air. Framed by the red metal, inside the blue churned and seethed, a deep pool of brilliance that seemed to call to me, to draw me.

Now I was stepping towards it, my hand slowly rising to the slot, fingers outstretched, holding a stiff envelope, stretching to place it, to slide it into the slot, into the light.

SLAM! The fist dug deep into my back, grinding into my kidney, rattling my teeth and buckling my legs as pain shot through my body. I crumpled, the envelope slipping from my grip. Now I was on my knees, on my hands, breathing heavily, my palms flat on the filthy black paving stones as I felt footsteps shift behind me, setting themselves, planting themselves apart, braced strong and heavy, ready to go, ready to fight.

A gurgling noise. From the gaps between the paving, blood began to rise, oozing out and over the black greasy stones, a deep red net that spilled out to flood the floor, rising to cover the envelope, filling the gaps between my fingers, submerging my hands, climbing my wrists.

Now the thick hand grasped at my collar and yanked me to my feet, then spun me round, dazed, unsteady.

A wide fist crashed into my nose, my teeth springing in and out, my eyes squeezing shut as another crashed in, smashing my cheek, my neck muscles snapping tight. Instinct.

I felt my feet move and plant firmly, my chin pull in, my fists raise into place, into position. My eyes opened. My eyes? It was in me. In front of me, a hazy figure formed in the blue light emitted by the post box, a haze of swaying shoulders and weaving hands, coiled in readiness, ready to spring. A blurred fist shot forward; I felt my head move, ducking to the side and then my own hand – a streak of motion – jabbed out. I felt its impact shudder through my shoulder as it landed. Aggression surged through me like electricity, hardening the air, numbing my skin. The fight exploded. Punches rained into me and from me, knuckles crunching against bone, arms flailing, and knees bending to absorb the brutal rhythm of the blows, deadening the punches and swallowing the frenzied energy as I looked on, like a passenger, from inside the maelstrom.

Then, like a great ball, the brawl rolled away from me, leaving me standing free and dead-headed as I watched it circle the space outside the doors, the two blurred figures furiously grappling with each other, spinning and shuddering, their hands jabbing and swinging, their heads absorbing sickening blows. Above the door, the ghost sign shone in the blue light, its letters clear and vibrant.

They stopped for a moment, their shoulders heaving up and down as they fought for breath. The figures slowly stalked each other. Then, with a sickening crunch, they launched into each other again but lurched in my direction, the rolling mass of arms and fists spilling across the blood-soaked floor to engulf me, to swallow my frozen body.

Rage washed over me again as I connected, my fists becoming his, my arms, my legs, my feet. Punches rained quicker and quicker, closer and closer, his breath against my face, mine hot on his, until our fists unfurled to grapple, to pull, to scratch, pulling in close, cheek against cheek, skulls clashing, writhing, an ecstasy of violence, our ribs thumping into each other, hearts beating together, beating and breathing in unison and then... I caught a cold, sharp breath, my eyes frozen open against his, as the steel entered my chest, the blade piercing skin, parting bone, pushing the air from me, his breath faltering desperately as he felt the life slip from me, felt me slump, my arms weaken, the fight done, the fights – all the fights – finally finished... but my hand fell and reached behind, to grasp the handle in my back pocket, to press down on the button, to feel the blade spring open and then to plunge it into his stomach. Our eyes locked together and, as the life leaked from me, I willed my hand to pull back, my knife slipping from his flesh, and then in again, and again and again and again and again as he too crumpled, our fists gripped around blades, but our faces pushed together, the fighting over as we slipped to our knees, then onto our sides to lie in the pooled blood, curled together like babes in the womb.

The pub sign creaked above.

TWENTY-SEVEN

Death Knock

The air was sharp with pine disinfectant, the paper-crisp bed sheets cool against my bare arms. Somewhere, soft shoes squeaked on scrubbed floors.

As I groggily blinked open my eyes, the bright ceiling lights blurred and streaked. Mom was at the side of the bed, her hand on mine, her head on the soft blanket, asleep. Gus, sitting at my feet, silently stood and stirred her awake with the gentlest of touches, his gaze on me the entire time.

Mom's pained expression dissolved into a relieved smile as our eyes met. Gus returned to his seat, offering me a cautious wink.

Over his shoulder, next to the door, a dark figure lurked, curled crookedly on a chair, sunken eyes studying me coolly. Realisation pulsed through me.

In an instant, I was sitting up, pointing at him, prodding a finger past Gus.

'You – you! Are you real? Are you alive or dead?'

Dr Sabapathy smiled sympathetically.

'Hello, Joseph, it is good to see you,' he said. 'I can assure you I'm very much alive. Just very old.'

Mom leant forward. 'Joe, it's OK, I called him. We've stayed in touch.'

I looked around. The décor was different but the familiar solemn hush of Westcroft pressed oppressively down on me.

'How did I get here? What am I doing here?'

Gus scratched his beard. He looked exhausted. 'I brought you here. You were found in London, on the street, unconscious. Some tour guide found you. The police said you may have been attacked. A mutual friend at the *Standard* called me. Your bag's under the bed.'

'But how did I get *here*? In this place?'

Sabapathy spoke calmly. 'You're here under my supervision, Joe – your mother asked me to help. To pull some strings. It's a private room. There's no need to worry.'

'But I can leave if I want to? I can go?'

He nodded. 'Yes, of course. We just want to make sure you are OK.'

I looked at Mom. 'Jesus Christ, you know how I feel about this place. I'm not staying here.'

'Yes, Joe, I know.' She glanced at Gus. 'What have you been doing, Joe? Where have you been? No one's seen you for days. I got up the other morning and my car was gone and… everyone is worried about you.'

I rubbed my face.

'I've been up north, then down to London but it's… hard, Mom, hard to explain. If I was to tell you what I have seen over the last few months, they'd never let me out of this place.'

Sabapathy stood up, slowly. 'Joe, can you tell me… has the voice returned?'

I ignored him and turned to Mom. 'I have to ask you some questions. About Dad, about our family, about why this is happening to me.'

327

She gripped my arm.

'Oh, Joe, we've gone over this – your father was unwell, but he was different to you. He was a good man who had a tough life, and had his reasons for what he became, what he did, but you are not him.'

Sabapathy stepped forward. 'Joe, has Wilko been talking to you again?'

'Yes!' I shouted. 'Yes! He's back and you know what? He's real. It's all real! I've seen them, I've talked to them!'

I pointed at Sabapathy. 'And you know what? I know now. I was never mad. What happened to me really happened. And it's happening again now!'

He gently shook his head at me. 'Joe, I suspect you are having a psychotic episode, probably brought on by a number of factors. Your mother has told me about your project; Mr Harper has explained what has happened with your job. You need to rest, to reset.'

'I'm not having a psychotic episode!' I growled. 'And the project's finished. I've done the last one, no more book.'

'Joe…' Sabapathy pressed his hands together.

There was a soft knock on the door, followed by another. Sabapathy opened it. There was no one there.

'No. He's n-n-not mad.' The weak voice floated into the room.

Slowly, Nipper's huge figure filled the frame.

The doctor's jaw dropped. 'Andrew?'

'Hello, D-Doctor,' he said. 'I'm glad you remember me. It's been a few years.'

Mom and Gus exchanged confused glances. 'Who is this… sorry… who are you?' she asked.

'This is Nipper, Mom, Nipper Mitchell – the boy from the catacombs.'

'The little boy? The little boy who…'

'Hello, Mrs Baxter,' he said shyly, shuffling into the room. 'Joe's telling the truth. He's not mad. I am, I think – or at least I am now. But he's not. And he's right. It's all true.'

Gus was staring at him in disbelief. 'Have you been here all this time?'

'I have, yes.' His blue eyes settled on Sabapathy. 'You might say they threw away the key. I refused to change my story, unlike Joe. I know what I saw. What we saw. It was real.'

He turned to me. 'J-Joe, you need to know that it is gone. The sleeper. I don't know where, but it is gone.'

Gus was exasperated. 'What on earth is going on? Joe, have you been talking to each other?'

Sabapathy walked briskly to the phone next to my bed and picked it up. 'Andrew, I think we should get you back to your bed.'

The old doctor spoke quietly into the phone and replaced the handset, then watched as Nipper lowered himself slowly to the floor to sit cross-legged in the centre of the room.

We all watched the bear-like man as he inspected his black fingertips.

'You know, l-last night I slept for the first time in a very l-l-long time. So did they. All of them. They told me he had gone, gone away. At l-least for a while. They said he was drawn away, by something bigger.'

Nipper licked a shiny fingertip and looked at me. 'A bigger fish.'

There was a flurry of activity in the corridor. The two orderlies stepped into the room. They stood back as, with a sigh, Nipper climbed clumsily to his feet.

'B-b-back to bed. Goodbye, Mrs Baxter,' he said before turning to Sabapathy, then to me.

'This isn't over y-yet. It's s-starting all over again. They said someone else is in danger like I was – like you was – someone young.'

Gus bristled with frustration. 'Who said? Who are *they*? Who do you mean?'

Nipper smiled sweetly. 'The dead, of course. My friends. They are the restless dead. They told me.'

The orderlies parted as he stepped through the door. 'B-back to bed,' he whispered, 'back to bed.'

With a nod, Sabapathy followed busily after them, the door swinging shut behind him.

The room fell quiet. Mom said, 'That poor boy.'

I swung my legs out of the bed.

'He's stronger than I am. He's never changed his story in all these years. Where are my clothes?'

Gus stood up. 'Where are you going? I don't think…'

'Where are my clothes!'

I looked at Mom. 'I told you I am *not* staying here. I am leaving, and I am leaving now. How long have I been here?'

'Gus brought you in this morning. You've been asleep all day.'

'Well, I'm not staying here a minute longer. *Where are my clothes?*'

Mom gestured to a wardrobe. 'I brought you some fresh things. They're in there.'

I strode over to it, pulled it open and began to pull on my trousers.

'OK, but I don't think you should be alone, Joe,' Gus said.

'Why? Because of what happened to Dad? You don't need to worry about that, believe me! I'm not going to do anything stupid. But Nipper said someone is in danger, someone is about to go through what I went through, and I can't allow that. I can't.'

'But who? Where would you go? I don't understand.'

'I don't know… Nipper said it was all starting again, so… the catacombs?'

Anger flashed across Gus's face. 'No, no! Nipper's clearly very unwell, Joe. You can see that. I mean, his fingers! You can't listen to what he says… I mean… the restless dead! The man's clearly insane!'

I pulled the sweater on angrily. 'You know, Gus, that's really not a term you're supposed to use in here these days. But let me tell you… after what I've seen over the last few weeks, there's a thin line between sane and insane. There's a thin line between everything!'

'So, what have you seen?'

'It's all real, Gus! All of it! The supernatural! Ghosts, demons, spirits, hauntings – I've seen them! *I've seen them!*'

Mom shook her head. 'You're talking like your father did. This is what he said.'

'And I think he's involved, I think it's him – I've seen him too, Mom.'

Slowly, her head sank into her hands.

Gus crossed his arms as I stooped to pull on my trainers. 'Joe, that's enough. Look at your mother. Look at what you are doing to her.'

'Mom, I'm telling you the truth, it's just the truth. Now, if you want, I'll stay at yours tonight, but I am not staying here. I can't stay here!'

I moved towards the door, but Gus stepped in my way, arms crossed, leaning into me.

'Wait a moment, just wait a moment. Think. Think about what you're saying, what you're asking us to believe. Show me, Joe. Show me your evidence. Make your story credible. Back it up. That's all I ask.'

'The rules? I'm not sure the rules apply anymore, Gus.'

'Well, if you want anyone to believe a word of what you say… ever… if you want to avoid ending up like that poor bastard Nipper… you need to remember to back it up. Think, man! Has anyone else seen these things? Is anyone else involved?'

'I don't know… maybe! Some of it, yes, but… someone is in danger – now. I can't let this happen to them too.'

He threw his hands up. 'Who? Who's in danger?'

'I don't know, but I'll find out once I've got out of this place!'

I grabbed for the door handle, but it turned as I touched it, swinging softly open.

Kate stood in the corridor, her face white with shock.

331

'Joe' she said, 'I can't find Helena.'

*

Kate sat on the end of the bed. She seemed lost. Now Mom was holding her hand.

'Helena is Kate's daughter – she worked with us at the *Post*,' Gus explained.

'Do you remember Kate, Mom? We went to school together.'

'I do, yes,' she said. 'When did you last see your daughter?'

'Last night. She didn't come home,' Kate said.

'Did she say where she was going?'

Kate gave me a dazed look.

'I was hoping she was with you – I've been looking for you too. I came here just in case you had come looking for me. I've looked everywhere else – and then they said you were here. I can't find her, Joe!'

'Did she say what she was going to do?'

'She said she had solved the puzzle you gave her.'

'A puzzle?'

'That mystery phone number. She said she'd figured out where it was and was going to check it out, because it didn't make sense. What was that number, Joe? That's where she is!'

'I don't know, I don't know – that's why I gave it to her. I've never seen a number like that before. Why did she go off on her own?'

Kate wrung her hands together. 'You know Helena, she just went. Said something about it being the closest to a death knock she'd get. A death knock?'

Gus nodded. 'Just a name. She never got to do one. We'll find her. We'll find her.'

'But how? The police won't even look, they said she hasn't been missing long enough.'

Suddenly, from beneath the bed, a phone began to ring.

I dropped to my knees and pulled my bag out. Inside, my phone screen glowed: 02135652108.

I stood, staring it.

'It's the number.'

'Answer it,' Kate said.

'Put it on speaker,' Gus added.

I hit answer. The speaker buzzed.

Helena's voice was a whisper.

'Hello?'

'Helena? Are you alright?' Kate shouted.

The line fizzed again.

'I can't hear you,' she whispered. 'This phone is so old. Mine doesn't work. Who is that?'

'Helena, it's Joe. Where are you?'

'Hello?' she said again. 'There's someone here. There's someone here and I think he's looking for me. I need to hide. I've got to hide.'

The little boy's words came back to me. 'Helena,' I said, 'Helena, hide under the stairs. Go under the stairs.' Kate looked at me, wide-eyed.

'Oh, OK,' Helena whispered. 'Joe? Joe, is that you?'

The line hissed angrily.

Gus butted in: 'Helena, sweetheart, where are you? We need to know where you are!'

'He's coming!' she whispered.

There was a dull thud, as she placed the phone down. We listened, frozen, as the static whirled in the speaker. Then, down the line, a voice emerged from the noise.

'Where are you, my dear? Is it playtime?'

Mom's eyes widened. She looked at me. Her hand moved to her cheek.

'Can't hide for ever. Waste of skin.'

The line went dead.

'Who was that speaking?' Mom said. 'Who was that?'

333

'You could hear it?'

Gus said, 'We could all hear it. Who was it?'

'I know that voice,' Mom said, 'my God. That voice.'

I looked at Gus. 'That was Wilko. That was Wilko. You all heard it?'

'Wilko?' Kate said. 'Wilko? The voice? How can it be Wilko? Wilko's not real! Where is she, Joe, where is she?'

'I don't know, I don't know – all I have is the phone number.'

'Let me look at that,' Gus said, grabbing the phone.

He stared at the number on the screen.

'That doesn't make any sense,' he said. 'The code doesn't exist.'

'I know. I know.'

'No, I mean that code doesn't exist anymore. It's an old Birmingham code. 021. They added an extra digit years ago. It's 0121 now. This is a phone number from thirty or forty years ago.'

Mom held out her hand.

'Let me see it,' she said.

She took the phone and stared at the screen. Slowly, the colour drained from her face.

'I know where she is,' she said. 'I know where she is.'

TWENTY-EIGHT

The Door

We drove in near silence. A winter fog had descended, lit white by a cold moon above. Only Mom spoke, guiding Gus through the deserted streets. The shuttered shops of the city centre gave way to row upon row of slumbering factories and warehouses, which skulked in the mist under security lights and behind fences. In the back seat, Kate gripped my hand.

Mom took a breath then whispered the final direction, turning us into a wide road lined with office blocks. The car glided along it. Huge, modern buildings swept past. The car came to a stop, as if on its own.

Between two pristine office buildings was a narrow gap.

Deep in the shadows, hidden behind modern security gates, was an old house, thin and tall, its windows clouded with dirt, its mottled brickwork dissolving into the darkness.

It felt like we were the first people to look at it in a very long time, to even notice it.

It felt like it was looking back at us.

'I don't understand,' Gus muttered. 'That's a slum – an old back-to-back. I thought they were all…'

335

'I can't believe it's still here,' Mom said, as if to herself. 'I was told it was demolished.'

She turned to me and Kate. 'That's the house where we lived when we first got married.'

'And you think Helena's in there?' Kate asked.

'That phone number... it was our phone number when we lived here. The call must have come from in there.'

I reached for the door. 'I'm going to go in and get her, but I want you all to stay here.'

Mom shuddered. 'Be careful.'

'You think he's in there?'

She closed her eyes. 'That voice, Joe... that voice.'

Gus said, 'I don't like this. We'll give you ten minutes. Then I'm calling 999.'

'The police can't help, Gus. Not with this.'

He produced a torch from the glove box and handed it to Kate. 'Ten minutes,' he said.

Determination burned in her eyes. 'I'm coming with you,' she told me.

We stepped into the deep shadows between the office buildings, the pavement giving way to grass then dirt as we reached the dilapidated gates. They sagged loosely on their hinges; a faded 'Danger' sign hung from them. We pulled them apart and squeezed through.

The black-walled house loomed over us. Above, between the upper windows, an iron cross, splayed out in a wide 'X' shape, gripped the wall like a great spider.

I pointed to it. 'We've got to be careful. This place is going to be dangerous. That thing's a tie rod – it's holding the walls together. Looks like it's been there a long time.'

If the front door had ever been painted, any colour had long since been bleached from it. Its grey wood was soft and fibrous, the grain bloated by rain and wind. Across it, faded notices were pasted.

We peered at the smudged lettering in the torch light.

'Keep out. Demolition Order – Condemned.
Preliminary historic survey site.
Archaeological Notification Area.
Building Preservation Order.'

A separate bill was pasted below.

'Warning: asbestos. Health and Safety Executive: Hazardous materials notice. Keep out.'

This house had been abandoned, then saved, then abandoned again.

I don't know how but I knew. Something inside me, something shaped by all the vigils, by the nights of listening, by the hours of darkness… something inside me just knew. The house was expecting us.

There would be no long wait tonight.

I took Kate's hand. I could feel her pulse pressing into my palm, her heart pounding.

'Can you feel it?' I asked.

'I-I can,' she stuttered. 'This house… it's like it's… vibrating?'

'Like a charge in the air. I recognise it now.'

'I can… I can feel it on my skin.'

'That's right. Every time.'

She looked up at the dark walls. 'We have to go in, Joe.'

I took hold of the door handle, then paused.

'Kate, you said once that you believed me, that you believed what I've seen. You're about to experience it for yourself. I want you to be ready.'

'I am.'

'One other thing. You remember that I told you I didn't know how to deal with life? How to deal with it when things go wrong? It's true. I don't. But I know how to handle what's behind this door. It's what happens when *death* goes wrong… and I've seen it all. This is real. We're going in to get Helena. But when we're in there, you must listen to me, OK? Will you do that?'

She nodded.

'Open the door, Joe.'

★

There was no hallway. The door swung silently open to reveal a low, uneven ceiling. The little room was icy cold and completely bare, only a crude fireplace visible in the faint moonlight. As we stepped in, the dusty floorboards moaned.

Kate swept the torch over the walls, into the blackened fireplace, through an open doorway and then down across the filthy floor. The air was fetid and damp, but something else hung in the atmosphere. Poverty. Deprivation was soaked into the dank plaster.

'Your parents lived here?' she whispered.

'Yes. They did,' I muttered. 'I had no idea.'

A cold silence descended on the room.

Then, hesitantly, Kate called out, 'Helena?'

We listened.

Somewhere in the house, there was a dull thud. Our eyes met.

'I think that came from through there,' I said.

Kate walked to the doorway and shone the beam into the darkness beyond. 'We've got to find the stairs. They must be through here.'

The next room was windowless and almost completely black. We stepped inside, our feet shuffling uneasily forward on the creaking floor. Carefully, Kate moved the torch in an arc, but the darkness seemed to smother it, condensing it to a weak, narrow spotlight. It swept across more crumbling plaster and another old fireplace, then stopped at the only piece of furniture – a heavy-looking sideboard. I heard Kate inhale sharply. In the little yellow circle of light, the black handset of an old telephone lay on its side. Slowly, she moved the circle on, on to the far wall. Now it picked out planks of knotted wood, nailed together to form crude panelling. She followed it upwards. The split rotten ends of steps descended between broken spindles. The staircase.

Quickly, Kate shone the beam around the panelling, looking for a door.

'Helena?' she hissed. 'Helena!'

There was no door. No handle.

'Helena? It's Mom!' she said.

We listened. And listened.

Listen.

Suddenly, a scream tore through the house, visceral and high-pitched, drenched in panic, drenched in fear. Drenched in pain.

'Helena!' Kate shouted desperately.

Somewhere, a door slammed violently.

The air shifted, as if the house had pivoted beneath our feet. A low, hollow whistling rose from the floor, thrumming from the walls, from the wood and then, as if a curtain had been peeled gently back at the top of the stairs, dim light illuminated the darkness, throwing the banister's skeletal shadow over the walls and across Kate's face.

The light pooled in her terrified eyes. 'What's happening?' she whispered.

'Don't panic,' I said. 'Just wait.'

Another ear-piercing scream.

Running. A frenzy of footsteps above.

At first, he was barely visible.

'Oh my God...' Kate whispered. 'My God!'

The gossamer form of a little boy, shining in the dim light, ran silently down the stairs, stripped to his waist, bare feet blurring on the crooked steps, his face wet with tears. We watched as he reached the bottom and stumbled into the room in front of us, before spinning away to face the wood panelling. The translucent skin of his back seemed to writhe and move. He stood for a second, the outline of his thin shoulders rising and falling. He seemed to glance fearfully up the stairs. Then he frantically grabbed for the panelling, his little hands searching along the wood's edge. With a twist, he slid a plank aside. The spectral boy squeezed silently into the space beneath the stairs then, from within, the plank moved back into place. The gap closed. The dim light evaporated. The room was plunged back into silent darkness, broken only by the weak beam of the torch.

Open-mouthed, Kate shone it at me, then back at the panelling.

A whimper came from inside.

'Helena?' she said.

'She's in there!' I shouted, and we lunged at the wood, my hands finding the plank, slipping into well-worn finger grooves, grappling at the old timber, twisting it and feeling it give and move, and then sliding it away, revealing the black cavity behind.

Dust shifted in the beam of the torch as we peered into the tight space.

A glistening red shape cowered in the corner. It was the little boy's back, his face hidden. But this was no longer a spectral figure – this was real, trembling skin that bled from two long, open wounds across his bony shoulder blades. The scars were real too. They covered his back in a mass of scarlet welts. He wept gently.

'Helena? Helena, is that you?' Kate whispered.

'No, it's not,' I said. 'It's not Helena. This is who has been making the calls.'

The little boy's back began to rise and fall with desperate sobs.

'Are you alright?' I asked. 'Can you hear me? I want to help you.'

I moved an arm inside the cavity.

'My name's Joe. You called me on the telephone,' I said softly, and reached out towards the pathetic little figure, my fingers stretching along the beam of the torch.

'I want to help you. I just want to help you.'

My finger touched his shoulder. The sobbing stopped. He turned slowly.

The boy's face was hidden behind his fingers, with only his trembling mouth visible in the torchlight.

His voice was fragile. '*Did you find the door?*' he asked.

A blinding flash. Our eyes snapped shut.

'Mom?'

Helena was sitting in the beam of the torch. The boy was gone.

As we helped her out of the cavity, her confused eyes stayed fixed on her mother.

Then Kate cradled Helena's cheeks, before pulling her into a desperate, relieved embrace.

'I couldn't find you,' she whispered, 'I couldn't find you.'

'I know,' Helena said, pulling me into the family huddle.

We stood for a second, the three of us, holding each other in the dark, protecting each other.

Then, wiping her eyes, Helena said, 'There was a boy. Here. There was a little boy. He helped me.'

'He helped us too,' I said. 'He showed us where you were.'

'We need to get out of here,' Kate said, leading her daughter towards the door.

Helena stopped.

'But what about the boy? And there's someone else here, Joe. Someone bad,' she said.

I looked up the stairs. 'I know.'

'Joe, come on,' Kate said.

I shook my head.

No turning back.

'I've got to finish this. I have to see. I have to know.'

She studied me for a second. Then she handed me the torch.

'We'll be outside.'

★

The stairs creaked. At the top, a short corridor waited in the gloom, a door directly ahead. I shone the torch along the narrow landing. A second door lurked further away, on the same wall, a black, tar-like puddle shining dully at its foot in the weak beam.

Two rooms down, two rooms up.

The house was silent. I put my palm on the door. It felt wet, cold. I pushed gently. It swung open. Stale air pushed past me. I aimed the beam in. The yellow spotlight moved across the wall opposite, and then reflected on a thin, black line that cut through the air below the ceiling. I followed it with the light. Its pitted metallic surface was twisted into a tight spiral. This was the tie-rod, an iron anchor line that passed through the house, pulling the sagging outer walls together. I stepped carefully into the bedroom and turned to swing the torch around.

It crawled across the window and a bare, metal bedframe then, behind the door, fell on a huge wooden wardrobe.

A chill ran up my spine. This had been my parents' bedroom.

Then, through the wall – from the room next door – came a soft scraping noise, like something moving across the floorboards. I stepped quietly back out into the corridor and edged towards the second door. The torchlight struggled to cut through the darkness. Mould coated the door.

I blinked at the dark puddle at my feet, then carefully pressed a toe onto it. It crunched softly.

I held my breath. Again, a soft sound of movement came from within.

No turning back.

I reached for the handle.

As my fingers gripped it, a whirling noise rose like a siren on the other side of the door, high and shrill, like a swarming, rushing mass of energy was pressing against it from the other side, furiously filling the air, rattling the wood in its frame. I looked down at the puddle between my feet – it seemed to writhe in the dark.

No turning back.

I pushed at the door. It swung open. The noise was gone. A sickly-sweet smell of decay filled my nostrils.

The same black substance seemed to cover the floorboards, gathered into pools that gleamed like oil in the light. I stepped inside, my steps crunching as if on frost.

Shapes loomed. This room was full. Full of junk. Like so many times before, my eyes raced to adjust. In the dim spotlight I saw a rough-hewn wooden chair and a rusting iron bedstead; a dust-covered hat rested on its soiled, sunken mattress. Above, the iron line of the tie-rod continued its path through the building. On the wall, a faded military uniform hung from a nail, more of the same black substance pooled on its threadbare shoulders. A pile of walking sticks leant, bonelike, next to the door. Over them, two leather belts hung, dried and curled up. Across the room, I could make out a desk, and the back of another chair next to it. I stepped forward and aimed the beam at the forms silhouetted on the desktop – picking out decades-old electrical equipment with clouded glass dials, switches swathed in cobwebs and an antiquated metal microphone on a cloth-bound wire. Radio equipment? Everywhere, the film of oily black matter glinted back at me.

Then I shone the beam onto the chair... and recoiled.

It was a commode. Faeces were caked around the hole in its plastic seat, dark smears climbing up the back and across the shell-like arms. A thin plastic bucket sat beneath, its warped rim speckled with dark stains.

Revulsed, I pulled the light away. It fell on a fireplace. More of the black sheen glinted on a white stone mantelpiece – thicker, like a layer of ash. I stepped across and, between finger and thumb, carefully took a pinch of the substance. Tiny legs and desiccated, veined wings poked out. Flies. I dropped it. Flies. Millions of flies. Dead. Everywhere. Instinctively, I rubbed my fingers against my coat, as my eyes followed the layer of dead insects along the mantel; it seemed to rise towards the centre, climbing to a little, sharp peak.

Up, up, up. On the wall above, directly over the fireplace, was a metal box mounted on a bracket. Behind a rusted grill on the front, a large electrical filament coiled in a double loop. I shone the torch on it. Some kind of bug killer?

This time I felt it coming. I felt the hairs lift on the back of my neck.

Crack! The room flooded with light. Blue-white light. I rocked back on my heels, my muscles tense.

Here we go.

Above the mantel, a piercing arc of brightness was threading its way around the old filament, slowly circling one loop then the other, before joining like a stream of molten metal to glow and throb in a shape I knew, a shape I'd seen before.

The figure of eight glowed and crackled behind the grill. The torch fell limply by my side.

Then, as if burning itself onto some great retina, the glowing shape detached from the box, lifting from the filament, floating into the air above the fireplace, out into the room, fizzing and quivering as it lit up the bed, the desk, the chair, making the pools of dead flies glisten as it roamed towards the far wall. Now there was noise too: muttering voices, confused and angry, rising from the floor, pulsing with the flickering figure of eight as it scratched at the darkness.

I watched, frozen, as it met the wall and then, with a fizz of static, passed through into the bedroom beyond, momentarily plunging me back into darkness, before re-emerging, stalking through the air in front of me again to hover above the bed, hissing and flaring as it flung shadows across the walls. The muttering voices dropped to a low hum as the shape hung there, as if scanning the room.

'It's looking for me.'

Wilko's voice rasped in the darkness. I saw him.

I saw him.

Behind the floating shape, a dark skeletal figure sat on the commode, silhouetted in the flickering light.

He waited for my response.

'Hello, Grandad,' I said.

His face hidden in darkness, he gave an almost imperceptible nod. I could see straggles of long, unkempt hair swept back from a leathery, balding scalp. A claw-like hand rested on the desk.

'It's looking for me.'

The shape crackled in the air as he spoke.

'What is it?'

He chose his words.

'You know what it is. A door. Attached to me, to this house. It comes every night, and it wants me to pass through. Why should I? I choose to stay. I choose to stay.'

It fizzed angrily. Through its loops I could see a curtain of smoke billowing and writhing. Another place.

My God. A door.

Find the doors. I had found the doors! I just hadn't seen them. The coffin-like drain in the Old Tunns, the flickering light of the Regal's projector room, the inky Saxon pit, the mercy stone, the elevator cage, the bent and mangled blast door of the *So Long Betty*... all of them portals searching for lost souls, tethered to where they had died, reaching out with ethereal light to tempt them through, to coax them to move on... I realised now that I had seen Mimms make her choice, accept the light and move up above but... some of them didn't want to go.

'Why do you choose to stay?'

He chuckled darkly. The muttering voices bubbled.

'I know what's waiting for me.'

'Judgement?'

'Judgement! I will not be judged. Do you judge me? You? Pathetic waste of skin. Just like your father. This is my house! I will not leave!'

345

His silhouetted head turned slowly, surveying the room.

'What do you know? With your pathetic, hopeless life. What have you seen? What have you done? What have you got to give up? What memories? What experiences?'

The shape fizzed angrily, as if it sensed his presence.

'Poor little Joe, poor mad Joe, locked up in the loony bin, abandoned by his own father, no one to love him, all alone, in his shitty little flat, no job, no hope. You were wasting your life – the life I gave you.'

I shook my head. 'I've worked hard. I've made a difference. I've helped people. Or at least I've tried.'

'Worked hard? Waste of skin, waste of breath, waste of time. Waste of life. You call yourself a man? You're just a boy... I can hear you now: Please! Please! I'll try harder! I'll do better! Just like your father. Pathetic! Call yourself a man? This man went to war. This man fought. This man changed. This man tasted things, saw things... learned new skills...'

His hand wrapped slowly around the old microphone and lifted it into the darkness.

'Wilco, Wilco, Wilco...'

He tossed it back onto the desk.

'And so he did things. In the war. Saw things. He finds he likes them. Has a taste for them. His blood rushes. Rushes! Then he comes back. Comes back to what? Who's waiting? A pathetic child. A weak woman. A filthy slum. Everything is boredom, numbing boredom. The blood is still. It clots with boredom. Where is the pain? That's not living. Everything is pain. Pain is life.'

He looked at the shape and, for the first time, I saw the contemptuous glint in his eyes.

'There's too much life here. I'm not going, why should I?'

'I know how it works now,' I said angrily. 'Why you're refusing to go through. But you will. You will.'

He laughed, coldly.

'No. I will not, and you can't make me. You're in the wrong place, boy.'

346

'I've met your kind. You're all cowards.'

'Oh yes, I know. I saw you. That fat, fingerless fucker in his bell tower. That posh, preening pervert scurrying around under the ground. Feeding like greedy little pigs. You liked meeting them, didn't you? Got a kick out of it! And don't think that black bitch was any better! She's had her feed too!'

'Oh no… she was different. Patience helped me! She tried to warn me, warn me about you! And what's keeping you here? What are you feeding on? Flies?'

He snorted.

'You don't get it, do you? You still don't see it?'

The black shape of his head tilted to one side. The figure of eight buzzed, sending a ripple through the muttering voices.

'Family business, this is. My life's work. My death's work. You have all been most helpful.'

'What do you mean?'

'What do I mean? Your father, that pathetic waste of skin. My so-called son. I sat on his shoulder first. Stayed in his head. For years.'

'No.'

'Yes, yes. All that anguish, all those breakdowns. Me. It was me. Talking to him. Reminding him. Reminding him he grew up here! Reminding him where he came from. Feeding off him.'

'Why? Your own son!'

He slammed his bony fist on the desk.

'Why? Because he left me to die in here, in this room, in my own filth, wasting away! His own father! His big, dirty secret! Then, with me gone, he moved back in here, with his young slut, with you in her belly. Only I wasn't gone. I'm not gone. I'll never go.'

From deep in my childhood, Dad's words came back to me: 'The person who had lived there before us – an old man – had died in the back bedroom.'

The shape seemed to judder and pulse as it hung over the bed, its light picking out deep creases in the old man's shadowy face.

I felt anger rise.

347

'The little boy,' I said, 'downstairs. Is that him? Is that my father? What did you do to him?'

'Little cry-baby. He went over. He didn't stay. But he's been trying to warn you, trying to reach you. Pathetic. He always did need discipline. He couldn't take it.'

'What do you mean?'

'I fed on him. He kept me here, and then when he died, I sat on your shoulder instead. Invisible friend! Wilco! Wilco! I fed on you. My flesh and bone. You and your father before you. I gave you both life, it's only right I take it back. Shame you're no use to me now, like him. I've used up your lonely little life. Time to move on. I have a new friend.'

'Who?'

'I like her. She's feisty, very headstrong. I'll have fun breaking her down. So much life. So young.'

'Helena? Do you mean Helena?'

'I've been talking to her for a while. She's started listening, just like you did, just like your father did. How do you think she found this place?'

My stomach turned. Realisation hit. Helena zoning out. Helena 'away with the fairies'. The familiar look of confusion, of fear.

'You will leave her alone!' I shouted. The shape juddered, as if stretching itself, trying to grow. Inside it, I could see the curtain of smoke broiling, lit by flashes of light. The door was opening.

The old man's voice boiled to a deep growl.

'Leave her alone? Or what?'

Slowly, he stood on stick thin legs, stepping in front of the pulsing light of the figure of eight, his face suddenly revealed by its flickering brilliance, his features stark and jagged, his sunken eyes clamping on to me, projecting their cruelty, a sinister smirk spreading across his thin mouth.

I felt myself shrink, intimidated, infantilised.

He jabbed a bony finger at me.

'*What are you going to do? You're just as pathetic as he was, just as weak. Mentally weak. Cry-babies. I spawned cry-babies!*'

Behind him, the shape flashed angrily and enlarged again. He sneered at it over his shoulder.

'*Oh, no. I'm not going anywhere. This is my house. Forever! My house! I own it – like I own you!*'

Suddenly, the wooden chair slid across the floor behind me, striking my calves and buckling my knees, forcing me to sit. Pinning me back, pulling me down.

The old man towered over me now, growing, filling the room, his thin legs stretching out, his bony finger jabbing at my chest. I saw his colourless tongue slide over his yellow teeth as he snarled down at me. I couldn't move.

'*What are you but a waste of skin! What are you but a pathetic cry-baby!*'

I looked down at my hands, the hands of a child, gripping onto tattered shorts, shaking with fear. Emotion welled.

'*You need discipline! You need to learn how to keep that emotion in! You're both the same!*'

His crooked hands reached out above my head then reappeared, clutching the two twisted leather straps. His eyes gleamed as he handed one to me. With a trembling child's hand, I reached up and took it.

Somewhere, I heard my father's voice say, 'Bite down on it, son, bite down on it!'

I slipped the dried leather into my little mouth as the shadow of the old man's arm fell over me, the strap held high, ready to lash down. I felt my naked shoulders brace themselves, felt the scars on my back stretch. I bit down.

'*This is my way! This is life!*'

The leather strap lashed down across my naked shoulders, violently whipping and cracking across my back, jolting my spine. I felt tears flood from my eyes, running hot down young cheeks.

But behind him the shape, the door – the portal – reacted; it flashed angrily and stretched further open, the vortex of swirling smoke beyond it writhing and twisting.

I tried to speak. I couldn't.

He raised the strap again.

'He belonged to me, you belong to me, she will belong to me!'

I bit down on the leather. Again, the strap whipped down, splitting the air, burning my skin and again the portal shook and enlarged, as the blinding brightness of its figure of eight edge looped and surged faster and faster, throwing off sparks as the vortex inside it shifted and swirled.

I spat out the leather as he raised the strap again.

'No, she won't! Not her! You have me! Use me!'

I saw the strobing light of the portal spin in his black eyes.

'No! Too late. I want her. You're finished. Spent. A waste of skin.

Just like him.

Just like your pathetic father.'

'I won't give in. I won't do what he did. You won't win that easily. I'll never make that choice!'

As I spoke, the portal throbbed and grew again, changing shape, its two loops merging into one, filling the room behind his crooked frame. He laughed, coldly, and dropped the strap.

'Choice? Choice? You think he had a choice? You think he had the backbone to do that on his own? That was me! I ended his pathetic life, just like I drank up yours!'

His spindly fingers reached out and grasped my arms and, pinning them to my side he lifted me with a jolt off the chair, my little feet dangling, my shoulders burning, my ribs cracking, and then he stood me, like a plaything, on the seat. He stared hungrily into my eyes as the portal pulsated behind him. I squinted into the swirling vortex of smoke, then looked up at the ceiling. Like a snake, a thick rope slithered over the tie-rod and descended, slowly curling to form a noose in front of my face.

The old man laughed.

'Like father like son.'

His thin fingers stroked the coarse fibres of the rope. Behind him the portal flared violently, the smoke churning and flashing. Now he was clutching the noose. I was frozen. I looked into his eyes and then stared beyond, into the smoke, into the other place, through the vortex. In the maelstrom, something moved. Now he was pulling the looped rope apart and raising it slowly. I blinked through tears as deep inside the smoke, a dark shadow moved, emerging, wading through, pacing. Now the old man was placing the rope over my head, his eyes fixed on mine, drinking in my helplessness but I still looked beyond, at the portal, into the smoke; yes – a figure, a black shadowy figure, was forcing his way through swirling clouds, pushing through as the muttering voices began to chant and shout as he came close, closer. Now the noose was slipping over my eyes and down, down, down as the old man's wicked mouth smiled but the figure was rushing closer now, stepping forward from the smoke, from the vortex, from the other place and, as the coarse noose tightened around my neck, squeezing my throat, he moved from the shadows into the blinding light of the whirling figure of eight. It lit up his face, glowing in brilliant blue-white. Inside the portal, my father stood behind the old man, determination flashing in his eyes. The old man's bony hands yanked the noose tight, my eyes bulged, I felt his foot push against the chair, I teetered, and the old man laughed but behind him... behind him my father's strong hands grasped the swirling edge of the portal and he swung his leg over, climbing through into the room, rising behind the old man as his old foot kicked at the chair; it tipped, I felt my feet scrape and scrape and scrape desperately then dangle free as the rope pulled tight against the tie-rod above, but then through bulging eyes, I saw my father's big hands land heavily on the old man's thin, cruel shoulders, his fingers digging in, and then he pulled at him, lifting him from the floor, and then he flung him – flung him like a rag doll – through the portal and into the smoke, a rasping scream trailing behind him as he disappeared into the swirling clouds. I hung helplessly, my little legs – a boy's legs – kicking and struggling as the rope tightened around my neck, but then his arms lifted me, my father's arms, strong and warm, the rope pulled away, the noose removed, my face buried in his beating chest. I sobbed. The room fell quiet.

The portal glowed warmly as I looked up into his face. His voice was gentle. It seemed to resonate through me.

'It's alright, son,' he said, 'it's not your time. It's not your time.'

His kind, loving eyes gleamed in the blue-white light as he held me.

Suddenly, a rasping scream tore from the portal as the old man's long arms shot out, his furious skeletal face emerging, lunging at Dad, at me, his bony fingers clawing into us both, pulling at us, pulling us towards the smoke, to the other place, as the vortex of smoke and light swirled violently again.

I only saw it for a second.

But I saw it.

White, smooth and marble-like, the expressionless face of the huge, hooded figure surfaced silently from the churning smoke, his arms reaching out to wrap around the old man's torso, before sinking back into the vortex, clutching his prey tight as they both vanished into oblivion.

We both watched as the smoke calmed, then the portal, as if it was spent, twitched and shrank back to its figure of eight shape, its light dying away gently, then it blinked, and blinked again, and then vanished.

I was a little boy, in my father's warm arms, in the quiet, dark room. He winked at me and then bent to pick up the dirty old hat from the bed, dusting it off against his side before placing it on his head with a mischievous, playful smile.

I laughed a child's laugh.

'Time to go to sleep,' he said, carrying me to the door, out into the hallway but then upstairs, upstairs not down, up the familiar stairs of my own childhood home, to my own bedroom, where he gently lay me down and pulled the blankets over me. He stroked my hair.

'I have to go now, son, it's time to go to sleep,' he said.

I saw tears well up in his eyes as they filled my own. He stood for a second, silhouetted at the end of my bed, the old hat clutched in his hands – the imaginary ghost I had conjured up so many years before. Then he turned and walked through the shining doorway.

'Dad!' I shouted.

I sat up, the rusty bedstead moaning. I was in the empty bedroom of the slum.

'Joe! Joe!' Kate's voice came from outside. I looked through the window; she was standing, waving her arms, beckoning me down. 'The cross! The cross, Joe, get out!'

Above my head, the black line of the tie-rod seemed to sag, as dust and mortar shook from the wall around the window as it bent outwards, the plaster cracking as bricks beneath separated and buckled.

I scrambled down the stairs, through the rooms below, out of the front door and into Kate's arms. Gus, standing by the car with his arm around Helena, pointed at the house. We looked up as the iron cross came apart, its black arms slipping down the wall as it began to crumple and fold.

We ran to the car as the old house collapsed in a cloud of dust.

TWENTY-NINE

The Frame

'How come I always end up carrying the monitor?' Gus said as we made our way up the driveway. 'And where's everything else? I was expecting you to have loads of stuff to move. I'm glad I didn't hire a van.'

Kate was standing at the door, squinting in the spring sunshine, her hair tied up. She cast a wry look into our boxes as we approached.

'Is that literally all you've got?'

'I'm leaving the furniture behind,' I said. 'For the new tenants. My clothes are in the car. But it's too late to back out now, Kate, I've handed over the keys. The contract's signed. I'm all yours.'

She smiled. 'I think we've got room for you. Anyway, your other stuff has come. From the *Echo*.'

Gus and I exchanged glances.

She led us through the warm hallway and into the empty home office, its barren shelves caked in thick dust. Two large boxes sat in the corner, heavily bound in brown tape.

Kate put her hands on her hips. 'The workmen who are stripping the newsroom dropped them round. They said they arrived this morning. They weigh a tonne.'

Gus inspected the label.

'Joseph Baxter, care of the *Midland Echo*,' he muttered.

'No idea,' I shrugged. 'Complete mystery.'

'Shall we open them, then?' she said.

Gus exhaled and put his box down. 'Do you mind if we have a cup of tea first?'

'First rule of journalism?'

He placed a hand on my shoulder. 'I have taught you well.'

Warm morning light flooded into the kitchen. My mom looked out at the garden, while Helena sat at the table, studying a copy of the *Echo*.

'Put the kettle on, Jeannie, I'm parched,' Gus said as he took a seat, peering at the front page.

She nodded.

Cups rattled; the fridge opened. I sat as the kettle began to stir.

With a hint of triumph, Helena showed me the front page.

'*VICTORY*,' screamed the headline, over a picture of the beaming Bentley family.

'Funding reinstated, apology from the council – the family couldn't be happier,' she said.

'Brilliant – you've made a real difference to their lives.'

'Proper journalism,' Gus said. 'And that's not the best part. She put it online, along with all the data about how the council was wasting money elsewhere. It went massive. It was a virus.'

'It went viral,' she corrected him.

'That's what I meant. It's gone international. Biggest digital story the *Echo*'s had this year. Nash is furious.'

'People do care,' I said.

'People are the story,' Gus said.

As usual, he was right. People are all that matter, all that count, all that really endure. Sometimes it's their ideas, sometimes their memories, sometimes their promises, sometimes their love, but as everything else decays and falls away, people hang on, despite everything, despite the passage of time. The secret, Alfred had taught me, was to find the right person to pass that time with.

Helena folded the paper and stood up.

'Anyway, it will go very well with my college application – which I've got to go and finish.'

She headed to the door as the tea arrived on the table.

'Don't forget, sweetheart, to put me down as a referee,' Gus said.

'I won't,' she said as she headed upstairs. 'And don't call me sweetheart.'

Kate sat next to me and slid a mug of tea into my hand.

Mom's kind eyes watched as I spooned in sugar.

Outside, magpies skipped on the lawn.

'Jeanette, why don't we go and open those boxes, I want to know what's in them,' Gus said gently.

Mom smiled at Kate. 'Of course,' she said, getting to her feet and picking up her tea. 'We'll go and open those boxes.'

Kate called after them, 'There's a knife on the desk, you'll need it.'

I felt her hand slip into mine, as we looked out at the garden.

'How's Helena been?'

'Fine,' she said. 'I haven't seen anything to worry about at all. And I would know.'

'She's not exhibiting any signs of...'

'No, nothing. She's back to normal. I tell you who is improving... Andrew.'

'Andrew?'

'Sorry... Nipper. I'm working with him one to one now. He's sleeping much better and after all these years of silence we can't shut him up. He's talking all the time.'

'Amazing. Should I go and see him?'

'I think he'd like that. Take him some art material, he can't get enough of it.'

'Is he still drawing faces?'

'No, not anymore. Get him plenty of paper and coloured paints. The brighter the better.'

'I will. I will.'

She sipped her tea. 'And what are you going to do now? What's next?'

'I don't know. Finish the book, I suppose. Try to make sense of it all. But it does feel like I've still only scratched the surface. Like there's more to learn, more to see. I've still got questions.'

'You're welcome to use the office, make it your own. I've no use for it. I hope you find the answers you're looking for.'

Hope. As I sat with Kate in the sunlight, that was what I felt. Hope for the future and a fresh start, but also hope anchored in the people I had met and the things I had seen. I hoped that the lonely soul I encountered in Cornwall would be reunited with her lost love. I hoped that mischievous little drummer boy was still happy in his sandstone playground. I hoped the lost warriors' long night watch would finally come to an end. I hoped that the Regal's most loyal customer would continue to enjoy the best seat in the house. I prayed that the Black Abbot would stay entombed in his wretched abbey, and that the miners of Hall End would escape the clutches of Josiah Alexander Rowlett the Second.

Above all, I hoped that Patience would finally get to finish her game of cards.

And I knew that, for each of them, a door waited – a door that hoped they would pass through.

'Bloody hell, Joe!' Gus shouted from the office. 'What are all these?'

'There's hundreds of them!' I heard Mom say.

Kate and I found them in the office, standing over an open box, dusty books clutched in their hands.

Gus held one up and read the spine: 'Morphic Resonance & The Presence of the Past: The Memory of Nature.'

Helena appeared at the door. 'Whose are all those books?' she said.

I smiled and took two out of the box. 'Alfred's. They're Alfred's books.'

'Who's Alfred?'

'An old friend. No, actually, he's a new friend – who's very old. Who *was* very old. He must have died. Oh, Alfred.'

'I'm sorry,' Helena said.

'No,' I said, 'it's OK. Really, it's OK. He wanted me to have these. We had a shared interest.'

'There's so many of them,' Mom said.

Kate looked around the empty shelves. 'Well, we've got room for them.'

I looked into the box. A single, empty photograph frame gleamed among the dusty books.

'Yes,' I said. 'I think they've come to the right place.'

Acknowledgments

This book is the culmination of so many elements, influences and moments of kindness. So many, in fact, it would be futile to try to list them. So, I want to mention a few people who have directly helped, as well as calling out the influences that have no doubt seeped into its pages.

First of all, my wife, Jane, daughter, Abbie, and son, Leo, who have had to put up with the sound of freakishly fast two-fingered typing hammering through the house at all hours. Abbie deserves special mention – she helped immeasurably by brain-storming ideas for ghosts with me, on long drives through the Staffordshire countryside. Thanks, Sweetpea, your wonderfully imaginative fingerprints are all over this book.

I want to thank Becky and Geoff Coleman for their input and opinions, which were suitably honest to effect change and suitably kind not to bruise my confidence.

And I want to thank all of the journalists I have worked with throughout my career. This book is something of a love letter to British newspapers and the characters who populate newsrooms across the land. There have been so many friends and colleagues, mentors and mentees, who I still hold dear. I marvel at the press's ability to change and move with the times and, in my new life in the

PR world, often see myself in the young reporters I come across.

Some of the ghost stories in this book are based on real tales spun in newsrooms or delivered down the phone by self-conscious readers trying to make sense of what they had seen or heard. Every newsroom has these stories if you dig deep enough.

As for influences, where do I start? As a child of the 80s, my horror chops were formed by reading about Carrie and Cujo, swarms of rats and giant crabs. King and Herbert led me through the cemetery to discover the wonders of Lovecraft, Blatty, Poe and co, and the ultimate fountainhead of sinister mundanity: Ray Bradbury, who else?

But as a fully paid-up member of Generation VHS (pre-Blockbuster), horror lingered on the pause button too, Landis, Carpenter, Craven *et al* providing the thrills, with not a CGI pixel in sight. Children of my generation listened for voices in the white noise at TV closedown, watched Damien grow up, said things into mirrors and dreamed that one day that pretty TV news anchor might actually turn into a werewolf live on air. Still waiting.

All of this head-guff is in *13 Doors* somewhere, along with the lost documents I stumbled across on later trips to Raccoon City, Silent Hill and beyond.

My home city of Birmingham also played a major role in the long-term gestation of *13 Doors*. As a small child, on the way to school every morning, we would drive past the crumbling graves of the Victorian cemeteries in the Jewellery Quarter. I would try not to look. Now, I love them, catacombs and all.

But the real thanks for *13 Doors* must go to my parents, Brian and Janet, who told me the true bedtime story that set this whole thing in motion.

Do I believe in ghosts? As a journalist, you're trained to be sceptical, demand evidence and place objectivity above all else.

Ghosts? Don't be ridiculous.

But when your parents tell you they have seen one, what do you do then?